CW00642334

# FATAL CURE

KATHY LOCKHEART

ROSEWOOD

Copyright © 2022 by Kathy Lockheart
All rights reserved.

No part of this book may be reproduced in any form or by any electronic or mechanical means, including information storage and retrieval systems, without written permission from the author, except for the use of brief quotations in a book review.

This book is a work of fiction. All names, characters, locations, and incidents are products of the author's imagination. Any resemblance to actual persons, living or dead, locales, or events is entirely coincidental.

Editor: Michelle Mead
Copy Editor: The Novel Triage
Proofreader: Jovana Shirley, Unforeseen Editing, www.unforeseenediting.com and Judy, with Judy's Proofreading

Cover design © By Hang Le

ISBN 978-1-955017-04-6 e-book
ISBN 978-1-955017-05-3 Hardcover
ISBN 978-1-955017-06-0 Paperback
ISBN 978-1-955017-07-7 Large Print

**Please note this e-book is exclusive to Amazon. If you are reading it from any other site, please be aware it is pirated and could result in Amazon removing the author's books.*

Published by Rosewood Literary Press

# FATAL CURE

*For my dad, my hero.*

# AUTHOR'S NOTE

Fatal Cure is an emotional, tension-filled romance. If you are looking for a lighthearted read, you will not find it in these pages.

While the romantic scenes are not extremely graphic, this forbidden love story contains violence and other content that may be triggering for some readers. I prefer you go into a story without spoilers, but if you would like **a list of detailed triggers**, you can find it posted on my website at KathyLockheart dot com, under FATAL CURE.

# 1

When a gorgeous guy walked into the otherwise empty elevator, I had no idea that in a few weeks, he would kill several men to protect me. He didn't strike me as a killer. He looked like a model with dark hair and facial stubble, a tall, muscular body and captivating eyes.

Eyes that locked on to me as he casually rested his hand on a Gucci gym bag slung over his shoulder.

"Morning." His baritone voice rumbled through the space.

I offered a polite smile but said nothing back. Not that I was trying to be rude. I just wanted to stay focused because today, my lifelong dream to dismantle the drug organizations that had destroyed my family was a huge step closer to coming true.

This all-consuming goal had guided my every move leading up to this moment. I'd worked three jobs to get my bachelor's degree from the University of Illinois, graduated at the top of my class from the police academy, moved to Chicago, and after gaining experience as a Chicago police officer, applied to and gotten accepted into a prestigious DEA task force. The first meeting? Was in one hour.

I ran through my checklist for the millionth time.

Police uniform ironed, crisp and waiting for me in the Chicago Police Headquarters locker room? Check.

Workout this morning to burn off nervous energy and help keep my mind alert? Check.

Showered, makeup and hair done here at the gym? Check, check, and check.

I glanced at my phone screen, seeing it was 7:03 a.m. Three minutes past my target time but still plenty of time to get to the precinct, change, and be in the conference room well before eight —nothing left to chance.

"I'm Dillon." The handsome guy extended his hand as the elevator began its slow descent from the fifty-fifth floor to the ground level. His unwavering eye contact and firm handshake brimmed with the confidence normally reserved for someone beyond his mid-twenties age.

"Fallon," I replied.

"Fallon," he said. "Cool name."

My name meant descended from a ruler. My parents, at the time of my birth at least, viewed me as their little princess, a miracle after a battle with infertility. From that moment on, their entire life shaped around me like the careful organization of the planets in our solar system, their baby the center of gravity pulling each decision they made. My mom packed lunches with little drawings, and Dad dedicated every Saturday to Fallon's-choice day, where I got to pick what we did. If I had to assign a word to those earlier years, it would be *bliss*, when I felt completely safe and love penetrated every cell of my body.

That was before it all got sucked into a black hole, and any semblance of life and of the parents who once loved me more than anything was destroyed.

"I've never seen you here before." Dillon snapped my focus back to the present.

"Maybe you have."

"No." His gaze glided over my lean five-foot-four frame, chocolate hair, and sapphire eyes. "I'd definitely remember if I did."

I would remember if I'd seen him, too. With a rugged jaw drawing you into a hypnotic smile, the guy was so hot that women probably literally fainted around him. He probably had to go around checking pulses left, right, and sideways with the hormonal devastation left in his wake. His extraordinary physique contoured his black T-shirt and gray pants like a walking advertisement for workout clothes.

But no matter how hot he was, there was only one priority today, and that was work. I wasn't going to be distracted by the embodiment of sex on legs.

I watched the floor number on the digital panel descend from twenty-eight to twenty-seven. But I allowed my eyes to wander back over to him, curious if he was staring.

He was.

Until the elevator bounced like a yo-yo. It took me a second to realize I was now on the diamond-patterned carpet, thanks to the elevator having jolted to a stop.

"You okay?" Dillon offered his hand.

*Of course Sir Sex Magnet managed to stay upright, the ridiculously perfect specimen that he is.*

On any other day, that charming way he looked down at me and extended his hand like a gentleman would've sent butterflies in my stomach. But not today.

Not. Today.

This first meeting of the task force was vital. First impressions were critical, and if I couldn't be early, I sure as hell couldn't be late, let alone miss it entirely.

"You have got to be kidding me." I jumped back up. "I don't have time for this."

I pushed the open-door button, several of the numbered floors, and the main-lobby button. When nothing worked, I tried the red emergency-call button. "Hello?"

Static. Crackling, like maybe someone was trying to answer.

I tried again. "Hello? The elevator stopped."

More crackling. I tried four more times.

"What the hell?" I held my phone up, irritated to see it had no signal.

I hated these older skyscrapers. Their elevators were like signal-blocking steel bunkers.

I moved around, desperate to hit the right spot so I could make a call. But as I tried each wall—the center, lower, and then higher above my head—I discovered it was fruitless.

"Can you try yours, please?"

Dillon fished his cell out of his back pocket and held it up. "Who would we call?"

"If we can get a signal, the phone number on the panel, for starters. If they don't answer, we call the fire department."

Dillon raised an impressed eyebrow.

His deltoids waged a war against his shirt's fabric as he held the cell above his head, squinting at the screen. After several moments, he sighed. "I'm not getting any bars, but I'm sure the elevator will restart any second. They probably know we're in here."

"I can't bank on *probably*. Can you please turn your cell off and back on?"

His lips curled up as he complied.

"What?" I asked.

He shook his head and ran a thumb over his smile. "Nothing."

After both our cells rebooted, I asked, "Are you getting any bars now?"

He frowned.

"Great." I pushed the emergency-call button again. "Hello?" I tried repeatedly but couldn't get a response.

If I missed this meeting, I might get kicked off the task force before I even started, and then all the work I'd done to get here would go up in smoke. On every future application, I'd have to disclose that I'd been let go from the operation, thwarting any realistic chance of joining another in the future. My ability to succeed on this task force was my ticket to establishing a successful career in the DEA, which was more than just a career move. It meant being able to stop other families from going through what happened to mine.

"Let's try to pry the doors open," I suggested.

Dillon raised his brows. "*Pry* the doors open? It's only been a couple minutes."

"We could be in here for a couple of hours if we don't do something."

Dillon bit back his smile, dropped his gym bag on the floor, and joined me by the doors. We tried to insert our fingertips between them, but after three failed attempts, we accepted it wasn't happening.

Dillon leaned against the wall and studied me with a playful gleam in his eyes as I paced and twisted my hands together, trying to calculate how long it might take them to get up to the twenty-seventh floor. At least, I thought that was what floor we were on. Someone probably heard us on the other end of that emergency button and was on their way. They had to be...

I might be a Chicago police officer trained in de-arming an assailant, firing a weapon with precision, and getting out of some seriously sticky situations, but no police training could help me if I missed the most important morning of my career if this damn elevator didn't start moving again.

"Are you claustrophobic?" he asked. "Because you're suddenly looking pretty freaked out."

"And you find that amusing?"

"Find it kind of adorable."

I glared at him, but it only incited a bigger smile.

Dillon watched me walk from side to side.

"So, is it a heights thing or a claustrophobic thing that's creating this"—he gestured toward my body—"situation?"

"Neither; I'm in a hurry."

I needed to calm down. I left myself a buffer for the unexpected, just in case. I just hadn't thought I'd actually need it. I didn't like cutting things close.

"You're not gonna faint or something, are you?" Dillon asked.

I glowered at him, and at least this time, he cleared his throat to hide his smile.

"You need to get your mind off being trapped in here," Dillon said.

"That's not possible."

"Do you live in this building?"

"No, I just come for the gym. And I don't want to do small talk," I said. "I want to get us out of here."

The lights flickered, and the space—which had been playing jazz music moments ago—grew quiet.

A new unease washed through me; a simple stuck elevator didn't have its lights flicker or lose power to the speakers.

"Why did the music shut off?" I asked.

Dillon shrugged as he continued to observe me.

"I'd really like to know exactly what is malfunctioning here. There's, like, twenty-six floors of air beneath us."

"Elevator crashes are very rare," he assured.

"He says to a girl in a broken elevator that's dangling from a cable."

Dillon bit his lip, clearly trying not to laugh at me. "They have emergency brakes for things like this."

"Do you hear that?" I asked. "It sounds like yelling."

As we listened, the yelling escalated into an all-out symphony of screaming and a stampede of running.

Dillon furrowed his brows.

"Do you smell that?" I asked.

Dillon sniffed and instantly stiffened his muscles just as the fire alarm blared.

I banged the heels of my palms against the cool steel. "Hello!" I shouted. "Two people are trapped in the elevator!"

Dillon pounded louder than I was able to, but our cries for help were drowned out by shrieks and the alarm.

"We're stuck in the elevator!" I pushed the emergency button again and screamed into the speaker. Not even static returned.

Meanwhile, Dillon dug his fingertips between the metal doors and tried to pry them open again. Unlike before, his movements were desperate. When it didn't work, I joined him—him standing on one side, me on the other, both of us pulling in opposite directions. Our fingertips couldn't get enough traction, though. They slipped off again and again.

The smell of smoke intensified, reminding me of something I'd learned in emergency rescue training. It only took three minutes for a normal-sized structure to become completely engulfed, less than that for it to turn fatal. And while the high-rise was bigger, we'd been tugging and pounding at the doors for a couple minutes already. And counting...

We shoved our fingers deeper into the crack and pulled so hard, sharp pains stabbed my fingertips like my nails might rip off. Finally, the elevator doors opened a couple of inches—just enough to see what was on the other side: a wall.

"We're between floors," Dillon said.

"Shit."

Black smoke billowed in from the ceiling hatch's seal. With a click, the space went dark, but a moment later, another click preceded the amber glow of emergency lights.

"How is the fire spreading this fast?" Dillon asked. "This building must have a sprinkler system?"

This was the exact question investigative journalists researched after a fire killed five people downtown a year ago. On one of the news broadcasts covering the story, the reporters explained that all new high-rises built after 2018 required sprinkler systems, and most older buildings were required to phase them in. But there were exceptions. It depended on the year the building was built and its intended use. Based on the pummeling smoke, this building was either one of those exceptions or hadn't come into compliance yet.

"Lift me onto your shoulders." I coughed, looking up at the escape hatch.

"That's where the smoke is coming in."

"It's our only way out."

Dillon only hesitated for a second before he knelt and let me sit on his shoulders, like we were two teenagers about to play a game of chicken in a swimming pool. When he stood back up, I discovered I still wasn't tall enough to reach the ceiling. With the smoke thickening and the screams and alarms blaring, I held Dillon's head as I carefully got my right foot onto his shoulder, then my left. He sensed what I was doing and grabbed my ankles.

As I stood up, I wobbled, trying to find my center of gravity. Dillon leaned forward and backward in sharp jerks to compensate for it until I was stable enough to stand.

Thankfully, I could now reach the escape hatch, but it didn't budge when I pushed.

With my eyes watering from the thickening smoke, I tried again and again until I realized a lever held it shut. I twisted it, and the escape hatch popped open.

Dense smoke flooded the elevator. The only way out was to go deeper into the worst of it, flames flickering a mere twenty feet above me.

*What could be burning inside an elevator shaft? Pipes? Electrical lines covered in years of flammable grease, maybe?*

The fire stung my eyes with its heat, cracking pops as it stretched down the shaft, reaching to take us in its grip.

I pulled myself up and threw my elbow over the lip, and with Dillon's shove, I yanked my knee up, then slithered my chest on top of the box.

I lay on my stomach and dangled my arm through the opening.

"Take my hand!" I shouted.

He was only three feet beneath my fingers, but when he jumped up, it might as well have been a hundred. He jumped again, and our fingers brushed.

"Higher!" I coughed.

He squatted, sprang up higher, and grabbed my hand. But with the heat, my skin was too sweaty to hold it. Dillon crashed to the bottom on his side, making the elevator jerk.

I risked a quick glance above me and saw the only cables that held us up from certain death were engulfed in the inferno. I wasn't an elevator-cable expert; I didn't know how long the fire would take to compromise its structure, but I had to assume not freaking long. And I seriously doubted brakes would withstand the fire's heat.

My lungs burned, my nose recoiled from the smell of burned rubber and oil, and my eyes stung so badly that I could barely see through the tears.

I leaned down again. "Come on!" I shouted. "You can do this!"

Dillon tried two more times before staring up at me. A minute ago, he looked so powerful and in control, but now, he looked small. Helpless.

"Just go!" he yelled.

"Grab my hand!"

"Get the hell out of here while you still have a chance!" he choked.

Something popped, and the elevator plunged a few inches before it yanked to a stop.

"I'm not going to have your death on my conscience, so hurry up and grab my hand!"

He jumped four more times, our fingers only touching once.

"This isn't working, so just go, Fallon! Now!"

"Get the strap off your bag!"

Dillon looked at his gym bag and must have realized what I was asking. He unclicked the strap, extended it as long as it would go, and then threw it up to me. I wrapped it around my wrists twice and dangled its end down the emergency opening.

I pushed my feet against the wall, and I had to brace my legs, back, shoulders, and arms so that I didn't fall when he jumped up and grabbed the belt. I clenched my muscles and held my body steady, allowing Dillon the seconds he needed to climb up the strap and grab the lip of the opening.

His elbow flung on top of the elevator, followed by the other.

I locked my hand around his wrist and grabbed his collar as he pulled, grunting from the effort until he finally spilled onto the elevator's roof.

The elevator plummeted a foot.

"Climb!" I pointed to metal rungs along the shaft.

I coughed, choking so hard, I thought I was going to throw up. Dillon did, too, and above our heads, the blue-and-orange fire made a whoosh sound.

*Backdraft,* I thought. Not on us, but nearby.

The heat singed my face as we climbed up to the floor above us. Two silver panels on gliders, normally opened with the elevator's doors, rolled apart when I tugged.

*Thank goodness.*

Another earsplitting pop, and the elevator dropped two feet.

Before I could get out of the shaft, though, a powerful snap cracked above our heads.

"Look out!" Dillon screamed as the elevator's cable whipped by our heads.

And then a metallic grinding sound accelerated, and I watched in disbelief as the elevator we'd been on only moments ago sailed into a free fall for twenty-some stories. Until it crashed with the force of a dynamite explosion.

"Come on!" I shouted.

I threw myself into the hallway, where the fire licked its walls. It was as hot as the inside of an oven, making it even harder to breathe through the hostile cloud of smoke. I covered my mouth with my shirt's sleeve, and Dillon pressed his forearm over his lips.

"Stairs!" I screamed and rushed toward the illuminated Exit sign.

The flames roared up the walls behind us and onto the ceiling as we sprinted to our only salvation.

A popping sound preceded Dillon's shriek. "Fallon!"

He tackled me to the ground and protected my head with his arms as a door-sized piece of fiery drywall crashed down from the ceiling. Right next to us.

"Come on!" He rolled off me and yanked me up by my shoulders.

The door was hard to get open—heavy as sin. As we both pushed, Dillon positioned his body behind me, shielding me from the incinerating heat. We coughed so hard, I feared we'd lose consciousness any second.

Finally, we got the door open and ran into the stairwell.

Just as a whoosh incinerated the rest of the hallway.

Several floors above us, the stairwell was already engulfed. We raced down the steps while I prayed we could make it out alive.

# 2

"Fuck," Dillon said, staring at the engulfed skyscraper.

After climbing down the twenty-some floors, we stood on the ground level, where fire trucks, ambulances, and a growing crowd of onlookers amassed around the structure.

Standing against the backdrop of the morning's pastel-pink sky, the seventy-story building chugged ebony smoke out of its top like a chimney, the upper floors glowing orange with flames crackling outside the windows. The putrid smell of burned metal and wood stung my already-raw nose, and the echoes of sirens racing to the scene silenced the cries of victims, whose once stampede of escapes slowed to a trickle. Then stopped completely.

"Do you think everyone made it out safe?" I asked. As a person trained to help protect people, I felt utterly helpless, unable to do anything but watch trained firefighters battle the blaze.

"I hope so," Dillon said.

*Oh gosh. Zoey.* I'd met her at the gym a few weeks ago. The poor girl had been through a lot lately, barely holding it together after suffering a devastating loss. And she was there today. I needed to make sure she'd made it out alive.

I scrolled through my contacts, grateful we'd exchanged numbers.

**Me: Zoey, are you okay?**

**Zoey: I'm fine. With a crowd on the north end of the building. Are you okay?**

I breathed a sigh of relief.

**Me: Yeah.**

**Zoey: Thank goodness! This was so scary!**

**Me: It was. Stay safe, Zoey.**

**Zoey: You too.**

**Me: Let's do coffee soon?**

**Zoey: Absolutely.**

I coughed, which made my esophagus burn even more.

Dillon put his hand on my shoulder. "Are you okay?"

I nodded, hypnotized by the scene before us. A fire truck extended its ladder as high as it would go, allowing a firefighter to climb up, break through the window with an ax, and enter a floor that didn't have flames sticking out yet.

"You go into a building like any other day," Dillon said, his emotions growing dark and reflective. "You never imagine you won't come out of it." He rubbed the back of his neck. "My brother would've never understood."

The gravity of his words weighted his voice down even lower until he read the questions rolling across my face.

"He's intellectually disabled. Needs round-the-clock care, so he lives in a facility. My mom and I are all he's got. I visit him every Sunday, and if I just stopped showing up..."

Dillon swallowed hard.

My eyes watered, but it wasn't from the flames this time. It was because of how touched I was, sensing Dillon's immense love for his brother. If I were honest, it was also because I was envious.

*I wish I mattered to someone the way Dillon matters to his brother.* To know that if you died, someone out there loved you so much, they would be destroyed. My best friend, Shane, would care, of course. At least I had that. And surely, on some level, no matter how much smaller it was than I wished, my dad would care, too. I shouldn't be so hung up on wishing I were someone's *everything.*

A pop drew our attention to another window that blew out and rained shards of scorching hot glass onto the thankfully cleared sidewalk below.

Fifty feet away, a police officer looked down at his pocket-sized notebook, tapped it with his pen, and nodded before walking away from a pedestrian.

"I'll be right back."

I walked away from Dillon and approached the cop. Chicago employed twelve thousand police officers, spread among various precincts, so it wasn't a surprise that I didn't know him.

The guy appeared to be in his thirties. He was thin with high cheekbones and a narrow jaw.

"Officer O'Connor." I extended my arm and shook his hand firmly. "Is there anything I can do to help?"

He shook his head, motioned to the nearby people. "We're taking witness statements." And then his eyes glided over my appearance, which must have been a dirty mess. "You were inside?"

I nodded and gave him an account of everything I witnessed while he jotted down notes and peppered me with clarification questions.

"I would tell the fire department to look into the elevator shaft. I'm not a fire expert, but I found it odd that it was engulfed when there wasn't any wood or drywall in there to burn."

He raised an eyebrow. "You thinking an accelerant was used?"

"I don't know," I answered. "But it was strange."

He nodded, and after leaving him with my information in case he had any other questions, I made my way back to Dillon.

"Make sure you give your statement before you leave," I said.

Dillon's lips twitched in amusement at my assertive tone when my cell phone buzzed with a text from my father.

**Dad: I know you're upset about what I did, but I love you more than anything.**

*Not anything.* If that were true, he would have shown up to my high school graduation, my college graduation, or my graduation from the police academy. Most dads would've shown up to all three, especially when they had no work conflict preventing them from going. I'd have settled for one, and that didn't even count all the ways he'd let me down before then.

Eleven-year-olds weren't supposed to have to raise themselves.

A stronger person would've cut him out of their life a long time ago, but I guess everyone needed to be loved by their parent, some of us having to chase it harder than others. I'd kept up that chase my whole life, pathetically savoring whatever measly crumbs of affection he'd throw my way. How many times had I gotten my hopes up that things would get better, only to be crushed into dust, rocking myself in the fetal position in tears? Yet I'd kept going back.

But this time was different because he'd gone too far.

For the first time in my life, I'd finally taken the experts' advice and cut Dad out. Addicts couldn't be trusted. Helping him the way I had—funding three rehabs, countless other bills, and groceries—was only enabling him, they'd said. Which, logically speaking, made sense. I'd walk out of those Nar-Anon meetings with my spine straight, ready to decline his calls and lay down an uncrossable line. And every time I'd hear his voice, see his face, or think of the dad before the disease changed him, I'd crumble into my prepubescent self, wanting nothing more than my daddy to come home. To hug me and tell me from this point forward, things would finally get better. They had to. And when he'd have no food to eat, all the expert opinions couldn't stop the haunting images of my father suffering. When his landlord threatened to kick him out, they couldn't stop me from envisioning him cold, living in an alley in the dead of winter. So, for years, I couldn't stop doing what they said not to.

But he crossed a line there was no coming back from, and, well, it was the wake-up call I needed. I couldn't enable him. As much as it gutted me and as many times as I cried myself to sleep because of it, I drew a line in the sand. If he wanted a relationship with me, he needed to be sober. Maybe, just maybe, it would finally give him the motivation he needed to get clean.

**Dad: PLEASE call me back. There's something I've never told you, Fallon. I need to tell you before I lose my nerve.**

"Everything okay?" Dillon asked, noticing the look on my face.

I swallowed the pain. "Yeah."

A tickle in my voice box made me cough—a barking, burning cough—and once I started, I couldn't stop. It turned into an all-out fit that drew the attention of a first responder.

"Miss." A guy with a Chicago paramedic patch stitched to his blue shirt approached me. He had a confident tone, but he was so young, I wondered if he'd ever worked a crisis of this magnitude before. "Let me look you over."

The appearance of the EMT snapped me out of my fog, making me realize I'd been here and let the clock tick forward for far too long.

"I have to go," I said.

"Fallon, you need to get checked out."

"I can't be late." I coughed, and this one turned so violent, I gagged.

"Let me at least check your oxygen levels," the EMT insisted.

"I'm fine."

"Breathing makes you barf," Dillon argued. "You're not fine."

I cut my eyes to him. *Traitor.*

"Look, no cabs are getting through." Dillon motioned toward the now-blocked-off roads. "And you can't walk unless you can breathe, so let him help you, and you can be on your way."

I coughed, but before I could argue further, I was ushered inside an ambulance, where I sat on a gray stretcher. I glanced around at all the cubbies filled with medical equipment to help save people: oxygen tanks, blood pressure cuffs, bandages, and defibrillators, among other things.

The EMT put a pulse oximeter on my finger and made me take deep breaths as he listened to my lungs with a stethoscope before doing the same for Dillon.

"You need oxygen." The EMT retrieved a mask attached to a green-and-silver tank and turned it on to the appropriate level of airflow.

But before he could place it on my face, a screaming woman burst out of the skyscraper's front doors. The sleeve of her right arm was singed off, exposing crimson welts that caused the EMT's eyes to widen.

I took in the scene around me, counting thirteen ambulances and noting more victims now spilling out of the building. If help didn't arrive soon to assist with the wave of new victims, this already-dire situation was bound to go from bad to worse. And in the meantime, our EMT appeared to have the least critical patients on his hands—us. He needed to help that lady. Now.

"I got this," Dillon assured and took the mask from the hesitant EMT.

In a typical emergency, an EMT would never let Dillon hold the mask, but this was escalating into a triage situation, and I would be considered green (walking wounded with minor injuries). That lady was probably a yellow (medium priority with moderate injuries) or maybe even a red (a high priority with life-threatening injuries). After a few moments, the EMT rushed to the more critically injured patient and guided her to an ambulance that was open, thanks to other paramedics treating victims where they'd fallen on the ground.

Dillon sat on the bench and positioned his body so we sat face-to-face.

Knees touching.

"Hold still, Fallon." He pressed the oxygen mask against my face, the tip of his finger grazing my skin as he did. Based on the rise and fall of his Adam's apple, the touch seemed to take Dillon a beat to recover from. "Now, breathe."

The air felt cool, going down my throat, hitting the bottom of my lungs. I coughed a couple of times, but it didn't deter Dillon from his mission.

"You need oxygen as badly as I do," I said.

He smirked. "You sound like Darth Vader with this thing over your face."

I took deep breaths in and out and had to remind myself to hurry. Though my boss would be the biggest dickwad in the history of dickwads if he didn't understand why I was late or missed it, I didn't want to give him that first impression of me not being there. Nor did I want to miss when assignments were handed out and volunteer hands shot up for the best parts.

Dillon's thick lips curled down into a serious line, full of fresh emotions.

"You really took charge in that elevator." Which, based on the look in his eyes, was something he was unaccustomed to seeing. Or maybe seeing other women do it, at least. "It was...impressive."

More like well-trained and self-sufficient. After taking care of myself for as long as I could remember, I learned the hard way that people weren't going to step in and solve my problems; I had to do it myself.

Dillon studied my eyes for so long, I thought he'd get lost in them. "You saved my life." He looked at my hair, my hands, my irises. "You could've left me, but you stayed. You saved me."

"Watching people burn to death isn't on my bucket list."

But he didn't smile at my joke. Instead, he scanned my face slowly, his breath hitching as his chestnut eyes locked on mine. I'd never had anyone look at me like this—staring as if the most important thing in the world was to learn everything about me.

And I had to admit...I loved it.

I pulled the mask off my face and pressed it to his. "Your turn to breathe."

His lips parted, and a slow smile spread across his face. "I want to take you out."

I couldn't deny my attraction to him. If I'd met Dillon earlier, I'd have gone out with him, no question. Enjoying the lighthearted company of a hot guy from time to time was fun, and romance provided color to an otherwise bleak existence. But I wasn't sure now was the best time to date someone, not with starting this task force.

"What?" Dillon asked. "You don't date?"

"I don't have a lot of time for dating."

"Make time," he implored. Not in a pushy, won't-take-no-for-an-answer kind of way, but a charming, I-promise-it-will-be-worth-your-time kind of way.

I couldn't help but smile. "And if I refuse?"

He pinned me with a seductive stare, his eyes glimmering with hope. "I owe you my life, so I'd have to become your indentured servant. Your love slave. Feed you grapes, massage your feet, whisk you away to an island."

I laughed.

But even if I made time to date, Dillon's good looks and confidence spoke of someone who probably dated normal people. Not someone like me, who couldn't even remember what normal felt like.

"My life is complicated," I said.

"So is mine," he reasoned, probably trying to put me at ease. "My world kind of imploded when I was thirteen." He shrugged. "So, I guess we have that whole complicated-life thing in common."

I raised my eyebrows. "What happened when you were thirteen?"

He grinned. "You'll have to let me buy you dinner to find out."

I hesitated.

"Come on. After saving my life, the least I can do is treat you to some ridiculously overpriced meal. I'll even splurge for dessert."

I sighed. "I don't even know your last name."

"McPherson."

I looked at his pleading gaze. "When did you have in mind?"

Dillon pulled the oxygen mask off his face and stared between my eyes and my mouth. "Is that a yes?"

CHICAGO'S POLICE HEADQUARTERS STRETCHED ALONG MICHIGAN AVENUE for an entire city block. Its five stories of sculpted concrete and perfectly spaced windows showcased clean architecture lines, a far cry from the dirty cases investigated inside.

I ran toward the conference room on the third floor. Past a dozen mahogany doors, past the wooden benches that lined the gray hallway, past the grouping of colorful flags perched along the wall, and when I finally arrived, I hesitated behind the door's frosted glass.

I'd managed to clean the soot off myself and change into my uniform in record time, but I was still a few minutes late, and my new boss had a reputation for being harsh. Praying I could contain the fallout, I took a calming breath, pulled the door open, and walked in.

# 3

Sixteen officers—a mixture of Chicago PD (including my best friend, Shane) and DEA agents—turned their heads and stared at me with tight faces that rolled tension through the air like a fog machine. They sat around an oval mahogany table, peppered with frosted water glasses that sparkled with sunlight from oversize windows, but one officer was standing, introducing himself to the man who stood in the front—DEA Sergeant Marcus Burch.

*The* Sergeant Marcus Burch. In the flesh. I couldn't believe I was standing in the same room as him. The man who'd kept going through a raid, even after a bullet had shattered his kneecap. The man responsible for taking down some of the biggest criminals in America. The man who'd written more training manuals than anyone in DEA history.

Rumor had it, he was three years away from retirement, and with thirty-six months left, he planned to eradicate one more drug organization on his way out. Which was aggressive. That gave him roughly six months to identify all the players, twelve months to investigate and gather evidence, and eighteen months to prosecute. I guess the way he saw it, you could either fade into oblivion at the end of your career or go out in a blaze of glory.

His pale skin reddened along his throat, and his lips tightened into a thin line beneath his silver-speckled mustache.

"Officer O'Connor, I presume?" he said in a gruff voice that reminded me of thunder.

He carried his tall, lean frame with the kind of authority that could make a grown man cower, his meaty hands clenched his hips, and his black hair was still thick, as if too scared of his wrath to succumb to the typical thinning for a man his age. But the most intimidating thing about him was his sharp eyes, which sliced through the room and stabbed me with animosity.

"Yes, sir, I apologize for being l—"

"Have somewhere more important to be than the official DEA task force kickoff meeting?"

"No, sir, I—"

"Meeting started seven minutes ago, O'Connor."

"I was detained by a f—"

"Do I strike you as the type of guy that gives a crap why you're late?"

Based on my research of him, this was a man who'd served his country, obeyed orders, and never taken BS from anyone. Let alone accepted excuses.

"Sir—"

"We'll talk about this after the meeting; I'm not going to waste everybody else's time."

*I wonder what the world record is for the quickest time in destroying one's career.*

I tried to hide my despair as I walked to the only open seat in the room—the one next to Shane, who must have saved it for me. But when I sat, the look Burch gave me—and by look, I mean, a glower that could've made an old lady drop dead from a heart attack—said he hadn't meant for me to wait *inside* this room.

I squared my shoulders, trying to feign confidence that I belonged here. If I missed the meeting, I would miss the entire case and investigation setup, which they hadn't even gotten to yet. They'd still been doing introductions when I walked in. If Burch accepted my apology and let me stay on the team, I couldn't afford to be behind everyone else.

"Sarge," another uniform interrupted from the doorway. "A word?"

Burch tried to murder me for a few more seconds with his death scowl before he exited the room.

Shane leaned closer. His wavy black hair looked a half-inch longer than normal, as if he'd been running a hand through it, his thick brows drew together, and his athletic frame tensed. "Where the hell've you been?" he whispered.

Shane Hernandez had been my best friend since middle school. Clarification: my only friend. We met in sixth grade after I'd moved from our beautiful brick home on its pristinely manicured lawn to the trailer park where I'd served the rest of my childhood sentence. And by trailer park, I don't mean one of those charming manufactured homes. I mean, the trailer park that gave other trailer parks a lousy reputation—disheveled and full of the one in four families that didn't have enough to eat each day. It was at this trailer park that I first saw Shane.

The son of a stay-at-home mother and a police deputy in Blue Island, Illinois, Shane was four when his father was killed. In the years that followed, his mother struggled. Two small kids and a mountain of debt were too big for the death benefits his father had earned, so eventually, she fell behind on their mortgage and rented the trailer next to us.

But at least Shane's mom ensured they always had food. She was good like that. Reliable. Getting food stamps and doing what she needed to do to ensure her kids ate. I, on the other hand, had fought against perpetual hunger during the first half of that school year.

Enter the day I talked to Shane for the first time. We'd been assigned seats next to each other in class, and as the weeks had passed, I pretended not to notice Shane's flashes of worry when my stomach growled. Especially when it still growled after lunch.

And on that day, the ache in my stomach was all I could think about. I watched the other kids with their overabundance of food throw half their lunch away—perfectly good food, thrown away—and bit my lip, wishing they'd just left it on the table so I could've discreetly taken it.

Looking back on it, what I did was stupid. I'd always been careful about dumpster diving *before* school and off school grounds, so I'd have enough to pick at in front of the lunchroom teachers to make them assume I was just a picky eater, not a kid going hungry. But that day, my dumpster dive had failed to produce anything, so when Jessica Roche threw her entire uneaten sandwich away and everyone cleared the lunchroom, I acted on instinct. Hunger was primal, and a clean, untouched sandwich, still in the bag, was too enticing.

It'd been sitting there, right on top of all the other trash. So, after one last glance around, I reached in and took it.

At the precise moment Shane walked in to retrieve his forgotten water bottle.

Instantly, my cheeks became a furnace.

He looked at my hand as it retracted from the can, then my face. His ocean-blue eyes pierced straight through my protective layers and exposed my hidden truth of all of those stomach growls. I felt naked, standing before him, terrified of the power he now had to destroy what was left of my life if he told someone about this.

"Fallon," Mrs. Swanson barked. Because suddenly, she was

there, too—because, for the love of all things holy, why wouldn't she also walk in at the worst possible moment? "Did you just pull that from the trash?"

"I—"

"No," Shane said. "I tossed it to her. She missed."

Mrs. Swanson looked from Shane to me. "Lunch is over. Did you not have enough to eat?"

Dad didn't take the best care of me anymore, but he was all I had left in this world. If they investigated, they'd take me away from him and make me live with complete strangers. I'd rather die than have that happen.

"I did. I just..."

"It's for after school," Shane lied. "We have a study hour planned."

Mrs. Swanson looked back to Shane's convincing face before pursing her lips. "Both of you, get to class."

Shane grabbed his water bottle, and we retreated into the hallway together.

"Thanks," I said quietly.

The next day, he plopped down across from me at the lunch table. I usually sat by myself because being poor made me unpopular. Shane opened his brown sack, pulled half his sandwich out, and placed it on the table in front of me.

"You don't have to tell me anything else," Shane said. "But I need to know one thing."

I looked into his severe gaze as the hum of voices around the lunchroom seemed to fade.

"Is anyone hurtin' you, Fallon?"

I blinked.

"Are you safe?"

I swallowed. "No one's hurting me," I whispered.

Shane tilted his head and chewed his cheek, clearly trying to decide if he believed me, before finally relaxing into acceptance.

"It has grape jelly," he said. "If you're not a fan, I can leave it off tomorrow."

And that was that. As much as I detested taking charity, Shane didn't make it feel like charity at all. He acted like we were just two friends, sharing lunch, and from that day on, we became as close as brother and sister.

Cut to today.

"You left before I was up," Shane continued.

Fun fact: thanks to sky-high rent, Shane wasn't just a friend and fellow cop; he was also my roommate. Two bedrooms, though—totally platonic.

"What happened?" Shane pressed.

"It's a long story." One I wouldn't go into right now. Right now, I had to focus on salvaging my spot on this task force, and I certainly didn't want Burch to catch me talking about this and misconstrue it as me trying to garner sympathy.

"You've never been late to work before. Let alone today."

"I know; I'll explain later."

"Are you okay?"

"Yes."

"Your voice sounds hoarse."

It'd sound a lot worse if Dillon didn't insist that I get an oxygen treatment.

"There was an incident," I hedged.

Before Shane had the chance to ask me more questions, the door swung back open.

"We're going to need to make this fast," Burch declared as he walked back inside. "A group of us needs to head over to a scene. Officers are processing it as we speak."

When he saw me sitting here, his eyes narrowed, and he opened his mouth like he was about to go off on me and kick me out of the room. But he must have seen the determination in my eyes and sensed I'd try again to explain why I was late. So...tick-tock. Crime scene.

"See me after, O'Connor," Burch snarled. "We'll discuss your future on this team."

Future. As in career-ending exit, based on his tone.

"We're in the preliminary stages of investigating the largest narcotics group in the United States," Burch began. "They're highly organized, extremely intelligent, and operate more like a Fortune 500 than an organized crime unit. They have a clear strategy, execute it with precision, and trade in volume."

Whoever came up with the idea for DEA task forces should be given the Medal of Honor. By partnering with city counterparts, the DEA could draw on the local expertise in this area, share resources, and increase possibilities with investigations. Plus, it gave us a great experience on our résumés, so I'd have a better chance to land a full-time role with the DEA, and Shane would have a better shot at one day becoming police chief.

"Now, in terms of narcotics," Burch continued, "we have the usual suspects: heroin, cocaine, diverted pharma, cannabis, but the ones that are on the rise right now are fentanyl—a key driver in the current opioid epidemic."

Shane gave me a worried look.

"And methamphetamine. Vast quantities of which are being smuggled in from Mexico. This is where the group we're investigating comes in: The Chicago Syndicates."

Burch moved to an eight-foot-long corkboard in front of the room and flipped it over. On the other side was an organization chart pinned up with rainbow-colored pushpins with two leaders, four headshots beneath it with the word *Captain* over their pictures, sixteen other leaders beneath them, and at the bottom, dozens of faces titled *Soldiers*. Only a third of the portraits, however, were of actual people with names. The others were a dark cartoon-like silhouette with a question mark under them.

"Our first goal in this task force is to put names and faces to every single one of these roles up here." Burch took a drink of water, plunked the glass down on the table. "This case ain't going to be easy. That protective layer they built by only distributing in larger volume means the typical play of going after the dime-store dealers and working our way up won't work. Further, one of our primary tools to vet operations like these is the use of confidential informants. We work with someone on the inside to get a baseline of the organization, but in this case, no one is talking. And when I say no one? I mean, no one. Not a word. One of the reasons for that, more than likely, is because of this guy."

He pinned a photo of a young man's mugshot to the board. "Christopher Cantrell—a soldier in the org—street name: C.C. Picked up on a narcotics charge, he was facing a life sentence due to his priors. After laying out his nonexistent future for him and his family, we offered Cantrell a deal—at which point he'd be moved into immediate protective custody, awaiting a detailed interview, where he was going to give up names, the structure, everything on a silver platter. Two hours before the interview, he's with two of the most experienced protection agents who, between the two of them, kept over sixty witnesses alive. But not in this case. We were never able to thoroughly interview Cantrell because he was executed right there in protective custody."

"How'd they get past those two guards?" an officer asked.

"They were executed first. As was Cantrell's entire family to send a message."

I picked at my thumbnail.

"This group runs a clean operation," Burch said. "No one's talked, and I'm tired of it. We need to find a good CI. Someone that can help us put names with faces if we have any shot at taking them down soon. We'll work leads. Establish rapport.

"Meanwhile, we need to get out there and start identifying these guys. I need names. Street names, legal names—I don't care.

Just get me something to work with. The only lead we have right now is this."

Burch took an eight-by-ten photograph out of a manila folder and pinned it to the board.

"This was obtained during a surveillance operation."

He pointed to the image. It was zoomed in and cropped to show the unclothed back of a man. He wore a hat, so we couldn't see his hair color, if he even had any—just his bare-skinned back.

And on it, a basketball-sized tattoo of a scorpion holding an American flag.

*Why would someone tattoo something like that on their body?*

"This picture was taken three weeks ago when my agents observed what was initially believed to be a possible narcotics move," Burch continued. "This tattoo was later shown to someone in interrogation, who confirmed it belongs to one of the captains in the Syndicates. Find the tat, we identify a captain."

Burch rubbed his chin, looking like he debated on adding something that was on his mind. He gazed over the group of agents and officers and put his hands on his hips. "One more thing I need to make clear, to give you a chance to back out now."

Back out now? What could he possibly say to us to make us reconsider being on one of the most elite task forces led by one of the best—if not *the* best—DEA sergeants ever?

"I believe they're about to make a major play," Burch said. He let his proclamation hang in the air, thickening the room with suspense.

With more busts under his belt than most anyone else in the DEA, his experience was something to be taken seriously. I knew there was the scent of an investigation. The gut feeling, hairs standing up in the back of your neck. Burch had seen things, probably started noticing patterns, and saw what ended up happening when those things played out. It didn't mean he was right, of course—only time would tell us that—but if he said they were about to do something big, then I absolutely believed they were.

I bounced my knee to get the excited energy out.

"My hypothesis?" he continued. "They're about to do a major expansion, which could mean war with the crews in New York or Miami, who are just as ruthless. There's never been a more important time to get in front of this," he said. "Now, little chatter that we did have came to a complete stop weeks before C.C. was killed. History says when that happens, it happens for a reason. People cleaning house, getting their ducks in a row for something. Whether it's expansion or something else, we need to figure out what it is."

The task force agents took notes, several nodding their heads.

"We'll be on the front lines, the faces of the people trying to lock up the biggest and most sophisticated narcotics criminals in the country. I don't need to remind you of the dangers."

As Burch looked around the room and allowed his ominous warning to wrap around our throats and strangle us, the cautionary tales they'd gone over in training flashed through my mind—shoot-outs, agents who had been killed in the line of duty.

"One more thing," he said. "This is not the case to try and be a cowboy. Later in the investigation, we'll be getting closer to the enemy, but listen to me when I say this: if you are not ready for something, do not volunteer. There's no honor in going undercover and getting yourself killed."

Undercover? I didn't realize that was a possibility. I thought this was going to be a ton of investigation. But being undercover and posing as one of them? Nothing would give me more satisfaction than getting to beat them at their own game. Thank goodness I'd taken all that extra undercover training. It'd give me a better chance at getting picked.

I sat straighter in my seat, tasting the opportunity ahead of us. *Well, if I'm still part of the team, that is.*

"All right, that's enough for today. Hernandez, Marks, Proctor, wait in the hall for me. You'll accompany me to a one-ten."

A first-degree homicide? The only reason the DEA sergeant would take his team there was if he thought it had something to do with this case. Talk about starting with a nuclear-sized bang.

I smiled, thrilled that Shane got called in to the action, yet wished I could be at that scene, too.

"Rest of you, you're dismissed for the day. Except you, O'Connor. You get your ass up here."

Shane put a hand on my shoulder before he strolled out the door with the rest of the officers.

I took a deep breath and tried to calm my nerves as I walked up to the front, knowing the fate of my career hung in the balance of what happened next.

As Burch moved the board to the side of the room, he said, "On a case like this, do you know what happens when an officer gets sloppy?"

I opened my mouth to answer, but he cut me off.

"Puts the lives of everyone else working with her in jeopardy." He turned around and flipped the board around so that anyone passing the conference room wouldn't be able to see the information. "I don't tolerate BS on my team, O'Connor."

"I was in a fire, sir."

Burch tensed. *Why?* He kept his back to me, though, refusing to show his cards, I guess. So, I continued.

"After finishing a workout, I was in an elevator with a civilian when it stopped, and the shaft filled with smoke. We gained access to the escape hatch and climbed out. Made it to the stairwell and escaped. I was treated on the scene for minor smoke inhalation and then came here."

Burch turned around and stared at me with the oddest expression. "The one on Wacker?"

"I—you heard about it, sir?"

"Word travels fast."

Why did it seem like he was holding something back?

"I was told I should be at the hospital, getting treated for smoke inhalation, but I refused to miss any more time than I already had. I want to be part of this task force, and I want you to understand how serious my intent is."

Burch tightened his lips and narrowed his hardened eyes, looking like he wanted to fire me. And something told me that from this point forward, he would look for any reason to do it. Inferno or no inferno, *not* letting me go would make him look weak in front of his team. And that was unacceptable. But he also had to know that dismissing somebody with undue cause—and holy crud, if almost dying wasn't undue cause, what was?—would open a ton of bureaucratic red tape for him.

Burch tugged at his ear and took a step closer, making sure he towered over me when he said, "When you're on my team? Don't put yourself in buildings that catch fire."

*Reasonable.*

But Burch earned his unreasonableness. You didn't get the kind of results that he did by being soft. Maybe by the end of the investigation, I could get him to hate me a little less. The more important headline was that I'd spared my job.

*For now.* What I needed to do was stay out of his line of sight. Let him cool down, give him space because Burch held all the power over the one thing that was most important to me—my career. He could end it with one phone call. And I had a feeling that if I did anything else to annoy him or made a mistake, he'd destroy my career, no question.

"Come on," he said. "You can ride with Proctor."

*What?*

I suppressed the panic that warned me that his invitation to work the scene wasn't a compliment; it was a penalty flag. I was officially on probation. Burch was going to keep an eagle eye on me, waiting for me to screw up so he'd have an indisputable reason to dismiss me.

And as if that weren't bad enough, I was about to share a ride with the one person who hated me even more than Burch did.

# 4

Proctor rested his right wrist on his cruiser's steering wheel and smirked as he peered at me. "Have a buddy who worked the scene of a fire this morning."

*Here we go.*

Proctor, who sported a blond buzz cut and stocky torso, was an officer from my precinct who I'd had the displeasure of working with. The guy's hobbies included weightlifting, checking himself out in the mirror incessantly, and trying to make my life a living hell.

Why did the guy hate me? To start with, Proctor had been offended when I politely turned down an invitation to go to dinner with him. Cue him throwing condescending jabs at me. Then, things got worse when I received high praise from our boss and severely escalated when I made the task force and he didn't. The only reason he eventually made the team was that one of the original officers had to move to Montana for personal reasons. Being waitlisted was a massive blow to his planet-sized ego, and I guess the only way to soothe it was to belittle me.

Constantly.

I usually tried to ignore it, but I was so not in the mood for it today.

"Said you were canoodling with some guy."

"So, you're keeping tabs on me now?" I asked.

"You gonna go out with him?"

He didn't give two craps about my love life; he just enjoyed antagonizing me.

"The light's green."

He took his foot off the brake. "You going to give this sucker a chance? Or shut him out like you do everyone else?" Proctor asked. Not in a sincere way, of course. In a you'll-screw-this-up-like-you-always-do way.

I clenched my jaw. "Still licking your wounds that I turned you down?" Because honestly, that was what this was about, wasn't it? No female could ever turn down Earth's gift to women.

Unfortunately, my uppercut provoked Proctor to double down.

"You've got *one* friend." Proctor tugged his thumb toward Shane's cruiser behind us. "And your longest relationship with a guy's been what, two weeks?"

"Maybe you should pay attention to your own lack of a love life instead of being obsessed with mine," I snarled.

I didn't want Proctor to know his words bothered me. I didn't shut people out; I dated casually because I was a busy, career-minded woman.

"Whatever," Proctor said. "Can't believe you're even on this team after the stunt your dad pulled."

Despite myself, I shrank two inches. I hated that any mention of my father had this effect on me. After all these years, I should have been stronger by now.

My cell phone buzzed with a text.

**Dillon: How are you feeling?**

Dillon's message was a welcome relief in a vehicle laced with so much hostility. I smiled and immediately answered him.

**Me: Throat feels raw. And I'm tired, but otherwise, I'm okay. You?**

**Dillon: If you start to feel sick, call me. I'll take you to the ER. Okay?**

**Me: Okay. Are you all right?**

**Dillon: I'm fine, thanks to you.**

As three dots blinked at the bottom of the screen, indicating that he was typing, I held my cell perfectly still, eager to see whatever text appeared next.

**Dillon: I can't stop thinking about you. I've never had a woman stuck in my head like this. It's very distracting.**

I smiled wider.

**Me: Maybe your fixation with me is just because I pulled you out of that elevator. Maybe it'll fade.**

This time, when he began texting back, I found myself leaning closer to the screen, watching every dot pulse as seconds ticked by.

**Dillon: It's not just because you saved me, Fallon. I noticed you the second I saw you and kept noticing you as everything unfolded. You impressed the hell out of me, even before the fire started. And no, it won't fade. It's only been growing since we parted. Feels like I've been away from you for a lot longer than an hour. I can't wait to see you tonight. Have a great day.**

I hid my grin from Proctor by looking out the window at the skyscrapers passing us by, grateful he kept his big mouth shut for the remainder of the drive.

Proctor parked his squad car behind several others on the south side of the Chicago River, which was flanked by seventy-story buildings that were home to some of the largest businesses in Illinois. Not the usual place for a crime scene. Yellow *Police Line*

*Do Not Cross* caution tape had already established a wide perimeter, causing traffic to bottleneck with curious drivers. Uniformed officers manned the nearby bridge to shoo away lookie-loos who might inadvertently drop something in the water and contaminate evidence. Water that smelled faintly of rotten eggs—a smell that would likely only intensify in this baking heat.

Shane, Proctor, Marks, and I followed Burch as he approached the bald homicide detective wearing a black suit.

"What've we got, Detective?" Burch asked, shaking his hand.

"Adam Terrell. Captain in the Chicago Syndicates," the detective started, looking at a credit card–sized notebook. "Witness out for a jog this morning saw the body under the bridge and called it in. Cause of death TBD. Body couldn't have been there long." The detective pointed to the surrounding buildings with his pen. "Someone would've seen it. Most likely dumped in the middle of the night."

"Still risky to dump it in this part of the city," Proctor said, trying to add his weight in.

"You don't think he was killed under the bridge?" Burch asked.

"No," the detective said.

"Why?"

"I'll show you."

He motioned for us to follow him, and as we walked, Shane positioned himself next to me.

"Heard the news on the way over," Shane whispered. "Please tell me you weren't at the gym this mornin'."

Shane appeared to hold his breath as he waited for my reaction.

"Close call," I admitted. "But I'm fine."

I hated when Shane looked worried like that; he'd done enough worrying for me when we were kids.

Before Shane had the chance to ask me anything else, Burch

stopped in the shade of the rust-colored bridge near the waterline.

My stomach twisted. Seeing the crime scene made the worst moment of my life flood back to me.

*I reach for the doorknob of our trailer, hearing that the television is on inside. I twist the knob and then—*

"O'Connor." Burch waved me forward.

It took me a moment to swallow my past and focus on the present.

"What do you see?" Burch asked.

*He's testing me. Get it wrong, and he might deem you incompetent —due cause for termination.*

The body that rested in six inches of water on the concrete base was nude, save for a single blood-soaked sock. His eyes and mouth were frozen open, as if he'd been screaming in agony at the exact moment of death, which, based on the immense amount of lacerations, burns, and other injuries, was probably exactly what happened.

"He was tortured." I finally found my voice, answering Burch's question. "There would have been a lot of screaming, so it had to have taken place somewhere remote. Or soundproof."

Burch nodded. "This is the only captain in the crime ring that we had identified."

"Which can't be a coincidence," I reasoned.

"I questioned this guy a couple weeks ago," Marks said. "I was doing patrol in a fairly abandoned area and saw him walking around. Turned out, he had a quarter of meth on him, so he got charged with possession."

"A quarter?" Proctor choked. "Why would a captain carry around anything, let alone something that small?"

Marks shrugged. "He never gave that up."

"And why torture him like this?" Proctor pressed. "Normal execution is two in the head, and you're dead."

"During his interrogation, he's the one that confirmed the tattoo belonged to a captain," Marks said.

"Why'd he give that up?" Shane asked.

"Was a slipup in a heated back-and-forth," Marks remembered.

Burch rubbed his chin. "Could explain why he was killed. The one thing the Chicago Syndicates do not tolerate is intel leaking."

"Or maybe it was because he got a possession charge," Proctor mused.

"Either way, this guy's been a loyal captain for years." Burch rubbed his mustache. "They could have buried the body where we would never find it." He glanced at the growing crowd of spectators. Then at the torture marks, the loyal captain, the very public location in the heart of the city.

"This isn't a murder," Burch said. "It's a message."

Shane, Marks, and I exchanged glances and then looked back at Burch.

"To the Syndicates?" Shane asked. "Or to us?"

A stylish guy wearing black slacks, a hunter-green button-down, and a detective badge on his belt interjected and waved Burch over.

*That's detective Fisher. In the past, I'd shadowed him for training purposes, but what would he be doing here?*

As they stood, talking twenty feet away, Burch glanced at me with that look people had when they were talking about you.

I twisted my hands together to massage away my anxiety. What could they be saying about me? And why did they look so irritated by whatever it was?

"You okay?" Marks approached me.

Thirty-three years old with blond hair and a thin frame, Marks was my mentor, assigned to me when I'd started the force. He was a man I admired for how much he adored his family, whose pictures blanketed his desk at the precinct.

"How's your wife feeling?" I managed.

I wanted to ask if he noticed Burch glaring at me, but I was too embarrassed to draw attention to Burch's animosity.

"Huge. I could get the call at any second." He held up a picture on his phone of his two little girls—a toddler and his four-year-old, both with baby blond hair, big blue eyes. "Jess took this yesterday."

"They're beautiful."

"They take after their mother. Maddie, the little one, runs up to me the second I walk in the door and hangs on to me like a monkey the rest of the night. Doesn't let me go."

A pang hit my chest. Those girls were so lucky to have a dad like him. But it was obvious that Marks considered himself the lucky one; he clearly went home every night to a house overflowing with love. Which made me think...

This morning, I'd been obsessed with missing out on my coveted seat on this task force, but after nearly losing my life, I was beginning to wonder if maybe I was missing out on so much more.

"Looks like you're being summoned," Marks said, nodding to Burch, who waved me over.

I swallowed my apprehension, straightened my shoulders, and approached the men.

"O'Connor," Burch started. "This is Detective Fisher."

"We've met."

I'd trained with Fisher around the time he'd worked the tragedy that unfolded in the city a while back with that girl Jenna Christiansen. News stories said she'd moved to the city to go after her dreams, only to find herself in a nightmare.

But Fisher was a homicide detective, one who wasn't working this scene, so why was he here?

"Need you to tell us exactly what happened this morning," Burch insisted as he scraped his thumbnails against his fingertips.

I glanced over my shoulder at the murder scene we were supposed to be processing—the urgent murder scene that was deteriorating by the second, thanks to the water. What could be more important than that?

"They *do* think it was arson," I deduced.

Burch exchanged a look with Fisher, who cleared his throat and said, "The initial report just came in. Confirms telltale signs of it, yes."

Okay...

And Fisher must be the lead detective on the case, which sadly meant someone must not have survived.

But why interrupt an active murder scene to talk about this now? And why did Burch take such an interest?

"You told the officer on the scene you were on the fifty-fifth floor, that correct?" Fisher pressed.

I nodded. "The gym. Got a workout in. Why?"

Fisher exchanged a look with Burch.

"Appears the fire started on that floor, right next to the elevator shaft."

Okay, I wasn't an arson expert, so what did that mean? Would it spread faster through the shaft to the other floors?

"You mentioned the stairwell was also engulfed," Fisher said, looking at his notebook. "That correct?"

"Yes. Is that a point in the investigation?"

"So, maybe they wanted someone dead enough to block all escape routes," Burch suggested.

Wanted *someone* dead? Arson was one thing. Attempted murder was another. Attempted murder that risked the lives of thousands? That was a stretch.

"There are a lot easier ways to kill someone than setting fire to an entire building full of people," I said.

"Unless you don't want police to know which person is the target," Burch said.

"Is that the theory you're working?"

"It's early," Fisher said. "Have to wait for the full investigation before speculating." Code for not willing to share his theory.

"And yet I know how important those first gut feelings are," I pressed.

Fisher evaluated me. "Has anyone threatened you recently?"

"Threatened *me*?"

Burch and Fisher exchanged a look. Fisher shook his head, urging him to keep his mouth shut, but Burch measured something else—something more important than this guy's annoyance.

"Eyewitnesses saw two men loitering near the elevator, O'Connor," Burch said. "Where the fire started."

There was something in the way that Fisher looked at me—fixed gaze, leaning into my words—that made me think this was more than just a routine follow-up interview.

"Meaning?"

Burch delivered the news like a doctor giving a sad diagnosis. "They may have been targeting you, O'Connor."

I blinked. "There were a lot of people in that gym," I said.

"We'll look into everyone," Fisher said.

But that would take time. In the meanwhile, I sensed from his tone that I was their focus.

Which didn't make any sense. I didn't have any enemies. "No one would have a reason to target me."

"Being a cop is a reason."

"I'm one of twelve thousand Chicago police officers. I'm too new to have pissed someone off bad enough to try a one-ten on a cop."

"You're on my task force."

*Oh. That's why he cares so much.* That was where his head was going, the hypothesis hitting me loud and clear.

"Along with almost twenty other people, sir, so why me? Why

not one of them? And how would anyone even know I'm on the task force?" And why now when we hadn't even started and had done absolutely nothing to pose any threat at all?

I guess when you'd been the leader of many missions, you'd seen some of the craziest stuff that people were capable of. And clearly, that made you a bit paranoid that any coincidence was no coincidence at all, that it was all related to you and your task force's mission.

"May not know the full motive yet, but I never discount facts. First day of this investigation, a Syndicates captain is found tortured, and one of my DEA agents almost gets killed in an arson."

Still.

"Why would *I* be a target?" I pressed.

"I don't know," Burch admitted. "But we better find out."

# 5

"Do you think it's true?" Shane's eyebrows pulled together.

I put fresh makeup on in our apartment's bathroom while Shane leaned against the doorframe, watching me.

"I don't think it makes a lot of sense," I assured.

"But *they* think you might have been targeted."

"Key word being *might.* I'm sure it had nothing to do with me."

Shane didn't look convinced, but I didn't want him to worry over a mere hypothesis.

"Can we drop it for now?" I asked.

We'd been talking about this for a while already, and all this wondering wasn't productive.

Besides, there was something else I wanted to ask him about before I left for my date with Dillon. I'd told Shane what Proctor had said but hadn't discussed how it'd made me feel.

As Shane scrubbed his face and let out an exhausted breath, I studied him—my best friend. The guy who'd hopefully be honest with me even if I didn't like the answer.

"Do you think I shut people out?" I asked.

Shane's jaw became a statue of frustration. "Don't listen to Proctor; he's just trying to get into your head, hoping it'll make you screw up at work."

"Doesn't mean he's wrong," I allowed.

In fact, now that I thought more objectively about it, what he said was true—I'd never had a boyfriend last longer than two weeks.

I thought the reason I'd always kept things casual was that I was career-focused, but seeing Marks today reminded me that a lot of career-minded people had significant others. Families even. So, what was my hang-up, then? Why, in all these years, hadn't I ever really opened up to anyone?

"I've never told anyone, except you, about my past," I admitted. "Don't you think that's pretty damning evidence that I don't let people in?"

"I think you're a very private person."

*That's a yes.*

I never discussed anything personal. "All I ever talk about on dates is work."

Maybe that was why I didn't get a lot of callbacks for a second date. If I tried to get to know someone but the only thing they would discuss was their career, I wouldn't feel a connection, either.

"Why do you think I do that?"

Shane sighed and regarded me in the mirror. "Honest truth?"

"No, lie to me."

Shane frowned, unamused. "I think it's because you don't like talking about what happened to you. About..."

How my dad being an addict wasn't even the worst part of my childhood.

"I don't like people pitying me, and I don't want to be a Debbie Downer." I evaluated myself in the mirror, and for the first time, I said out loud what I never wanted to admit to myself. "Maybe I'm afraid people will never look at me the same when they find out what I came from."

That tasted awful coming out of my mouth. Giving a damn about what other people thought of me was weak and pathetic.

"Your history shaped you into the warrior you are today, Fallon. You should be proud of everything you've overcome and wear it as a badge of honor."

My eyes stung as tears threatened to form. "What if other people don't see it that way? What if they look at me like the trailer trash I was when I was younger?"

Shane tightened his lips. "A, you were never trailer trash, Fallon. And B, if someone ever, ever looks at you like that, they don't deserve to be in your presence, or your life. Better to find out the guy's a douchebag now than later."

I bit my lip. "So, this is what normal people talk about on dates? Their super-depressing past?"

"Opening up is a vulnerable thing," Shane said. "You don't have to do it if you're not ready."

*Maybe I'll never be.* But if I didn't change things, I would wind up alone.

Just like when I was a kid...

I didn't want to feel alone like that ever again.

I wasn't sure if I was ready or even wanted anything more than casual dating. Part of me wondered if I was too broken for it, but I was willing to at least approach things differently with Dillon and keep an open mind.

"You going to tell him?"

I sighed. "I don't know."

Knocking on the door interrupted us and made butterflies float through my stomach. Shane stood in the living room, watching as I danced to the front door, and as soon as I opened it, my mouth went dry.

*Holy smokes.*

Dillon was sinfully gorgeous. His dark hair complemented his sexy stubble and eyebrows. Lean muscles pushed against the high-end fabric of his white button-down, as if the cloth were incapable of containing his rugged strength, and each curve of his chiseled face drew my gaze to his magnetic eyes. I'd never dated anyone so dangerously handsome. No, handsome was an understatement, an insult to someone of his caliber. If sexiness were an Olympic sport, this guy would win the gold medal, hands down.

I'd never had anyone look at me this way, as if he'd thought about me every moment since we'd parted. His brown eyes drifted through my skin, as if able to see every part of me.

"Whoa." Dillon's gaze skimmed my knee-length red dress, my twisted-up hair, and dangling earrings. He leaned down and pressed his lips against my cheekbone—holy moly, the spark from his mouth on my skin unleashed a tsunami of pleasure—and he murmured, "You look amazing."

Dillon handed me a bouquet of two dozen pink roses in a crystal vase. No guy had ever given me flowers before, let alone something this nice.

"They're beautiful, thank you." I looked at Shane standing there and motioned with my chin. "Dillon, this is my friend and roommate, Shane. Shane, Dillon."

Dillon raised his eyebrows, clearly surprised to find a guy in my apartment.

Shane walked up and shook Dillon's hand. Hard, by the looks of it.

"Nice to meet you." Dillon smiled.

"Same." They finished shaking hands, and then Shane went into his bedroom to give us privacy.

"Hungry?" Dillon asked.

"Starving."

. . .

This restaurant was gorgeous. White tablecloths. Women in high-end dresses and even higher heels. Champagne flutes, waiters in tuxedos, lighting carefully crafted to replicate the warm glow of candlelight.

Dillon pulled my chair out for me, and as he walked around and took his seat, he didn't even glance at the other women in this restaurant even though many had movie-star looks. In fact, his piercing gaze never left mine, not even when our waiter came by to take our drink order.

"Do you like wine?" Dillon asked me.

I hesitated. "I'll just have water."

The way he tilted his head made me wonder if he'd ask me why I didn't drink alcohol, but I hoped he wouldn't. It would open a depressing explanation before we even opened the menus.

When the waiter scampered off, Dillon leaned forward and rested his elbows on the table as he smiled at me.

"You live with that guy?" he asked, surprised amusement lacing his words.

I nodded. "Shane's a friend. Platonic," I clarified. "We're like brother and sister." Any doubt to the contrary had been answered in tenth grade when we kissed, curious if it might spark romantic feelings. It didn't for either of us, though. We laughed about it, and it never happened again.

"If I lived with you"—his eyes wandered down my body—"there's no way in hell I could keep my hands to myself."

*I wouldn't want you to.*

"He's protective of you," Dillon continued.

"We've been friends since we were kids. Went through some heavy stuff together."

Dillon's gaze cascaded over my face like he wanted to uncover each puzzle piece of me and put it together.

My chest warmed.

"I have a confession to make," I said.

"Just one?"

"I looked you up on social media."

That wasn't the extent of it. I'd run a basic background check, looking for warrants and criminal records, and he had none. And then I thought to myself, *What the heck am I doing?* Investigating my date couldn't be something a normal, healthy person did.

"I'm not really into the social media thing."

"So I gathered. You have, like, five pictures, and four of them are of sporting events."

He offered a smile. "What can I say? I prefer living in the moment versus posting about it to get likes." Then, he added, "I have a confession to make, too."

"Just one?"

"I looked you up on Instagram, too, and you also only have a few photos. I have to say, it was a breath of fresh air. Most women I've dated are obsessed with putting their whole lives up on social media."

Well, cops were a lot like teachers in that regard. One wrong post could cost you your career, so why take the chance?

"I'm not a social media person. And even if I were, the things I find value in are things I'd never post about online."

Dillon tilted his body closer to mine, his energy glistening through the air like embers cast from a flame and gliding across my skin like silk. My stomach flickered as he enveloped me in his gaze, his chestnut eyes like polished amber, so beautiful, they brightened the entire room.

"So, did your day get better?" Dillon asked.

"After escaping certain death?"

"After that." He smiled.

*Houston, we have a dimple.*

I opened my menu. "Not particularly."

Dillon's smile fell. "Why?"

*Take your pick: a pissed off boss, crazy conspiracy theory that the fire was an attempt on my life, and as an added bonus...*

"A guy was a complete dickwad to me. I'm pretty sure he intends to make my life miserable."

A protective edge sliced through Dillon's eyes as his mouth morphed into a tight line.

"Your waters," the waiter said.

As the waiter stood at the side of the table, Dillon seemed to recalibrate, that momentary edge fading as we placed our dinner orders.

Once the waiter left, Dillon held his glass up toward mine and smiled. "To second chances."

He clanked my glass, and I took a drink.

I stared at the ice cubes, his toast to second chances scorching my heart.

Celebrating our escape from the inferno should have felt great, but it brought a tug of sadness. It wasn't fair that we got to sit here and celebrate having lived when others would never get to do this again. How many families were out there, mourning right now?

Dillon read my expression and cleared his throat. "I heard on the news that seven people didn't make it."

Seven families destroyed after losing a mother, father, sister, brother, son, or daughter.

"Would have been eight if you hadn't saved me." Dark sadness lingered in his tone. "I know I said it before, but thank you. I owe you my life."

"Anyone in my position would've done the same thing."

"We both know that's not true," Dillon challenged. Then, after several seconds of silence, he admitted, "I haven't been able to stop thinking about you all day, Fallon."

Dillon's gaze was so intense, it made my nerves crackle beneath my skin.

"I've been waiting all day to get to learn more about you," he said.

I wasn't used to being the source of someone's absolute attention. So acute, it was like an electric current surging through my veins, erupting goose bumps in its path.

"Like what?"

"Everything."

No one had ever had this kind of insatiable curiosity about me before, and it was exhilarating. Because it was *him* wanting to get to know me.

But as I stared at Dillon, I instantly understood how much I had, in fact, used my work as a crutch in the past. Steering every conversation to my career time and time again had created an emotional barrier that prevented anyone from seeing the real me. A crutch that I'd undoubtedly lean on tonight—and any other night—the second talking about myself felt uncomfortable.

I didn't want to be that closed-off person with Dillon.

It was time I pushed myself past my comfort zone because he was different than other guys I'd dated. Selfless. When he almost died, his first thought wasn't of his own life; it was how his death would shatter his brother. A brother he made time for every Sunday. I wanted to try to open up to Dillon, but to do it, I needed to lock my crutch in a closet.

Plus, now that I was on an official DEA task force, it wasn't like I could discuss details about my job, anyway.

"Would it be okay if we didn't talk about work?" I asked.

Dillon blinked. "Tonight? Or in general?"

Based on my tone, he must have sensed the latter.

"I have a stressful job," I hedged.

Dillon's beautiful lips seemed to know exactly what to say. "We won't talk about work," he conceded. "Any other topics you want to keep off-limits on our dates?"

*Dates. Plural,* I noticed. I smiled, knowing he already liked me enough to want to see more of me, but a swelling panic came right behind it. Did I really have the courage to talk about my dark, twisted childhood?

Dillon seemed to sense my apprehension and leaned his forearms on the table. "I just want to get to know you better," he assured.

Right. This wasn't an interrogation. It was a date with him, the guy whose eyes instantly calmed my nerves.

Before figuring out where to start explaining "everything" about me, I got distracted by my buzzing cell phone. When I saw it was another text from my father, I couldn't hide my grimace.

"Everything okay?"

I sighed. "My dad and I aren't speaking right now," I admitted. Some of which was my fault. I'd cut him off, refusing to speak to him. "He's an addict."

A better daughter wouldn't feel embarrassed by his addiction, that she didn't have a normal parent. Yet heat seared my cheeks and tunneled into my chest, scalding my ribs.

When Dillon's eyes touched mine again, though, they extinguished the flames because his expression wasn't pity. It was poignant sadness, the recognition of someone else who must be battling complications. Complications that were easier to admit to someone who must have also gone through something terrible based on his comment earlier.

"He's promising to get clean again. For the millionth time."

"Has he been an addict your whole life?" Dillon asked.

"He started when I was eleven."

That was when those drug dealers murdered him and replaced him with a zombie mutant whose only purpose was to sprinkle the occasional, irrational hope that he might recover. But instead, he had me living in constant fear of every phone call and every knock on the door that it would be *the one* that told me my father overdosed.

"And your mom?"

I twisted my fingers together. "My mom was a stay-at-home mom. In the beginning, they both doted on my every move." I traced my finger along the circular lip of the glass, the happiness of those times now hurting with how much I missed them. "Those were my original parents."

Dillon shifted in his seat, his gaze morphing into worried curiosity. "What changed?"

The winds of my past carried me back to the place I'd tried so hard to leave behind.

"When I was nine, my mom had to have shoulder surgery. We didn't think too much of it." I picked at my nail. "The doctor prescribed pain pills for after. This was before we knew anything about opioids, let alone how addictive they could be."

Dillon's expression grew apprehensive.

"After, something seemed different in my mom."

To say the least.

Nine-year-olds can't reconcile suddenly going from their parents' first priority to their last. They can't understand why a mom used to greet them with a huge hug when they got off the bus but then won't even say hello when they walk in the door. No. Those nine-year-olds blame themselves, wondering what they did to make their parents fall out of love with them. And they pathetically try everything to regain said love, no matter how many times they cry themselves to sleep after failing.

"I was worried something went wrong with the surgery because she just couldn't get out of the pain. Kept going back to the doctor to get more pills. She became withdrawn and stopped taking me to the park. Eventually, she just stayed inside all day, even on the nice days. Our medical bills must've been piling up, too, because my parents would argue about money. By the time I was ten, we had to move into a trailer park. Dad promised it was temporary, that it was just until Mom got better, so he could pay for her to go to a special shoulder treatment place." I shrugged. "I didn't realize until much later she was going to rehab. Or that she'd switched from pills to heroin since heroin has the same opioid base she'd become addicted to."

I nibbled the inside of my cheek before I continued. "I eventually realized she'd become an addict and felt sorry for her because she never saw it coming. She hadn't sought out drugs or done them to party or something. She'd taken pills her doctor gave her for her surgery, and that was it. What I really couldn't forgive was when my dad became an addict. He'd seen exactly what it'd done to my mom and me, and despite that, he became an addict by choice."

Dillon leaned closer and spoke in a gentle tone. "You said he started using when you were eleven?"

I picked at my nail. "Still in the trailer park, of course. Only now, I was basically an orphan. My mom had died, and my dad was almost always high, and when he wasn't high, he was sleeping or coming down. He'd stopped working, so we lived hand to mouth on whatever government assistance he managed to get ahold of, but the drugs came first. Always first."

Dillon watched me straighten all my silverware even though it didn't need tidying.

I worried he'd ask me questions about my mom, but maybe he sensed I would refuse to discuss the circumstances surrounding her death.

That was something I'd never talk about with anyone. Ever.

Instead, he asked, "How long has it been since you've spoken to him?"

"Three months." After he'd humiliated me and almost ruined my career. But if I were honest, my anger ran deeper than that. "I've never understood why he started doing drugs, and he's always refused to answer that question. Like finding out why my whole life crashed and burned around me is of no consequence."

And now, he kept texting me that there was something he needed to tell me. I didn't care that my gut told me this time was different; I didn't trust him. All his empty promises over the years were daggers that would strike the second my hopes got up. He never followed through with any of them. We never even left that run-down neighborhood.

"He still lives in that trailer. Blue Island is a nice enough town, but that trailer park..." I pursed my lips. "Oasis Homes makes it sound like something beautiful."

Dillon paused and took a tight sip of water. "You lived in Blue Island?"

I nodded. "Why?"

He hesitated. "No reason."

But he wouldn't look me in the eye, and before I could ask why, the waiter brought our food over. Each plate looked like a work of art with asparagus crisscrossed in a pinwheel pattern over steak, parsley flaked on top, and a rich oil dripped along the outskirts. It looked too beautiful to eat, but the smell of its rich, buttery flavor moistened my mouth.

As soon as I cut into my steak, however, my shoulders sank.

"What's wrong?"

"Nothing," I lied and even put on a smile. He was treating me to a nice dinner, and I wasn't about to ruin any part of it.

But Dillon looked at the meat and flagged down the waiter.

"Dillon, it's fine."

"She ordered her steak medium-well, not rare. Please have the chef cook it longer."

"I'm sorry, sir."

"Take my plate, too."

"Sir?"

"I won't eat until the lady does," Dillon declared.

I stilled. How could such a small act make me feel so cared for?

The waiter issued apologies and vanished with our plates,

returning a few minutes later with both of our dinners cooked the way we had ordered them.

Dillon picked up his utensils and unleashed the electric current of his stare onto me that glided past my skin and magnetized its voltage inside my chest.

"I'm glad you made it out of that fire, Fallon."

My eyes prickled because I understood his double meaning. The fire of my past and the one that almost took my life.

"I assumed you were going to look at me with pity."

But wonderfully, he raised his eyebrows and shook his head.

"Pity? No. Admiration? Hell yes. I respect someone else that had to pull themselves out of a sinkhole."

I blinked. "Someone else?"

# 6

Dillon cut his steak. "My dad took off when I was thirteen without so much as a phone call or a dollar. He claimed he had some big career opportunity, but I think he couldn't handle the responsibility of my little brother.

"Dex's bills—that's my brother's name, Dexter—his bills were adding up. It became quicksand, and it wasn't long before we lost our home and moved into government-subsidized housing. Gangs infested that place. Loved to talk crap just to assert their alpha dominance, and sometimes, they even beat you up for no reason."

*I can't even imagine.*

"They loved to ridicule Dex, who still lived with us at the time. I knew we had to get out of there. Mom did everything she could, but there just wasn't enough money to move, especially since Dex needed care that cost more than my mom could make. I had to wait until I was fourteen to apply for jobs. State law. Spent my fourteenth birthday applying for every job I could. Took years, but I got my mom out of that hellhole and bought her a home in a good neighborhood. Found a great place for Dex, too, where he gets the care he needs."

Wow. I bet most teenage boys would've become bitterly angry and rebelled in his situation. Maybe even run away. No one could've blamed Dillon for doing that, and no one could've expected him to step up and become a surrogate parent at such a young age. But in the face of a crushing situation, Dillon took action. I admired that he refused to accept his circumstances and not only managed to free himself, but freed his mother and brother as well.

My affection for him became a power surge, blazing through my veins and lighting up everything in its path. It was more electrifying than anything I'd ever felt on a first date—or a second or third, for that matter.

"Do you mind if I ask what Dexter's condition is?"

"Complicated pregnancy, followed by oxygen deprivation at birth," he said. "Suffered brain damage."

"I'm sorry."

He offered a weak smile.

"And you visit him every weekend," I remembered.

"I bring him gummy bears." Dillon smiled. "Our mom would never let us have much candy, growing up. We couldn't afford nonessentials. Dex is a perpetual little kid, so when I roll up with a bag of gummies, it makes him so happy, I can't help myself."

*I think my ovaries just exploded.*

My pull toward Dillon only increased through the rest of dinner. Afterward, Dillon drove me home in his silver 2021 Mustang GT Premium Convertible and walked me to my apartment building's entrance.

I hated that our date drew to its end. Saying good-bye felt like being expelled from a warm bubble bath and stepping into the icy air.

"I had a nice time," I said. "Thank you."

Against the blackened sky, towering buildings with checkered lights sparkled in gradients of whites and grays. It almost looked like a sophisticated, life-size Lego set, complete with cars rumbling along the roads as a light summer breeze danced across my arms, leaving goose bumps in its wake.

Dillon bit his lip and, standing a solid ten inches taller, smiled down at me.

My lower belly warmed. His presence pulled at me, his body just inches from my own. I longed to feel his chest against mine, his lips on my mouth, tasting me, his powerful arms holding me.

"I had a great time tonight, too." His voice glided over my skin in a low, sexy rumble. "And for the record?" He brought the back of his fingers up and trailed them down my cheek. His touch was soft and gentle, awakening desires deep within me. "I've never enjoyed a date as much as this one."

*That makes two of us.*

He cupped my cheek, his thumb in front of my ear.

*Lord, his touch.*

My breathing quickened as my body heated. His lips came closer, but they were going too slow. I needed them on mine—now.

*Hurry.*

He looked from my mouth to my eyes as he tilted his head.

And then an explosion of intoxication as he took my lip between his.

I could no longer feel my legs. I swore him grabbing my lower back was to keep me upright. I moaned—holy mother, it was a moaning type of kiss—and wrapped my arms around his neck, pulling our bodies together. He was warm and delicious, and when he opened his mouth, I accepted the invitation. I touched his tongue, relishing *his* moan as our kiss intensified. Our hands wove through each other's hair as our mouths opened and closed, our tongues connecting deeper and deeper.

I wanted him on top of me, under me.

Kissing him and being in his arms made everything feel lighter, the heaviness that once pressed on my chest evaporating.

Dillon eventually pulled back and smiled, bringing his hand up to my cheek. "I'd like to take you out again."

Was I imagining it, or did that slight crease to his brow make him look worried?

*No, not worried*, I realized. Overwhelmed by whatever this was buzzing around us, between us, and through us. It was comforting to know this sensation must have been as unique to him as it was to me.

I'd never been this excited or eager to go on a second date with anyone. It was thrilling, but it also made me a little nervous because, in the past, I didn't care that much if a guy didn't call me back or never wanted to see me again. But if Dillon ghosted me like that, it'd hurt a lot. And that was after *one* date. What would it feel like after two? Six? Thirty?

I leaned into the warmth of his touch and swept my apprehension into the shadows of my mind.

"I'd love that," I said.

# 7

Shane scrubbed his face and blew out a breath.

"Are you okay?" I whispered, so no one else in the conference room could hear. "You haven't been yourself lately."

At first, I attributed his stress to work, but now that I thought about it, his smiles had become less frequent over the past few weeks, even outside of work.

Before I could press Shane further, Burch stormed into the conference room.

"May have just caught a huge damn break," he declared.

DEA agents and officers leaned forward in their seats.

"Autopsy results came back from Terrell," he said. "Turns out, Terrell swallowed something before he died." Burch rubbed his chin. "A USB drive." He looked around the room. "Medical examiner says it was ingested about thirty minutes before the first wounds were made."

"Before he was tortured," Proctor clarified.

Burch nodded. "I sent it to our IT team. Stomach acid ain't too friendly on electronics, but the thing was wrapped in rubber, so we have a shot at finding out what was on it."

"You think it could have some intel for this case," Marks said.

"I don't think people swallow digital family pictures," Burch answered.

"Why would he have a jump drive with vital information on it?" Shane wondered.

*Seriously*. Seemed risky to hold on to evidence like that.

"All businesses need to keep records," Burch said. "Even illegal ones."

"Why would he swallow it, then?" I asked.

"Maybe he threatened to leak it, and they fed it to him to make a point," Proctor, the ever-butt-kisser, offered. As an added bonus, he threw me a snarky look as if we were on a high school debate team and he'd just won the round.

"Too risky," I argued. "If they fed it to him, they risked letting the ME find something that could take them down."

Burch's nod agreed with my logic. I was almost mature enough to *not* relish Proctor's frown. Almost.

"Maybe Terrell sensed he was in trouble," Marks offered.

"Still doesn't explain why he swallowed it, though," Shane added.

"Maybe they found out about it. Showed up at his house to get it," Proctor offered. "So, he swallowed it to get rid of it before they'd confirm he had it."

Burch rubbed his face, as if exhausted by this back-and-forth guessing. "We'll likely never know why he did it, but that doesn't really matter. What matters is what's on it and if IT can salvage any of it."

"How long will it take them?" Shane asked.

"They said a few days, maybe longer."

Whatever was on that USB drive had to be pretty damning to the Syndicates. I couldn't wait to find out what it was.

Burch spent the rest of the morning giving us the overview he'd intended to yesterday. It wasn't until I was on a coffee break that I saw a missed text from Dillon.

**Dillon: I have a surprise for you.**

I smiled and replied.

**Me: What kind of surprise?**

I didn't expect him to text back right away, especially since so much time had passed since his first text, but his response was immediate.

**Dillon: I've been thinking about everything you said at dinner, and I planned something special that I think you're going to love.**

Our conversation, though lovely, had been rather heavy. What fun idea could've sparked from it?

*As long as it includes spending time with him, the date will be incredible.*

**Me: What is it?**

**Dillon: I'll pick you up on Saturday.**

Which was only four days from now. How could four days suddenly feel like an eternity?

**Dillon: And, Fallon?**

What was it about this man that could make me stare at my phone with this much anticipation?

**Dillon: I cannot wait to see you.**

# 8

Dillon picked me up in his convertible—top down, thanks to the city's seventy-degree temperatures—and as the evening sun tilted in the cloudless sky, he struggled to keep his eyes on the road. His hungry gaze glided over my face, my body, making me feel wonderfully desired.

When we arrived at his secret destination, I smirked.

"Seriously?" I smiled.

"What?" Dillon said.

"We're not thirteen."

"First of all, that's a travesty if you're under the misguided belief that only people the age of thirteen can enjoy this place. Second of all? This is fun."

It wasn't Navy Pier itself that I found amusing. Navy Pier was a 3,300-foot-long concrete peninsula that extended from the shoreline out into Lake Michigan, peppered with brick shops and restaurants, emerald-green landscaping around gorgeous walkways, and a 200-foot-tall Ferris wheel that held over two thousand people an hour. It was the temporary carnival that made me grin.

Dillon watched my reaction as I took in the magic of it all. The rows of multicolored booths with games and prizes. The clowns on stilts that wobbled through the packed pedestrians, trying not to get taken out by a rogue child. The sea of people and the rumble of their voices overriding the city traffic. The smell of fried treats and kids clutching prized stuffed animals as they chomped on pink cotton candy. Other than a serious banner that promoted an upcoming awards ceremony—where the mayor would honor Chicago's chief of police—the place had transformed into a child-like fairyland.

My chest tightened as memories of my tween years crept into my mind. A time that should have been filled with innocence, optimism, and dreams of a prince on a white horse sweeping me off my feet. Instead, I'd peered through the gate of a carnival just like this one at the carefree kids overflowing with laughter with their best friends and crushes on boys. I'd felt so alone on the outside of that gate, looking in on the life and feelings I'd so desperately wanted but would never have.

"I've never been to a carnival," I said.

"I figured." Dillon tried to shrug what he said next off with a nonchalant smile, but his words delivered a powerful blow to my heart. "That's why I picked this. Sounded like you kind of got robbed out of your childhood. Thought it'd be fun to give you a little piece of it back."

My eyes watered, and I had to take a deep breath to keep them from leaking.

Dillon's chestnut eyes cut straight through my camouflage, which made me wonder if he saw all the emotions I usually hid from other guys. The hurt that this was what a tween should have been doing on her Saturday nights, playing games at a carnival with a boy she had a crush on, instead of being a prisoner to that trailer, too scared to leave because she was terrified her dad would overdose.

Dillon took my hand and laced his fingers through mine, and instantly, every ounce of sadness washed away. In his embrace, I only felt bliss.

I felt like a piece of my soul was a butterfly in flight, feeling magnificently free for the first time.

"Come on." He smiled, his lighthearted tone back. "Let's have some fun." He pulled me through the crowd until it came to a clearing, where the song "Iko Iko" blasted through speakers while street dancers dressed in white T-shirts, backward baseball caps, and skinny jeans danced to the music.

The street performers were invigorating, rocking their bodies to the thrumming beat as the crowd clapped and shouted along to the lyrics. All the smiles, the kids squealing with laughter. It was as if someone had put pure happiness into a bottle and released it for everyone to breathe. And I wasn't immune to its intoxicating effects.

When Dillon let go of me to clap to the cadence of the music, my hand had never felt emptier. The omission of his touch and the warmth that radiated through my blood was profound.

We watched the street performers for a full minute. Well, I watched them; Dillon watched me, his smile growing wider, the more I enjoyed myself.

"Come here," Dillon shouted, pulling me by my hand to an open space.

"I can't dance," I said, seeing his intention. But dancing meant I'd get to feel him touching me again, so I wasn't about to put up a fight.

"I can't, either!" He smiled as he spun me around and dipped me, holding my hand and upper back for several beats as he gazed into my eyes.

"Liar."

Dang, the sexiness of his mouth and those beautiful full lips when he chuckled.

With one arm, Dillon effortlessly snatched me back to a standing position. I followed the momentum of his hands' pushes and pulls, moving me away from him and pulling me back. Spinning me one direction, then the next.

I laughed as he spun me again, and this time, he pulled my back to his chest and put his hands on my hips, swaying to the music. Geez, his chest and abs were granite ripples yet warm and inviting, a perfect mold around me.

*Heaven help me. I'd volunteer to be a human crash test dummy to see him without a shirt.*

How did it feel this exhilarating, having my body pressed against him?

When the song ended, everyone erupted into applause for the professional dancers, but Dillon continued to hold me, putting his mouth near my ear. The heat of his breath tickled against my neck. "Keep dancing, food, or games?"

I leaned my cheek against his chin's whiskers. "I've never had cotton candy."

"A tragedy we'll rectify immediately. Come on."

The absence of his chest took a second to recover from, but luckily, he slipped his hand into mine and guided me toward a booth.

"Two cotton candies," Dillon said. He pulled his wallet out of his back pocket, slapped a ten down, and handed me a pink cloud on a stick. He examined my face as I took a bite. "Well?"

It was the strangest sensation, a fluff ball that melted into sugar granules. "Heaven on my tongue."

Dillon's lips curled. "Come on. I need to win you a teddy bear to complete the experience."

He pulled me through the crowd.

Amid the rows of carnival games stood an unsuspecting pink booth with upside-down purple cups spread across four shelves. A rainbow cloud of stuffed animals packed the booth's roof, and below them, a gray-haired man with arms like twigs looked about as thrilled to be there as a plumber called in to unclog a toilet.

Unlike the other booths, this one didn't have a single player. Certainly a bad sign. Humans were quick students, spotting which games were unlikely to win prizes.

"Five dollars," the game guy said.

Dillon placed his money down, and the guy handed him a gun.

*Five bucks, and a guy hands anyone a gun. Every officer's worst nightmare.*

"Well, this seems safe," I quipped.

Dillon smirked. "It's just a BB gun," he said, and then he asked the guy, "How many do we have to knock down to get that?" Dillon pointed to the largest stuffed animal—a three-foot-tall pink teddy bear.

"Fifteen."

"How many shots per turn?"

"Twenty."

Dillon arched a mischievous eyebrow at me.

"Ladies first." He handed me the gun and stood behind me.

Like, inches behind me.

I knew how to handle a weapon, but I didn't tell Dillon that. My hormones were having too much fun, letting his hands caress my hips, then glide sensually down my arms to adjust my grip. He tucked a fallen hair behind my shoulder and lowered his mouth next to my ear.

"Relax," he whispered.

*Dang it, is he trying to make me misfire?*

Impossible when I could feel the thump of his heartbeat. But I tried.

I wanted to impress him, so I aimed toward the center shelf, took a breath in, let it out halfway, and pulled the trigger.

A *ding* sounded, but the purple cup didn't fall.

Cup, my butt. Those things were solid steel.

"They're screwed down," I accused.

Game Guy gave me a look of annoyance and lifted one of the cups, trying to make it look like it didn't weigh seven tons.

Dillon tried not to laugh. "They make the games a lot harder than they look."

"Apparently."

"Try again."

I tried two more times with the same infuriating outcome and then frowned. "There's no way to knock them down."

"You have to hit them right in the center."

"You think I'm *not* aiming for the center?" He didn't know that I went to target practice regularly, but evidently, this cup required sniper-level accuracy to knock down the steel drum.

Dillon chuckled a delicious, throaty laugh.

"You think you can do better?" I challenged.

"Without question."

"Ten bucks says you can't knock even one down."

To this, he raised a flirtatious eyebrow. "I have a different wager in mind." He bit his lower lip. *Lucky lip.* "I knock down fifteen of those before my turn is up," he started and lowered his mouth to my ear. "I get to take you home and have my way with you."

*Holy crud.* My lower belly tingled, my hormones grabbing the steering wheel and performing a hostile takeover. They tried to convince me to jump over this counter and sucker-punch fifteen cups, so he could carry me to bed.

"And if I win?"

He put his mouth by my ear again. "I'll let you have your way with me."

He dangled his mouth over mine, and instantly, a nervousness swept through my body. Part of me wanted to go to bed with him —a gigantic part, actually—but we'd only been dating a week. A week that had already been a whirlwind for me, and gunning the gas pedal even harder risked us crashing and burning out. I liked Dillon too much to let that happen. It would be better for us to wait a little longer.

I didn't want to ruin the moment, though, because honestly? I enjoyed this flirtatious, sexy banter too much.

I grazed his lips with mine and answered seductively, "While I admire your confidence, you're not getting me into bed that easy."

His lips pulled into a smile.

"And I know you can't knock down fifteen."

He pulled his beautiful mouth back and offered a sexy grin as he rolled up his sleeves.

Man, he was hot, taking his stance. Feet shoulder-width apart, propping his butt up.

*I could totally build a display shelf and fill it with nothing but molds of that fine ass.*

His shoulders exploded out of his shirt when he raised his arms up to aim the gun, and the bands of muscles covering his forearms tightened.

*Bam.* A purple cup fell.

*Bam.* Another fell.

*Bam, bam, bam.* Three more.

I stood with my mouth falling open as Dillon knocked down seventeen cups in what had to be less than ten seconds.

"How do you know how to shoot like that?"

The game guy looked completely uninterested as he yanked the pink teddy down and handed it to Dillon, who passed it to me.

Dillon shrugged. "Bad neighborhood, remember? After something horrible happened, I needed a way to protect my family. Started going to target practice. Got really good at it."

I wondered what horrific event could have made him so worried about their lives that he became obsessive in learning how to shoot. But I wouldn't spoil his mood with my curiosity. I'd save that question for another day.

"For the record," he said, slinging his arm over my shoulders. His embrace sucked me in like a cyclone, whipping everything around us in gusts while we coiled together in the eye of the beautiful storm. "I was only half-joking with the bet."

"Half, huh?"

"My upper body was joking."

I laughed.

Dillon pulled me over to a line of people. It didn't take long before it was our turn on the Ferris wheel.

"Ever been on one of these?" Dillon asked as the cart slowly ascended.

"No."

Dillon's mouth tightened, but he shook it off with a smile as the Ferris wheel rose to the top. And what a climb it was. As we ascended twenty stories in the air, the gorgeous Chicago skyline sparkled against the now-black night like twinkle lights. Swarms of people swam through the booths like a river beneath us, and just as our cart reached the highest point, a burst of orange and red exploded in the sky and shimmered over the ebony water.

Right. Fireworks in the summer every Saturday. And we had the best seat in the city for them.

"Did you time this?" I asked.

Dillon shrugged. "Tried to. Wasn't sure I could pull it off."

*Geez.* He put so much thought into this night. First, he picked something so special, then made sure I danced, played games, tried cotton candy, and now this. I'd never had anyone do so many thoughtful things for me before.

Dillon's kindness was like a warm blanket on a cold winter night. It enveloped me and dethawed parts of my heart I didn't even realize had been frozen.

Red, white, then blue fireworks lit up the night sky as people cheered and clapped.

With each burst, Dillon's face glowed in various colors, but he wasn't even watching the fireworks. He was watching me, absorbing my glee and wonder. When his gaze settled on my mouth, a hunger flashed through his eyes that lingered until it seemed he couldn't resist his desires anymore. He cupped my face, stroked my cheek with his thumb, and then moved his hand to the back of my head.

*Please kiss me. Please put your mouth on mine, put your hands on my body.*

After one last agonizing second, he finally brought his mouth to mine.

And licked my tongue.

*Good Lord.*

The taste of pure sugar from our cotton candy intensified as our tongues connected over and over.

I licked his tongue and pulled his mouth tighter against mine. Taking things slowly with him would be a lot harder than I thought because right now, I wanted far more than just a kiss. I wanted to straddle him and feel him beneath me.

When Dillon's fingers skated along the base of my shirt, I could tell that he wanted more, too. I wasn't about to deny him, either. We were at the top of the Ferris wheel, two hundred feet above the prying eyes of people below, in a glass-enclosed bubble. We didn't have much time—once we descended a bit more, the people in the cart behind us would be able to see us—but the wheel moved incredibly slow.

Affording us a minute or two.

Beneath the fabric of my top, Dillon's hand slid up my stomach slowly, leaving a trail of fire in its wake. When his grip reached my chest, I squirmed and growled into his mouth as he squeezed.

If his touch felt this good with his hand over my bra's fabric, I couldn't even imagine how good it would feel to have his hands on my bare skin—with no clothes on, when we were alone and had all the time we wanted to caress each other.

I moved my hand to his back and skated it up his shirt, exploring the ridges of his tantalizing muscles with my fingertips.

He pinched me, the sensation jolting through my chest.

Our chemistry was dangerous; it could tempt me to misbehave in ways I never had. I needed to control myself, but it was hard, not just because of our passion, but also because of how special Dillon made me feel.

I ran my fingers through his silky hair, feeling the *boom, boom, boom* of each firework vibrating in my chest while a different explosion erupted through the chambers of my heart.

# 9

Burch stood at the front of the room with an expression on his face I'd never seen before. It almost looked as if he was biting back...a smile?

"IT was able to recover some information off that USB drive."

I sat up straighter. Everyone in the task force's conference room did.

"They're still scrubbing it, hoping to come up with more, but for right now, we got three names off the drive. Which might not sound like a lot, but it might be enough to make a huge freaking dent."

*Giddy-freaking-up, buttercup. Here we go. A break.* A huge break, judging by the look on Burch's face. Maybe we'd take down the Syndicates a lot sooner than we thought.

"Now," Burch said as he flipped over his corkboard of mugshots, "we need to divide and conquer, research everything about these guys. Cross-reference the names with any drug busts in the last thirty years, arrest records—misdemeanor or felony. Also want a team working with the IRS to pull their tax records because my guess is that these guys just happen to make a crap-ton of money. On paper, the earnings might look legit, but let's tear into them to see if we can prove money laundering."

I studied the three names he had pinned to the top of the board.

"One name in particular caught my eye, though." Burch pulled the name off the board and pinned it to the side. "Rodrigo Ramirez," he said. "Ramirez used to run narcotics in the Midwest, but he vanished fourteen years ago. Figured he was dead. He might've changed his name, but the question is: what's his role in the Syndicates? And where the hell's he been for the last several years?"

Out of all the names I could have been assigned in the research, I was thrilled I got his. Because his seemed the most out of place and therefore might be an essential clue in our investigation into how the Syndicates ran their operation.

# 10

"I can't talk right now, Dad. I'm heading out."

I hadn't even wanted to answer his call, but evidently, he wasn't going to stop until I acknowledged him—something I did via text, to no avail.

"I understand." The defeat in his voice tugged at my traitorous heartstrings. "I'd rather talk to you in person, anyway, if that's possible?"

The thought of seeing him again after everything he did made me uneasy. I was just starting to find my stride with work and personal life. A bird taking flight for what felt like the first time, soaring through the clouds and leaving the hurricane behind. But here he was, ready to suck me back into his dark vortex.

"I'm swamped."

"It's important," he insisted.

But my life wasn't. The one time he bothered to show up for something important to me, he almost cost me everything. And now, he expected me to be at his beck and call and, what, drop everything the second he asked?

"I'll look at my calendar for the next couple of weeks and text you a time that might work."

"Thank you." He breathed a sigh of relief. "And, Fallon?"

I waited.

"I love you, sweetheart."

I punched the End button harder than I needed to, just as Dillon pulled up to the curb to pick me up for our date.

He hopped out of his running convertible and opened the passenger door for me, his smile fading when he picked up on my tension.

"You okay?"

He waited for me to talk, not even caring that an impatient driver was already honking at him for holding up traffic.

"Dad drama," I hedged and climbed inside.

A moment later, Dillon entered the car, too. "Want to talk about it?"

I shook my head.

Dillon's lips tightened into a concerned line as he threw the car into gear and jetted out into traffic. As we tunneled through the skyscrapers, my muscles relaxed now that I was with him, and somehow, he knew exactly what I needed. He let me process my dad's call in silence as the city's buildings faded behind us, twilight setting in over the darkened interstate. He had the convertible's roof up this time, which was good, considering he gunned his car.

Dillon evaluated me.

"Could go straight to O'Hare," Dillon suggested. "We could be in the Bahamas by morning."

Despite myself, I smiled.

"You'd go to the Bahamas with me," I said incredulously. "Right now?"

"Wouldn't have to twist my arm."

I rolled my eyes. "We have no luggage," I countered. "I don't even have a swimsuit."

"If you don't want to go, you should stop sweetening the pot."

I laughed this time and accepted his embrace when he took my hand and kissed the back of it.

My tension melted even more.

"No international escape," I said.

"Do you still want to grab food?" he asked. We'd planned to get appetizers somewhere casual.

When I nodded, Dillon smiled and pressed the accelerator harder.

He drove to a smaller town outside the city—away from the noise and the congestion of people. When we arrived at the bar, I couldn't believe how empty the parking lot was. Yes, we'd come at an off-hour, and yes, this place was low-key. But still. In the city, you'd never find a near-empty parking lot like this.

We went inside and found the entire space was gift-wrapped in wood. Seriously, every square inch of the place? Wood. Floor? Wood. Walls? Wood. Counters, stools, and bar? Wood. Heck, even the light fixtures were made out of wood. I felt like I was in a log cabin–slash–biker bar with peanut shells on the floor, grungy rock music blasting over the speakers, and the smell of beer and man wafting through the space.

I was probably overdressed for the place—in my black skirt and emerald top—but I liked being away from the chaos of the city.

"Want a beer?" Dillon asked me.

I straightened hypothetical wrinkles out of my sleeves. "I don't drink," I admitted.

To this, Dillon raised an eyebrow.

"Why don't you drink?" he asked, but when his face fell, I could tell he immediately suspected the reason.

"I don't want to turn out like my parents."

His stare felt like it burrowed past my eyes and into my thoughts, medicating any lingering anxiety about my admission. With Dillon, I didn't feel ashamed or embarrassed by my past. His serene presence made me feel so comfortable with exposing all the layers that made me who I was that I might even tell him the rest of the story someday.

Something I thought I'd take to the grave.

A waitress with flaming red hair and tattooed arms appeared. "Can I get you two something to drink?"

"Water," I said.

"Make that two," Dillon added.

"It doesn't bother me if you drink," I assured.

He waited until the waitress walked away to answer me. "You're more important to me than a beer, Fallon."

My eyes burned as tears formed behind them. He couldn't possibly know how his proclamation both scorched my heart—for it reminded me of when I'd desperately longed to be more important than drugs had been to my parents—and spread soothing balm on it. Because to him, I was the priority.

Dillon leaned his sexy forearms on the table and took my hand in his. It was incredible how he could simply stare at me and make me feel so desired and adored and how his touch was like magic pixie dust, sprinkling calm through my body.

"If you don't mind me asking," he said, "what was it like? Growing up with addict parents?"

I'd never been asked this question. "Your childhood was far more challenging than mine."

He studied my gaze. "Somehow, I doubt that."

The tightness of his eyes showed he was as curious as he was anxious to hear my answer.

I ran a hand through my hair and thought back to that time when the whole world seemed like a scary, unsafe place.

"When I was younger, it felt like they didn't love me enough to stop doing drugs. Like I wasn't important enough to them." I tried to fight the wrenching sadness that still existed in fragments of my heart, splinters from a little girl, broken and sobbing in her bedroom because her mommy would rather get high than play with her.

"Then, I became convinced that my parents did drugs because they couldn't stand to be around me."

Some might find that absurd, but when you were rejected incessantly in favor of drugs, the excruciating fear that no one wanted to be around you cemented itself into your DNA. And when you spent almost every non-school hour in your room, alone...

"It made me feel unlovable, like no one would even notice if I ceased to exist."

And many days, I didn't even want to exist.

"That paranoia still creeps up sometimes," I admitted. "Even now."

Dillon shook his head, as if I didn't see myself clearly. But I guess that was what it was to be human. Beneath the layers of confidence and strength lay hidden insecurities, regret, and self-doubt. On any given day, it was just a question of which one rose to the surface.

"I've never talked about this with anyone," I said. Not even Shane.

Dillon raised his brows slightly, looking as surprised as he was flattered that he was the first person I'd opened up to. "Why?"

I considered this as he rubbed my palm with his thumb in soothing circles. "I put up a strong front with most people, so they don't see how broken I actually am inside. Even with Shane, I find myself putting up my armor because it bothers me that he met me at a time in my life when I was so frail. I guess I feel like, with him, I have this image I need to overcome of me being a weakling. It's all in my head, though, not his," I assured. "He's never done anything to make me feel that way. It's just the reality of our relationship. So, I don't like to talk about any of that stuff that left me vulnerable. But with you..." I looked into Dillon's gentle brown eyes. "When I'm with you, I feel like it's okay for me to be all the pieces of who I am. The strong ones and the weak ones. It's like I can just...exhale and be my raw, imperfect self."

I realized how strange that would sound to anyone else but Dillon—that I felt safer with him than anyone else. But our connection had been virtually instant. Maybe almost dying put a lot of things into perspective for me, including living my truth without caring as much about what people thought of me. And maybe that raw honesty, in turn, broke down some of Dillon's walls, and he opened up to me in ways he normally wouldn't have. Or maybe it had nothing to do with a near-death experience, and this was just what it felt like when you met someone extraordinary.

Regardless of the reason, revealing my hidden truths to Dillon was exceedingly significant to me. The look in his eyes told me the magnitude wasn't lost on him, either. He locked his gaze with mine for several beats of my heart, and it felt like nothing could ever break the intimacy of this moment.

Until a guy walking past our table bumped my shoulder. Hard.

He hadn't meant to do it; he was just texting and walking, but that didn't seem to matter to Dillon. Especially when the guy didn't even acknowledge it.

"Hey!" Dillon snarled.

The guy snapped his head around at the sound of Dillon's tone.

"Dillon..."

"You just hit her!"

A quick glance at the guy's body language warned me this might be a bad night to lecture him on social graces. His muscles were tense, and his face contorted in fury as he squeezed his cell phone in his hand, perhaps arguing with someone on the other end.

"Like I give a shit."

When he turned to walk away, Dillon opened his mouth, but I squeezed his hand.

"Let it go," I insisted.

If there was one thing I'd learned from being a cop, it was that small acts of hostility could escalate quickly over nothing at all. I once worked a scene where a fight had spiraled into a stabbing over a spilled beer. Something like this wasn't worth the fight.

Dillon rubbed the side of his nose with this thumb, trying to annihilate the guy with his eyes. His anger didn't surprise me. After how protective he'd been with his brother, defending me from someone's mistreatment didn't feel malicious or dark. It simply felt protective.

Luckily, Dillon let the guy walk away without a further argument. What he didn't know was that Text Guy circled back and took a seat directly behind Dillon.

And proceeded to glower at us.

Dillon rubbed his now-hardened jaw and recalibrated to what we were talking about before the interruption.

"I hate that you had to go through that," Dillon growled.

"Sadly, a lot of kids have it way worse than I did," I said. Addiction didn't just destroy the user; it hurt everyone they loved, too. Kind of like the addict was the epicenter of a bomb's explosion, but all their loved ones were in its blast radius. "My parents never beat or abused me."

"But there was nobody there to keep you safe. The way you've been treated by people upsets me. Makes me want to beat the shit out of anyone who's ever been unkind to you."

His eyes hardened with a longing for vengeance.

"And for the record," he added as he held my gaze, "you're very lovable."

My chest warmed under the weight of his adoration. I wanted to freeze this moment. Come back to visit it, feel it, anytime I wanted.

Dillon kissed the back of my hand, and I wished he could leave his lips there forever. I studied the curve of his mouth, his affection breaching my skin. How could a simple touch emit so much emotion? Emotion that pirouetted through his eyes as he rubbed his thumb along my palm.

But after a few seconds, his eyebrows pulled together. It was so slight, no one else would have noticed, especially when he tried to camouflage it with a smile. But it almost looked like he was...worried?

"What's wrong?" I asked.

He hesitated. "Nothing," he claimed, and then his momentary change evaporated.

I wondered if I should press him on it, but the guy sitting behind Dillon shifted in his seat and glared at the back of Dillon's head. Judging by the droop in the guy's eyelids and the tightness of his jaw, he'd had too much to drink and looked like he'd been stewing over Dillon's earlier attitude, now wanting to settle a score.

I could taste the sudden energy change in the room. And both my sixth sense and my police experience warned me to get out of here before something bad happened.

"We should go," I said.

Dillon looked at the time on his phone. "Let me use the men's room and settle the check. I'll be right back."

I wanted to tell him to stay and wait to use the restroom until we were out of this place, but I worried that explaining why would only compound Dillon's anger with this guy. That would escalate the tension even further, to a point that there would be no hope of avoiding a brawl.

Text Guy waited until Dillon was out of sight before slurring something. "Tell your boyfriend to mind his damn business."

I wasn't being baited into a fight. "Will do."

"I don't appreciate him talking to me like a damn child."

I stood up to leave. Problem was, I had to walk right next to him to get to the door, and I needed to do it before Dillon came back.

"I'll let him know that." I began walking.

Text Guy stood up and grabbed my wrist. "You're a smart-ass, aren't you?"

"Get your hands off me, or you'll be arrested for battery," I said.

"Threatening me now," he said, as if I'd just made this even more interesting for him.

"Let me go," I warned.

He squeezed harder.

"She said, let her go," Dillon growled, suddenly at my side. The fact that he kept his tone calm and deep made it sound all the more threatening.

"Or what?"

Instantly, the guy was no longer holding my wrist. He was pinned against the wall with Dillon's forearm to his throat.

"Touch her again, I'll knock your fucking teeth in," Dillon growled.

"Dillon!" I shouted.

Dillon stared at the guy for a beat—and by stare, I mean, he looked like he had to convince himself that beating the guy to a pulp wasn't worth it. And then he shoved off the guy.

"Come on," Dillon said to me.

Dillon threw a fifty down on our table, glared at the guy one last time, and then took my hand and led me out the front door and to his car.

As soon as we were safely inside, I made sure the raging

lunatic hadn't followed us out before turning my focus back to Dillon. "I don't need you to protect me."

Dillon took a deep breath and put his hand on my cheek. And this time, when he spoke, his voice was softer. "I know you don't. You're the strongest woman I know. But it's about time someone protects you, anyway, Fallon. And I want to be the guy who protects you."

Instantly, my lower belly warmed, and his touch became fire. He released my face, unaware that his words had tunneled past my skin and through my pulsing heart, sparking desires deep within me.

Dillon put his finger on the push-button start, but before he could press it, I leaned over and crushed my mouth to his.

His head jerked in surprise, but after a moment, his lips tightened into a smile before he kissed me back.

And my goodness, did he kiss me back. Fingers in my hair, tongue slipping into my mouth, but it wasn't enough. I needed more. It was like handing a person dying of thirst a water bottle and trying to get them to stop drinking after just one sip.

A greedy need took over my body, my inhibitions, my logic even. Tucked into a back-corner spot of the dark parking lot—thanks to Dillon not wanting to get it scratched—his car was surrounded by trees on two sides. No one would see us. Even so, this was insane. I was more responsible than this. A cop, for crying out loud.

And yet, with his words and fierce protection, something primal and deeper took over. Water bottle in hand, dying of dehydration, I became desperate to satisfy my thirst.

I climbed on top of Dillon's lap and straddled him. He growled and pushed the button to move the seat back to give me more room. His hands skimmed the skin of my thighs, drifting beneath my skirt, causing a surge of heat to erupt inside of me.

As our kiss deepened—our tongues connecting in perfect,

delicious rhythms—his hands worked to my backside and squeezed. Hard.

I wove my hands into his hair as he kept one hand on my butt while the other shifted beneath my shirt, found the front snap of my bra, and unhooked it.

When he cupped my bare chest in the strength of his hand, I arched my back. His entire body tightened like a rubber band demanding a release. His desire swelled beneath me as he lifted my shirt and took me into his mouth.

*Holy...sweet...*

"If you want to stop, we need to do it now," he growled breathlessly against my skin.

I risked a quick glance around to ensure no one was nearby. We *should* stop.

But then his hand slid down my stomach and inside my panties. When it hit its mark, I grabbed his shoulders. Even with my eyes closed and my head tilted back, I could feel his gaze on me, watching my reaction to every pulse of his finger, every movement of his palm, hitting my every cadence with just the right note.

I'd never been with a guy who knew how to incite so much pleasure. It was like he knew my body better than I did, making it feel like this was my first time with a man.

Dillon wrapped his free hand around the back of my neck and brought my mouth back to his.

"Tell me what you want," he commanded against my lips.

I couldn't think about anything but his hand. I couldn't catch my breath, couldn't think. All I could do was feel. And need. And want more.

"I want you," I whispered. And then I took his lip between my teeth and nibbled.

That was all it took. In an almost frenzy, Dillon lifted my hips, undid his zipper, pulled his pants to his knees, and slipped protection onto himself that he'd pulled from his pocket.

Then, he grabbed my hips again with so much force, a flicker of pain preceded the pleasure.

As I slid my panties to the side and lowered myself onto him, I looked him in his eyes and savored the groan that escaped his mouth.

My lips were back on his, his hands roaming beneath my shirt as I began to move.

Man, he felt so, so good. Full, blazing fire raged through me as our bodies moved with each other exquisitely, as if designed perfectly for one another.

I'd never felt anything this incredible. Never felt this connection with anyone, this uninhibited as I rocked my body against his. If it felt this good now, I could only imagine being nude and alone with him in a bed

with hours for us to explore each other's bodies.

As we moved, kissing and touching, pushing and pulling for several glorious minutes, Dillon sensed my rise and grabbed my chest, growling as I leaned back. When I hit my release, I looked right into his eyes, watching him follow with a release of his own.

# 11

"This is so frustrating." I tossed my pen onto my precinct desk, which was cluttered with papers and notes that had proven unhelpful in my research.

"Walk me through it," Marks said. "I'll be your sounding board." He leaned on the edge of my desk and crossed his arms over his chest.

I let out a huge sigh. "Okay, so we know Rodrigo Ramirez was a suspected narcotics criminal fifteen, twenty years ago, right?"

He nodded.

"But then fourteen years ago, he upped and vanished."

"Presumed dead," Marks agreed.

"Right. But now, his name shows up on that USB drive along with other *current* names of the Chicago Syndicates. So, he must still be alive, doing something. But I haven't been able to find anything on him."

"What have you searched so far?"

I pinched the bridge of my nose. "I scrubbed all the criminal databases in the United States, even misdemeanors and traffic tickets. I thought maybe he relocated to the Miami or New York crews."

Marks raised an impressed eyebrow.

"But that turned up empty. So, then I went back and looked at his financial records to see if I could find a clue. What his activity was, leading up to his disappearance."

"And also came up empty," Marks presumed.

"The data is spotty. Not all financial databases go back fifteen years. We could assume they looked at all this when he first disappeared, but if he was presumed dead, maybe law enforcement didn't look as hard as we're looking right now."

"Plus, databases are a lot more sophisticated than they were fifteen years ago."

Exactly. "But I've found absolutely nothing to explain where he's been or why he would turn up on this USB drive."

Marks chewed the inside of his cheek while I tapped my pen twenty times on the desk.

"You know," he said, "in the cartel, sometimes, they have certain members whose identities are a carefully guarded secret, even from within their own organization. Like the bookkeeper, for instance. Those are the guys controlling the money needed to fund wars against police, hire soldiers, and pay hit men. Because money is the lifeblood of the organization, they're often the right-hand man to the leader but work completely behind the scenes. Keeping their identities confidential is another protective layer from law enforcement and any other cartels who might want to overthrow them. Maybe the Syndicates followed the cartel's playbook and buried this guy's identity. Maybe he's been here all along as their bookkeeper or something."

I nodded, chewed the cap of my pen.

"Keep at it. You're doing a great job, O'Connor."

I frowned. I didn't feel like I was doing great. I wanted to contribute to this investigation, not just hit dead ends. I rolled my pen between my fingers, considering what Marks had said.

And then bolted straight up in my chair, my eyes darting from side to side. I clicked around on my computer until I finally found the contact information I needed and placed a call, explaining what I was looking for.

"How many years of data are stored in the database?" I asked.

"Fifteen."

*Hallelujah.* "Can I get an extract of any passengers that departed Chicago O'Hare from 2007 to 2009?"

"That's a lot of data." She paused. "It'll take me some time to put it together."

I gave her my information to send it as soon as possible, and then I hung up with new hope in my chest.

But that hope took a backseat to a new set of emotions when I saw the time and realized I had less than an hour before Dillon picked me up. Dillon invited me over to his place tonight, which was both exhilarating and also a little terrifying because this time, being intimate with him wouldn't be some frenzied, unplanned moment of passion. It would mean something more—a deliberate step in our relationship. One that was important to me.

I'd already grown to care more about Dillon in three weeks than I ever had with anyone else. In fact, I hadn't been able to stop thinking about these feelings that had grown inside of me. A light had cracked open in my chest and flooded with happiness whenever I was with him. His every text and phone call sent my heart into flutters, and I found myself thinking about him before I fell asleep and as soon as I woke up.

And while I was almost certain he felt the same for me as I did him, I couldn't take that deliberate step in our relationship on hope alone. I needed to know where I stood with him.

Tonight, I was going to lay it all out on the table. Tell him how I felt and find out if he felt the same for me, too.

*It's funny how, for weeks, you can feel confident that the emotions you've developed for another person are mutual. Yet when you're about to put it all on the line, you feel incredibly vulnerable. Because opening your heart to that person gives them the power to hurt you.*

# 12

"Hey, gorgeous." Dillon cupped my cheek and brought his lips to mine, the rest of the world evaporating instantly.

I tasted his tongue and groaned as he pressed his hand to my lower back. In his arms, my heart floated in ecstasy.

Dillon pulled back and rubbed his thumb over my cheek, making me feel like the most majestic thing he'd ever laid eyes on. "You okay?"

I offered a weak smile and nodded. I loved the way he looked at me, the way he always held me for several seconds after he kissed me, like he couldn't bring himself to let me go. I loved the way he smelled—of clean soap and joy. I loved the feeling of his body against mine when he hugged me.

"You didn't have to pick me up," I managed.

Dillon simply smiled and grabbed my hand as we walked out of my apartment complex to his convertible parked just outside. I savored the feeling of warmth and happiness radiating from his palm to mine.

He held the door open and shut it once I sat down. He walked around the hood, got inside, and held my hand as he drove.

"I've never had a guy cook me dinner before."

That had to be a good sign, right? Surely, you didn't go through that level of effort for any girl.

On the drive over, Dillon cheerfully talked about how his visit with Dexter had gone yesterday, but my mind was only half-listening. It was too busy assuring myself the impending conversation would go the way my heart needed it to.

When Dillon arrived at his apartment complex, he let me out of the car by the building's entrance while he went to park. I cherished his chivalrousness.

As I stood outside the front doors of the building, I looked at the sun dipping behind the skyscrapers, anxious to realize that my next chapter with Dillon would begin by the time that sun set. Hopefully, it would be a good chapter and not an ending.

After parking a block away—which was close, by Chicago standards—Dillon headed toward me. Man, he was gorgeous, wearing jeans and a white T-shirt. I adored how, even a half-block away, he fixed his eyes on me with a commanding stare, as if he were coming to claim me. Amid a chaotic city full of traffic horns, crowded sidewalks, and skyscrapers, I was the only thing he had eyes for.

Suddenly, those eyes abandoned mine, and his grin fell. He halted when a man approached him. An unwelcome man, based on the tightness of Dillon's face. I could only see the guy's back. Six feet tall. Brown hair. Thin, wearing a navy suit.

As he spoke to the guy, Dillon flashed his troubled eyes to me but only allowed them there for a fleeting moment.

*He doesn't want the guy to notice and look my way.*

Did Dillon need help?

I stepped forward, but Dillon flipped his hand around, so his palm pointed to me. He did it discreetly and only held it there for a second, so whoever he was talking to wouldn't see. But I saw it and stopped.

I wasn't sure what to do while the guy talked to Dillon. Why did I get the sense I should hide? I willed the guy to turn around, so I could look at his face, but after a minute, he walked away in the opposite direction.

And when Dillon reached me, his mood was dark and possessive.

"Come on." He guided me by my elbow inside. He smiled and took my hand as he flashed some card that activated his building's elevator, but the tension radiated off of him in waves.

"Who was that?" I asked as the elevator ascended.

"Just a guy from work."

"What did he want?"

Why would he come to Dillon's apartment building instead of, oh, say, his office or call him?

"Just work stuff." Dillon squeezed my hand.

The cop in me knew he was lying.

It made my stomach twist as the elevator rose and opened to Dillon's apartment. As in the elevator opened *into* his apartment.

"You live in the penthouse?" I raised my eyebrow.

"You like it?"

The floor-to-ceiling windows surrounding the central area exposed the city's buildings that stretched out as far as I could see. The roads below had tiny cars and people scuttling around like little bugs while in here, his white kitchen with a sofa-sized center island stretched into the dining room area. Next to that, a navy sectional couch faced a flat screen that hung above a gas fireplace, which crackled flames with fake sounds of burning wood. Gray and black accent colors polished the decor with a shag rug, throw pillows, and black-and-white images of Chicago, circa the early 1900s when the city had rebuilt after the Great Chicago Fire of 1871.

Dillon poured us each a glass of water and handed it to me without a smile.

"I'm going to start cooking," he said. Also sans smile.

"Is everything okay?"

"Yeah," Dillon claimed as he busied himself about the kitchen. "It's fine."

But as I sat at one of the stools along the overhung center island and watched him cook, it didn't seem like everything was fine. Something weighed on his shoulders. He'd stir the sauce and then stop, just staring into the pan. He'd cut up onions and let several beats pass before washing his hands.

I wanted to ask him again who that guy was, but he clearly didn't want to talk about it; doing so might sour his mood even more. I'd come here with a mission, and I needed to fulfill it before I lost my nerve.

I took a deep breath and prepared to speak, but Dillon stopped cooking, shut off the stove, and spoke in a low tone. "Fallon, there's something I need to tell you."

Something bad, by the sound of his voice.

His troubled eyes locked on mine, and he looked like he didn't want to spit out whatever it was.

But suddenly, I suspected what it was—he was going to end things. He had to have sensed my feelings for him—feelings that weren't mutual after all—and he must have prepared this meal as a thoughtful way to let me down and end things.

I'd been so lost in my head when he picked me up that I assumed he was acting normal with his kiss and holding my hand. But he'd been lost in his own head, too, knowing he was going to break it off with me. That was probably why he didn't want that guy to meet me—the pathetic girl who'd fallen for him.

"I was wrong, then," I said, looking down at my hands.

Dillon came to me and pressed his finger to the base of my chin, pulling it up until I looked at him. "Wrong about what?"

I hid my embarrassment. "I was going to tell you tonight. Make sure it wasn't all in my head."

His eyebrows pulled together, and he searched my face for understanding. "Tell me what?"

*Maybe I shouldn't tell him.* What would be the point now?

But as I stared into his eyes, I couldn't stop the pulses of affection or the desire to let him know how much he meant to me. Even if it would be the last thing I ever got to say to him. Especially so.

"I..." I bit my lip. "I'm falling for you."

Dillon looked stunned by my emotional stab, his shoulders sinking.

Not the reaction a girl longed for after professing her feelings. This was a huge mistake. I bit back the stinging in my eyes, grabbed my purse off the counter, and walked to the elevator. Pushed the button.

"Fallon." Dillon turned me around by my elbow, and when he stared at me, the look on his face wasn't sympathy. More like a dark, penetrating sadness. He looked as if he was fighting his own internal war, though his creased eyebrows relaxed as he bit his lip.

Dillon took a step closer, staring at my mouth as he put his palms flat to the wall on either side of my head. And when he spoke, his words sounded strangled. "You shouldn't be with me."

*Shouldn't.*

"Why?" I asked.

But my heart didn't care about *why* at this moment; what it cared about was that, with that one word, I could tell he felt this, too. And that he wanted it—I could see it in his eyes.

He stroked my cheek and confessed, "I'm falling for you, too, Fallon."

His words tunneled through my ears and into my heart, penetrating my soul. I wanted to savor them, put them in a bottle and consume them anytime I wanted to hear them again.

For the first time in my life, I left my comfort zone and embraced the possibility of having a serious boyfriend. In the past, this idea had felt foreign and induced anxiety, but with Dillon, it was like soaking my emotions in a soothing bubble bath.

Dillon stared at my mouth for one, two, three seconds, and then he crashed his lips to mine.

I dropped my purse and welcomed the fire that cascaded down my throat and into my belly. Our hands twisted in each other's hair with urgency, and without breaking our kiss, Dillon turned me around and walked me backward.

Ushering me through a doorway into his bedroom.

The only light came from the fireplace outside the room. The sounds of the city—of rumbling engines and the metallic grind of the "L" train—faded in the distance.

Desire spread through my veins, pulling me to him, making me ache for him to touch and kiss me everywhere. He nibbled my lip, kissed down my jaw and neck, licking my skin with his hot, wet tongue as he tugged at the hem of my shirt and pulled it over my head, tossing it aside, followed by my bra.

Dillon stared at me like I was a gorgeous work of art whose beauty deserved a moment of silence before he kissed me. On my mouth, my jaw. My chest.

I pulled at his shirt in desperate jerks, but with one fluid motion, he reached behind his back and tugged it up over his head like a slow-motion music video.

Heaven help me; he was even more gorgeous than I'd fantasized. A body carved of perfection, his shoulders cut into biceps, a rounded chest with a delicious line drawing my eyes lower, down his ripped abs.

He unfastened my zipper and kept his insatiable eyes on mine as he slowly pulled my pants down, one inch at a time until they finally fell to the floor. Repeating the same intoxicating dance with my panties.

His eyes glided over my body with a hunger to taste every morsel of it. “You’re stunning, Fallon,” Dillon whispered as he stripped out of the rest of his clothes.

This time, when he kissed me, he was more forceful.

I groaned.

He grabbed the backs of my thighs and wrapped my legs around his waist. When he walked me over to his dresser and set me down, I relished how my body was his trophy. He palmed my chest, making me gasp as he moved his lips down my throat, his mouth needy, kissing me everywhere.

He trailed his kisses down my stomach, along the inside of my thigh, closer and closer to my core. With his lips hovering over my center, he looked me in the eyes as he moved his mouth until it—

*Holy hell.*

I grabbed his shoulders as he worked his tongue on the epicenter of my desire. I ran my hands through his hair and watched him savor my body as my legs began to quiver. Our bodies moved with each other, wanting more—so much more—but he made me wait for it, building me up until he could feel me approaching ecstasy.

And when I hit it, he grabbed my thighs, riding my wave until its ravenous end.

He let go of me, leaving me yearning for him as he reached into the drawer, opened a wrapper, and stood between my legs after a second.

“Fallon,” he whispered. “Look at me.”

His stare pierced my core as he pushed his hips forward.

*Oh my word.*

I gasped and grabbed the dresser’s edge and watched the beautiful pleasure spread across his face as he worked our bodies together, pressing his hips against my inner thighs. Dillon knew how to move, knew how to make the beats hit all the right notes, and as he found his rhythm, I climbed higher and higher.

What he'd done a moment ago was ecstasy, but nothing could top this.

Not breaking our connection, he pulled me off the dresser, laid me down on the bed, and climbed on top of me. He kissed my collarbone and chest. I climbed higher and higher, feeling his lips on mine as I broke over the edge. When a moan escaped my throat, one followed from his.

After, I laid my head on his chest, relishing the warmth of his arms wrapped around my body. It was so peaceful, hearing his heart thump beneath my ear, that I could sleep for days in this position, and it wouldn't be enough.

I AWOKE TO THE SMELL OF BACON AND EGGS AND THE BUZZING OF MY CELL phone the next morning.

Burch just sent a group notification that we were not to report to HQ this morning; Instead, he required us to report to an address I didn't recognize. Immediately.

*Something must be going down.* I needed to get home, get into uniform, and be on the scene quickly. The last thing I needed to do was piss Burch off more by being the last one to show up.

I tossed on one of Dillon's T-shirts and went into the kitchen to tell him I had to go. Wearing nothing but a pair of jeans, he rested his butt against the counter next to the stove, sipping coffee as breakfast sizzled next to him. The view gave me an incredible look at his abs, chiseled out of stone, set beneath a broad chest.

When he saw me, he smiled and arched a hungry eyebrow as I approached him. "Just when I thought you couldn't get any sexier." He kissed my neck, ran his hand up my thigh to my backside, and growled. "You're not wearing any panties."

"You're making me breakfast."

"Forget breakfast," he said, cupping my butt harder and planting his lips on my collarbone. "I want to ravage you instead."

I smiled. "I have to get to work."

"I can be quick."

I laughed. "As enticing as that is, I can't be late. But we could get together later?"

Later, I wanted to ask about that creepy guy, his mood after, and why he said I *shouldn't* be with him.

"Do you want to take a shower with me?"

I smiled. "I wish I had the time."

Dillon's lips curled down slightly. "You eat while I shower. Then, I'll drive you home."

"I'll just grab a cab. Save you the round trip." Plus, I needed to hurry.

"What kind of a gentleman would make love to you and not drive you home?"

*Make love...not have sex.* My heart danced.

"The kind who has a woman who has to go."

Dillon cupped my cheek. "My woman," he said. He grazed my lips with his one last time and pulled back, leaving me breathless.

"Don't let breakfast go to waste," Dillon insisted. "Eat. I'll be in the shower, praying you change your mind and join me."

I grinned as Dillon gave me a quick wink. He turned around to lift the food off the stove, and when he did, I froze.

Ice surged through my limbs.

The whole time we'd been nude, I'd been facing him, so I hadn't seen him from behind. Until now.

There, across his skin, was a tattoo I hadn't seen last night—a scorpion holding the American flag.

# 13

My breath lodged in my throat so severely, I thought I might pass out. Unaware of my sudden shock, Dillon scooped eggs and bacon onto a plate and set it on the dining room table along with a fork and a glass of orange juice. I had to focus on keeping my facial expression composed as he kissed my cheek.

This time, his touch felt completely different—ice instead of fire.

"I'll call you later," he said.

When his mouth pressed to mine, I couldn't move a muscle. Luckily, it was just a quick peck, and he didn't seem to notice my statue-like stance as he walked into his bathroom, stripped naked, and got into the shower.

Which had a glass surrounding. With the door open, he had a full view of the kitchen and me. As the water cascaded over his hair, fogging up the glass with heat, I tried to calm my thoughts.

*There's no way. He can't be a captain of the largest drug organization in America. It's not possible.*

When Dillon found out about this, he'd laugh his butt off. He was probably the vice president of some corporation, maybe a lawyer or something.

It was embarrassing how little I knew of Dillon, though. I had no idea how someone so young earned an apparent abundance of money.

Or why he'd have a giant tattoo of a scorpion holding the American flag.

I sifted through all the conversations we'd had, looking for clues.

Imagine the fallout of a cop, a DEA agent—never mind the technicality that it was a temporary DEA badge for this case—letting the very person they were hunting into their bed. Falling for him, for the love of all things holy. My career would be over. How would I ever tell Burch and my precinct boss how stupid I'd been?

If any of this was true, I didn't deserve to be a cop, let alone a DEA agent.

My blood froze. What if he knew I was on this DEA task force? What if he was working me to see if I'd give up intel?

"You okay?" Dillon suddenly shouted. He peered at me through a spot in the shower he'd wiped free of fog, obviously noticing I hadn't moved an inch.

"Got spaced out," I lied with a smile, walking toward the plate of food.

Sadly, lying had become a strength of mine in life. When you had two parents whose addiction you tried to keep a secret, it became an important tool, one that I was grateful I had now.

My cell phone buzzed with an alarm, reminding me I had to hurry to get to work. If Burch was furious that I ran late from being in a fire, he'd never accept this explanation.

*Oh, sorry, after a night of lovemaking, I started to wonder if my boyfriend might be the drug kingpin that's the target of our investigation, so it slowed me down, sir.*

There had to be some simple explanation for that tattoo. A lot of people got tattoos, and while that seemed unique to me, maybe a scorpion holding the American flag was a symbol of something, a symbol that surely more than one person had.

I'd research it and run a more thorough background check on Dillon to prove he wasn't a drug dealer.

Like the ones that had come to our trailer. I shut my eyes, fighting against the barrage of memories.

*My pulse quickens when the knock comes. Mommy opens the door and lets him in. I don't like how he's dressed in baggy pants with that chain around his neck, and I hate how he dangles that cigarette from his lips like he's forgotten it's there. I want to run into my bedroom and hide under my covers, but I'm scared to leave her alone with him, worried he'll do something to hurt her, like last time.*

*"Got my money?" he snaps. He stares at Mommy like she's an irritating errand he needs to get off his long list of traumas.*

*Mommy blinks rapidly, holding out messy bills. "I have most of it. I couldn't get—"*

*She doesn't finish her sentence. He's backhanded her so hard that she falls to the couch in a yipe, and I hear someone screaming, realizing after a few seconds, it's me.*

*"I made myself clear!"*

*"I'm only twenty dollars short," she cries. "I can get it by tonight, I swear."*

*"That's what you said last time, bitch."*

*He takes out a knife, and I know what he's going to do, and I'm screaming.*

*I'm only ten years old, but I charge him, yelling at the top of my lungs as I smash into him. I'm not strong enough to overpower him or even knock him down, but I bite his arm so hard, the coppery taste of blood pricks my tongue.*

*And then something slams into my head. I'm on the floor, no longer screaming.*

*Mommy is.*

*He hits her again.*

*"Help!"*

*Are any neighbors home? Can they hear my cries? If they can, will they be brave enough to come?*

*I try again to charge him, but he throws me across the room like a rag doll, and now, all I can do is hug my knees and cry as I watch him hit my mommy again.*

*He pulls a gun from his waistband and points it at her. "Next time, I blow your head off in front of your kid."*

*He turns around and glares at me.*

*Even though I'm terrified of him, I refuse to give him the satisfaction of showing how afraid I feel. So, I stare at him. I even consider charging him again to bait him into a fight because, maybe, if he hurts me bad enough, Mommy will call the cops this time, and they'll lock this monster up, so he can't hurt anyone else's mommy. But if he hurts me that bad, Mommy might get into trouble, too, for allowing him in our home. Daddy will probably leave her, and then no one will be able to protect her. So, I don't bait him; I just look at him with pure hatred until he leaves.*

I wasn't able to shield Mom from a fallout, though. I had to get ten stitches from when he threw me across the room. Dad was enraged when he got home. After he thought I was asleep that night, he and Mom had the worst argument yet about the drugs being more important than the "damn safety of your own child," and "if one more thing" happened, that was it. He was kicking her out and getting a divorce for my own protection. A drug dealer was never allowed anywhere near me, he'd said, and if he ever found out otherwise, he'd divorce her.

Drug dealers had turned my once-happy childhood into my own personal horror movie. They ruined my family, sabotaged any feeling of safety I had, and became the bogeyman I spent the last several years training to take down.

And now, I wondered if the man I had fallen for might be one of them.

If he was, I had no idea what he was capable of.

I'd witnessed some of the horrific things drug dealers were willing to do to avoid discovery by the police, let alone a DEA agent.

Alone in his home.

*I should get out of here. Run.*

But I couldn't leave here without answers.

I walked past the bathroom, seeing his foggy frame scrubbing his underarms.

I went into his bedroom, unsure of what I was looking for yet terrified of whatever it was. I pulled out each drawer of his dresser, careful not to leave evidence that I'd rifled through his neatly folded clothes. The drug dealers I'd met in my childhood would never have this kind of clothing or organization. But they were the lower-level people, weren't they? The guys above them probably had all the money.

What was I even looking for, anyway? Did I expect to find a brick of cocaine?

In the fifth drawer, I found a Smith & Wesson M&P. But that didn't mean anything. Lots of people kept guns for protection.

But if it was just for protection, why have a gun that held two seventeen-round magazines?

When the sound of the water shut off, I glanced in the direction of the bathroom, hurried to his nightstand, and pulled out its drawer. There were several watches in a fashionable case. But in the back of the drawer, tucked away as if he didn't want anyone to find them, were three phones still in their packaging.

Burner phones.

My throat became sandpaper. Why would Dillon have burner

phones? My police training had taught me there were two primary reasons people bought them: people couldn't afford a cell phone plan or to use the phone for criminal purposes.

Dillon entered the bedroom and eyed the open drawer.

And then his eyes cut to me.

# 14

Dillon stood in nothing but a white towel fastened tightly around his hips, his dark hair tousled, casting a few water drops onto his shoulders. The sculpted muscles encasing his arms and chest, which had unleashed pulses of desire only hours ago, now fired off a silent warning—how easily he could overpower or crush me if this confrontation turned violent.

Not to mention that if, Heaven forbid, he was a drug lord, he was in an organization that guarded secrets with bloodshed. And he had a loaded gun a few feet away.

He stood between me and the door—blocking me from escaping the room. On accident or on purpose, I wasn't sure. I looked past him at my purse lying on the kitchen counter, where I kept mace.

Dillon glanced at his nightstand. "Were you going through my things?"

As he waited for my answer, I curled my fists in rage that had taken root at the age of nine.

When drug dealers had brought bag after bag of drugs to my

mother and anytime she tried to muster the strength to quit, they capitalized on her weakness by offering a free dose, disguised as a *thank you for being a loyal customer.* She was their ATM, and the price tag? Her life and the welfare of her family.

And then came the incident that draped me forever in darkness and extinguished all my childhood innocence. Leaving me a mere shell of who I once was.

*I've decided to beg Mommy with my whole heart. I will tell her I'm scared every waking second of the day and that I've been having nightmares that something terrible will happen to her. The nightmares wake me up with a pounding heart, and I always have to go into her room and see that she's still breathing before I'm able to go back to bed.*

*I approach my trailer's front door and hesitate when I hear the television on inside. Mommy uses the TV whenever she gets high because she knows it makes me feel less scared to see her spaced out, looking at a TV than staring at nothing. Even though she gave up a long time ago hiding her addiction from us, she never gave up her TV trick, and that means she still cares about me. It's my only evidence she still does. She might not greet me with a warm hug when I get off the school bus anymore, she might not want to spend any time with me, but she still cares enough to leave the television on when she gets high. And right now, that means the world to me because maybe she'll start caring about me a little more each day until she loves me again.*

*But the sound of the television doesn't explain my strong hesitation to open the door.*

*It's so strong, I even wonder if I should wait for Dad to get home from work, but it's three thirty, and he won't be home from work until nine.*

I'm probably being silly.

*I twist the doorknob, and it opens into the living room, if you could call it that. A two-person couch along one wall with the television on the opposite wall, separated by six feet.*

*Mommy is lying on the couch. And the second I see her, my heart gallops like a racehorse.*

*Her face is a ghostly white I've never seen before. Her eyes are open, her mouth ajar, and a needle is hanging out of her left elbow, the skin on top of it bulging slightly from the syringe's weight pulling the tip up.*

*"Mommy?"*

*She doesn't move. Doesn't even blink.*

*Somehow, my heart beats even faster. "Mommy!" I shout louder.*

*No response.*

*I toss my backpack down and approach her slowly, noticing that in her right hand, she's clutching a photograph of Dad and me—like she was missing me when she got high. But I'm here now, and I need to wake her up, so she can tell me if she needs an ambulance.*

*I shake her shoulders, but her head only wobbles. I shake harder, but she's not moving. Her eyelids don't even flutter. What are you supposed to do if someone is so high, they don't respond?*

*"Mommy!" I shout, shaking her harder, so hard, the needle falls out of her arm and onto the floor.*

Overdose. *The word echoes through my mind.*

No. She's fine. She's just, like, so high, she can't feel anything or something.

*"Mommy!" I slap her, but her eyes remain an empty cavern of life.*

*I begin to cry. I shake her so hard, I'm worried I'll hurt her. Her chest isn't moving up and down.*

*"Mommy," I cry, moving the hair away from her face. "Please wake up! Please, please!"*

I don't know what to do. Why isn't she moving?

*I root around the couch cushions in a desperate hunt for her phone, not even caring if I get stabbed with a dirty needle that may lie in the crack, and when I find it, I call 911.*

*"Lay her flat," the operator tells me.*

*I heave her off the couch, which is super hard because she's so heavy.*

*I do the chest compressions they tell me to do, but I don't think I'm strong enough because she isn't waking up. And she's cold.*

*So cold...*

*"Please don't leave me!" I sob.*

*Nothing that I'm doing is working. I'm pushing and pumping and breathing in her mouth and screaming at the operator.*

What is taking the ambulance so long?

*And all this time, Mommy is not breathing. She's not waking up, or moving, or fluttering her eyes or anything.*

*Realization tries to invade my heart, but I fight it. I won't let this reality unfold.*

She can't be gone. It can't be true. It isn't true. I won't let it be.

*I pump her chest harder and faster, and I hear the sirens in the distance, but Mommy is cold and floppy, and her eyes are just...they have no light in them at all. She reminds me of one of my toys that ran out of battery.*

*My arms are so tired, but I keep going, and I hear the siren growing louder, and with each failed pump against her heart, I can't stop the reality from crushing my spirit into dust.*

*I want to run out of the trailer and come back another day when this isn't real. I want to hide under my covers until this scary nightmare stops. But I can't.*

*Because it's too late.*

*My mommy. The woman who was the best, most loving mother in the whole wide world for the first nine years of my life, the mommy who used to write a special note in my lunchbox every single day. Who used to read to me for an hour every single night. Who stood at my old bus stop—rain, snow, or shine—breaking out into a huge grin and hug the second my feet got off the bus. Who reminded me daily that I was her miracle baby and there was nothing she wouldn't do for me. Who I knew would come back to me one day, just as soon as she got this addiction thing under control. Is gone.*

*I was too late to beg her to stop using drugs.*

*"Mommy," I cry. I sob so hard, it feels like my ribs are cracking, and part of me wants to take that needle and jab it into my arm because this hurts too bad.*

*I don't want to be alive anymore, either.*

*I stare at an empty orange prescription bottle that lies in the corner of the room, at what was supposed to be medicine to treat her recovering body from surgery. But that medicine didn't cure her pain.*

*It turned fatal.*

*As the sirens grow closer, I lie down next to her and tuck my head onto her chest, pulling her arm around me the way she used to hold me when I was scared.*

This will be the last time Mommy ever holds me.

*I close my eyes and sob as pain devours me, and I hold my breath, hoping it'll stop my heart before the paramedics arrive.*

"Fallon?" Dillon asked.

The brokenhearted little girl inside me needed confirmation he wasn't the devil I had once hidden from, then hunted down, for most of my life. If he was, my whole world would implode, and my heart would be irrevocably destroyed.

But I wouldn't confront him here.

"Why were you going through my things?" he demanded, and this time, his tone had a flare of anger to it.

"I have to go."

I tried to walk past him, but he stood in front of me.

How dare he block my path. Was this supposed to intimidate me?

"Why were you going through my things?" he asked more forcefully this time.

"Move!" I demanded.

"What were you looking for?"

"Move!"

"Tell me why you went through my stuff!"

"Why are you so upset? Do you have something to hide?"

"You think I'm dating other women? Is that it?"

"As if it were that benign!"

"What the hell does that even mean?"

"Are you a drug dealer?" I snapped.

I wasn't sure who was more shocked at my outburst—him or me.

His head tilted back. "What?"

He'd heard me just fine, and it was too late to retract my accusation. I'd shown my cards, and now, the only hope to get an honest answer was to shove more chips into the center of the table before he had time to overthink his response.

"Are you involved, in any way, in dealing drugs?"

Dillon's chest rose and fell faster than it had before. He looked around his room, clearly trying to figure out what sparked my question.

Or my discovery...

If it was a discovery, would he be honest?

Drug lords surely never told people what they did for a living. It had to be as closely guarded a secret as being in the Mafia.

I thought back to how gladly he'd let me stop the conversation about work, and therefore, we'd come to an inadvertent agreement to not talk about what we did for a living. I thought he was doing that for me since I was the one that didn't want to discuss it, but I'd made it so easy for him to hide his profession.

He rubbed the back of his neck, and I eyed the drawer that concealed his weapon, noting I was closer to it than he was.

"Are you a captain in the Chicago Syndicates?"

His eyes rounded slightly.

He chewed the inside of his cheek, probably sifting through his possible answers, playing each scenario in his head. If he was involved with drugs and yet cared about me as much as he claimed, he couldn't hide this forever. So, if he did want a future with me, he couldn't deny it once confronted.

He stared at me. His voice was low and gentle when he spoke this time. "Yes. But let me explain."

# 15

The numbness was temporary. I knew the avalanche of hurt and pain was headed right for me, but anger came first.

Look at him, staring at me with those worried eyes. He'd let me fall for him, and the whole time, he was the big bad wolf.

Images of Dillon mixed with memories from my childhood in flashes. *The man who stinks of cigarettes chases me to my bedroom, where I dive under the bed. His tattooed arm reaches for me, grabs my ankle, and pulls me out as I scream. Dillon's kissing my neck, his hand cupping my chest. The man slaps Mommy, and she yipes, holding her cheek. Dillon cups my cheek before he kisses me.*

I couldn't picture Dillon doing the awful things that Mom's drug dealer did, but I couldn't picture him being a drug lord, either.

Dillon left the room and returned with a glass of water. "Please drink."

He was clearly worried I was going into shock, but he could wipe that look of concern off his face. Drug dealers didn't have souls. They were the devil in plain sight.

I threw the glass across the room, where it shattered and splattered everywhere.

"Fallon..." he said.

"This whole time we've been dating, you didn't think I had a right to know the kind of person I was falling for?" I demanded.

"We didn't talk about work, and even if we had, this isn't exactly something I can open up about," he said sternly. "People who find out stuff they shouldn't are a liability in my profession, and I didn't want to put you in danger. I was trying to keep you safe. How do you even know about the Syndicates, anyway?"

If he thought that made him noble, he was wrong.

"I lost my family because of someone like you."

I stared into his gaze, struggling to reconcile this. How could the man who seemed like the most caring, wonderful person I'd ever met also be the vile, repulsive drug dealer that he was?

"Fallon, please let me explain."

All the other times the foundation collapsed from under me, I was never afforded the answers as to why it happened. I shouldn't listen to a damn word he had to say, but I needed to know how this could be real. If I had any hope of leaving my broken heart behind me, I needed closure.

"I'll give you five minutes," I said. "Not a second more."

For five more minutes, we could wear our relationship hat. But then I would walk out that door and build a case against him and his criminal enterprise.

I stormed past Dillon and plopped down at his kitchen table at the end, wanting distance between us. But the lack of clothing —me still in nothing but a T-shirt, Dillon nude, save for a towel— was a reminder of the intimacy we'd shared.

Dillon took a seat and scrubbed his face with his hands. "What I'm about to tell you, I've never told anyone. You have to promise me you won't tell anyone, Fallon. No matter how mad you are, my life is on the line here."

*So is mine, asshole.*

He must've interpreted my silence as complaisance. Probably thought he could weasel his way past my new brick wall. Fat chance.

"First of all, I need you to know that I didn't set out with the goal of becoming who I am today," he started. "One decision sort of led to the next, and..."

I crossed my arms over my chest. Four minutes, thirty seconds left.

Dillon studied me. "I told you about my dad leaving us with nothing. My mom worked her butt off, but she couldn't leave Dex unsupervised. We didn't have enough food and certainly didn't have enough to pay Dex's medical bills, not even with the help of Medicaid. And not even close to enough for his therapy, which he needed a lot of," he said. "I had to step in and help."

Dillon ran a hand through his hair, provoking a water drop to plop onto his shoulder. "Fun fact: the system isn't set up for a fourteen-year-old to support a family of three, especially one with medical bills. I tried working mainstream jobs. Worked my ass off to try and make ends meet, but it was impossible. Our neighborhood was infested with dealers on every corner, and they were constantly recruiting kids to join in. Kids make good dealers. Don't get charged as an adult, have clean records, aren't on cops' radar. I resisted as long as I could, but...a couple things happened that were so bad, they made selling drugs an acceptable sacrifice."

He blew out a huge breath when he thought back to it. "Dex didn't understand why we had to ration food the way we did. Food pantries weren't enough, so he was always hungry. Me and my mom gave him part of our meals but it still wasn't enough. He kept crying that he was hungry, and it was just so damn..." Dillon hesitated, clenching his jaw. "His unrelenting hunger was the first domino."

He leaned forward in his chair, put his elbows on his towel-covered thighs, and rubbed his hands together. Then, his face hardened into a rock of disgust at whatever he was about to say. Even thinking about it invited a rage into his darkened eyes that I had never seen.

"Second one came when a gang jumped Dex and me outside our home. Not sure if it was random or if it was a gang initiation, but either way, they held him down and made him watch as they beat me up. Bad. Broke three ribs, my arm, but the worst part was hearing Dex's screams as they did it. I kept trying to get to him, but eventually, I was in so much pain, I couldn't move. When they were done with me, I didn't even care about that pain. I was just so relieved Dex wouldn't have to endure any more of it. But I had no clue what they were going to do next was even worse..." he choked.

"They laid into Dex so badly, he sounded like a wounded animal being murdered right in front of my eyes. The adrenaline helped me get up, but two of them held me down as the others stomped on Dex's face and torso until he stopped moving." Dillon swallowed over the terrible memory. "I thought he was dead. He was in a coma for two days and in the hospital for almost three weeks. It was in that hospital room that I vowed I would do whatever it took to get us out of that hellhole. Whatever it took even if that meant selling drugs."

Dillon ran a thumb across his lip.

"I got good at it. I wasn't like most dealers; I was methodical. Professional about it because I wasn't in it for the flashy jewelry. It wasn't long before bigger opportunities came calling, which meant more money for Dex's care. Took over an entire Chicago region, and then by twenty-five, I was one step down from running the entire Midwest."

Dillon cleared his throat and looked at me—a person whose family crumbled under the weight of narcotics.

"I never meant to fall for you, Fallon. And not just because it's too dangerous; I tried not to fall for you because after what you've gone through, you deserve someone who isn't wrapped up in the drug trade."

"*That's* what bothers you? That you fell for me? Shoving drugs into people's hands didn't bother you?"

"I never pushed them on anyone, Fallon. They came to me."

"You did not just say that."

"I didn't recruit customers. And the only reason I got into this was to save my family. I can't apologize for that."

"Wow." Just when I thought I had an ounce of empathy for him. "That's just what you told yourself for years, so you could sleep at night. It's the only way that you don't see a monster staring back at you when you look in the mirror."

Dillon cringed at my words. "I'm not exactly proud of what I do for a living, Fallon."

"You certainly fooled me, and in case you forgot? My parents were both addicts, and some of those drug dealers that came around my house? They beat me. They pulled me, kicking and screaming, out from under my bed when I was a nine-year-old girl and terrorized me. They beat my mother in front of me, and got high in front of me, and made me feel scared every second of my life!"

I hadn't realized I'd stood up or that I was shaking until this very second.

Dillon rubbed his jaw harshly. "They beat you?"

Judging by the look in his eyes, the boyfriend in him was enraged by it; the narcotics boss in him looked like he wanted names to find out if the sons of bitches were still within his vengeful reach.

"You hurt people for a living, Dillon. I don't understand how you can be okay with that."

It took him a moment to answer. "In my line of work, when someone breaks the rules—if they steal a large sum of money, for example—we can't exactly go to the authorities. So, you're not wrong. There are enforcers in this organization run by my bosses, but I'm not one of them, Fallon. Fear keeps people in line, and I would argue ninety-nine percent of the time, people don't even try to pull something that'd get 'em hurt. It's that one percent who know the rules, know the consequences, and break them anyway."

"Just because *you* don't pull the trigger doesn't mean the blood isn't on your hands, Dillon," I said. "Those dealers? Their bosses? They didn't wait for my mom to come to them. They showed up, over and over, and gave her freebies to keep her hooked anytime she wanted to quit."

Dillon's jaw hardened, and he licked his teeth. "They came to her?"

"Proactively. Like clockwork."

Dillon recoiled, looking sickened.

*Good. That's how a normal human being is supposed to feel when they realize that they've been delusional in thinking that eating gourmet food, driving nice cars, and keeping distance from the dirty, filthy business that they actually operate in makes them any better than the people who attacked a scared little girl.*

He rubbed his hands together for several silent seconds. "Fallon, I think you should leave."

I blinked. "Excuse me?"

After hearing that story, *that* was his reaction? How many ways could he disappoint me?

"Did you even want to stop doing this?" Or did he like the money too much?

"I tried to get out, for my brother's sake. If something happens to me—if I'm in prison or dead—he'll be thrown out of that home and into a state-run facility, best case. Worst case, homeless. Mentally impaired. You do the math on what would happen to him. But even if that wasn't true, I figured out a long time ago, I have a lot less control than I thought. Didn't realize what I was getting into, Fallon. I'd been so tunnel-visioned on getting Dex and Mom out, I didn't stop to consider what this looked like long-term. I never meant to deal drugs forever. It was a desperate stop-gap that got out of control, and by the time I understood what I'd gotten involved in, it was too late."

Dillon spoke in a low tone. "They don't let people out of the organization. You're in, or you're killed, cleaned up as a precaution. I have to watch my back every single day. They watch people. Just wait for someone to slip up. Three weeks ago? They killed my colleague. He'd dedicated his whole life to the organization. Got hit with bad luck, got busted with minor possession. That was it." He shut his eyes and blew out a breath. "You can't get out. And you can't make mistakes."

And yet here he was, unknowingly having made the biggest mistake he could ever imagine.

I stood up, retrieved my purse, pulled out my badge, and set it on the table in front of him.

Dillon stared at it for several seconds, and then his gaze locked on mine. He blinked. Twice. Rubbed a thumb along his nose. "You're a cop?"

"I'm not just a cop; I'm on the DEA task force investigating your organization."

Dillon's gaze sliced through mine, his mind undoubtedly racing.

A better person wouldn't have taken satisfaction in his squirming.

"I figured it out when I saw your tattoo," I said.

Dillon stood up and paced in his kitchen. "Fallon, you need to leave right now. If they see us together, they'll kill you."

"They'll kill you, too," I pointed out.

"You have to leave. Now."

"Turn yourself in," I insisted.

"What?"

"You're a good person who's trapped, right? So, turn yourself in. Make a deal to keep your brother and mom safe."

"You think I haven't considered that? If you're on the case, you know what they did to the last witness and his family."

I gritted my teeth. Did he really think I'd let him go back to breaking the law? No matter what his reasons, if he wasn't willing to cooperate, he left me with no other choice.

"I'm not leaving until you're in cuffs."

I'd let a drug dealer into my bed. The only way I could make this right was to have Dillon arrested. If I didn't arrest him, it would mean he'd won, that *they'd* won. It would be proof that drug dealers could do whatever they wanted, to whomever they wanted, and get away with it. They couldn't. I couldn't live in a world where the balance of justice always tipped in favor of the criminals.

I reached into my purse and pulled out the metal restraints.

Dillon glared at me. "You're joking."

"Not even a little."

"You have no grounds to arrest me."

"Probable cause of a felony crime; you just admitted to being involved with a drug organization. Last time I checked, that's slightly illegal."

"I wasn't Mirandized."

I tightened my lips. I could already hear the district attorney. *Have any evidence of drugs in his apartment?* No. *Any other evidence of a crime being committed?* No. *Any specific evidence at all?* No. *Then, get out of my office and don't waste my time until you have some.*

"And an officer needs a warrant to arrest someone in their home," he added.

These types studied their rights, didn't they? To keep themselves out of jail.

"Exigent circumstances. You let me in."

"Still no grounds for an arrest."

I glanced at Dillon's bedroom. "You have a permit for that gun?"

"The one you found without a search warrant?"

I clenched my jaw. "Then, I'll detain you until a judge signs an arrest warrant," I said, holding the cuffs.

"On what basis?"

"Reasonable suspicion you're trafficking narcotics with the Chicago Syndicates. The tattoo on your back is sufficient evidence."

"You can't detain me," Dillon said.

"While I wait for an officer to obtain a warrant, yes, I can." Especially with concerns Dillon could destroy evidence while we waited. "Put your hands behind your back."

Dillon put his hands up in surrender and backed away. "I can't let you do that, Fallon."

Dillon backed up closer to the wall.

I pursued him, cuffs in hand.

"I let you bring me in, I'm dead, just like my coworker."

"Well, maybe you should have thought of that before you worked for a bunch of psychopaths."

He looked hurt. "You'd really be okay if I died?"

*No. But I should be.*

I reached for his hand, but suddenly, the room spun, and I wasn't facing him anymore; I was facing the wall, my chest pressed up against it. My hands behind *my* back.

Dillon stood behind me, holding my arms together. He hadn't hurt me; he'd just been quick. Quicker than me.

*Dammit.*

"Fallon." His breath warmed my ear.

I sensed the rise and fall of his pectorals, my wrists wedged against his hard, bare abs, and in the struggle, my shirt's hem had come up a couple of inches.

I turned my chin over my left shoulder and looked up into his eyes. His warmth was back. The warmth that had kissed me last night. He stared at me—at my nearly exposed backside, at my lips—with desire swirling through his eyes.

As if he had to fight the urge to kiss me.

"I can't let you take me in," he whispered.

I yanked my wrists, but he tightened his grip and pressed his chest against my back.

"Don't move," he said. "I don't want to hurt you."

"Let me go!"

"I let you go," he commanded, "you walk out of here and never see me again."

My chest ached as I looked up above my shoulder at his chestnut eyes. "Is that really what you want?"

He looked at my mouth, then back at my eyes, and when he spoke this time, his voice was softer. "I need to keep you safe."

The hurt inside me dulled a little, and then I got mad at myself. I shouldn't care if he cared about me. I was a cop; he was a criminal.

"Just let me go."

My cell phone rang with Burch's ringtone, but I remained Dillon's captive. He held me for several more seconds before backing away, but by then, my cell had gone to voice mail.

He retrieved a black bag and placed it on the counter. Packed a wad of cash and a burner phone into it and shoved it into my hands.

"What are you doing?" I asked.

"You need to leave town. I'm calling you a ride."

"No! And by the way, you think I'm that stupid to get into a car *you* put me in? It'd blow up or drive off a bridge."

He looked annoyed at my accusation. "I would never hurt you, Fallon, but the guys I work for would in a heartbeat. If they find out you were dating me, that you know..."

I'd be killed.

We both would.

"Maybe they already saw us together," I challenged.

A fresh look of alarm flashed across his face. He shook his head. "We'd be dead already."

My cell phone rang with Burch's ringtone. I needed to tell Burch everything. Even if he didn't forgive my stupidity, I'd give him every piece of intel I had to help his investigation and let the cards fall where they may.

"Sergeant," I answered.

My intent must have been written all over my face because Dillon took a step closer.

"Fallon," he whispered.

"O'Connor," Burch snapped. "Ever hear of answering your damn phone?"

"Don't do this," Dillon added.

"Yes, sir," I said. "I have something—"

"An officer is missing."

Silence.

"I...what?"

"He left his house for an early morning meeting. Never made it to the station."

*Holy crap...*

"Get down here—now. Texted everyone the address. I took over as IC, and I want the whole task force on this."

Incident commander meant there was an official crime scene, which meant they thought something happened to him. And if Burch was the IC, then it had something to do with the case.

"And, Fallon?"

"Yes, sir?"

"When I call? You answer."

The call ended.

I tried to call Burch back five times. I wanted permission to stay here and detain Dillon. I wanted Burch to confirm the tattoo was sufficient enough evidence to get a warrant. But Burch didn't answer, and with an officer missing, I was left with two bad options: no-show at the crime scene or rush there and tell Burch everything.

I despised the idea of forgoing my original plan, but leaving wouldn't change one vital fact: I now knew the identity of this Syndicates captain. I had Dillon's name, address, and make and model of his vehicle—all things we could use to find him and put him behind bars.

"Looks like you got a temporary reprieve," I choked. "Key word being *temporary*. As soon as I see my boss, I'm telling him everything."

I walked into his bedroom and threw my clothes on. When I came out, Dillon stood with his arms crossed over his chest.

"I wouldn't do that if I were you."

"Is that a threat?" I grabbed my purse.

"It's a warning. Do *not* tell him. You'll be putting yourself in danger."

"More like your life in danger," I said as I put my shoes on.

"You really think I'm saying this to save my own ass?" he snapped. "I don't give a shit what happens to me! If it weren't for my brother and mom, I'd have done something to just let them..."

He stopped and shoved a hand through his hair.

I couldn't process all this right now. Right now, I needed to go, so I pushed the elevator button.

"Fallon."

I turned around and saw the *boyfriend* Dillon again. The man who had broken down all of my walls and made me think that I had finally found happiness.

"I trusted you," I managed over the lump in my throat. "I never trust anyone, and I trusted you."

He opened his mouth but clearly realized there was nothing

he could say to undo any of it. Instead, he held the escape bag out and pleaded, "Please reconsider."

The elevator door opened, and I stepped away from the landscape that once held my happily ever after and into the empty shell that was my heart's future.

# 16

I couldn't believe I fell for Dillon. Love was complete bull, making you savor it when you thought you had it, only to rip it away each time and watch you bleed. What the hell was wrong with me, letting the wall come down I'd safeguarded for years? I finally let someone in, I trusted him and gave him my heart, and look what happened. My soul was put into a wood-chipper.

Why? Was I so broken that I only attracted darkness into my life? Was I cursed?

Or maybe...maybe I didn't *deserve* love.

I bit back the tears.

Right behind the pain came anger at myself because I was stronger than this. This whole experience with Dillon just proved my original priorities were right.

Priorities that did not include love but did include rushing to this crime scene.

When I arrived at the address Burch had texted us, I was overwhelmed by the number of uniforms on the scene. When a cop disappeared? Police took that very seriously and spared no expense in looking for one of their own. The top detectives and crime scene units joined us, ready to comb every square inch of this place.

Before I could join them, my cell phone buzzed with a text.

**Dillon: Fallon, please tell me you're okay. I heard a cop is missing.**

Another buzz.

**Dillon: I know it's not fair of me to be worried about you, but I am. I'm so damn worried, so please. Just text me back one word. Tell me to go to hell, anything to let me know you're safe.**

The audacity of him to act like he cared.

**Dillon: For the record, I would give anything to be the guy you deserve, Fallon.**

But he knew all along he wasn't the guy I deserved. How could he let me fall for him?

I clenched my fists. I wanted to hit something. Beat something. My enraged heart thrashed around in my rib cage, pumping an unhealthy desire for revenge, for vigilante justice, through every cell of my body.

"Sir." I approached Burch, who stood near the command center.

Proctor was near him, of course, lips firmly planted on his butt.

I'd quickly changed into my uniform at home before rushing here, where yellow police tape roped off an abandoned parking lot with asphalt so faded, you could barely make out the yellow stripes. Weeds sprouted between its network of cracks, and its fifty parking spots were all empty, except for one police car. The parking lot was flanked by industrial buildings to the north, a patch of weed-infested land to its south, and Lake Michigan on its east, which had once been home to shipments that arrived on a now-broken boat dock.

Burch glanced around at all the other officers, then returned his steely eyes to me. “You’re late, O’Connor.”

Proctor smirked, making my cheeks warm in anger. I’d never met anyone who savored someone’s suffering like Proctor did.

“I know. I can explain. It has to do with the case. I need to tell you something.”

“It’ll have to wait,” Burch said.

Proctor had to act like he was wiping his lips to keep them from smiling too wide.

“All right, listen up,” Burch shouted to everyone else, thwarting any possibility to talk to him.

What if Dillon was telling the other captains right now? Getting the jump on this information? I needed Burch to listen now.

“Officer Anthony Marks was last seen at six o’clock this morning when he left his home.”

The shotgun blast of shock rocked me back on my heels. The missing officer was Marks? Kind, family-loving, about-to-have-a-third-child Marks? My mentor?

“Told his wife he was heading to an early morning meeting at work—a meeting his commanding officer confirms was on the books. Marks never showed, which is out of character. An hour ago, his empty squad car was found ten miles away in this abandoned parking lot. Which, as you can tell, is the opposite direction of the precinct. We tried to trace his cell,” Burch continued. “But it was shut off ten minutes after he left home.”

No cop ever shut off his cell, let alone one with a wife about to have a baby any second.

“Upon an interior search of his vehicle, we found small traces of blood on the steering wheel.”

*Oh no.*

“We need to work fast,” Burch said. His implication—that the clock was ticking to find him before he was killed—twisted my ribs.

If Burch thought this had something to do with the Syndicates, he needed to know about Dillon ASAP. Dillon could be telling his bosses everything about me right now, jeopardizing our case. Maybe even putting Marks in more danger.

"Sir," I pleaded, "I really need to talk to you."

"I'll come find you in a few minutes," he said with an edge. "Right now, I need to get everybody assigned to their grid because minutes matter."

Burch walked away, and Proctor had the nerve to step into my path like some douchebag excuse of a bodyguard protecting his boss from some crazy woman who might otherwise follow Burch around. The look of complete satisfaction on his face made me clench my teeth so hard, they might break.

"Did you know you were the last one here out of forty officers?" Proctor sneered. "You're making it pretty clear this job isn't a priority of yours."

"I don't have time for your petty BS today, Proctor," I snapped. "So, leave me the hell alone."

His nostrils flared. "Maybe we should discuss your tardiness with your commanding officer."

"You know what?" I snapped. "Let's set that meeting up. Because there's a very good reason I was late today, but there's no good reason for why you won't stop harassing me at every turn. Maybe we should discuss *that* with our commanding officer."

Proctor's jaw ticced. "You're turning into an embarrassment, you know that?" Proctor spewed. "Just like your dad."

My fingers twitched. It took every ounce of self-control to not shove him to the ground and pummel him.

I walked over toward Shane, but because the universe evidently wanted to make today a living hell, Proctor was assigned to our little group working the grid on the nearby small field.

"Do me a favor," Shane hissed quietly. "Next time you decide not to come home at night, give me a courtesy text, so I'm not worried somethin' happened to you."

Shane had never snapped at me like that before.

"I thought you knew I was with Dillon."

"You've never spent the night before," he spat. "For all I knew, something might've happened to you on your way home from his place. Courtesy text. All I'm askin'."

Before I could apologize for worrying him, Shane stomped away.

I dug my nails into my palms, fighting back tears of fury.

"Maybe Marks took off," Proctor suggested with a dismissive shrug.

I bit down on my teeth. "He wouldn't take off, Proctor. His wife is about to have a baby."

"Exactly," Proctor said. "Nagging wife, screaming baby on the way. What guy wouldn't want out?"

"How can you be so ambivalent about a missing cop?" My voice rose.

If he didn't take this seriously, he might miss clues that could save Marks's life.

"Geez, chill!"

"He's missing, and there's blood in his car. Did you flunk common-sense class?" I demanded.

"I can't wait for Burch to fire your ass. You're such an embarrassment to this force!"

I clenched my fists. "You don't care about Marks! Or any other fellow officer, for that matter!"

"*You* don't care about what a shit stain you're leaving on our uniform. I can't believe I ever asked you out. If I'd known you were the offspring of some lowlife junkie piece of s—"

I growled and slammed my fist into his cheek.

Suddenly, I wasn't standing anymore. I was on the grass, holding my face. He had hit me back—hard.

"The hell is going on?" Burch barked.

I stood up, and Proctor wiped his bloody lip.

"Look, I don't know what the hell is going on, and frankly, I don't care. Both of you, go home now," Burch ordered.

He walked away.

"Sir," I started.

"That's an order," Burch said.

Proctor gave me the look of death before walking off, and as badly as I wanted to just get away from the scene, I couldn't leave yet.

"Sir, before I go, there's something I need to tell you."

Burch's lips tightened. "You'd better make this fast, O'Connor."

Burch marched over to the water and expected me to follow, out of earshot of everyone else.

"Sir, I've uncovered the identity of the captain with the tattoo."

Burch stared at me as I willed the words to come.

"I discovered his identity this morning, but for the past three weeks..." I swallowed. "I've been dating him."

Burch didn't move. Didn't blink. Didn't do anything.

"What the hell are you talking about?" he demanded.

"I had no idea he was involved with drugs."

Burch scrubbed his face. He looked like he couldn't believe what a cluster-F this investigation was turning into.

"This morning, I saw his scorpion tattoo. Confronted him."

"You confronted him without backup?"

"It happened fast."

"And let me guess. He didn't give up any evidence we can work with."

I tensed. "No permit for a weapon."

"A slap on the wrist. You should've waited for us to properly interrogate him. You blew our element of surprise."

Something inside of me swelled up, and my backbone snapped straight.

"Maybe," I allowed. "But my guess is, he'd have never admitted he was a drug captain to anyone else. But he admitted it to me because I built up a rapport with him."

Burch smoothed his mustache as he looked to the side. When he spoke again, his tone lost some of its edge. "You tell him about the investigation?"

"I never even told him I was a cop until this morning. But now he knows I'm on the task force investigating his organization."

"There any chance you slipped and gave up details?"

"No."

"Any chance he was working you this whole time?"

"I don't think so. If anyone in the Chicago Syndicates knew he was dating me, he'd have been killed. So would I."

Burch considered this. "What's his name?"

I hesitated. But the protectiveness that came over me was absurd.

"Dillon McPherson."

"Will he still talk to you?"

What? "I...I don't know. Why? You want me to interrogate him?"

"No. I want you to make him an informant."

An informant. Not only a role where I'd be forced to talk to Dillon regularly, but it'd be an intimate, secret relationship between a cop and a CI on top of that.

"No one talks in this organization," he said. "You've just cozied up to a captain in the Syndicates. This is our best shot to get information."

"But we got names off that USB drive, and IT still might get more."

"A CI would be a game changer that we can't afford to pass up."

"Sir, there's no way he'll tell me anything else now that he knows I'm a cop. And even if he would..." It would be too damn painful to tug at the emotions I'd let myself have for him. "We wouldn't be able to trust a word he says."

"Didn't say it'd be easy to sift through the truth, but we need answers."

He must have assumed my sigh was hesitation.

"O'Connor, Officer Marks arrested a captain, and that captain turned up in the river. If the Syndicates *are* responsible for Marks's disappearance, he might not be the last."

Burch was right. Our team, if successful, would continue to put massive dents in the Syndicates' plans. Which meant more officers could be in danger. Even Shane.

My skin prickled at the thought.

He let the fear bounce around inside my head for a full thirty seconds.

"What do you want me to do?" I asked.

"Call him. Set up a meeting."

# 17

The diner screamed the 1950s with red and black walls, where framed Blackhawk jerseys and autographed pictures of celebrities surrounded the casually dressed crowd in Chicago nostalgia. The undercurrent of voices competed with Elvis Presley music that pumped through the stuffy air. Behind a wall opening, a short-order cook with sweat shining on his forehead slapped a set of white plates piled high with pancakes onto the counter—the scent of eggs mixing with the smell of stale coffee.

Dad stood up when he saw me come in, motioning to the empty chair in front of him.

*Like I need his help.*

I plopped down and tossed my cell on the table faceup. If any word surfaced on Marks—any—I wanted to see it right away.

Yesterday, the techs dusted the entire car inside and out for prints and found it clean. Not a single print, not even one from Marks himself. Which pointed to a professional job, one I prayed was not a hit.

Marks's cell phone remained off and unfound. No suicide

note, nothing unusual in the initial review of his financial records. Nothing to suggest that whatever happened was self-inflicted. There wasn't a single clue as to what happened to him or where he was. Not even a hair out of place. And now, a day later, the team was no closer to finding him.

And here I was, having to carve out time for breakfast before work because Dad's incessant calls finally made me cave.

"What happened?" Dad motioned toward my bruised cheek and had the nerve to look worried. The hurt he'd caused me in just one of his episodes was nothing compared to the force of Proctor's fist.

"I'm here, so just say whatever it is you want to say because I really have to get going."

*Geez.* When had I gone from the loving daughter who'd fight to the ends of the earth to help her father conquer his disease to this bitter human?

Dad cleared his throat. "You look good," he said, nodding to my uniform, using the same proud tone as when I'd come home with an all-A report card in grade school.

He reached for my hand just like he used to do when I was a kid—before he'd traded his love for me in for drugs.

At dinners, he'd hold my hand, tell me how much he loved me, and ask me to tell him everything about my day. "Don't leave anything out," he'd say with an eager smile. His affection used to be the brightest spot in my day.

The key phrase being *used to.*

I snapped my hand back before suffering the burn of his once-pleasant touch and crossed my arms over my chest.

"What do you want, Dad? And what was so urgent it couldn't wait a few more days?"

"I've missed you," Dad said. He looked like hell, worse than I'd ever seen him. His eyes had dulled to a gray, as if their luminosity was chained to his dwindling spirit, his skin puddled around his elbows, and his hair had further succumbed to balding.

"Here are the coffees you ordered," the waitress interrupted. She wore her hair in a messy bun and smelled like she'd taken a recent smoke break.

"Thought you might want a cup," Dad explained.

"Will you guys be ordering food?" she asked.

"No," I said. "We won't be here long."

She walked away.

I glared at my dad, becoming more impatient as he gathered himself.

He leaned his arms on the table. "I have something to say. It'll just take a few minutes, and then if you never want to talk to me again, I promise I won't bother you."

The fear of losing him kicked my ribs. I was the one shutting him out, so why did it hurt so much that he might stop trying? Maybe it was because the only constant in our relationship—in my life, really—was Dad's pursuit of my love, his promises to recover echoing through the halls of our lives. The thought of that going away terrified me. It was all I had left of him.

"First of all, I need to apologize, Fallon. Last time you saw me..." Dad ran a hand over his head, unable to finish before his lips quivered.

That was the thing about getting high; when you came down, the hurt you'd caused people crashed through you, unable to hide behind the fog of narcotics.

After what he'd put me through, part of me was glad he fought back tears. Especially since his moment of being the good dad, the dad that actually cared if he hurt me, had become less frequent with each dose of drugs.

The soft old Fallon would smile weakly and accept his apology. Anything to preserve the possibility that a morsel of his affection might be thrown my way. Anything to maintain the delusion that things would get better one day. That the foundation of my world would finally be repaired, and what I'd desperately longed for year after year would finally come back to me—the stability of my father and his love for me. If I were honest, I needed it now more than ever. It felt like my life was spiraling with Marks missing and Dillon's shattering revelation. But each time I'd hoped Dad would start to love me how I needed to be loved, my heart was sliced. And now, I couldn't handle being forsaken again.

"What you did was low," I growled. "Even for you."

Dad gripped the white ceramic mug tighter, staring at the brown liquid in shame.

I was an awful person because at this moment, I wanted him to hurt the way he'd hurt me. I wanted him to feel the suffering of a terrified child, devastated over her mommy's death, desperate for her dad to assure her everything would be okay. Only to discover him using Mom's leftover drugs to get himself high.

I hated thinking about that time, filled with a mixture of terror—how could we live without Mommy?—and hope that Daddy would take care of me.

*I'm holding Daddy's hand, watching Mommy's casket lower underground.*

This is all happening too fast.

*Life doesn't seem like life without Mommy. It feels like my world cracked in half and filled with lava, and nothing is ever going to be okay.*

*But Daddy said we'd be okay. He tells me that every night when he tucks me in. And I trust Daddy. He's never failed me, not once.*

*"Things will be okay, kiddo," he says. "I promise."*

*"I'm scared you'll leave me, too," I say.*

*He looks at me super seriously and squeezes my hand. "I will never leave you. I will always take care of you, Fallon. I promise."*

Fast-forward to reality, sitting in a diner.

"I'm ready to answer your question, Fallon." By the tone of his voice, I knew which question he was referring to.

"Really? So, hell has frozen over, then."

His lips tightened, and he tried to hide the sag of his shoulders. "I deserved that."

"You deserve a lot of things."

He cleared his throat. "In my meetings, they've been telling us we need to accept the anger from our loved ones. You have every right to hate me after what I put you through."

"You're going to meetings," I said incredulously. As in plural. As in more than one, without me shoving him through the door.

"For three months."

I glared at him. He expected me to believe this? The last time I saw him, he was so in love with his next fix that he'd finally destroyed me. Almost cost me my coveted seat on the task force.

"Fallon, after what I did to you..." He rubbed his hands, trying to disguise their trembling. "It was rock bottom. After that day, I went to an NA meeting and never touched the stuff again. Never will, either."

Yeah, right. How many times did I have to get my hopes up before I learned my lesson?

"You embarrassed me," I growled. "In front of my boss. My colleagues. Police officers, for crying out loud! That night was special to me, and you could've cost me my job."

I should've known better than to invite him. But that was me—pathetic old Fallon, desperate for my father to care about me. Desperate to get his attention and his approval, thinking if he saw the celebration of me having made the task force, we would have some kind of a happy moment together for once. A happy moment that would bring us closer. I had pictured him walking in and putting his arm around me proudly, maybe even saying a few words on my behalf. But my boss was the one saying a few words on my behalf when my dad stumbled in, high as a kite. In that instant, I was overcome with dread as I watched him lumber through the group of officers, and once he got close? He was so high, he fell into a waitress and knocked her tray of drinks on the ground. The whole restaurant stared at my dad on the floor. And there, lying next to him? What had fallen out of his pocket for all my fellow law enforcement officers to see?

A baggie of heroin and a needle.

As if that wasn't bad enough, the needle had no protective cap. No cap. He could've infected the waitress with Lord knew what when he bumped into her. He could've infected any colleague there—my boss even—if they'd bumped into his pocket.

*Mortification* wasn't even the right word. All the disappointments he'd caused had been brewing inside like a volcano, and that was it. My anger erupted. I was so furious, I didn't even feel bad for him when he was arrested.

I was angry that he'd made me so angry. He'd unleashed some bitter, horrible version of myself.

"I'm sorry, Fallon."

*I'm sorry.* Two words wouldn't undo everything he'd done.

"Is that it, then?" I asked. "Because I have somewhere I need to be."

Dad offered a sad smile. "I have some things I need to say to you, Fallon. Before it's too late."

"It's already too late. I don't care about your apologies or if you're trying to get clean for the zillionth time. I give up on you, Dad," I declared. "I finally don't give a crap why you picked up the drugs because you know what? It doesn't matter. It took me a while to figure out that I don't care."

Dad's gray eyes shimmered, so he looked down.

Evidently, not all of me was on board with hurting him; a sudden rush of compassion made me want to wrap my arms around him because I'd never seen him look so...broken. Not even when Mom died.

And I'd never seen him look so ashamed. It contorted his face, and his body folded in on itself.

"Fallon, you deserve to know why I started taking the drugs in the first place."

My heart stilled in the silence.

"Before your mom died, I'd argued with her so many times about her addiction. In the beginning, I was patient. Understanding. But it was scary, watching the woman I fell in love with change like that. Sent her to rehab multiple times, but nothing worked; it just kept getting worse. I think the first time I felt true anger was when we lost our house. I guess in my mind, it was one thing for her to lose her job, her friends. She was hurting herself, and I hated that, but it was confined to her. Until it wasn't."

Dad took a sip of his coffee, as if willing it to give him courage. The door to the café opened, and a handful of people stomped in, greeting friends with loud hellos.

"When we lost our house and drained our retirement accounts, I got mad and insisted she get a grip on it. If not for her sake, for yours. You were just a little girl, and she'd be passed out when you got home from school."

Dad rubbed his face. "No matter how much I tried to understand, she was crossing lines I couldn't tolerate. Endangering you with drugs in the house. The people she brought over." Dad cracked his knuckles. "After you left for school one morning, I went off on her like I'd never done before. The years of anger finally exploded. I told her she was being a horrible mom, destroying your life. If she didn't get clean, I was going to file for divorce, take primary custody, and never talk to her again."

When my dad spoke next, I could hear the tears he choked back. "She said maybe we'd all be better off without her." Dad stopped and squeezed his eyes shut. "I said maybe we would."

The air around me became poisonous, stabbing my lungs because I understood where this was going.

"I'd said it out of anger. I was sick of her playing a perpetual victim and flipping the tables like that. What I'd meant was that I couldn't keep an addict in the house with you. But she..." He gathered himself. "She got this look on her face I'd never seen before. Something about it worried me, but I was too pissed to ask her about it. So, I just stormed out and went to work."

Dad rubbed his eyes, taking several moments to gather his emotions.

"That was the last thing I ever got to say to her," he explained. "And to this day, I don't know if her overdose was an accident."

*Oh my gosh.*

All these years...I had no clue that there was a chance her OD was intentional.

I'd later learned the same statistics she probably did in treatment. While the relapse rate for substance abuse disorders was between forty and sixty percent, the rate for heroin specifically was as high as ninety. With a ninety percent chance she'd continue to hurt her daughter, did she think she was doing me a favor, that a life without her was better for me?

How hopeless must she have felt in her final dark hours, the disease of addiction suffocating her spirit. It had to have devastated her to think of the mom she was once capable of being and seeing the anti-mother she had become. It must have destroyed her, realizing her existence caused so much pain to the two people she loved more than anything in the world.

Even though rational people may have seen that with time and the proper treatment, there was plenty of hope she could beat her addiction, perhaps she'd grown too depressed to believe it.

Maybe when she stuck that needle in her arm, it had not been a selfish act at all. Maybe, in her hopeless mind, it was a sacrifice to free me from unconscionable pain. If I was a mother and the only thing I ever did was hurt my child and thought there was no hope of it ever changing, maybe I wouldn't want to be alive, either.

Then, I remembered it—the photograph of me and Dad that had been in her hand when I found her. I'd never told Dad about it. After we got home from the hospital, I'd put it in my jewelry box. But it had always puzzled me why she was staring at Dad and me as she took her final hit—a hit that was so powerful, it must have killed her before she could even get the needle out of her arm.

That had to be why she was holding it. She was looking at the two people who would be better off without her. Maybe it gave her the final motivation she needed to take what she knew was a lethal dose.

"That's why she had that picture..."

I suddenly felt so ill, I had to focus on my breathing to not vomit. I'd resented her for all these years, never comprehending the depths of her suffering. And all the while, she must have sensed my disappointment in her and my hurt that I wasn't enough for her to want to get clean.

When in fact, I meant so much to her, she'd rather die than cause me any more pain.

"What?" Dad's eyebrows furrowed.

Dad's voice snapped me back to the noisy diner. I'd been so lost in thought, I hadn't meant to say that out loud.

"Nothing."

But I could tell he wasn't about to let this slide.

"Fallon, I can tell it's something, so just tell me."

I took a sip of coffee. It was lukewarm and bitter. "I don't want to upset you."

He'd just blame himself more, and even though a minute ago, part of me had wanted him to hurt, there was a considerable difference between that and giving him news that had the power to destroy him.

"Was there a suicide note?" he pressed, trying to hide his growing edge of panic.

"No."

"Did she do something to you?"

"No."

"Fallon, tell me."

It was strange how we could slip back to father-daughter roles with him in command in a snap. I sipped my coffee, trying to think of a way out of telling him. He already suspected suicide, and maybe the photo didn't confirm it with certainty, but it was pretty damning. I looked at the determination in his eyes and realized there was nothing I could say to get him off the scent. The best I could do would be to soften the blow.

"When I found her, she was holding a picture of you and me."

I didn't need to say more. Gut-wrenching understanding washed across his face.

"It might not mean anything," I insisted.

But I could see my words just bounced right off of him.

"More coffee?" the waitress asked.

I offered her an uncomfortable smile as she topped off our mugs.

Dad looked stunned, like he had been emotionally tasered. I didn't know what to say, but when I opened my mouth, my cell buzzed.

**Dillon: Tonight. 10 p.m. I'll text you the location.**

It had taken him almost a day to respond to my request to meet.

The text must have reminded Dad we were on limited time because he forced himself to resume the conversation where he left off, to finish saying whatever it was he wanted off his conscience.

"When your mom died, I went to a really dark place. Blamed myself for her death. At best, I hadn't gotten her the help she needed in time to save her. At worst, saying we'd be better off without her made her..." Dad blinked back tears. "I should've been stronger. I was all you had, and you were hurting." He paused. "And I swear, I tried to be strong, but my mind...wasn't working right. Felt like I'd been drowning for two years and an anchor pulled me under."

Dad's eyes were haunted at the memory, glazing with tears. "What I did next, there's no excuse for. I should have gotten help, but I was just in so much pain. She was the love of my life, and I couldn't stop thinking about the last thing I'd said to her."

Dad let a more extended silence pass this time. He wouldn't look me in the eye as he repeated in shame, "I should have gotten help."

Unease wrapped its unwelcome blanket around me, sensing a far more sinister explanation for what took place after my mother died.

"A few weeks after her funeral," Dad finally continued, "I couldn't look at her stuff anymore. I went around the house, shoving all her stuff into bags. That's when I found a pill bottle wedged between her nightstand and the wall. It was still full of pills, so obviously, she'd gotten high and forgotten they were there or lost them. I shoved the bottle in the bag so hard, it ripped a hole and fell right back out. Lying there on the carpet, taunting me."

Dad rubbed his eyes.

"Wasn't in my right mind. Wasn't sleeping or eating, and every day hurt worse than the last. I'd find a voice mail from her and listen to it repeatedly for over an hour. I'd find old letters she'd written when we first started dating and read them over and over. It made it hurt so much worse, but I couldn't stop myself. Went into a...kind of spiral, missing her so badly, I'd hunt for any piece of her, but that piece would just rip my heart open wider. It felt like a walking wound that I couldn't stop ripping the scab off." Dad paused, and his voice dropped its pitch in shame. "I just wanted the pain to stop."

He rubbed his thumbs together and braced himself.

"I swallowed the entire bottle of pills, Fallon."

My breath caught in my throat. Of all the hypotheses I had come up with over the years as to why he'd first tried drugs, this was one I had never considered—attempted suicide.

Dad may have disappointed me and hurt me throughout the years, but I would never wish pain so unbearable that you wanted to take your own life on to anyone. And knowing he went through that broke my heart.

I thought back to those dark days, but I was hurting so badly that I assumed Daddy's pain was normal. What was normal, after all, when your world was destroyed by a nuclear bomb?

"Guess it wasn't enough to..." Dad said. "So, it just...got me high instead."

"And the high let you escape your pain," I realized. "That's why you started using."

He shook his head. "I'm not going to say that wasn't a welcome side effect, that it took me away from my pain for a bit. But I've, uh...since learned that some people—and they don't know why it's some and not others—get exposed to drugs, and addiction takes place fast. After just one try..."

I'd read up on addiction, about the theory that some people had an addict gene. It aligned with what Dad had experienced. Some people could take a hit with no problem. But others with the gene...one time, and their life as they knew it ended. Especially if they ingested enough heroin-laced pills to almost die. That flood of narcotics must wreak havoc on brain chemicals.

"Never forgave myself for trying to take my life, for almost leaving you an orphan. And then to become an addict on top of that. To become the very thing I'd fought against for two years..." He bit his lip. "I tried so hard to fight it, for your sake. And each time I failed, I felt guilty. That guilt would eat me alive about how much I was letting you down, and that guilt was so overwhelming, I'd give anything to stop it, and the only way to stop it was to take a hit. The worse I felt about myself and how badly I failed you, the more I sabotaged it to escape it."

On the outside, everything had looked so black-and-white.

*Just don't take the drugs*, I'd thought. *You don't need them to stay alive, and each time you choose them, you are choosing them over me.*

I'd been so wrapped up in my own grief, confusion, and hurt that I hadn't seen what he was going through.

If I had understood, this anger would not have snowballed all of those years, and when he fell down at my celebration toast, I would have felt worried instead of angry. This didn't take away all of Dad's mistakes, but it sure as heck explained a lot of it and opened up forgiveness and compassion in my heart.

I wiped a stray tear from my cheek and took a deep breath.

"I'm sorry for all of it, Fallon. I'm sorry for failing you. For letting drugs ruin our lives."

I battled the tightness in my throat, my eyes stinging harder.

"I'm sorry I didn't ask the doctor the right questions when your mom had that surgery. I should've asked if the drugs could be addictive. It just never crossed my mind. I let it come into our house, and I've never forgiven myself. You deserved better."

I'd just heard everything I'd ever needed to hear and felt so much lighter, as if a vise squeezing my body had released.

I could see Dad had changed. He was clean. He was...Dad.

And while the cautious part of me reminded me he could relapse, I was ready to begin building something that we'd been missing for years. It would take a lot of time, but I was willing to put in the work.

I reached across the table and held his hand. And when I did,

Dad sobbed. He looked so fragile, childlike almost, as his shoulders shook.

I could see by his pained stare how badly he needed my forgiveness. And by the shrinking of his shoulders, how unworthy he felt to receive it.

He squeezed my hand. "I love you, baby girl."

We sat like that, holding hands and just staring at each other. I hadn't seen him—the old dad—for years. The him that had been overtaken by his demon, and now, here he was, finally sitting across from me.

He'd been so insistent on meeting with me these past few weeks, and now, I could see why. After undoubtedly getting pushed to apologize and come clean in his NA meetings, this was quite the burden to unload, and he must have needed to do it while he had the nerve.

My cell phone buzzed with the location where Dillon wanted to meet.

"I should let you go," Dad said, glancing at my phone.

I wished I could stay longer, but it was a workday.

"Let's do dinner this weekend?" I suggested. "I can buy some groceries and cook for you. Provided I don't have to work," I clarified.

By then, hopefully—please, for all things holy—Marks would be back home safe with his family.

Dad smiled. "I'd love that."

When we both stood, I walked around the table and wrapped my arms around him. I could feel his bones as he shook in tears, and his hug wasn't as tight as I'd once remembered. But for the first time in a long time, peace came over me. No matter what happened with Dillon later, I could handle it now that I had my dad back.

I let him go and, after saying final good-byes, reluctantly walked away. But quickly turned around.

"By the way," I said, "what are you doing downtown today?"

When he asked to meet, I'd assumed it would be out in Blue Island, which was an hour from here. But he said he would be in the city this morning, which was odd. He didn't own a car, and public transportation was expensive.

Dad hesitated. I didn't like the look on his face as he put his hands into his pockets. "I was getting chemo, Fallon."

# 18

There was his name. Right there on the list.

I shoved the notebook off to the right side of my desk and typed the name of the airport into my search bar. And confirmed my hunch that it was within driving distance of Baja, Mexico. Then, I searched all the nearby airports until I confirmed that this was the most direct route from Chicago to Baja.

I covered my mouth with my hand. After fighting tears all morning from my dad's revelation, I needed this win.

I hustled to the task force conference room, where Burch stood, huddled with the team of investigators working Marks's disappearance. Chicago Police invited the FBI to help with the investigation, and the rest of us were told to stand down, but it wasn't easy to sit on the sidelines when someone you cared about was out there somewhere. I had a whole new respect for what families went through with missing loved ones.

"Sir, I think I found something."

He looked up at me.

"It's not about Marks," I clarified.

Burch motioned for me to come to the other end of the room, out of earshot of everyone else, where he stood with his arms crossed over his chest.

"After a few dead ends, I cross-referenced Ramirez's name against the PNR."

He raised an eyebrow.

"The US Department for Homeland Security keeps the names of passengers, among other things, in their database for fifteen years. Turns out, Ramirez is on that list. Fourteen years ago, he boarded a one-way flight to Los Cabos International Airport."

Burch looked to the side for a moment before returning his gaze to me. "He went to Mexico."

"And never came back."

Burch rubbed his chin.

"Los Cabos International Airport is the closest international airport to Baja, Mexico." I paused. "I think he joined the Baja Cartel fourteen years ago and has been living there ever since."

Burch picked at his thumbnail. "What's your theory on what this has to do with the Syndicates?"

"At first, I thought maybe he was responsible for smuggling drugs over the border to them." But after I'd put in the request to see the passenger list, I'd had more time to think about it. "If he's been working with the cartel this whole time, he wouldn't still be that low on the totem pole. He would have either moved up the chain of command or been killed, and since his name is on the drive, I think it's the former."

"The DEA doesn't have his name on the list of suspected cartel members."

"Which might suggest he's their bookkeeper."

Burch was silent for several moments before he nodded. "This is excellent work, O'Connor."

The approval in his eyes made my cheeks warm. "Marks planted that idea in my head." He deserved to get credit for that.

"In any case, if we're right, it provides further evidence that the Syndicates must be about to make a major move, likely expansion, like you said. The bookkeeper would need to be aware of a huge change in the financials."

Burch rubbed his mustache. "We'll bring in the other two Syndicates we found on that drive for questioning, but it's unlikely they'll talk. You meet with McPherson at ten?"

I nodded. "I don't know if he'll agree to be our CI."

"Get him to agree. Meanwhile, poke around about a possible expansion but come at it from the side at first. Not head-on. We don't want to tip our hand. Expansions often mean promotions for leaders, so feel him out there. But the first priority is to find out anything you can about Marks. We need intel. Fast, if we have any shot of finding him before it's too late."

"I'll try like hell, sir."

"You sure you can handle this?" Burch pressed.

Emotionally? No. Tactically? "Yes."

Burch hesitated. "I'll post a car a block away. Anything seems off, anything at all, you get the hell out of there."

"I will, sir."

When he nodded, I turned to walk away.

"O'Connor."

I turned around.

"Be careful. He's had a day and a half to process this. I don't want to have another missing agent on my hands."

# 19

Darkness encased the pothole-infested alley, concealing anyone who wanted to hide in its shadows, making it challenging to find the metal door. It rested inside a brick wall with a single bulb dimly illuminating its notebook-sized window, covered with a metal slab. As directed, I knocked three times and then scanned my surroundings with uneasy eyes.

The door's window creaked open, and a set of murky eyes peered at me, waiting for a password.

"Dibs." Today's password was a word frequented by Chicagoans, who used it to claim difficult-to-find parking spaces. And today, the ticket to enter was an homage to the past.

Speakeasies—illicit bars that sold alcohol during Prohibition—were a significant part of Chicago's history, a scattering of them peppering the city today. Like the 1920s, their locations were kept secret, passwords changed daily, making it one of the safer places to meet Dillon.

In theory.

It wasn't foolproof, though. Far from it. The risk of being

discovered together surged through the air like electricity during a storm threatening to strike.

And that didn't include another danger: I was about to meet a confessed drug lord, a drug lord who may have admitted his mistake to his bosses. If he did, would they step in to clean up his mess?

Was I really meeting Dillon, or was I walking into a trap?

I touched the bulge under my arm, wishing it were winter so I could've hidden my Smith & Wesson better beneath a baggy sweater.

The door groaned open, and the guy manning the entrance allowed me past him, through a crimson hallway, down a flight of concrete stairs, and through the door marked *Enter at your own risk.*

*Ironic.*

It opened into a room draped in chestnut wood and red velvet. Crimson chandeliers that looked like open umbrellas with yellow tassels hung overhead, illuminating the mahogany bar with soft, romantic light that made all the alcohol bottles glow. The ornamental rug next to the bar drew me toward the back, where Dillon told me he'd be waiting.

As I walked deeper inside, I glanced over my shoulder to ensure no one followed me, looked at me, or gave me any indication something was off. But the place was virtually empty. I slowly made my way through two draped doorways, observing every person and their movements until I finally entered the back room.

It was in here, on the far side of the room, where Dillon stood.

I savored the quick bolt of relief that it was him waiting, not some hit man. But I was instantly overwhelmed with how complicated seeing him made me feel. How could the guy I'd fallen for inhabit the same body as a drug captain? How could I want to punch him in the face yet also want him to kiss me?

It didn't help that he looked so...sexy, dressed in Diesel jeans that hugged his hips, a white T-shirt stretched over his muscles, and a baseball cap that brought attention to his striking eyes. Ordinary choices for another man, camouflage for someone trying to blend in with pedestrians on the streets.

*He's the enemy, Fallon. Enemy. Enemy. Just because he's here doesn't mean it's safe.*

"Fallon." His face flooded with relief to see me, and his mouth —the same one that had explored parts of my body I hadn't even seen myself—turned up slightly.

Until his gaze sliced through the room to my cheek.

Rage rippled across his muscles as he stormed over to me and brought his hand up to my face before catching himself and putting the distance between us that now existed in our hearts.

Why did it feel good to think of him touching me? Did a heart have muscle memory it had to outgrow?

Dillon balled his fists at his sides. "Who did that to you?"

"It wasn't one of your minions, if that's what you're worried about."

"Who did that to you?" he repeated, firmer this time.

I did not have feelings for Dillon anymore.

I didn't.

I couldn't.

"Fallon," Dillon pressed.

"Disagreement with a coworker."

Dillon's jaw locked, and his lips tightened into a line. He took my chin between his thumb and finger and tilted my face to the side for a better look.

"Coworker," he growled.

"What can I say?" I added. "Guy's an asshole."

Dillon's eyes snapped to mine. "A *guy*?"

*Uh-oh.*

"A guy *hit* you?"

"I hit him first."

"What's his name?" Dillon demanded.

"Irrelevant."

"Like hell. Give me a name."

"Why?"

"Because I'm going to find him and fucking pulverize him."

"Unwise."

"Name."

"This isn't what we're here to talk about," I said, moving away from him. Distance would help fight the pheromones' effects.

I stood on the other side of the room, but Dillon followed and put his palm on the wall next to my head.

"Coworker, as in a cop did that to you?"

"Doesn't matter."

"So, that's a yes. Give me his name."

"And then what?" I challenged.

"He'll be dealt with."

"I thought you didn't hurt people."

"Willing to make an exception when some asshole hits my girlfriend."

"I'm not your girlfriend."

"If you think I'm gonna let this slide, you clearly don't know me very well."

"No," I agreed. "I don't."

My emotional slap silenced him for a few seconds, and when he spoke next, he softened his tone. "You might not like what I do for a living," he said, his mouth distractingly close to mine. "But you know I'd protect you with my life."

I'd been so angry ever since I found out who he was. Angry when he confessed. Angry when I worked the crime scene where Marks's car was found. Angry when I met my dad. But now, I was just...exhausted. I guess anger only had so much runway before it ran out of steam, and with Dad's terminal prognosis and Marks missing, my anger dwindled.

"Look," I said. "I asked you to meet with me because I have some urgent questions I need to ask."

Dillon chewed the inside of his cheek. I could tell he wasn't going to let the bruise go, but for now, he appeared to recalibrate. "Does anyone know you're here?"

Only Burch. I hadn't told Shane about Dillon. We'd been too busy, talking about my dad.

I was devastated that Dad only had a year to live, but thank goodness I had that time with him. If he'd been cut out of my life abruptly, it would have been unbearable. We had time. Not much, but enough to bookend our relationship with bonding and happier memories. Well, as happy as they could be, fighting stage four cancer. I'd go to every chemo appointment I could with him, I'd take care of him when he was sick from its side effects, cook for him when he was well enough to eat. We'd flip through photo albums to cement the good memories, to remind him of what he was fighting for. The doctors said we'd have only one more Thanksgiving and Christmas, but maybe his body would respond better to treatments, and we'd have more.

My cell phone rang with Shane's ringtone, which was odd since we were scheduled to meet in an hour. Maybe he had to cancel, but I needed to focus, so I turned my ringer on buzz.

"Fallon, I can't answer your questions. Anything I tell you puts you in even more danger." His voice was steady and calm.

Mine was high-pitched and desperate. "Officer Marks is my friend," I said. "He's missing! He was taken—"

"I don't know where he is," Dillon said.

"You could ask."

"Asking around for something like that won't get answers; it'd just raise suspicion. You've seen what they do to people they don't trust."

"Why did you agree to meet me if you wouldn't answer any of my questions?"

"Because I needed to warn you. Something big is going down." But he didn't know that we already suspected as much.

"What is it?"

He shook his head. "The point is, they're cleaning house, and you can't get in my bosses' way."

"That's why you're here?" I couldn't blink back the tears this time. "Because I'm complicating your business?"

I shoved myself away from the wall and steeled myself to get answers. Dillon must have thought I was about to leave, though, because he grabbed my arm to stop me.

"I don't care about the business. I care about you," he said.

I looked down where his hand gripped my skin. With our faces separated by only inches, I could smell his minty breath ripple across his plump lips. The soft lighting darkened his bronze skin and facial stubble, accentuating his jaw and his eyes, which erupted in desire as he stared at my mouth. It looked like it took every ounce of control he had to stop himself from kissing me.

His brows furrowed, and sadness cascaded through his features as he released me. When he finally spoke, despair infected his tone. "I'm sorry, Fallon," he said. "I shouldn't have let myself get involved with you. In my line of work, anyone that gets too close to me could become a target. Leverage if someone wants to get back at me or punish me." His Adam's apple bulged with a swallow. "But I couldn't stop myself." He hesitated. "The truth is, I felt something the first time I laid eyes on you, and then every moment after crashed into the next. And the more time I spent with you, the less possible it felt to cut you out of my life. I told myself to walk away from you many times." He shook his head. "But I couldn't get myself to do it." Dillon looked down. "It was selfish and reckless of me. I'm sorry."

I thought back to that night I'd told him what it was like,

growing up with addicts, how he'd reached across the table and linked his fingers with mine, and then that look of worry flashed across his face. And how he'd said I *shouldn't* be with him the night I finally told him how I felt. Looking back, I could see him struggling.

Maybe he thought he could keep our relationship casual; someone he didn't care deeply for could never be used as leverage against him. But his feelings for me had become a runaway horse.

Just like mine for him.

I realized I believed him, that he never set out with ill intent to knowingly put me in danger. And I felt his sorrow pulsing through my veins.

Especially when he reached his hand up and cupped my cheek and stroked my skin with his thumb. "I still care about you, Fallon. And I'm not gonna let anything happen to you," he vowed.

Dillon's gaze fell to my lips and back to my eyes, as if silently begging for permission. Before he tilted his head and drew his face closer to mine.

I was surprised that any part of me wanted him to kiss me, wanted him to wrap his arms around me, if only for a moment.

But I wouldn't allow that to happen. No matter how confused my heart was right now, Dillon was still a Syndicates captain and I was in law enforcement.

I lowered my head before his lips connected with mine and stepped away from his confusing touch.

Dillon sighed deeply but nodded in unsurprised understanding. Several moments of silence passed before he spoke again. "You need to leave town, Fallon."

"Just because Marks is missing doesn't mean I'll go missing."

Dillon picked up a bag off the ground—the same bag full of cash he'd tried to force on me yesterday—and tried to make me take it. "This is the only way I can protect you."

"If you're so worried about what they're capable of, why

aren't you leaving town?" I demanded.

"Because it's too late for me," he said. "There are only two paths ahead of me, Fallon. Prison or a coffin."

My eyes watered at his devastating destiny. And when they did, Dillon's gaze shadowed in sadness.

"I'm sorry I was ever involved with any of this, Fallon."

"You could go into witness protection," I whispered.

Dillon gave a sad smile; he didn't need to say what I already knew. These sociopaths got to the witnesses faster than if they went to prison. At least in prison, they lasted a few months before being slaughtered in the showers.

But maybe there was another option. Maybe Burch's idea would give Dillon the benefit of legal immunity with the discretion of his associates not knowing he was helping us.

"I want you to be my CI," I announced.

His eyes shadowed in anger. "Are you kidding me?" His voice was a cool frost over my skin, a whisper of his darker side percolating beneath the surface.

"Unlike witness protection, a confidential informant is just that—confidential. The only people who would know about it would be me, you, and my boss. That's it."

"It'd never work," he snapped. "They'd find out. They always do, and any cop who worked with a CI? Would get killed, too."

He set the bag closer. "I have a car waiting to take you to O'Hare."

"I'm not going anywhere."

"Yes, you are. You're in danger here."

"So are you."

"*You* don't need to be. There's still hope for you."

"Is that what this is about? You've given up hope?"

"You can't be here," he repeated. "It's too dangerous. The guys I work for have started taking things to a whole new level. That fire you were in? Wasn't an accident."

I blinked. "How do *you* know that?"

"That guy you saw outside my apartment? Heard something he wasn't supposed to—the fire was set on purpose. He didn't know what it meant, but after I thought about it, I did. They started in the elevator shaft, right after *you* climbed in. You, who's on the task force trying to take them down. You, on the same team as another officer who's now missing."

It made no sense, yet the cop in me had to acknowledge if two independent sources—my boss and now a captain in their organization—believed I was the target, discounting its possibility was reckless.

"Maybe they were after you," I said. "You're the captain in a drug organization, not me."

"If they wanted me dead, they'd simply send a car for me and put a bullet in my skull. They wouldn't need an elaborate fire to take me out. And if they wanted to kill me and failed the first time, they'd have tried again; I'd be dead by now."

Still, I'd mention it to Burch to make sure that angle was looked at, just in case.

"If they were coming after you before," Dillon said, "what do you think they'll do now that you're deeper into the case? Or if they find out we've been together? Think about it, Fallon. The stairwell on fire? The elevator? It was to make sure you didn't escape."

"How would they have known about me being on the case to begin with, especially since I hadn't even been briefed on it until later that morning? And how would they have known I was in that building?"

"That's what I'm trying to find out," Dillon said.

So, he was working on some information.

"But in the meantime, can you think of any reason they'd be targeting you specifically, out of all the cops on the task force?" Dillon asked.

I hesitated. Burch had shared a hypothesis he'd been piecing together with me. He said there was a difference between having a *passion* for locking up drug criminals and having it be your life's mission. Ever since the fire, he'd been quietly digging through my cases, trying to find a motive, and recently discovered that my vendetta against drug criminals was evident and frequent. For example, it came out when I gave testimony as the arresting officer of low-level drug charges to push for the maximum sentence. Or in the handful of speeches I'd given. Burch now believed the Syndicates may have vetted the cops joining the task force and saw my crazy level of determination as a threat.

"No," I hedged because Burch's theory was just that—a theory with holes in it. He didn't know how they'd get the names of the people on the task force to begin with.

In any case, if Dillon was willing to snoop around this, maybe there was a way for him to ask questions to the right people to get vital information.

"Be my CI," I insisted.

"No. You're leaving town." He kicked the bag closer to me, clearly accustomed to people obeying his commands.

I kicked the bag back. "I'm staying and working this case."

Dillon eyed me like a caveman about to throw me over his shoulder and drag me out.

"Fallon." He seemed to choose his next words carefully. "My bosses have connections with the cartel."

We'd already suspected this, but still. Hearing Dillon's confirmation was unsettling.

The cartels in Mexico were the most dangerous drug organizations globally, known for brutal violence of not only fellow and rival drug members, but also innocent men, women, and children who had nothing to do with their organization. Murder and torture were their weapons of mass destruction, used to incite fear and keep police so afraid, they would never go against them.

One time, a cartel even bombed a school full of children simply to send a message to the police.

It was well known most drugs came from the cartels, but those business transactions concluded once the drugs were across the border. Which meant there *was* something bigger going on with the cartel. Was it expansion, like we suspected? Or something else?

"How is the cartel involved in this?"

My cell phone's buzz burst through the silence, and now that I was looking, it was the *tenth* time Shane had called.

*Oh no. They must have found Marks...*

"Shane?"

"Fallon, where are you?"

"Is he alive?" I could hear it in his voice—something terrible.

"I...come home. I need to tell you something."

"Tell me now."

"I'm not doing it over the phone, Fallon."

"Is Marks alive?" I repeated.

"This isn't about the case. It's about...look, just come home."

"You're scaring me."

Shane's silence only heightened my growing panic.

"Tell me what's going on," I begged.

"Fallon, I—"

"Just say it!"

I could feel Dillon's worried stare.

"Fallon...two uniforms came by, looking for you. It's...your dad. They need you to go down to the medical examiner's office."

Two uniforms—textbook death notification procedure.

Medical examiner, as in morgue.

Dad.

After a sleepless night and barely any food, that was all it took for my blood pressure to plummet and for everything to go black.

# 20

In the darkness, the cold floor beneath me wobbled.

"Fallon," a gruff voice echoed.

It took several seconds to open my eyes. Dillon's face stared down at me, his eyebrows crinkled in worry.

He held my cheek. "Fallon, say something."

I was spilled across his lap on the floor of a room decorated circa the roaring twenties, and when I touched the back of my head, I hissed.

"You hit it pretty good. You need to go to the ER."

"I'm fine."

In the warmth of his embrace, everything felt peaceful. For a second, I forgot about the call that had made me pass out.

"I have to go."

I tried to get up, but he held me down with a hint of a smile.

"As if I'd let you in your condition."

But my cell phone was already buzzing.

I yanked myself free from Dillon's protective limbs and stood up. Too fast. I wobbled, so Dillon jumped up and steadied my arm.

"I have to get to the..." I choked over the last word. "Morgue."

When Dillon's eyes grabbed hold of mine, they penetrated my irises, but after a few seconds, he picked what he believed to be the more urgent priority.

"You could've cracked your skull; you need to get it looked at."

But I was already walking away, willing the dizziness to stop. Through the doorways, the hall, back up the stairs, and out the same door I came in.

Damn, my head throbbed. Each beat of my heart launched a cannon into the back of my skull.

I texted Shane.

**Me: Cook County ME office?**

**Shane: What happened? Your phone cut out.**

It annoyed me that I had to repeat myself.

**Me: Cook County, not Will County?**

It was unlikely he'd traveled outside Cook County, but I wanted to be certain.

**Shane: Let me pick you up and take you. Where are you?**

**Me: Which county?**

**Shane: Fallon, you shouldn't do this alone.**

**Me: WHICH COUNTY??????**

I walked down the alley, intending to hail a cab.

"Wait." Dillon's voice came behind me.

I kept walking.

When Shane's text confirmed it was the Cook County office, I ignored his pleas to let him pick me up and lifted my hand, grateful a cab rolled toward me. I opened the door, but Dillon's palm grabbed the top of it, blocking my ability to get inside.

He had the bag slung over his shoulder. "I'll drive you," he insisted.

Did I seriously need to state the obvious right now? Even if I wanted the company, which I didn't. "If you're seen with me, they'll kill you."

"I'm not letting you go to the morgue alone, Fallon. So, either I'm driving you or I'm coming with."

"Hell-lo?" the cab driver barked impatiently.

"I don't need a chaperone."

"You just knocked your ass out. If you think I'm taking no for an answer, you're sadly mistaken. So, we can stand here in the open, debating this, or we can be on our way."

"Yo! Lady! You in or not?"

With a huff, I got into the cab, and Dillon climbed in next to me.

"Where to?" the cabbie barked.

I told him the address.

When the cab pulled off, Dillon's lips tightened in worry for me. "Is it your coworker?" His concern for me deepened when he noticed my lips quiver and my eyes well with tears.

My voice grew weak. "It's my dad."

Dillon's eyes softened into heartbreaking understanding, and he reached over and gently laced his fingers with mine.

With a black hole swallowing me up, I couldn't refuse his comfort.

The cruelties of having feelings for a person who I could never be with receded behind my wall of suffering. At this moment, we existed in a space where all the complications that remained outside of this taxi temporarily faded to black, where Dillon was simply and wonderfully the guy who cared so much about me that he refused to let me go through this alone.

"Incorrect identifications happen sometimes," I said. "Person carrying someone else's wallet, for example. Like if you got robbed and that robber sort of looked like you and died, they'd preliminarily think it was you."

Dillon didn't say anything.

In desperation to prove my theory, I called my dad, but it went straight to his voice mail. Maybe he forgot to charge his cell phone, or maybe he turned it off, sleeping off the long day of chemo.

Chemo.

Cancer. Could it have snagged him suddenly? Stopped his heart after all those years of drug abuse? But the address Shane gave me was to the medical examiner's office. MEs are for things like gunshots, stabbings, and, well, drug overdoses.

I shook my head.

That couldn't be the case. Dad was fighting cancer, and he'd been clean for three months. You didn't fight cancer and turn around and gamble your life away with a high.

And he couldn't die. Not now. I had been waiting for him, my old dad, since I was eleven. He just finally returned to me, and we had so many years to make up for, so much hurt to eradicate through our long-lost love.

"It can't be him."

When we arrived, a silver-haired man approached me.

"Officer O'Connor?" Wearing blue scrubs and a white lab coat, he carried himself with confidence despite the mustard stain on his collar. He extended his hand. "Dr. Archer. I'm the medical examiner. Normally, I have my assistant do this, but when I heard it was an officer coming in..." He must have seen the blank stare on my face because he appraised Dillon—who lingered near my shoulder like a bodyguard—and then cleared his throat. "I'm sorry we're meeting under these circumstances. Please, follow me."

The white walls of this place reminded me of my childhood elementary school, made of giant bricks, painted with so many layers that the paint itself served as glue. Fluorescents buzzed overhead, turning the doctor's skin a jaundiced yellow.

He led us into a dark room with white ceiling tiles, shut the door, and motioned for us to take seats at an oval conference table, where he placed a manila folder in front of him. The place smelled like stale coffee, and icy air blew down from the vent above my head, coating my skin in invisible frost. Four feet of scratched mahogany wood separated me from the doctor.

I picked at my fingernail, trying to appear calm, but whatever happened in the next few minutes was going to change my life forever.

"Before we proceed"—he opened the folder, pulled out a pair of royal-blue reading glasses from the breast pocket of his coat, and put them on the tip of his crooked nose—"I need you to confirm your father's name, please?"

"Philip O'Connor."

Dr. Archer nodded. "I'm going to show you a photo of the man we brought in, and I need you to tell me if it's your father. Do you understand?"

"I thought I'd get to see his body."

"People prefer photographs. Seeing the body can be upsetting."

"I need to see his body."

No way I was looking at a photograph. What kind of closure was that? No way.

"Officer—"

"I appreciate your concern, but I've been around dead bodies before." My mom's, for one. "I'd like to identify him in person, not in a photograph. It's what I drove all the way here to do."

Dr. Archer was clearly about to put up an argument.

"She'd like to see him in person," Dillon commanded, making it clear he had my back in whatever I needed. And unlike my shaky voice, Dillon's forceful tone came off like a warning.

I could suddenly see this other side of Dillon. The one that could calmly make demands and intimidate people with his dominating presence.

Above the table, he screamed power, sucking all the energy out of the room and using it to silently threaten the man sitting across from me—the man attempting to not give me what I wanted. The hint of danger expanded from Dillon's body and thickened the air like a poisonous fog. Beneath the table, he placed his hand on my knee and squeezed tenderly.

And while the normal response might be fear, his demeanor incited a different and unexpected mix of emotions inside me.

Dr. Archer seemed to process the request for a couple of seconds, pulled a cell from his pocket, and placed a call. "Megan, can you get Mr. O'Connor's body prepared for identification?" There was a long pause. "Thank you." He hung up and returned his attention to me. "It'll be a few minutes, then I can take you down."

"What happened to him?" I asked. "Assuming it *is* my dad, what happened?"

Dr. Archer looked at a report. I knew the drill; he knew what happened but wanted to speak the facts precisely as they were. One didn't play the telephone game when it came to death.

"Says here a neighbor saw him lying on the ground, facedown, through the window of his residence."

That nosy neighbor had moved in two years ago. I couldn't blame the guy for disapproving of my dad's obvious drug use, but I did fault him for treating my father like a less-than, a deadbeat, and for always looking for reasons to call the cops. Peering through his windows, taking pictures of any comings and goings.

"Got worried when he wouldn't respond. Couldn't gain entry because the door was locked from the inside. First responders arrived at the scene approximately six minutes later. Upon gaining forced entry, they found no pulse, and the skin was cold. A n—"

He stopped. Looked at Dillon, as if hesitant to say something that might aggravate him.

"A what?"

He looked back at me and sat up straighter, as if to remind

himself he was a doctor, delivering information. "A needle was found in his arm."

"So, he overdosed."

"We won't know until we get toxicology back." Standard jargon for, yes, he overdosed.

It was a good thing I was sitting down because the room swayed.

"Somebody must have gotten to him," I declared.

The ME looked confused.

"Fallon," Dillon started.

But the glare I gave him could have cooked his skin. "You said yourself you thought I was in danger. I'm working on a drug case with violent criminals who have ties to the cartel. If something happened to him, it must have been them because my dad was doing great. I just saw him at breakfast, and he was happy."

Dillon opened his mouth but thought better than to disagree.

"Cause of death can't be determined until toxicology comes back in a few weeks," Dr. Archer said. "But there were no bruises, nothing consistent with a scuffle. Nothing at the scene indicated a struggle. And the dead bolt, it says, was still locked from the inside."

"Maybe you just saw all the track marks and jumped to a conclusion," I insisted.

He frowned.

"He was fine," I continued. "He'd been clean for three months. He was starting a new chapter in his life, so none of this makes any sense! He wouldn't have gotten high, not after our talk."

Dillon was kind enough to tighten his lips and nod, letting me hang on to the delusion that my dad hadn't *actually* overdosed for a little bit longer.

*This is how addicts are, unpredictable, never knowing when they'll go off the wagon, the disease always waiting in the wings to take them from you*, a little voice reminded me.

But I didn't listen to that voice; she was wrong. The medical examiner was wrong. Dad would not do this. Not now, no matter how much denial they'd claim I was in.

"They're ready." Dr. Archer stood up, looking at his phone.

I followed him out the door, down a long hallway, and into a medical area. White linoleum flooring, scuffed white walls, gray cabinets, and air-conditioning so cold, it could double as a walk-in refrigerator filled the room. Which was hauntingly quiet. The place smelled of sour pickles, and in the center, lying on a shiny silver table, illuminated beneath a large bulb, was a body, covered by a white sheet.

"Do you need a minute?" Dr. Archer asked.

When I shook my head, Dillon inched closer to me. He probably would have waited in the hall if I'd asked him, but I could see him bracing to catch my fall.

Dr. Archer slowly pulled the sheet down a couple feet.

And there—with his gray skin the only indication that he wasn't simply asleep—was Daddy.

*"Daddy?" I'm holding his hand, staring at Mommy's body in the coffin. I'm studying her face, desperately memorizing every cell of it, because I'm terrified that someday, I won't remember what she looked like. I cried for hours last night, just thinking about it.*

*"Do you still love people when you're dead?"*

*He looks at me with tears in his eyes. "What do you mean?"*

*I know Mommy hasn't been herself lately, but before that, her love for me was so big, it could fill the whole entire planet. It was like it was its own living, breathing force, but...what happens to it when that person dies? Does the love die, too?*

*"Does Mommy still love me?"*

*Daddy's lips tremble. "Always," he assures.*

*Tears form a river down my cheeks.*

*"Will you always love me?"*

*Because I feel so empty and so very sad. Like the floor could just vanish and the ground could swallow me up.*

*"Always," he promises.*

*"Even when you die?"*

Shock was a good thing. It helped you keep speaking, even when your insides had been gutted and set on fire.

"I don't understand how he could've overdosed. Even if he relapsed...he knew his way around drugs."

Dr. Archer's tone was empathetic. "We'll know more when the toxicology comes in, but sadly, this kind of thing happens all the time. Particularly when someone's been clean. Sometimes, they miscalculate how much they can handle. Sometimes, they get a batch that's purer than what they're used to."

I couldn't move.

"I'll give you a few minutes," he said, vanishing from the little hell room.

All those times I'd worried about something happening to him. I thought I'd built up a thick enough skin, especially after losing Mom, that it wouldn't affect me this badly. But this meant I was an orphan. No one tethering me to this world. Like being on a shipwreck as the lone survivor, floating out into oblivion on a raft.

My knees weakened a heartbeat before Dillon caught me under my arm. He gently lowered me to the ground and helped me sit with my back against the wall.

"Breathe." Dillon squatted in front of me, his eyes round with worry. He put his hand on my cheek. "Breathe, Fallon," he repeated.

Fear gripped my bones like a deep winter freeze, fear that I wasn't sure I could endure. I wasn't sure I had any more fight in me.

I'd tried to be strong my whole life. But right now, with my soul crushed, I needed Dillon to have been a stand-up guy, a person I could have leaned on for support. So he could've held me. Told me I wasn't alone in this, helped me with every step to come—the funeral arrangements, the pain that would continue rolling in.

I needed him to have never been involved with the narcotics organization.

I stared up at my father, thinking of all the drugs he'd pumped into his body, all the money he'd given to people to get those chemicals. Those people who didn't give a rat's ass about him.

People like Dillon.

"How can you be involved with a business that does this to people?" I choked. Betrayal pumped toxins through what was left of my heart.

I was ashamed of myself for crumbling and turning into this pathetic weakling. I never even wanted a Prince Charming, but once Dillon came along, I fell in love with the fantasy that he would sweep me off my feet and we would live happily ever after.

But he wasn't the prince. He was the bad guy.

"Fallon," he whispered. "I'd give anything to go back in time and make different choices."

How dare he look at me with watery eyes.

I slapped him.

"This is what you do." I pointed to my dad's body, wishing I weren't sobbing as I yelled. "Stay the fuck away from me, Dillon. You disgust me. The world would be a better place without people like you in it!"

I stood up and stormed out of the room.

# 21

"Do you think they'll find Marks alive?" I asked.

Shane's lips turned down. "I think the FBI is doing everything they can."

The critical forty-eight-hour window had passed already, and even though I knew what that likely meant, hope was a lot harder to extinguish than I thought.

"Has Burch said anything else about that fire?" Shane asked.

I shook my head. He'd relayed the angle that Dillon was in the elevator to Fisher, but nothing had come of it. Burch echoed Dillon's thoughts; if they wanted to execute one of their own, he'd be dead. And there'd be no reason to set an entire skyscraper on fire to try and pull it off.

Shane's chest rose in frustration. "It's been weeks."

My cell phone's buzz interrupted with a text.

**Dillon: Fallon, I'm so sorry about your father. If there's anything I can do…**

And then a second later.

**Dillon: I don't blame you for never wanting to talk to me again. Please know I'll always be here for you, Fallon. Always.**

**Don't hesitate to reach out to me if there's anything you ever need.**

"That from your boyfriend?" Shane asked, turning off the interstate.

*Boyfriend.* I had never used that term to describe Dillon to Shane, but I guess he could tell that was what it had developed into.

Had.

"We're not dating anymore," I said, tucking the phone into my pocket.

"What happened?"

I laughed over my tears. "That's a long conversation."

"Did he hurt you?" Shane growled.

"Does my heart count?"

Shane gripped the steering wheel tighter. "Tell me what happened."

How did one explain that they'd been cut in half and left to bleed to death in disbelief? Even to themselves? Maybe I shouldn't have expected a happy ending. I mean, even though the circumstances were extreme, did I honestly think that my first relationship wouldn't end in heartbreak after all those years of hiding behind my impenetrable shield?

"Proctor was right; I do shut people out." I looked out the window at all the homes that were probably filled with happy families. "At first, I thought the reason I was afraid to get too close to people was that I was afraid of getting hurt. But it's more complicated than that."

Shane waited patiently for me to choke this out.

"When I was a kid, in many ways, I felt abandoned by my parents." My throat clenched at the memories of their loving arms going from reaching toward me for a hug to reaching for the baggie of drugs while my arms remained open, aching for my parents' embrace. "Opening myself up to people makes me vulnerable because it means I have to trust them to never abandon me like they did."

And that abandonment wound, I discovered, was a deep abyss of suffering, so intense, I'd sink to the Mariana Trench to avoid it. That was why confessing my feelings to Dillon had wrapped my body in icy tendrils of fear. All those drugs my parents had taken poisoned my belief that anyone could ever fully love me.

"And he abandoned you?"

I bit my lip. "No. It just...didn't work out."

He looked at me fiddling with my hands. "But you still care about him."

"I don't want to. I made a huge mistake when I fell for him."

Concern radiated through his face. "Why?"

"It turns out, he's a bad guy."

"Did he cheat on you? If he did, so help me, I'm going to rip his freakin'—"

"No, nothing like that. It's just..." I bit my lip. "Can we talk about it later?" Because telling Shane that Dillon was a drug lord would open an exhausting firestorm, and that was the last thing I could handle right now.

Shane's squad car's tires crunched along the gravel in the trailer park we'd once called home. The rectangle-shaped trailers were surrounded by overgrown oak trees, grass so tall that a small child could hide in it, and abandoned cars with rusted wheel casings that made the dilapidated land look like a junkyard. The loud metallic hum of an ancient window air conditioner buzzed through the baking summer heat as we came to a rest just outside my dad's home.

Next to it sat the brown trailer Shane had grown up in, though his family had long since moved away. I suppose most families didn't make this kind of place their forever home.

But Dad did. This trailer had become his prison of defeat, his self-imposed sentence to solitary confinement. It broke my heart that, out of all the stunningly beautiful landscapes in the world, this sad little trailer was where he'd taken his last breaths.

Shane clunked the gear into park, and we went inside.

Even in broad daylight, the interior was dark, encased in chocolate wood paneling. A coffeepot that looked to be from the 1990s sat on the kitchen counter, still filled with four cups of unconsumed coffee Dad must have made the morning he'd died, saturating the stale air with its bitter smell. The kitchen slash dining room-slash living room was so small, you could make it from the sink to the couch in eight steps. The same couch I'd found Mom slumped on.

Shane ran a hand through his dark hair. "I'll start in your dad's closet. See if I can rustle up something decent for the funeral."

I opened a garbage bag and dropped trash into it. Cans of pop, food wrappers. I had to choke over tears when I washed the dishes in the sink. Based on the can on the counter and the stain on the plate, it looked like the last thing he'd eaten was a can of beefaroni. The cheap brand, at that.

If he had to have a last meal, I wished it had been something special.

"Do you think either of these will work?" Shane came out of my dad's bedroom, holding up two outfit choices—a blue sweater with a pair of gray pants and a long-sleeved black shirt with a different shade of black pants. All of them looked like they'd been plucked off the clearance rack at a thrift store.

I frowned.

"I know," Shane said, looking closer at them. "But it's the best he had."

Again, I had to fight over the tears. I wished he'd had nicer clothes to wear, a nicer place to live.

A better life.

"I'll buy him a suit," I said.

Dad deserved a suit. He might have morphed into the diseased dad, but inside was still the loving father who used to check under my bed for monsters. Bought me ice cream for getting straight As. Did his best to shield me from Mom's addiction.

Shane nodded, put the clothes back into my father's room, and then leaned against the doorframe. He tucked his hands into his pockets and studied me the way he'd been doing all morning, like he was worried I was about to shatter.

Which, in fairness, I was.

"How can I help?" he asked. "Put me to work."

"Would you be willing to help pack up his clothes? I'll donate them to the homeless."

"Of course," Shane said. "Anything you need."

Shane deserved a medal for excellency in friendship; I hoped I was as good a friend to him as he was to me.

"You still haven't told me what's been bothering you," I said.

"Who says something's been botherin' me?"

"I know you, so we can skip the coy part and get to what's been eating you."

"Today's about you."

"And I need to get my mind off this. Distract me with your problems."

Shane tightened his lips.

"Please?"

He sighed and seemed to measure how badly I needed to focus on anything other than my life.

"It's work stuff."

"What stuff?"

He pinched the bridge of his nose. "Feels like we're always one step behind, you know? It pisses me off, the things people get away with. And then the ones that do get caught? Overcrowdin' in prison makes them get out before they've even served their full sentence. Meanwhile, the drugs, the killing...it just never ends."

Shane's biggest obstacle to his career was his heart. Seeing the worst of what people were capable of took a lot out of you. I knew it would be an adjustment for him to join the Chicago PD, but looking back on it, I think I'd missed clues he might not be handling the adjustment very well. Like when he first moved to Chicago, his tone had changed.

"The violence," he'd said. "Can't believe some of the stuff people do to each other here. For, like, nothing. It's insane."

"Are you second-guessing wanting to become chief one day?" I asked.

"I don't know," Shane admitted.

Whoa. That was a big change.

Shortly after joining the force, Shane decided he wanted to move up the ranks and be the one setting strategies to keep the city safe one day. But in this job? Some days, it felt like the bad guys were one step ahead. It was only natural to feel discouraged.

"You don't have to be chief of police to make a difference in this world," I assured.

His cell rang.

"Take it," I insisted.

Shane looked at me like he didn't want to prioritize anything else above me, but even off duty, police work never ended.

"Take it," I repeated.

Shane let it ring one more time and then reluctantly answered. "Hernandez," he said, retreating into my father's bedroom.

I ran my hand through my hair and looked around. For a small place, it sure felt overwhelming—how much I needed to organize. I wondered where to begin, and when I scanned the kitchen and living room with its sea of browns and grays, a flash of purple caught my eye. Curious, I walked closer, picked up the notebook, opened it to the first page, and saw my father's handwriting.

*Kim,*

*My sponsor insists that journaling assists sobriety. According to her, it gives us "freedom to express joy, sorrows, and frustrations without pressure or judgment." She asserts that it helps manage the difficulties of recovery as well as anxiety and triggers that can cause a relapse. I hate the suggestion to focus on emotions I have bottled up because isn't that the ultimate trigger? Nothing else has worked, though, so I suppose I have nothing to lose by giving it a shot.*

*But you know me. Talking to myself about my feelings? I can't do it. But I can talk to you. Because I miss you terribly, and you're the only person who understands what this feels like.*

*Oh my gosh.* The front page was dated nearly a year ago when he had a stint in rehab. The one-subject notebook was filled with his entries. I wanted to sit down and read the entire thing front to back, but it'd take hours, so, for now, I skimmed around, desperate to read it.

My dad—through his messy black handwriting—was still alive on these pages.

*August 27$^{th}$*

*Kim,*

*Insufferable pain is assaulting my entire body inside and out. I can't stop vomiting or shaking from vicious chills that feel like I'm standing naked in a blizzard. I don't want to get high. I just want to stop this torture. I don't know if I'm strong enough to do this. Was this what it was like every time you tried to quit?*

I skimmed ahead.

*October 25th*

*Kim,*

*Withdrawal never ends. It only gets worse. I may not have muscle cramps or diarrhea anymore, but the subsequent depression that's commenced is unendurable, and I'm told it might not go away. How much of it is because, without a filter, I feel the suffering I've caused? How much is because I destroyed the chemical balance in my brain? I'm not sure. All I know is that I can't even remember what happiness feels like.*

I couldn't hold back my tears. He was hurting so much worse than I ever knew, and then I went and laid into him yesterday? Why couldn't I be more sensitive to him? I thought we left on good terms, happy terms, but what if...oh Lord, what if what I'd said to him sent him over the edge?

I shuffled through the pages until I found the last page, which was dated yesterday.

*Kim,*

*I thought nothing could hurt worse than the day you died, but I was wrong. Today, my grimmest fear was confirmed. You were holding a picture of your daughter when you took your fatal dose. Intentionally. Because you thought she'd be better off without you.*

*Because I made you feel that way. I was your husband, and when you were drowning, I held your head underwater.*

*I deserve to let the anguish of this revelation eat me alive, but I am a weak, pathetic excuse of a man because I cannot endure this. The anchor is pulling me down again, and this time, I want to let it pull me under.*

*I'll try to get clean tomorrow. But right now, I need something to take this pain away. Because I cannot bear it.*

That was the last entry in his journal.

He wasn't killed; he relapsed and accidentally overdosed.

Because of what I'd said to him.

I ran to the bathroom and barely got the toilet lid up before the bile came up.

"Fallon?" Shane appeared at the bathroom door.

Dad had seemed so clearheaded, but clearly, the disease was still the driver in Dad's sick head.

Even in a healthy body, taking drugs was potentially lethal.

But a man whose body had been weakened by chemo? Chemo didn't just hurt cancer cells; it also damaged the lungs, kidneys, and heart. I was sure his nurses warned him to stay clean—especially after years of drugs already damaging his body—but an addict clearly couldn't be reasoned with. Any dose was a fatality waiting to happen.

"I'm taking you home," Shane declared as he put a hand on my shoulder.

I didn't have the energy to argue. I didn't have the energy to read the psychological roller coaster my dad had been through in the months leading up to his death. Even though I deserved the painful lash from every word.

Shane helped me into his cruiser and watched the trailer grow smaller in the rearview mirror as he pulled away.

"Tell me about the douchebag."

"What?"

"The ex-boyfriend. Tell me about him."

I took a deep pull of oxygen. "You're just trying to distract me from my dad." I looked at the road passing beneath us, feeling utterly empty. Void of anything.

Numbness. It felt better than before.

"So, what if I am? Tell me what he did."

I laughed, and Shane looked at me like I was going crazy.

*Maybe I am.*

"I screwed up so bad."

"You never screw up," Shane said. "If he made you think that..."

"I fell in love with him."

Shane fell silent.

"I've never been in love before. Not like this. That," I corrected. I huffed my hot breath on the passenger window and traced a heart into the fog. Then, I drew an X over it. "He was"—I sighed—"everything I could want in someone. He made me feel alive and like life was going to be okay. Like as long as I was with him…"

Why was I even explaining any of this? I shut my eyes and got to the part where I screwed up.

"So, I see his back for the first time, and guess what I see."

"Nail marks from another chick?"

"Nope. Tattoo of a scorpion holding an American flag. Turns out, my ex-boyfriend is a captain in the Chicago Syndicates."

Shane jerked to the side of the road so fast, the person behind us nearly crashed into us, honking as Shane threw his cruiser into park.

"What?" Shane snapped.

"Life's a bitch, isn't it? It's like you think you're getting a happily ever after."

Shane's vein on his forehead bulged like it might explode beneath his skin. "He's a fucking drug dealer?"

"Technically, he's a captain, so he's the dealers' boss's boss."

"Does he know you're a cop?"

"He does now."

"Maybe he knew all along. You're on the task force. Maybe he inserted himself to work you. Get info."

"No," I said. "At least, I don't think so. We could both get killed if they knew he was dating a cop."

Shane gripped the wheel so tight, his knuckles turned white. "What's his last name?"

"Why?"

"Because I'm going to hunt him down and stab him in his ear with a screwdriver."

"I don't think that'd look good on your résumé."

"This isn't funny, Fallon!"

"I know, but I'm not going to let you get in trouble over it, so I'm not about to tell you his name."

"First name's Dillon," Shane said, pulling up his phone.

"Or is it?" I challenged.

Shane scowled at me.

"Please," I said. "I don't want to pull the dad-just-died card, but there it is. Flopped down on the table. Please don't give me another thing to worry about."

Shane clenched his jaw and looked out at the windshield. He took deep breaths as a dozen more cars drove past us until he finally glanced back over at me. "So help me, if I ever see that son of a bitch, I'm going to fuckin' kill him."

# 22

W*hat is* he *doing here?*

I stepped out of Shane's cruiser and onto the uneven pavement at Rosewood Cemetery, staring at Dillon in disbelief.

I couldn't believe he'd risk his life by coming, just as I couldn't believe this was happening. *Again.*

The first time I'd buried a parent, I was too little to fully comprehend that this was the last profession of love you'd be able to give your family member. But the adult me understood the gravity of this moment with tragic clarity.

Everything felt different—the texture of the air rolling across my skin, the sun warming my face, even the sounds of birds. A red-winged blackbird's throaty call—a lazy *deeeet-deeeet, yak-yak-yak*—sounded sad. It was as if the earth knew that the only person left that I'd loved since I was a baby, my anchor to this world, was gone. Along with the hope that Dad would one day find his way through the darkness.

"Ready?" Shane asked.

I nodded but welcomed the support of his extended elbow as we walked toward my father's final resting place.

Tucked into a sanctuary of trees, Rosewood Cemetery was tragically stunning. Well-kept emerald lawns sat beneath tidy rows of granite stones, and flowers peppered the area with their rainbow of colors. They worked together to veil death and heartbreak with the illusion that catastrophic loss was somehow beautiful.

The grounds were as lovely as the weather. It didn't seem right to have something so heartbreaking on a gorgeous, sunny July day; it should be raining. Thundering.

The walk around the other tombstones felt like it took forever, yet it was too short, all at the same time. Like time slacked in slow motion and prolonged my anxiety over giving Dad's eulogy yet simultaneously plunged me in fast-forward through the last chapter I'd have with my father.

When we reached the site, I was surprised. Dad didn't work, and he had no friends. All night, I'd been haunted by the hollowness of saying kind words about my father when there'd be virtually no ears to hear it. Dad deserved for people to hear it, and now, thirty people stood in loose groups.

Cops. Some of them I'd known from the precinct, every one of the DEA task force, and even some cops I didn't know.

My lips quivered. "You did this, didn't you?" I whispered to Shane.

He shrugged, as if his thoughtful gesture was no biggie. "Burch invited the task force."

I could picture Burch saying, *You all are invited to come to Fallon's father's funeral. And by invited, I mean, show up. Period. We have each other's backs on this team.*

Even Proctor was here, fat lip and all—though I knew it was more to do with obeying a boss's order than to support me emotionally. Nonetheless, it was another set of ears, so my dad's life wouldn't feel like it had ended in vain.

I made my way over to them, and as I did, I couldn't stop my eyes from sweeping across the field to a tree forty feet away, where Dillon stood, wearing a black suit.

Leaning against the bark of an ancient oak, he blended into the shadows of the trees. People had to have noticed him, but hopefully, they'd assumed it was a strained relative, someone who wanted to pay their respects, but maybe wasn't welcome to sit close. But it was also possible they'd start asking questions and find out the very captain they were hunting was among them today.

Our eyes locked.

The last time I saw Dillon, I told him the world would be a better place without him. Most people would've told me to F off, but Dillon didn't. And I wondered if the tragic reason wasn't just because of how much he cared about me...but because he believed what I'd said. Just like my mother believed what my dad said the day she'd taken her own life.

*I should never, ever have said something so cruel.*

And he shouldn't be here. We couldn't be seen together, not by the cops, not by anyone, or else someone could tip off his bosses and put Dillon in grave danger.

But at the same time, I was...relieved he was here. I needed him—the *him* that was my boyfriend, the him that had feelings for me—to care enough about me to come.

I didn't understand how I could go from wanting to never see him again to feeling comforted by his presence. I guess it was because, though other horrible things about Dillon might be true, his actions and words made it clear that his feelings for me were genuine. I could feel it all the way over here, his affection wrapping around me with his gaze. And it made me breathe easier.

As Shane left my side to talk to the pastor, I noticed Dillon type something on his phone before mine buzzed with a text.

**Dillon: I'm so sorry about your father.**

I met his gaze again.

**Me: You shouldn't be here. As you can see, there are dozens of cops.**

Dillon tilted his head while he typed.

**Dillon: I don't want to make your day more stressful. That's why I'm hanging out back here.**

My chest ached. He was willing to subject himself to standing there like an outcast just to make my day less stressful. To make this easier for me. If the tables were turned, would I have that level of selflessness for him?

**Me: Well, if any of your colleagues see you at a cop's father's funeral, there'd be no way to explain that.**

Dillon looked at his phone, then up at me, and shook his head.

**Dillon: You lost your father. The only thing I care about right now is being here for you.**

My breaths grew easier still as his words warmed me.

**Dillon: I hope this isn't wrong for me to say, but I wish I could hug you right now.**

My lips trembled. I wished he could hug me right now, too. I wished he could come sit with everyone else. I wished I hadn't told Shane about Dillon because I was hurting so badly right now, I didn't want to be rational. I wanted Dillon to hold me.

**Me: My friend Shane knows about you.**

Another eye lock. Yet he didn't look upset with me. Why?

Before I could ask, Proctor came up to me. Honestly, of all the people in the universe I wanted to see right now, he was the last. He conveniently looked over his shoulder to ensure Burch saw him making nice.

"Sorry for your loss," Proctor said.

How vindictive of me to feel gratified that his injured lip looked worse than my cheek.

"Thanks," I managed.

When I returned my gaze to Dillon, he looked at Proctor as if it hurt, not being able to come closer to me like Proctor could. Not being able to just walk up to me without fear of putting me in danger.

But that envy quickly vanished when Dillon's gaze fell to Proctor's fat lip, to my bruised cheek, then back to Proctor's mouth. And then his free hand tightened into a fist.

*Shit.*

But that wasn't my only problem. As Proctor walked away from me, Shane marched over and threw a death glare toward the oak tree.

"Is that who I think it is?"

Dillon took one step forward but suddenly froze.

So did Shane.

Because a black Mercedes SUV rolled to a stop on the pavement, and a man emerged, wearing a royal-blue suit. A man who didn't appear to belong here. Nor did the guy in the black suit, who also stepped out.

"Hey, O'Connor." Burch approached. Other officers started to look at the men, but the SUV was to Burch's back. "Sorry for your loss."

"Thank you, sir. And thanks for having the team show. Means a lot."

I studied the mysterious guy, who buttoned his jacket and scanned the cemetery. Maybe they were coming to pay respects to someone else?

"If you need anything," Burch said, "you let me know, okay? No one will think less of you if you take some time off, Fallon."

It was the first time he'd used my first name, and it felt wonderfully endearing.

"No," I insisted. "I want to work more than ever." It'd keep me busy, give me somewhere to point my energy.

Pride flashed across Burch's face, pride that meant more to me than he could imagine.

"In that case, you'll be glad to hear we put two of the captains behind bars this morning," Burch said.

"You did?"

"Tax evasion. Still building the narcotics case, but losing two of their leaders will hurt like hell."

*I'll say.*

"I know it feels like we're chipping away at a huge chunk of ice, but we're turning up the heat on these guys, Fallon. Homicide detectives have been pulling people in for questioning. We found the USB drive. Whether they suspect we have it or not, who knows? But they have to know that it's missing—that's for damn sure. And that's a huge blow itself. Plus, they know we've brought in those guys for questioning, related to this narcotics string, so they know we're onto them. They can feel the walls closing in, rest assured. There's anxiety in that organization right now. We all should be proud of that."

I nodded.

"And," he added, lowering his voice, "IT got another hit on that USB drive. An address. Working on getting the warrant now, so we can go in first thing tomorrow. Do a search."

"Seriously?"

"You want in?"

"Hell yes."

He smiled at me, but after a few seconds, his smile faded when he turned and spotted the men in suits lurking in front of their Mercedes. They hadn't gone to pay any respects. They'd locked their hands in front of them and proceeded to stare at us.

"Who is that?" I asked.

Burch tightened his lips and tried to give me a smile, but it didn't reach his eyes. "Don't worry about that. Focus on your dad today."

Like I could just stand up there and ignore them. "Who is it?" They looked familiar.

Burch shoved his hands into his pockets.

Shane approached us, and I dared to take a longer look at the men. "Are those guys from...the Baja Cartel?"

The Baja Cartel was the most ruthless, aggressive drug cartel in Mexico. They didn't just traffic drugs and kill people; they'd go after rivals so aggressively, some of the smaller cartels simply folded up shop as a preemptive strike. But why would they be here?

Cartel members lived in Mexico and didn't show up on American soil like this. Not openly, anyway. Certainly not in front of a group of cops like this. And if they *did* decide to show up in the United States, why at my dad's funeral?

"We're here to pay respects to your father," Burch said. "Let's not allow them to interfere with that."

"Am I right?"

Burch sighed. "That guy sucking the toothpick," he said, nodding to the guy in black, "name's Lopez. Street name: Peeps. He's a falcon in their organization. Eyes and ears of the streets, supervises and reports activities of police, military, and rival groups."

"So, he's here to spy on us?" I asked.

Burch shook his head. "You don't spy out in the open like this." He hesitated. "And you don't bring him." Burch looked at the guy in the blue suit. "Juan Sanchez, aka The Enforcer, is a hit man in the Baja Cartel. Part of an armed group who carries out assassinations, kidnappings, extortions."

"Well, if they wanted to hurt us, they wouldn't send two guys against thirty armed police officers," I reasoned. "So, what does it mean?"

"I don't know," Burch said. "But I need to find out." He turned to me and put a hand on my shoulder again. "*After* today. Try not to let them get under your skin."

*Oh, sure. A cartel hit man and his eyes are just here, stalking us, while my ex-boyfriend is hiding in the trees, waiting for a moment to come after Proctor, while Shane wants to pummel Dillon. No distractions here.*

"I don't like this," Shane said. "We should reschedule and get the hell out of here."

"You guys can leave. Hell, maybe you *should* leave, but I'm saying good-bye to my dad. Those two can flop their dicks on the table in front of police another day."

Burch's mouth curled up.

I marched toward the pastor, and as he asked everyone to take their seats among the rows of folding chairs, I risked a quick text to Dillon.

**Me: Do you know why they're here?**

His answer was quick.

**Dillon: No. But I think I know why they're in the United States.**

I didn't like this, and Dillon could not be anywhere near here.

**Me: Leave. Now, Dillon.**

"Are you ready?" the pastor asked me.

As everyone sat and the pastor began citing Bible verses, I noticed Dillon remained in his position.

The sun warmed my shoulders. I probably should have worn a dress instead of a black pantsuit. As I listened to the pastor talk, the sounds of birds chirping echoed through the nearby trees. They sounded so free, so happy—the opposite of what my poor father's life had been.

The closed coffin's shiny wood reflected the afternoon sun and hovered over the hole they'd pre-dug yesterday.

I placed my hand on the wood grain, noting how warm it was.

Knowing it was the closest I'd ever be to touching my dad again for the rest of my life.

And then it was my turn to recite the words I'd written and rewritten twenty-five times over the last few days. I pulled the two pages from my suit's breast pocket and unfolded them, wishing my hands weren't trembling from sadness as I started to say good-bye.

"When people see my dad, many only see the drug addict. They didn't see the person he was before drugs performed a hostile takeover of his life, and they didn't see the guy that battled addiction harder than many battle cancer."

My throat was so tight, it burned as I tried to swallow.

"I'm sorry, Dad, that you endured this terrible battle every day of your life. I'm sorry that in our race for time together, the drugs won. And we lost. And I'm sorry I wasn't more understanding during the storm.

"But I understand now that you were never choosing drugs over me. Just the opposite. You spent every single day battling against an impossible current that was trying to pull you under, and the only reason you fought that hard and that long was to get back to me. How strong is a love to wake up every single day for 5,500 days and fight for someone's love?"

My eyes watered.

I looked over at the cartel guy, who was twisting the toothpick in his mouth, his beady eyes staring right at me as he smirked. Those scumbags had some nerve, showing up here. Like they didn't cause enough hurt in this world, supplying drugs to millions of people. When one of their victims lost his life to their narcotics, they couldn't even let the man rest in peace. They had to take away the last moments I had with my father.

Those were the criminals keeping Dillon imprisoned in his occupation, and the only reason they'd stand there like this was to try and intimidate us. They weren't just killers; they were bullies.

I squared my shoulders.

"I couldn't save you, Dad." I glowered at the cartel guy. "But I'll do everything in my power to stop another family from going through this."

The Enforcer stood there for three seconds. And then he grinned at me like I'd just started the most delicious game and slithered back into the SUV with his thug and drove away.

*Crap, what did I just do?*

Burch approached me. "You sure that was wise?"

I swallowed. "There are a lot of ways to help families with addiction," I reasoned.

"Yeah. But you looked right at him when you said that. Judging by the smile The Enforcer gave, he took what you said as a threat. And the Baja Cartel don't take too kindly to threats."

# 23

I wondered what everyone would do if I walked out the door and never came back. *It'd be rude,* I warned myself.

All the cops had come to this post-funeral dinner to show support for me, which I appreciated more than they could imagine. And with only a handful of cops remaining—Shane, Proctor, and three other officers from our precinct—I only needed to wait a little longer.

But grief was exhausting, and after watching my father's casket get lowered into the earth, after taking a fistful of cool dirt and sprinkling it over his coffin, I could feel myself cracking. I'd had to fight to hold it together on the drive over when I picked dirt residue from under my nails. During every encounter with folks offering condolences. I fought to hold my composure when the officers spent most of the meal talking about the cartel showing up, speculating what it might mean—a topic I'd regain interest in as soon as this awful day was over. But now, my sorrow was like that elevator fire. Spreading. Engulfing me. Weakening me.

All I wanted to do was escape. Go back to my apartment,

where I could draw a warm bath and release the pressure of tears building inside me.

The problem was, I didn't think I was going to make it that long.

The longer I sat here, the more memories assaulted my heart.

*I'm on a swing, my shoelaces wiggling through the air as my feet pump up toward the sun. "Daddy!" I squeal. "Higher!"*

*As soon as I come down, his hands push my back again as he laughs.*

*Mommy and I are playing hide-and-seek, and I jump out from behind the door and shout, "Boo!"*

*She holds her chest. And then she gives me that look—the one that says,* I'm going to chase you. *And I take off, running up our staircase, laughing, and when she catches me, she tickles me for a full minute.*

*When she's done laughing, she kisses my forehead and says, "I love you, baby girl."*

*Mommy's at the park with me. "Fallon!" she shouts in horror when she sees I've climbed up on top of the monkey bars, walking across them like a balance beam. "Get down—now!"*

*"I'm fine!" I assure.*

*I'm nine. I'm a big girl now, and I have excellent balance. But Mommy climbs to the second story of the equipment faster than a rocket. She's standing at the opening of the fire pole when my footing slips. Her arms shoot out and grab me, swipe me to safety, but she loses her balance. And after pushing me to the playground's second-story floor, she tries to grab the lip of the wall. But it doesn't stop her from falling through the opening. After a seven-foot drop, she crashes to the ground and onto her shoulder.*

*"It's okay," Daddy says to me as we wait in the waiting room. "It's a simple surgery."*

*"It's my fault," I cry.*

*"It's not," he assures. "It was just an accident."*

*But it wasn't. She fell because of me. And as soon as she gets home from the hospital, I'm going to wait on her hand and foot to make up for it.*

*Daddy pulls me into a hug and kisses the top of my head. "This will all be behind us before you know it."*

What if the reason I'd been so determined to blame drug dealers for my family's demise was because the truth was too painful to accept? That the real person responsible for it all was me?

I bit my tongue. I couldn't hold this in anymore. I didn't care if it was rude. I needed to leave now.

My cell phone buzzed.

**Dillon: Meet me in the women's restroom.**

Confused, I looked around the restaurant.

**Me: What? What restroom?**

**Dillon: The one in the back of this restaurant.**

My heartbeat accelerated. What the hell was Dillon doing here?

I looked at Shane. He'd behaved at the funeral, but if he found out Dillon was here, I highly doubted Shane would hold back his wrath toward him now.

I kept my face neutral as I casually stood up and followed the signs to the restroom. Nobody stopped me as I walked to the other end of the main dining room, down a small corridor, turned left into a narrow hallway, and stood outside the door to the women's bathroom.

I glanced up and down the empty hallway before opening the door and walking inside.

The place was immaculate. Gray porcelain tiles blanketed the floor, butting up against white subway tiles that stretched halfway up the walls, reflecting the pink glow of the bathroom's soft lighting. Three stalls were to my left, two black sinks to my right. Dillon leaned against the far wall between them. He still wore his suit pants, button-down, and tie, but not the jacket.

I held up my finger and did a quick search of each stall.

"No one's in here," he said.

But someone could come in any second, and there was no lock on the door.

"What are you doing here?"

Dillon's eyebrows drew together, and he glanced down at my fidgeting hands. Before locking his chestnut eyes with mine.

"You were trembling when they lowered your dad's casket into the ground," he said. "I wanted to make sure you were all right."

Pain radiated through my nerves. He couldn't be this kind and caring with me. It made it harder to do the right thing and push him away. "How did you know I was here?"

Dillon hesitated. "I followed you."

"Someone could've seen you."

"All the other cops left the cemetery before you." Because I'd stayed behind to say my final good-bye to Dad privately.

Shane had waited for me down the hill, and Dillon was no longer at his post by the tree by that point. He must have been in one of the vehicles we passed in the cemetery's main parking lot on our way out. Maybe if Shane hadn't been preoccupied, attempting to console me, he or I would have seen Dillon.

"The cartel could've followed you," I said.

"I was careful. I'd never put you in danger, Fallon."

"I'm not talking about *me*. Plenty of officers came here." I gestured with my hand. "If the cartel wanted to know where I was, they'd have plenty of people to follow. But you showing up puts you in danger."

"I had to make sure you were all right," he repeated in a tone that declared it was all that mattered right now.

Which made my eyes sting.

As I stared at him, something shifted inside of me.

I realized Dillon had this effect on my heart that could never be tamed by rationalization. I felt warm in his presence. The armor that I worked so hard to keep up faltered around him, no matter how hard I tried to glue it back together.

As he studied me, he could've asked me anything or insisted we talk about the cartel's shocking move today. But the question that took priority for him was, "Are you okay?"

Sometimes, when you're breaking inside and it takes every ounce of energy to hold it together, that one question has the power to shatter your resolve.

And just like that, the rest of my bricks crumbled. The avalanche of suffering I had contained in the four days since my dad's death finally broke free.

My dad was gone. Just like my mom was. They would never hold me again or be there for any holiday or milestone for the rest of my life. I would never get to say all the things I wished I had before it was too late.

*What I wouldn't give for just one more day with them on this earth.*

I brought my hand to my mouth and tried to silence my cries, but the moment the first tear broke over my cheek, a flood rushed out behind them. My entire body dissolved into grief. My bones hurt. My chest burned, and my arms ached for my dad's embrace.

I'd managed to be strong in front of everyone else, but I no longer had the energy to hold up the dam. Instead, I covered my face with my hands. I cried so hard, it suffocated the last of my strength, and I slithered to the floor.

After a few moments, an arm reached around my shaking shoulders, and Dillon's hand pulled my head against his chest.

He sat on the floor next to me and held me in silence as I mourned the loss of everything. He didn't rush me or remind me that someone out there might come looking for me. Nor did he mention what the consequences would be for him if Shane found us together.

Instead, I got the sense that Dillon would hold me for as long as I wanted him to.

When my sobs finally slowed, I could hear his beating heart, feel its slight thump against my ear. I could feel his fingers run through my hair and his lips kiss the top of my head.

"I'm sorry for what I said at the morgue," I eventually managed. "And for slapping you."

Dillon chewed the inside of his cheek. "I deserved it."

No, he didn't. He didn't deserve me blaming him for my dad's death, either, or listening to my radical conspiracy theories about what might've happened, as if I could somehow blame Dillon for that, too.

"My dad's death"—I hesitated—"turns out, it was an overdose after all." I took a deep pull of oxygen to brace myself for the next part. "I finally found out the reason he did drugs in the first place."

Dillon tightened his grip on me, fully aware of how important it had been for me to get that answer.

"It was a suicide attempt."

He tensed.

"He blamed himself for the death of my mom. And when we were talking about it, I basically confirmed his fear." How could I ever forgive myself for that?

"Fallon—"

"I should get back to the dinner," I said even though I wanted to stay in Dillon's arms. I wanted us to be two ordinary people free to date, not hiding out in a women's restroom.

I wished Dillon and I could have pursued our relationship. "I wish you had a different occupation."

He kissed the top of my head again. "I do, too."

I loosened myself from his grip, so I could look up at him.

Geez, I'd almost forgotten how exquisitely beautiful he was. The warmth of the light turned his skin golden and made his facial hair—a few days thicker than a five o'clock shadow—look darker, framing his jaw. His shoulders and biceps tried to break out of his shirt, which was rolled to his elbows, revealing muscular steel bands along his forearms.

Dillon's gentle eyes drew my heart closer, reminding me that beneath his flaws and bad choices was the man I'd fallen for. A man that cared more about me than his own safety.

He brushed his thumb across my left cheek, then my right, wiping away the last of my tears. And then, as he stroked my skin, he allowed his gaze to drift from my eyes to my lips.

In that instant, I wanted his mouth on mine. Maybe it was because it was the only thing capable of momentarily soothing my grief. Maybe it was because the old Dillon was sitting with me right now, and I needed him back, if only for a moment. Maybe it was because we'd never had a proper good-bye. And if this was the last time he touched me, I wanted more of him than just his embrace.

Dillon's chest rose and fell quicker, and then he moved slowly, perhaps waiting to ensure I was okay with it before he finally lowered his face.

And pressed his lips to mine.

The flames of desire sparked my mouth to open, allowing his tongue to connect with mine. I shifted my body, so I could wrap my arms around his neck, relishing it when he deepened the kiss.

I knew it was wrong of me. Made me a lousy agent, at the very least. A traitor to law enforcement even. A hot mess of a person, certainly. But I didn't care. No one could understand how complicated this felt—trying to shove all the emotions we'd developed for each other into a box and never allowing that box to open, if only for a few minutes.

Surrendering to this passion felt like when we'd escaped that fire, bursting through that exterior door—leaving the suffocating smoke behind in exchange for fresh air. It made the agony of loss dim, so long as our lips stayed connected.

I pushed myself up onto my right knee and turned myself around. Dillon's hands clenched my outer thighs, steadying me as I straddled him, and I twisted my hands through his hair.

He didn't deny me when I deepened our kiss, when I opened my mouth wider and let my hands roam down his back. Instead, he followed my lead and let his hands roam, too. Wonderfully so.

Beneath my unbuttoned suit jacket, Dillon tugged at the undershirt until it released from my pants. And then his fingers glided up my stomach, to my chest before he squeezed.

I groaned and moved my hips, rocking against him, feeling his desire beneath me. I wanted to run out the door with him. Go back to his place and be selfish and irresponsible and wrong, if it meant I'd get to spend the night with him.

But just when I allowed myself to escape into that fantasy, a knock ruined it.

"Fallon?" Shane said from the other side of the door.

I pulled back, out of breath, staring at Dillon's bronze eyes.

"Are you in there?"

"I'll be right out," I said.

"Is everything okay?"

"Yeah. I just needed some space. Can you tell the waiter I'm ready for the bill? I want to leave."

Shane hesitated. "Okay. I'll let everyone know we're wrapping up."

Dillon cupped my cheek gently and kissed me one last time.

"I'd better go," I whispered.

If Shane found Dillon in here, it would turn into a massacre. I'd have no idea how to explain what I'd just done with Dillon.

Even to myself.

Dillon and I could never be together. I knew that.

So, why couldn't my heart seem to get the memo?

# 24

The DEA task force gathered with anticipation a block and a half from the address the IT team had recovered. The industrial neighborhood had been abandoned years ago after the real estate crash, its rows of rectangular buildings now empty. That meant the place in question—a three-story brick warehouse—most certainly wasn't being used for legitimate purposes. A sentiment echoed by the men prowling its outside, appearing to guard the place.

The minute we'd arrived at the gathering point, I could tell this wasn't going to be a typical raid. Heck, I'd already gotten that vibe when I heard we'd struggled to secure the warrant. Probable cause was trickier than some people might think—you couldn't simply get one based on an officer's subjective beliefs. Burch was able to provide reasonable suspicion, though, since the three names on that hard drive *were* linked to illegal narcotics, and the officers who'd completed brief surveillance of this address witnessed guards surrounding a box truck as it backed up to the side door. And witnessed what they recognized, based on their experience and training, to be drug activity at two o'clock in the morning.

Now daylight, the cloudless sky offered no shield from the sun, no breeze in the eighty-degree heat. The only sound I could focus on was from the straps of bulletproof vests tightening and quickened breaths from those of us taming our nerves.

I wished this search worked more like the movies and that we'd roll up with dozens of SWAT officers because the ten men walking around the warehouse's perimeter were undoubtedly armed.

Even Proctor seemed nervous.

"Are you okay?" I asked him. He'd winced when he put his vest on.

"Fine," he grumbled.

But he didn't seem fine. It looked like every twist of his ribs caused a great deal of pain. Yet he'd looked fine at the dinner yesterday.

"Remember, everyone is detained *before* we enter," Burch repeated.

He'd gone over this plan in the conference room two dozen times. Had the blueprint of the building pinned up on the wall, broke us up into teams, gave us assignments of where to enter, spreading out teams along the structure. We were to cuff the guards first and detain them for our safety and also so they didn't have the chance to destroy evidence. But planning to do this was nothing compared to this adrenaline of getting ready to possibly confront some of the most dangerous men in the world—armed men who had nothing to lose if they got busted with whatever was inside that warehouse.

"You think Marks could be in there?" I prayed even though I doubted the FBI thought so. If they did, they would have sent more than two men to join us in the raid. Probably reasoned that any address placed on a USB drive *before* Marks went missing was unlikely related to the disappearance case. Still, I hoped otherwise.

"One way to find out," Burch said. "Okay, let's go."

As instructed, we filed into marked police vehicles. It felt like we plunged into the scene at fifty miles an hour, and we had the place surrounded within a minute. Four of us—me, Proctor, and two other officers—jumped out at our mark and pointed our guns at two men on the structure's east side.

"DEA!" Proctor shouted. "Hands up!"

The men stood frozen for a moment, taking in the scene before them with the building now surrounded by cop cars and officers. There was nowhere for the perps to get away, so the only question was, would they surrender peacefully or go down in a blaze of bullets?

"Hands up!" I repeated.

And then shots rang out on the other side of the building. So much for plan A.

The perps exchanged a look. And then suddenly, the suspect with the square head gritted his teeth, yanked out his gun.

And fired.

His shot missed us, but when his buddy joined him, a barrage of gunshots forced us to take cover behind the SUV and return fire.

*Bam. Bam-bam. Bam. Bam. Bam-bam.*

It was hard to see what was happening. The four of us tried to poke our heads out as bullets sprayed the air with impending death. Gunshots continued to pop on the other sides of the building, too.

Plan B was going to hell.

The suspect on our right jerked and went down, but one of our agents screamed, grabbed his bleeding thigh, and let go of his weapon.

I crawled over him and aimed at the guy to the left. Square Head. I lined up my shot. Fired. And missed.

The other officer positioned himself at the vehicle's back, lined up his shot, and fired.

The second perp thumped to the ground.

Both suspects were down, and within seconds, all the other gunfire ceased. Making me wonder who won the fight on the other sides of the building.

We waited for the all clear—the signal to go inside—but there was nothing.

The sound of silence was haunting when we didn't know what awaited us on the other side of it. All I could hear were my labored breaths, the thumping of my erratic heart beating in my ears.

For what felt like an eternity.

And then, like a rainbow after the storm, Burch's voice commanded us to enter.

When we got inside the building, there were no other suspects. They must've had an escape route. Knew this building and the area better than anyone and had designed ways out in case something like this ever happened.

I'd hoped we'd find Marks inside, but we found something even more shocking.

Surrounding twenty rows of tables were shelving units on all four sides of the massive structure. Where hundreds of white plastic bricks sat. I had no clue how much cocaine we were looking at, but based on the whites of Burch's eyes, I had to assume it was more than any other bust he'd been a part of.

We'd just found the Syndicates' distribution hub.

# 25

I descended the cement stairs, sinking deeper into the darkness of the basement with each step. As the dank smell of mold tickled my nose and my eyes strained to see my footing, the most overwhelming sensation was the room's insidious quietness. I could hear the intake of oxygen flowing into my throat, the thud of my footsteps.

For the millionth time, I looked over my shoulder to ensure I hadn't been followed. I'd been meticulous during my journey here—switching "L" trains two times, walking in circles around three blocks, and walking into the building across the street, only to sneak out its hidden emergency exit to come here. But still. Eyes could be anywhere, especially now that I'd threatened the cartel.

I wondered what Dillon wanted to talk about and why he'd grown so paranoid that he no longer trusted burner phones to do it. If someone was looking for evidence as to who you were communicating with, they'd have to know the identity of *both* phone numbers. And thus far, the Chicago Syndicates hadn't been *that* sophisticated.

Then again, we'd just confiscated a massive amount of narcotics, so paranoia was probably at an all-time high.

At the bottom of the staircase, I turned on my cell phone's flashlight and scanned the space. It was an unfinished basement with concrete walls, stained with years of white and gold mineral deposits settling onto the stone. The concrete echoed each of my breaths in the damp, stale air, steel beams running along the ceiling, propping up the forty-story structure above my head. Save for a small folding table and chairs in the corner, the room was completely bare. I could see why Dillon had picked it—nowhere for someone to hide and eavesdrop.

Or ambush us.

I pulled my .40 caliber Smith & Wesson out as I took a further look around because, hell, maybe I was wrong; maybe there *was* somewhere to hide.

I illuminated the wall by the stairwell, where cobwebs blanketed the corner, and a spider shimmied away from my light. Then, I swept my inspection across to the far wall, where a car-sized water stain bled outward and intensified the smell of must as water dripped from an overhead pipe.

Suddenly, footsteps padded down the stairs, as if the person was trying to obscure the noise of their approach. I shut my light off and tucked myself into the corner with my gun drawn.

The footsteps thumped louder, and then, at the bottom of the staircase, the shadow of a man's outline spun around.

And turned on a flashlight. The light darted around the space until it found me and assaulted my eyes, rendering me blind to whoever was with me down here.

"Will you lower your gun, please?"

He shifted the beam, so it bounced off the wall to my right, illuminating the side of his face.

Dillon.

I let out a gulp of air I'd been unconsciously holding and

lowered my weapon as he turned the light off, pulled something out of his backpack, and flipped it on. A portable lantern, the kind that you had for camping, casting off an orange glow.

When he held the lantern up to get a better look at me, Dillon's eyes locked with mine, and something passed between us. Something profound, a bond that hadn't severed despite our opposite positions in this war.

He cleared his throat. "Shall we sit at the table?"

He set the lantern on the folding table in the corner and nodded toward the chairs.

I chose the seat with the best view of the staircase, so I could watch anyone who might come down.

Dillon sat opposite me.

The last time I saw him, he'd held me and comforted me in my time of need. I'd felt grateful and warm, but today, I had a bone to pick with him. And I was going to do it before he had the chance to get into why he'd called this meeting.

I crossed my arms over my chest and said, "You beat up Proctor."

That was why he'd winced in pain the other morning and why he was fine at the dinner. Because he *was* fine. Until someone must have confronted him and changed that. Someone who'd had a score to settle.

Dillon wiped his nose with his thumb. "I'm sure whoever did it wanted to do far worse to him."

"That's not a confession."

"Confessing a crime would put you in an uncomfortable position."

I frowned. "I told you I hit him first."

"I'm sure the only relevant fact to whoever did it was that he laid hands on you."

"Strange that whoever did it was smart enough to leave no

bruises on his face to avoid drawing unwanted attention to it. And even stranger that Proctor didn't report it," I said.

"A lot of guys feel embarrassed after getting their ass kicked."

"He could change his mind," I warned.

Dillon locked his steely eyes with mine. "Perhaps the assailant wore a ski mask. So that scumbag didn't see his face."

I glowered at him. "I don't need you to fight my battles for me."

"I know you don't need me to," Dillon said. "But anyone who messes with you can expect to deal with me."

"That's teetering awfully close to a confession."

Dillon tightened his lips. "This isn't what we came here to talk about," he said. "I told you something big is going down..."

I waited.

"I found out what it is."

Okay. He got my attention. "And?"

Dillon reached inside his backpack and set down various items on the table. A stack of cash thicker than the seventh book of Harry Potter. Credit cards. Passport. Plane ticket. I looked closer, examining the passport, realizing it was mine. Kind of. The picture was of me, the stats of my height and weight. But the name was wrong. *Samantha Bowen.* Which was the same incorrect name on the credit cards and plane ticket—which was one way, to Dubai.

"You realize this is all illegal," I said. "And you're handing all this evidence of your illicit activities to a cop."

He was silent.

"How did you even get my picture?"

"The Syndicates will not take that raid lying down. Cost them a lot of money. Plus, those two men at the funeral? The ones leaning against the Mercedes? They belong to the Baja Cartel."

When I said nothing, he tightened his lips and kept talking. "When the Baja Cartel moves into a new area, it becomes extremely dangerous for all the cities and towns nearby. First thing they do is infiltrate the police to get them out of their way. They start with bribes, and if that doesn't work, they resort to violence. Lot of people have tried to stand up to them. Cops. Military. But the Baja Cartel's been too powerful because of how violent they are and the lengths they'll go to, to stay in power. They'll bomb buildings filled with civilians if that's what it takes."

Dillon studied my face. "Those are the people you basically declared war on. So, yeah, if you didn't consider leaving before? You need to now."

I stared at him.

"These guys are vicious. And good."

"So are we," I said. "I trust my people."

A look flashed through his eyes.

"What?" I asked.

Silence.

"What?" I repeated.

Dillon seemed to weigh his next words carefully. "Fallon, I think you have a leak on the inside. Someone leaked that funeral to the cartel."

"Funeral information is public. You found the funeral information without getting it from a cop. Maybe they did, too."

"Maybe," Dillon allowed. "But if someone is under the thumb of the cartel? You need to be careful. They could be just as dangerous if you find them out."

I swallowed.

"You cannot get in these guys' way, Fallon. That cop that was taken?"

Marks...

My stomach rolled with nerves. For ten days, police had completed one of the most thorough investigations in Chicago's history. Street cameras from all over the city were reviewed—even national searches. Airports, parking structures. Thousands of people were interviewed, tip lines worked. And nothing had come of it. His pregnant wife was still in front of the media, keeping his story alive in hopes it would lead to his safe return. But the cops were no closer to figuring out what happened to him.

And now, Dillon knew something about it, which meant he'd stuck his neck out and asked around. Someone might grow quite suspicious of Dillon's loyalty if they hadn't already...

"The one thing the cartel needs to be successful is for the cops to stand down, back off. Not turn up the heat. That cop became a problem the moment he arrested one of our captains."

A captain with a USB drive in his stomach. Was that why they took Marks? To see if the captain had given it to the cops?

"They got nervous the captain mighta given up intel."

Like a USB drive.

So, they eliminated the threat? Or were interrogating Marks to find out?

"And they were trying to expand operations," I deduced. That had to be the big move Burch was sensing.

Dillon nodded.

"And Marks complicated that," I reasoned.

First, when they couldn't find the missing USB drive, and then it only got worse, even after he was abducted. The interrogations. The arrests. The domino had all started with Marks's original arrest of Terrell.

Another nod. "Plus, they'd be damned if they didn't send a message to cops about what happens if you get too close."

I swallowed. In my gut, I knew something awful happened to Marks, but sending a message made it all the more ominous. I thought back to the torture victim in the river and shuddered.

"And they can't *not* send a message after what you said."

Fear turned my voice to a whisper. "Is Marks still alive?"

Dillon blinked. "I don't know."

I leaned back in my seat, my mind taking in the scope of the threat. Marks. The body in the river. The thugs at the funeral.

Dillon rubbed his temples. "Fallon, I know you want to take down these guys. But getting yourself killed isn't going to bring your father back."

I squared my shoulders. "So, we're supposed to what, let the bad guys win?"

"What's happening is so far above all of us that there's nothing we can do to stop it. It's too late. Fighting it will only get yourself killed."

Dillon looked like a thin thread fraying at the edges, deriving its only strength from getting me to safety.

"Please," he whispered. "I need you to know that I really do care about you, Fallon."

My shoulders shrank.

"And I can't exist if something happens to you. Even if you didn't threaten them, you can't be here because I found out what's about to go down. And it's so much worse than I ever imagined."

"What is it?"

He paused. The space seemed to chill with his words. "Fallon, the Baja Cartel is moving to the United States."

The damp air blanketed my skin in goose bumps. I couldn't imagine a more devastating blow to the war on drugs, nor a larger influx of violence.

"Turns out, your DEA task force has been a little...too successful. The Syndicates were supposed to be expanding, but the DEA's disrupted that. When the cartel saw what a mess we'd made of things, they made a decision. To take over. Here."

"We have some of the best defenses in the world," I said. Best police. Best military. "Our government will never let that happen."

"They'll fight," Dillon agreed. "But the Baja Cartel will fight back, and they don't play by the rules."

I bounced my knee under the table.

Dillon leaned closer to me. "You need to leave—now. Don't go home. Don't collect any of your stuff; just go straight to the airport and buy what you need once you get there," he said, shoving the cash, credit cards, passport into the backpack and setting it next to my foot.

"And what about you?" I didn't agree with what he'd done, but I didn't want him to die over it.

He looked haunted by something as he shook his head.

I studied him. "You're keeping something from me."

He didn't deny it.

"Tell me."

He looked down, shook his head. "You'd never look at me the same."

"Have you killed someone?"

"No."

"Then, what is it?"

"Look, it doesn't matter. What matters is that you need to get the hell out of here."

"And then what?" I challenged. "What happens to Shane? And my colleagues and the innocent people of this country? And what happens to you?"

"Right now, I'm focused on getting you out. I'll figure out my next steps after."

This was a lot of information to process. If what he was saying was correct, it meant a war was coming to this country. With many lives lost.

The balance between good and evil would be as much on the line as the lives of innocent people throughout this country. The face of our nation as we knew it, the sanctuary of freedom.

"Leaving town might be safer for me," I started. "But if what you're saying is true, I'd be abandoning the very people I swore an oath to protect."

"Fallon—"

"I can't leave when my country needs me the most. I have to do everything in my power to stop it from happening."

I shifted the backpack across the floor with my foot.

He stared at me intently, and then he took my hand.

His touch sparked an electric current inside of me.

"For the record?" he said. "What you're doing right now is incredibly reckless."

He brought my hand to his lips. Would my heart ever *not* respond to his touch? Or the way he looked at me like this—his expression brimming with emotion?

"I want you to know something." Sadness choked his words. "I've always known I couldn't let myself get close to anyone." He paused. "But I never felt the weight of that sacrifice until I met you."

My insides wrenched because suddenly, worry for *his* safety ripped through my core.

"I'm sorry for being a bad guy, Fallon. For being any part of this."

"You need to take that cash and bolt," I said.

Amusement danced across his features. "You're encouraging a known criminal to leave the country?"

Was I? Where was *my* moral line?

"I'm going to get my mom and brother out," he said. "But I'm not leaving."

"Dillon—"

"A war is coming, and you're on its front lines. I'm not leaving, Fallon. I'm going to stay and do whatever I can to protect you."

# 26

Blood was splattered across the ash-colored doors. That was what led to the call, what led police to investigate the warehouse that we'd raided only days ago. What led to the discovery of the slaughter inside.

What happened to the victim, however, didn't take place in that building's entrance. Crime scene experts said the blood on the door had been planted there, perhaps to ensure someone would find the body.

New crime scene tape roped off the area along with twenty law enforcement and FBI vehicles, the medical examiner's car, and dozens of cops meticulously marking any possible clue with a yellow cone and a number.

The life this building once had—with its once-immaculate bricks, overflowing light from vast windows wrapping around its three stories—was drained, just like the victim inside of it. The burgundy color of its stones had faded, parts of them flaking off after years of abuse in Chicago's harsh winters, and the first-floor windows were broken and concealed with spray-painted wood.

"O'Connor." Burch waved me inside, where I joined Burch,

Shane, and Proctor, who stood in the center while investigators and the rest of the task force scattered about.

The space was vast. Concrete floors echoed my footsteps off its three-story ceilings.

It was there, on one of the ceiling's steel beams, that Marks hung by his neck. The rope was long enough to suspend his nude body four feet off the ground.

Vomit soared into my esophagus, threatening to erupt. I had to focus on breathing for several moments to regain control.

"Fuck," Shane said.

My mind flashed to my first day at the Chicago Police Department when I'd been feeling like a small-town nobody walking into the major leagues.

Officer Marks was the first one to look me in my eye, extend his hand with a warm smile, and say, "Welcome to the team."

Now, that smile was replaced with an open mouth, frozen in the screaming position. His eyes that had welcomed me with kindness were wide enough to show the whites above his irises, and the hand that had shaken mine was bound with the other behind his back.

The state of his body was even worse. His shoulder's skin bubbled with crimson divots—undoubtedly burned slowly, by the looks of it. Nails speckled his arms—so deeply, it had to have been done with a nail gun—and his skin had been shredded with dozens of gashes.

I took a deep breath, shoving the second wave of puke down. And then I clenched my fists with fury.

"How'd they get past the police car parked outside?" Proctor asked, referring to the one that had been assigned there since the raid.

"They knew this place well enough to get out during the raid; probably knew how to get back in without being noticed," Shane reasoned.

"I've seen the work of a lot of drug organizations in my career," Burch said. "But I've never seen anything like this before. It looks like what you'd see from—"

"The cartel," I finished.

Burch looked at me, and then, as the crime scene photographer snapped three more photos of the body, Burch seemed to consider my assertion. He had to see the evidence was insurmountable that the cartel had a hand in this. The blood on the door inciting attention. The dramatic posing of the body, the torture Marks had clearly endured, and the symbolic location—the abandoned warehouse where we'd confiscated their precious narcotics. As if to say, *This is what happens if you mess with our business.*

Seeing Marks should have scared me into accepting Dillon's plan—or at the very least, lying low for a while. But it did the opposite. As I thought of Marks's poor wife and children who would never see him again, a rage grew inside me.

"There has to be something more we can be doing," I said.

"We will," Burch said. "It'll just take time. We'll start putting an undercover team together next week and ramp it up quickly. In a few months, we'll be ready to infiltrate 'em and take every last one of them down."

"We don't have a few months," I said. "I have a credible source that claims the Baja Cartel is planning to move to the United States."

Burch's gaze cut to me.

"I just heard about it," I said.

I could see it in Burch's eyes that he was putting together clues that hadn't quite fit until this piece of the puzzle came into focus. And as it did, an unprecedented reality formed before us all.

Shane's body tensed.

"You think it's true," I said to Burch.

He glanced at Marks's body and rubbed his mustache.

"It would certainly explain some things," he allowed.

"You think they'd really come here?" Proctor asked.

Burch rubbed his jaw. "The Baja Cartel's wanted to move to the United States for years," he said. "More money, domination. They think that if they can take the US, they can take any country and expand their operations exponentially. Kill off all rivals in the market. Chatter has increased about it since last year when a guy named Gutierrez took over."

Gutierrez. I read he'd waged a bigger war than Escobar had.

"And lately, they've been cleaning house, killing off even the slightest perception of a threat to their operations."

Burch looked like he was searching for evidence that would contradict it because the reality of what we might be facing was so dire, no one wanted it to be true.

"This intel," Burch started. "Does this mean we have ourselves a CI?"

"He still won't do it. I got lucky, getting this piece of information."

"If they did plan on it, why come to the funeral then?" Shane pressed. "It blew their cover."

"They wanted us to see them at the funeral," Burch answered. "And they want us to know Marks was tortured for information." Even though he wouldn't have had much to say.

"Marks would never give up anything," I said.

"Body temp says he was killed just a few hours ago; he'd been tortured for ten days."

It took me a second to recover from that and refocus on the conversation. "He'd never talk."

Burch regarded me. "You have kids, Fallon?"

This was undoubtedly a rhetorical question on his part; knowing all the stats of the team he'd assembled, he had to know the answer.

"No."

"Well, I do. A wife, two kids. And one can only imagine the lengths someone's willing to go to in order to save them. Especially if they threatened to do all of this"—he gestured to Marks's body—"to one of his kids."

Seeing Burch rattled made me feel scared.

"We need to get more intel before we run this all the way up the ladder," Burch decided. "Some sort of proof." Burch paced. "This has to be why the Syndicates are hosting that national meeting. They're probably going to discuss it there."

"What meeting?" Proctor asked.

Burch looked like he'd forgotten we were there for a moment. "In six days, Chicago, Miami, and New York are meeting here in Illinois. If the cartel is planning to come, that'd be bad for business for these guys. Could put 'em out of business, maybe even mean their execution—for those that aren't already on the hit list because of the raid, that is. So, maybe that's why the meeting was called."

"Can we get into that meeting?" I asked.

"Undercover? No," Burch snapped.

"Sir—"

"Undercover operations don't work like that," Burch said. "You don't just waltz into a meeting of that caliber on a whim. You slowly build up an identity over months—years sometimes—before you make a play like that."

"But this meeting is happening now," Proctor pushed. "Think about what they'll probably talk about. Those organizations will have some huge decisions to make with the missing contraband and, more importantly, with the cartel coming. They'll surely talk about the timeline they have to play with. How long till the cartel arrives, who's coming, when, and where. We need that information to fight their invasion, and we can't let this opportunity slip by, sir."

Burch didn't disagree with Proctor's assessment. Surely,

whatever they discussed at that meeting would be vital. Decisions would be made. Orders given. But he did disagree about an undercover mission on such short notice.

"It's too dangerous," Burch said. "There's a reason we don't do half-assed missions. They fail." His tone closed the door to the conversation.

"This might be the only shot we get," I added. "How long do you think we'd have to wait until they meet up like this again?"

Months, maybe years, based on the look on his face.

"Look, I know this is a long shot," I said. "But it's the only play we have right now, and any chance is better than none. I'm willing to at least try."

"Doesn't matter. Those crews are dangerous. You know how many people they've killed in their careers? Besides, this Saturday's manpower is going to be light; half the task force and hundreds of uniforms will be at Navy Pier for the mayor's award ceremony."

"If we go slow, let someone build up an identity, even if we do get another opportunity like this, by then, it'll be too late. The cartel will have already moved here, planted and watered roots, and started the war. Do we really want to be the team that knew this was coming and didn't strike before it was too late?" Proctor pushed.

I wondered if Burch's legacy flashed through his mind and if he asked himself a tough question. Would he be remembered as the guy that sat back and allowed the most ruthless cartel in the world to move to the United States and didn't do everything in his power to stop it?

"No undercover agent would be willing to jump into something like that in as little as six days," Burch said.

I looked at him intently.

Burch chided, "You've never even been undercover before."

"I have," Proctor said. "I'd like to volunteer."

"No one here is ready," Burch said.

"Sir," I started, suddenly feeling like I was in a job interview, desperate to woo over an objection, "I've taken extensive training on being an undercover operative, both with classes offered by the Chicago Police Department as well as the Undercover Association. I progressed into advanced techniques, including a focus on narcotics, vice, and street crimes. Tactical training, covert missions, human trafficking. All of it." Because I wanted to be on the DEA, and training for their undercover arm increased the chances of acceptance. Not to mention the satisfaction of it. *Think of showing up on those drug criminals' turf, invading their life for once.*

"You haven't logged a single hour of actual experience," Burch argued.

"Maybe not officially, but from the ages of eleven to eighteen, I had to fool every official," I admitted. "Teachers. Principals. Social workers, police officers there to check up on my family. I learned how to be a chameleon, sir. How to think quickly and lie effectively."

Burch had to suspect some of this; he knew about my dad's addiction and was smart enough to imagine what a child would go through, hiding it.

"That, combined with all my training, I'm confident I can handle myself at this meeting."

"This is too dangerous," Shane argued. "We just raided this warehouse and confiscated a shit-ton of cocaine. They might know our faces."

"Their security team is sitting in jail. And there was nobody inside the building," Proctor said.

"Bull," Shane said. "There were most certainly people in the building. They just got the slip on us."

"They were probably too busy getting away to stay behind and memorize faces," Proctor argued.

"They had surveillance all over this place," Shane said, pointing to the cameras posted at every corner.

"Which IT confirmed had been disabled by the time we got in," I said. "To cover their own ass, no doubt, and erase their own faces from the footage."

"They could have footage backed up somewhere. Could be reviewing it as we speak to identify everyone involved in that raid. If they did this"—Shane gestured toward the body—"to Marks because he arrested Terrell, what do you think they're going to do to us? The people that took hundreds of millions of dollars of cocaine from their pocket?"

"I think they have more urgent matters right now," I said. "Namely trying to keep themselves alive after losing all that product. Something they'll surely have to discuss at this upcoming meeting."

"Sarge..." Shane pleaded.

I wondered how many gambles Burch had had to take in his years. Cases didn't always magically align in the perfect sequential order, so leaders were forced to balance risks. Burch had to see the more considerable risk was letting the cartel get an even bigger head start. And I knew how this worked; a threat this big needed more evidence before other agencies would get involved. The word of one unofficial CI wasn't enough for the United States to gear up the military and other forces needed to fight this war. We had to get inside that meeting, find out what they knew, find out a timeline, find out next steps, and get evidence on tape.

Burch rubbed the back of his neck; I could see him strongly considering it.

"We'll wear wires and transmit everything to a nearby command center. If it gets too hot, we'll get out," I said.

Burch chewed the inside of his cheek, took several breaths, and eventually regarded us.

"Proctor, I'll give some thought into sending you in."

Proctor perked up.

"Without an identity, the only way in would be as staff of some sort. Waiter, something like that," Burch pondered. "Still a Hail Mary, at best. We'd have a lot of work ahead of us in the next six days to prepare."

"I'd like to go undercover," I insisted.

"Fallon," Shane chided.

"You're not ready," Burch said. "And in case you forgot, you declared war on the cartel."

"This meeting is between the United States organizations. I'm no more of an enemy to them than anyone else here."

"Unless they're already under the thumb of the cartel," Proctor said. "I'll go, sir."

*Dick.*

"I can do this, sir," I repeated.

"Can't do it, O'Connor. You made a spectacle of yourself at that funeral, and we have no idea if that got back to any of them."

"No one will discuss anything significant in front of a waiter," I insisted.

Burch knew that; he could see the holes. He knew the only legit opening we had, but clearly, he wasn't going to suggest it.

"When I was doing research on these organizations, I read that these 'meetings' are more like parties. And you know who they invite to these parties," I insisted.

Burch stared at me.

"They have a few drinks; they may slip and say something around a hooker," I said.

"Hell. No," Shane snapped, seeing where I was going with this.

"I'm the only female on this task force, sir."

The fact that Burch didn't immediately shoot it down was a good sign.

"You freaking kidding me?" Shane said.

"Maybe one of them will get drunk and sloppy enough to give up something. A name, location. Date. Something to help us fill in the gaps when I'm alone with him. I can get a lot closer than the waitstaff."

"This is absurd," Shane said. "What if those two guys from the funeral circulated your picture to the US members?"

"I'll wear a wig. If I suspect my cover might be blown, I'll leave, and if I can't, I'll use the code word, so reinforcements can come."

"She's not wrong," Burch conceded.

Proctor's shoulders squared in jealousy. "I'm sure I can sly my way into conversations," he protested.

"A female is our best shot."

Proctor scowled at me. "But it's dangerous as hell."

"You know this is our best chess move," I said. "Give me a chance. Worst case, we come out of it with no intel, and we're no worse off than we were before."

His reluctance washed away.

Burch finally said, "Proctor's going in, too."

"What?" I asked. He'd rat me out and enjoy watching my death.

"He has experience undercover, and I'm not sending you in there alone."

"I'll go," Shane said.

"You'd stare at her the whole time, which would only tip them off to her being a cop. And for the record?" Burch looked at me. "Worst case isn't getting no intel. Worst case is that you'll be killed before any of my agents can get to you."

# 27

"Don't do this," Shane demanded. "This is a suicide mission."

Wearing a bathrobe and a towel on my freshly showered hair, I wiped away the mirror's invasive fog and glared at his reflection. Shane leaned against the doorframe of our apartment's bathroom with his arms crossed.

"We have a solid plan." A plan we'd gone over countless times.

The task force had spent days in briefing rooms, preparing for it. Listing out strategies to get information. Undercover operatives gave Proctor and me a crash-course refresher in staying in character, including backstories, details, and the like.

Was it scary? Yes. Did I feel a hundred percent ready? No.

"A million things can go wrong. You know that."

"Six agents will listen in at all times, just a short drive away. If anything happens—"

"They won't be able to get to you quick enough, Fallon! Takes one second to shoot you."

"Proctor—"

"Hates you. I don't trust that piece of shit to save you. And certainly not if it means riskin' his own neck."

I applied the makeup as I'd seen in a tutorial yesterday.

"You're taking this too far, Fallon. What are the odds you get some information that helps stop them tonight? Do you think you're gonna walk into the party and get some nugget of information that all our federal agencies have been unable to get?"

"Maybe you're right, but I still have to try," I said, blending the thick foundation.

"I'm just trying to give you a reality check. Before you get yourself killed on some Hail fuckin' Mary that has a microscopic chance of succeeding. Candidly? I can't believe Burch is crazy enough to go along with this. He's so desperate to end his career on a high note that he's getting reckless."

"Maybe it's reckless, but I'm doing my job."

"This is suicidal, and you know it."

I spun around. "If every cop ran the second things got dangerous, we might as well hand our country over to criminals and be done with it."

"You're takin' this too far!"

"Says someone who doesn't seem to believe the cops can have an impact anymore. If you're reconsidering your police chief career aspiration, that's fine, but stop projecting it onto me!"

"I did reevaluate because it felt like we could never do enough to make a difference," Shane snarled. "But once I realized how close these guys can get to the people that I love? My mind was made up."

He looked at me, letting his silent accusation bounce off the walls.

"I'm super glad you worked through your career-life crisis, but I'm a big girl, and my mind is made up."

Shane stared at me silently for ten heartbeats. Then, he tightened his fists and started to walk off into his room but paused. "Will *he* be there?"

I stiffened. "I have no idea."

I hadn't told Dillon I was going tonight; he might've been able to block my entrance somehow.

And I really hoped he wasn't going to be there. Because the last thing we could afford tonight was for any complication.

# 28

"How come I ain't never seen you before?"

As the windowless white van that reeked of paint fumes bounced along what felt to be an unpaved road, the redhead wearing an emerald-green miniskirt with a blue bikini-style top stared at me with suspicion. Seven sets of eyes joined her.

I gripped the edge of the bench tighter. The other hookers were used to this, being carted into the party's secret location, packed together hip to hip like fresh meat going to a slaughter-house. But I wasn't. And the farther we got from the remote parking lot we'd been picked up at, the more anxious I grew.

An undercover agent had worked her network of escorts with the cover story that I was her cousin in need of a good gig to bail out my baby's daddy. Luckily, it worked, and one of the escorts vouched for me to get me into this party. But she'd warned it was high pay, high risk. So high risk, in fact, that she wasn't even willing to come tonight.

"Asked you a question," the redhead snapped.

"Don't pay no mind to her," the platinum blonde to my left said. "She just jealous 'cause new girls get the most attention."

Great.

Before the scowling hooker with glossy lipstick clapped back, the van stopped. The front doors opened with a metallic squeak, banged shut, and then footsteps crunched on gravel.

When the doors opened, the girls delivered sexy, come-hither smiles as two men helped us out.

The burly guys with thick beards led us to a gate, where three guards carrying AK-47s began to pat the girls down.

My palms began to sweat. If someone touched me firm enough, they'd feel the button-shaped microphone hiding in my bra that transmitted everything to agents parked nearby. The one that I could use to relay my code word—*Christmas*—if something went horribly wrong.

Guard Man patted down Girl Number Two, touching her hips, looking in her shoes, even feeling her hair. He was thorough. And that was with girls who, based on that *how come I ain't never seen you before* comment, must've come here regularly. I was new.

"Come on," Guard Man snapped.

Someone shoved me from behind so roughly, I almost tripped.

Guard Man gripped my hips, pawed both of my legs, even though they were bare—*a-hole*—and moved to my shoes. Then back up, feeling my stomach. Could he feel my heart punching my ribs? His fingers felt my breasts. Had he done that with the other girls?

"All clear," he said lazily.

The AK-47 squad parted, so all eight of us hookers could glide through the gates like gazelles waiting to be claimed by lions. I tried to mimic the confidence of the other girls.

"Name's Layla," the girl who'd stuck up for me in the van whispered as she walked next to me.

"Candice," I lied. "Got any advice?"

"Keep your eyes to yourself, don't get nosy, and you should make it out in one piece."

*Should.*

My mouth ran dry.

Guards led us to an enormous patio encircled by four buildings.

At first glance, the courtyard looked romantic. Bubble lights swooped between single-story rooftops and ornamental trees, casting the summer night in a soft golden glow. Moss bubbled between uneven patio stones, meeting ivy that crawled up the sides of the stone buildings, and a bonfire tossed embers into the sky in the center of the patio.

But this place was the opposite of romantic. At each of its dozen doors, a guard stood watch with a semiautomatic rifle. More armed guards peppered the space, actively scanning like lifeguards watching a pool for signs of trouble.

"Is there always this much security?" I whispered.

I could see her worry.

"No," she answered quietly. "Not even close."

But then they didn't have three big organizations come together very often, so it was probably just beefed up because of that.

Still, I evaluated my surroundings. The entire area was enclosed by a barbed-wire fence, and the only gate was armed on both sides with several men. Security even flanked the bar.

Where Proctor walked away, carrying a tray of appetizers.

We made eye contact.

And I could see with the slight roundness to his eyes that even he—with his undercover experience—was nervous.

*So am I.*

The door to the main building opened, and three dozen men spilled out into the courtyard.

Between them and the guards, I counted twenty armed men,

sixteen automatic rifles, twenty-six pistols, and ten grenades—and that was just what was out in the open.

To protect thirty-some guys? Made no sense. It was overkill; something was off. But then Miami and New York bosses were here. Maybe Chicago was showing off.

I turned to start walking, and that was when I saw him. Standing with his back to me, he said something to the bartender and then leaned on his elbow to look around.

When his gaze reached me, it came to an abrupt freaking halt. To anyone else, his eyes were impassive, but to me, I could see his shock at seeing me here. And then his stare glided slowly, methodically over my legs perched atop stiletto heels, my dress wrapped tightly around my hips and stomach, my breasts pushed up and playing in the air, and my red wig. Before finally returning to my face. Where they lingered in angry disbelief for what felt like an eternity.

Dillon watched as a tall guy with shaggy blond hair, who smelled of cigarettes and whiskey, approached me.

"Hey there." He traced my arm with his finger.

I smiled flirtatiously and had to will my eyes away from Dillon, who now clutched his drink so tightly, I wondered if the glass would break.

"What's your name?" I asked. His face wasn't one I recognized from my studies.

"You can call me John."

"Cute."

"What's yours?"

"You can call me Candice."

"I've never seen you here before."

*So, he's a regular. Must be from Chicago, then.*

He trailed a finger down my collarbone. When his fingertip inched toward my breasts, I had to smile as if I wanted it. And pretend Dillon didn't look like he was going to storm over here and pound the guy's face in.

"You want a little snow?" he asked, motioning toward another bar on the far side of the room, where the other hookers and some men were lined up, sniffing the white powder.

I tensed my lips, nervous that my refusal to participate would make them suspicious. Equally alarming, if these violent men snorted coke, how much more unpredictable would they be?

My throat was instantly dry.

"Maybe later," I managed.

"I'm going to do a quick line," John said. "You get us some drinks. I'll have a whiskey."

I eyed the bar, where Dillon stood alone. I wanted to insist John go with me; approaching Dillon wasn't a smart move. Even though everyone seemed engrossed in conversations and flirting with the escorts, you never knew who could be watching.

But if I pressed the guy to go with me, he might either grow suspicious—why would a hooker be that clingy?—or insist I go with him to the drug table. Where more people could press me to do a line—at which point, I'd get made.

John tilted his head in curiosity at my hesitation, so I smiled and said, "Sure. I'll be right back."

I sashayed over to the bar, careful never to look at Dillon.

"Two whiskeys, please," I ordered.

The bartender nodded and went to the other end of the counter, fishing around for the bottle.

Dillon stared forward, so it wouldn't look like we were talking, his voice quiet when he spoke. "What the hell are you doing here?"

I discreetly glanced around. Made sure no one else had come within earshot, and when I answered, I continued looking at the back of the bar. "Working."

"You can't be here. Not *tonight*," he growled.

*Tonight.* The word bounced around my skull with its implied threat. "Why not *tonight*?"

"You need to get out of here," he insisted.

"I can't leave, so stop wasting your breath. We don't have time to argue about this." I ran a hand through my hair, feeling the thick fibers of the red wig trail between my fingers.

Dillon took an angry sip of his drink.

"He's looking at you," Dillon said, nodding over my shoulder toward the shaggy-haired guy who'd been flirting with me. "It's taking all of my restraint not to fucking kill him."

"You need to behave."

"How the hell am I supposed to do that with you sauntering around in that dress?"

The other women wore even more revealing outfits. I nodded toward them.

"Have you ever partaken?" I asked.

His lips twitched. "I'm glad I'm not the only one jealous tonight."

I pursed my lips.

"No," he answered. "Not that kind of guy."

The bartender set down the two drinks, and when he walked to the other end again, Dillon resumed whisper-talking to me.

"You don't know what you're getting yourself into. You have a weapon on you?" he asked even though he knew it was rhetorical. He could tell there was no place to hide one in this dress. " 'Cause they have several on them and more in the rooms they'll take you to."

"Tell me who to flirt with," I said. "Who has information."

"No one's going to talk to a hooker. Your plan is flawed. You, and that asshole," he said, glaring at Proctor across the room, "put yourself in danger for nothing. Only a matter of time before your cover is blown."

"Thought you were getting us drinks." John appeared by my side.

I smiled, handed him one of the glasses.

But he didn't take a sip; he was too busy, looking over my body, like someone evaluating a car before buying it. Out of nowhere, he grabbed my ass.

Dillon coughed and grabbed the bar's edge.

"Come on," John said. He grabbed my hand and pulled me toward one of the buildings. "You'll get me off in the back room."

In the pre-operation briefings, had I been educated on evasive tactics to avoid sexual acts? Yep. Had I been given a list of excuses to use, depending on the situation? You bet. But it was so dang early in the night that I wasn't sure any of them would work, which created a couple of huge problems.

First, the only kinds of illegal activity the DEA approved for undercovers were for things like buying drugs to catch them in the act. Me having sex with these suspects wasn't authorized. Not that I'd do it if it was; I'd rather light my panties on fire. But the point remained—if I couldn't get this guy to accept no for an answer, the officers listening nearby would terminate this operation immediately. The second, and far more significant problem, was that blowing my cover could get me killed.

The guy tugged me away from the bar, but Dillon stepped into the guy's path, scowling at his hand on my hip. "This one's mine," he claimed.

John looked surprised by Dillon's threatening posture, but he didn't argue. He simply relinquished me and walked away from us.

"That guy reports to you," I realized.

Dillon eyed the other men scattered around the courtyard carefully. "You need to get the hell out of here before it's too late."

"Too late for what?"

Dillon's brown eyes suddenly widened slightly as he stared at the gate, where ten new men strutted into the courtyard like they owned the place.

The guards stiffened.

My hands became clammy.

We were wrong about the real purpose of this evening. This wasn't a meeting between Chicago, Miami, and New York.

It was the welcome party to the Baja Cartel, whose top ten members had just officially arrived in the United States.

And with them were the two men who'd come to my dad's funeral—Lopez, the toothpick-sucking falcon who was the eyes and ears of the organization, and Sanchez, aka The Enforcer, the hit man who'd smirked at me when I threatened the cartel.

# 29

"Fuck," Dillon whispered. "You need to get out of here. Only way is an underground tunnel in the back that's there in case cops raid the place."

Sanchez's gaze locked on me from his position across the patio. Did he recognize me? I looked nothing like the proper police officer with little makeup and hair twisted into a bun. My red wig was full of sexy waves; my makeup was thick tonight, contouring my cheekbones to look higher and thinner. Not to mention, my outfit made my body look like an entirely different shape than that pantsuit at the funeral. But if he looked close enough, he might make the connection.

The Enforcer walked up to us, coating us with suspicion. If I didn't handle this right, I wasn't the only one in danger; Dillon was, too.

"You look familiar," The Enforcer accused.

Did he know? Was he playing with me or grasping for an explanation?

"I get around," I deflected.

The Enforcer smiled a toothy grin. "Have we partied before?"

"If we had, it would've been memorable."

He remained silent for a second and then smirked. "Funny," he said, though I still couldn't tell if this was lighthearted or if he already knew.

Even if he didn't already recognize me, it felt like it was just a matter of time.

"Was just about to take her in the back for a spin," Dillon said.

The Enforcer traced his fingertip down my breast. "No, this one's mine."

He pulled me by the hand over to his group of men, deeper into his Baja Cartel circle, and just as Dillon's subordinate had to let go when Dillon claimed me, Dillon was lower on the pecking order. And had no choice but to watch me, helpless from across the patio.

I was as scared as I was angry. Facing the Baja Cartel was terrifying, but it was also rewarding. Because I'd get to look them in the eye before helping take them down.

"Can I get you a drink, baby?" I asked.

"Something stronger." He snapped his fingers.

A waiter rushed over with a glass tray containing white lines of cocaine.

"Ladies first." He studied me. My every movement was under investigation.

"I prefer a drink," I said.

"I'm afraid I'm going to have to insist."

It felt like I was under a spotlight, interrogated by The Enforcer. Making me sense that I wasn't in control of this conversation; he was. I was a minor league player trying to outwit the major leagues.

He squinted his eyes and seemed to evaluate my facial expression, my mannerisms. Like he knew that if I was a cop, if he insisted on me doing illegal drugs, the operation would be immediately called off. And I'd either be stuck trying to escape or forced to lead backup into what might become a fatal trap.

"Why's that?"

He leaned in with a smile and whispered, "I have it on good word there's a cop at this party."

Needles surged through my fingers and toes, all while he watched me for my reaction. How would he have it on good word?

"I know all the men here," he said, releasing my hand and trailing his finger down my arm. "So, that leaves the security, the waitstaff, and the hookers."

Someone was hearing this down the street. Assessing the danger. Analyzing the risk. If things were getting too hot, they'd come in.

And even though it felt damn hot, this was fine. It was okay. It felt scary, like he was playing with me, but that didn't mean he was. He could just like to throw his power around and watch people squirm. That was what these types liked, wasn't it? Maybe it was what got him off.

I risked a glance at Dillon, who stood across the courtyard, trying to hide the worry on his face.

"Who do you think it is?" he asked.

"This place is a fortress," I said, keeping my sexy tone in place, like this was part of a hooker's job—to reassure the paranoid leader. "No one could've gotten in here."

"Let's say, for argument's sake, a pig did get in here," he pressed. This time, his tone was tighter. Angrier. His gaze cut through me like a knife to a Jell-O mold. "Who do you think it is?"

I didn't like the way he was smiling, as if he was about to do something wicked. "I think I'll have more fun with someone else."

I made it one step before he grabbed my arm and pulled me back, squeezing it in punishment.

Dillon tensed.

"Point to someone," he demanded.

I yanked my arm, but he wouldn't let it go.

"Why are you asking me? If I thought a cop was here, I'd have to run. I can't get arrested again."

He squeezed my arm harder. "Last time I'm going to say it. Point to someone."

Maybe he assumed I was a frequent hooker here and knew all the faces. Maybe he was asking for help in his bully-like fashion.

"I don't know. What about him?" I nodded toward a random waiter.

The Enforcer motioned to someone, who pistol-whipped the guy in the head.

I gasped and watched blood pool on the guy's face. I could feel The Enforcer's eyes on me as the cartel guy ripped open the guy's shirt, searching for a wire. When none was found, the cartel guy kicked the man in the mouth, cutting open his lips.

Everyone stopped talking, sensing the dangerous shift.

"Try again."

"I'm not playing your sick game," I snapped.

The Enforcer tilted his head, eyeing Proctor across the room. "What about that guy? He looks familiar, too."

If he found Proctor's wire, he'd kill him before anyone could get here.

It was time to abort the mission.

"What is this to you," I said, "some kind of a *Christmas* game?"

The Enforcer smirked at me while I waited for the sounds of the cavalry who were now on their way.

*Hurry. Please hurry.*

"Bring him here," The Enforcer said.

A tall guy grabbed Proctor by the arm and carted him over. Proctor tried to look indifferent, but I could see the panic settling in as they forced him onto his knees.

His white pants ground into the stones.

"Search him."

The cartel guy patted Proctor down.

The Enforcer added, "Remove his shirt."

If they did that, they'd see that one of his buttons was fake—the microphone. I needed to do something. Create a distraction, buy him some time until the agents burst in.

"I know who the cop is," I blurted out desperately. "And it's not him."

The Enforcer looked at me.

"How would *you* know who the cop is?" he asked incredulously.

"I'm a working girl. It's our job to know our johns."

Proctor took deep breaths.

*Where the hell is the cavalry? Maybe they didn't hear my code word.*

"People aren't your own personal *Christmas* gifts to unwrap," I said. It was a lame line. But it had the code word, so whatever.

A hairy guy approached The Enforcer and whispered something in his ear. Whatever it was made him smile wickedly.

"Seems my men found a truck of pigs nearby," he said. "Took 'em to the slaughterhouse."

*What? They found the agents? They...*

*No.*

*No, no, no.*

They were parked in a secure location, nowhere near a road. They had been meticulously careful about that, so they wouldn't be found. Dillon's suspicions of a leak echoed inside my head, but my panicked thoughts prayed The Enforcer was lying, trying to scare me and Proctor. We couldn't be on our own.

With the Baja Cartel onto us.

The cartel guy ripped off Proctor's white jacket, followed by his shirt, sending his buttons flying like M&M's bouncing along the stones. One of which The Enforcer picked up and stared at.

*Shit.*

The cartel guy looked to The Enforcer for an order, who nodded.

When the cartel guy raised his semiautomatic to Proctor's head, I lunged in front of Proctor.

It wasn't a smart move. I could see that now with all the guns that were now aimed at me.

And then came the gunshot.

Warm liquid exploded from my back. I must've been in shock because it didn't hurt. At all. I waited for the darkness to swallow me, but when I spun around, I saw Proctor lying on the ground with a bullet wound to his head.

Blood hadn't exploded from my back; it had splattered *onto* it —from Proctor's wound—and now, it became a crimson river, pooling between the cracks of the stones.

*Proctor!*

A lanky guy grabbed my arm and yanked me through the courtyard, past a horrified Dillon, and into the back building, where he tossed me onto the concrete floor of a storage room, whose shelves were lined with gallon-sized chemical bottles. It smelled like chlorine in here.

The guy padded around my dress and bra until he found my microphone and stomped on it.

Four murderous men surrounded me.

*Why didn't they just kill me when they killed Proctor?*

With a kick to my ribs, The Enforcer asked, "How much does the DEA know?"

How did they know it was the DEA, not the cops or the FBI? A good guess that the DEA would be the division working drug crimes? Still...he'd said it with certainty.

"I'm not going to tell you anything," I declared.

They were going to kill me, no matter what I did, and I certainly wasn't going to help the enemy.

"Wrong answer." The Enforcer grabbed a fistful of my hair

and pulled a knife to my neck. "Tell me everything they know, or I'm going to slit your throat from ear to ear and hold your head up, so you watch yourself bleed to death."

"What the hell is going on?" Dillon growled.

*He can't be here. They might sense he's on my side. They'll kill him, too.*

"This bitch is working for the DEA."

The Enforcer kept the knife to my neck while he turned to look at Dillon, as if assessing his reaction.

Was this a test? Did they know Dillon's relationship with me? Or that he'd met with me? Would they murder him, too?

And that was when I saw a different look in Dillon's eyes. He looked at me with disgust. "We'd better find out what she knows, then."

The Enforcer hit me upside the head with his Smith & Wesson, and I thumped to the cold floor. When I regained my bearings, I noticed the guy to my right had an ankle holster.

"Go on. Hit her," The Enforcer said to Dillon.

Silence infected the space as Dillon stared down at me. "What are you going to do with her?"

"Get her to talk," The Enforcer said. "Then slit her throat." He turned to Dillon again. "Go on. Take the first swing."

Was it a test? To see if Dillon's loyalty was with them or me? Or was it some kind of a prize, a welcome-to-the-team gift to partake in the killing of an agent?

Either way, five against one, I knew this was the end for me. But if they thought I'd go down without a fight, they were even more arrogant than I thought. I'd grab the gun from the guy's ankle holster and start firing, killing as many of them as I could.

Starting with The Enforcer, who'd slaughtered so many.

Dillon approached me and raised his left hand.

But just as quickly as he'd raised his left hand, his right suddenly grabbed the gun from his waistband and fired four rapid shots. The four men—who'd been watching my face for the coming blow—slumped to the concrete.

Dillon squatted in front of me and inspected the side of my head, where I'd been pistol-whipped. His lips tightened, and his worried eyes met mine as he cupped my cheek. "Are you okay?"

My thoughts raced, trying to keep up with it all. "I thought you were going to kill me."

His gaze plunged deeply into my eyes, and his body stiffened in shock. "I'd never hurt you, Fallon," he said in a deep voice that sent pulses to my heart. "I'll always do everything in my power to protect you."

He looked at the doorway, where a commotion of shouting grew louder. Killing an unarmed hooker didn't take four shots. Footsteps stampeded down the hallway toward us.

"Come on." Dillon pulled me to my feet. "We need to run."

# 30

As footsteps grew louder behind us, I grabbed the semiautomatic lying next to The Enforcer, whose blood stretched on the floor toward my high heels, and accepted Dillon's hand.

"The Syndicates have had a few meetings here, but the cartel hasn't. They don't know this place as well as I do," he said.

Dillon led me to a six-paneled white door, which I had assumed was a closet, but when he opened it and ushered me through, I discovered it was a narrow, ventless hallway. Footsteps and voices grew louder as Dillon rushed me through a second door, into what appeared to be an office with two bookshelves overflowing with books and a ten-foot mahogany desk with a bullet hole in its wood.

"Fuck!" a man growled two rooms over. "Where's that girl?"

Dillon grabbed the left bookshelf and slid it three feet over, revealing a rough cutout in the drywall.

"Saw McPherson come in here after her," another voice growled.

Dillon helped me step through the opening and into a dark

cavern of uncertainty. My shoes clicked on the stone floor, and cold, damp air that smelled of wet leaves slithered over my skin.

When Dillon quietly pulled the shelf back into position, all light ceased. I could hear my breathing echo off the walls, and I swore I could hear my heartbeat reverberate through this unfinished hallway.

"McPherson's working with that DEA bitch!" a voice shouted.

Dillon activated the flashlight on his phone and pointed down the corridor, motioning for me to follow as he began walking.

I took a step. My high heel clicked against the concrete so loudly, Dillon and I both froze. I looked at the spot we'd entered, praying it wasn't about to open in a sea of bullets.

"This is on fucking Delgado," a voice snarled back in the area of the original room. "If he'd done his job, McPherson wouldn't even be here right now."

Dillon allowed himself a quick look of shock but forced himself to refocus on escaping before it was too late. He motioned toward my shoes.

"What the hell is going on here?" a new voice demanded.

I stepped out of my high heels and onto the cold slab of concrete.

"We have a problem," a voice back in the room said.

"No shit."

"That DEA bitch is missing," he said. "With one of Chicago's captains."

I could only imagine an angry glare preceded, "Who?"

I took my first step, following Dillon.

"McPherson. He and that DEA bitch ran off."

A pause. "Find them. NOW. You," he said. "Go get Delgado, bring him here. Slit his throat for screwing up that fire."

*That fire?*

I tried to hear what they said next, but their voices became harder to hear as the passage descended, and the ceiling's height shortened until we had to crouch. It smelled like dirt, and the air grew colder, sending a shiver across my skin.

Suddenly, Dillon stopped.

We'd hit some sort of dead end. I glanced behind us, watching for any sign of a light breaking through the darkness. I couldn't hear them anymore. Were they still back in that room? Or asking a Chicago crew member where we might escape?

A metallic groan drew my attention back to Dillon, who grunted as he slid an iron circular plate off the floor and revealed another man-made tunnel beneath this one. I looked down into the hole but couldn't see anything. I couldn't tell how deep it was, which direction it went.

Dillon used his phone's flashlight to illuminate it, motioning toward a ring of bars that functioned as a ladder into the space.

"Come on," he said. "Hurry!"

I slipped my lower body through the hole, thighs scraping stone on the way in, and tapped my toes around until I found the rung beneath the ball of my foot. It was bumpy, like its metal had rusted and chipped, and when I began to climb down, those chips stung the skin on my feet and palm of my free hand—my other hand clutching the semiautomatic. I could hear drips of water echo off the underground tunnels' walls. I could feel its dampness in my bones.

After five rungs, my foot couldn't find the sixth.

"Drop," Dillon whispered. The fact that he whispered worried me; it meant he could hear them getting closer. "Ground's, like, three feet down."

I took a deep breath and let go.

I only fell for a moment before the unforgiving ground slammed against my feet and threw me off-balance, tossing my right hip to the floor. My gun scraped against the concrete as it slid from my grip and was eaten by the shadows.

I patted around the pitch-black space, unsuccessful in

locating my weapon, as Dillon descended the rungs, replaced the manhole cover, and jumped to the ground. Easily landing on his feet.

Shouting erupted in the tunnel above our heads.

"Come on!"

Dillon grabbed my hand, and we ran.

With his phone light only affording us a few feet of visibility, the darkness swallowed us. The men's voices grew louder. We ran for what had to be twenty seconds, and then my heart lodged in my ribs.

The manhole cover clanked.

"Here." Dillon handed me his phone.

And that was when I saw it—a door. Dillon worked the hatch and shoved it open.

A rush of warm outside air flooded over me as the moon's silver light became our beacon.

Behind us, flashlights cut through the pervasive darkness as men jumped into the passage.

"There!" one of them shouted.

A gunshot blasted off the walls as Dillon and I lunged through the opening and onto a lawn. Dillon slammed the metal door shut behind him and fastened it with a titanium lock that had dangled from its exterior hook. Probably there for the same reason the tunnel was built—to escape a police raid and block their ability to come catch you.

The problem was, *these* people knew where this tunnel system let out—in a field fifty meters behind the property with nowhere to hide. Only grass and trees and a road sixty feet ahead.

A road where an SUV hurtled this way.

"Run!" Dillon demanded.

The vehicle groaned closer while a stocky torso stood through its sunroof, holding a rifle as he scanned the area.

Our only hope of hiding—and that hope was pretty damn

dismal—was to make it to the field just behind the road, where the scattering of trees offered a little cover. But getting to it meant crossing the very pavement the SUV thundered down.

My lungs burned, and adrenaline surged through my muscles as my bare feet pounded the cool grass, then thumped against the pavement.

"There!" The guy sticking out of the vehicle pointed at us. Just as the SUV fishtailed to a stop.

We bolted and took cover behind a forty-foot oak tree. Against the backdrop of rustling leaves, the sounds of three sets of footsteps clunked against the pavement as they jumped out, no doubt guns drawn.

Hunting us.

"I lost my gun," I whispered.

Dillon pushed my back against the spiky bark and stood protectively in front of me.

Flashlights swept the air and grew brighter, the closer they got. Judging by the swishing of grass beneath their steps, our hunters were about sixty feet away.

I looked around for another tree, or road, or something, anywhere we could go. But there was nothing, save for the running SUV they'd come in. But to get to it, we'd have to make it past all three of them.

Forty feet away.

And even if there was somewhere to go, running would expose us.

Ten feet away.

I clutched Dillon's back.

Twigs snapped beneath the men's boots as they closed the last steps.

Dillon lunged from the sanctuary of the tree and fired in rapid *pop-pop-pops*. The taller guy thumped to the ground immediately, but the second and third guys fired back.

In what felt like slow motion, bullets exploded through orange embers from the ends of pistols, cracking the silence. The blasts seemed to echo off the stars that canopied the earth with their beauty.

A second body smacked the ground as the third guy lined up another metal death bomb at Dillon. I charged the figure with my shoulder, but before I made contact, his bang rang out.

Dillon's body jerked.

I wasn't big enough to knock the guy to the ground, but my attempt averted his attention long enough for Dillon to line up his shot.

And pull the trigger.

The man's head snapped back. His body stood hauntingly still for a half-second before dissolving to the ground.

"Come on!" Dillon sprinted toward the SUV.

In the distance, another vehicle plowed toward us. The door to the tunnel lurched with kicks from the people on the other side, and more men ran from the back of the property toward us.

We ran to the vehicle the dead guys had used, and I jumped into the passenger seat just as Dillon threw it into drive. And floored it.

The back window exploded.

As he hurtled the truck away from a mob, Dillon's body pumped blood onto his shirt with every beat of his heart.

# 31

The road flew beneath our tires at a hundred miles per hour as a black Mercedes SUV pursued us a few hundred feet behind. Dillon cut the lights, making it harder for them to see us, but also harder for us to see the road as we thrust into the murky ambiguity that was our future.

The road T'd so sharply, Dillon missed it, thumping into a field before cutting the wheel so tight, we almost flipped over. I looked behind us. The headlights grew smaller and then became taillights as the other vehicle lost sight of us and made the opposite turn.

I sighed, relieved for our reprieve yet unsure of how long it would last.

The only light we had came from the dashboard, illuminating Dillon's eyes that darted between the rearview and side mirrors.

"You okay?" He clutched my hand.

"You've been shot."

"Did they hurt you?"

"You're bleeding. Heavily." I could only see the general location of the wound in his shoulder area, now drenched in blood. "We need to go to a hospital," I insisted.

"We can't. Left a trail of blood on the way to the SUV. They'll look for us there."

I touched his shoulder, which was covered in warm liquid. "You're losing a lot of blood!"

Dillon growled in pain when my fingers explored his chest. "We go to a hospital, they could get to you, Fallon," he groaned. "I'm not risking it. We need to keep moving, get a few hundred miles behind us."

"You're not going to make it a few hundred miles. You might bleed to death before we make it much farther."

He cast his rounded eyes over my face, then the rearview mirror, as if more concerned about leaving me alone and unprotected than he was of his own well-being.

"I don't think it hit anything major," he claimed.

"Well, *that's* comforting. In that case, by all means, just keep driving until you lose consciousness, then. I'll sit here while we both become cartel bait."

Dillon glared at me, and I glared right back.

"A pharmacy," I compromised. "Stop at a pharmacy. I'll grab medical supplies, and we'll stop and clean the wound."

Silence.

"If you don't do it, I'll just jump out of this moving truck, so help me."

Dillon tightened his grip on the steering wheel, looked in the rearview, the side mirrors.

"Let me drive."

"I'm fine," he insisted. "We'll come across a main road in a few minutes, and then it's just a few more minutes to town."

We drove in silence, Dillon constantly glancing at the rearview mirror, watching for any sign of being followed. Eventually, the road bent to the left, then the right, and then we came across a handful of buildings—one of which was a pharmacy.

Dillon parked the SUV behind the building, hidden behind the dumpster, and I grabbed a crumpled T-shirt from the floor, wiping the blood splatter off my back from Proctor's gunshot. Luckily, my dress was dark, so whatever remained would hopefully not be too noticeable.

"You have cash?" I asked.

Dillon fished his wallet out of his back pocket, wincing from the pain of moving his arm. "Less than a hundred bucks."

I grabbed the cash, and he shut the engine off and opened the door like he was about to climb out.

"You can't come in with me," I said.

"I'm not letting you out of my sight."

"You go in, looking like that," I said, pointing to his blood-soaked shirt, "they'll call the cops."

Dillon tightened his lips.

Which, now that I thought about it...

"My opinion? It'd be a good thing."

They could get him an ambulance.

"The cartel has police scanners. Might even have the cops out here on payroll already. We call police, we might as well call the cartel." Dillon weighed this for a moment, then said, "This was a bad idea."

He shifted to put the truck into gear, but I jumped out first.

"Fallon!"

"You need medical supplies."

"You're not going in there alone!"

"Two minutes, tops," I said.

"You're going to draw attention, dressed like that," he argued. "You don't even have shoes!"

Nothing I could do about that. We needed to stop his bleeding.

Dillon looked at me in exasperation as I walked toward the front door and scanned the road for headlights one more time before ducking inside the building, where I loaded up on medical supplies. Water. Snacks that I grabbed near the register.

Did the cashier look at me funny? Yep. But he seemed too preoccupied, staring at my cleavage, to call the police over my frazzled appearance.

When I exited the building and walked around the dumpster, Dillon's injured shoulder sagged in relief when he spotted me. His eyes shot around in frantic bursts to the road behind me, the parking lot, even the field off in the distance before returning to me. He watched my every step as I neared the truck.

I hadn't seen or heard anyone following us, and while I knew they were out there somewhere, prowling, hunting, the most urgent thing on my mind right now was looking at Dillon's wound. If I thought it was critical, I was going to call an ambulance, whether he liked it or not.

I climbed inside.

He squeezed the steering wheel. "You're the most stubborn person I've ever met, you know that?"

"Says the guy who won't get medical attention for a gunshot wound."

I fished around the bag, reviewing all the medical supplies.

"We need to go somewhere with light and running water, so we can clean your wound."

Dillon started the engine. "We'll drive for a while, and then you can look at it in the truck."

Like I'd let him drive any farther in his condition.

He shifted the gear from park to drive, but I was faster. I opened my door and hopped out, pharmacy bags in hand.

"Where are you going?" Dillon growled.

I walked toward a one-story building just off the main road, turning to explain. "Running water. Light. A place to clean your wound without worrying you're going to pass out at eighty miles an hour."

"We need to put miles between us and them first, so get back here!"

"You can come with me or sit there and bleed to death."

Dillon clenched his jaw. "If they drive past, they could see the SUV."

"So, leave it behind the dumpster. They won't see it from the main road. And if they do"—I pointed to the building across the street—"we'll see them first."

I continued walking, making it clear this wasn't up for debate. His bloodstain was getting bigger by the minute.

"Damn it," Dillon snarled, stomping out of the SUV.

The building appeared to be turquoise, though I couldn't be sure without the benefit of sunlight. Surrounded by trees and an almost-empty parking lot, the structure had six doors separated by fifteen feet. An arrow with red and white letters that said *West Point Motel* pointed to the main door.

I went into the lobby and paid for a room with the leftover cash Dillon had given me.

Room six.

Dillon followed me inside, shut and locked the door, and closed the blinds to the only window, which overlooked the empty parking lot.

I hauled the pharmacy's plastic bags into the bathroom, removed the wig that made me sweat, and quickly organized all the medical stuff from them as well as a washcloths from the motel.

"We need to get your shirt off," I said.

Dillon peered through the blinds, looking to the left before making a slow, methodical sweep to the right. He didn't come into the bathroom until he did his scans twice.

Now that we had some decent lighting, I could see his shirt

had a basketball-sized blood-soaked section that was coming from his left shoulder area. It was on the front *and* the back.

I pulled at the hem of his shirt and tugged it up slowly, feeling his gaze on me as the fabric revealed his lined abs with its belly button pulling at the skin stretched around his muscles. When his shirt made it to his chest, sticky crimson peeled with it as Dillon hissed.

"Sorry," I whispered.

I pulled it up delicately, stretching my arms as high as they would go to get it up and over his head. And in that instant, the terrifying reality of his injury slapped me.

The entry hole was a half-inch, penetrating his body roughly two inches below the top of his shoulder, where blood dribbled from the crimson void. I turned him around and found the exit wound behind his left shoulder, in roughly the same position. Blood actively leaked from this one as well, but the location of it made me feel a little better. Nowhere near the heart or lungs, and if it'd hit an artery, it'd be gushing blood. Hell, he'd be dead by now.

But that didn't mean he wasn't in danger.

"There could be internal damage that we can't see," I said. "We really need to get you to a doctor."

Dillon turned around and stared at me with that damn stubbornness.

"I'm going to clean the wounds," I said. "And it's going to hurt. Sit." I closed the toilet lid and pointed to it.

He obliged, but his lips twitched up on one side.

I pulled out the antibacterial soap. "I don't know what you have to be grinning about. We narrowly escaped death, you got shot, and now, we're kind of up shit creek here."

As I wet a washcloth and doused it in soap, Dillon trapped me in his gaze's snare. Until I wiped the cloth across his chest.

"Gah!"

"Sorry." I put the rag under the sink, waiting for the water to turn from crimson back to clear. Then, I added more soap and, as gently as possible, wiped his skin again.

His shoulder muscles tensed with each pass.

"Is this going to take long?" Dillon asked.

"I don't know. I've never cleaned a bullet wound before; we should ask a *doctor* how long it takes."

I cleaned the washcloth and continued my cleansing on the entrance wound.

"We need to hurry," he said, glancing toward the front door.

"And go where?" I challenged as I pressed the cloth against the wound. "The cartel has targets on both our backs now. Where could we possibly go that we'd be safe?"

"Another country," Dillon hissed through the pain. "Run back to my place, grab some cash, get your passport and mine."

"They've probably got people watching your place."

He tightened his jaw. "The clock is ticking to get you out of town."

"Me?"

Dillon hesitated. "Us. Us out of town." But the look on his face told me there was more to the slip than he was letting on.

"Why did you say me and not *us*?"

"I meant us," he claimed. "Look, we need to hurry," he insisted.

I hesitated but had him turn around, so I could work on the back wound. This one was dripping blood at a more constant pace. A slow drip, which I couldn't decide if that was good or bad. If the wound was slowing its bleeding or if the bleeding was mostly inside his body.

I stared at the tattoo as I cleaned his skin, the tattoo of the scorpion holding the American flag. The one that forever redefined us to each other, on opposite sides of the fight. The drug lord and the DEA agent.

"What does the scorpion mean?" I wondered aloud.

"What?"

"The tattoo. What does it mean?" I asked, wiping his skin.

Dillon allowed a small silence to pass. "Scorpion is an expression of great strength. Ability to control and protect oneself."

Ah. The dad that left his family vulnerable. "And the flag?"

"Asshole father left for some job opportunity in another country. Felt like a *screw you, I'll stay here and protect our family*."

I rinsed the washcloth and wiped more blood off his skin. Dillon hissed when I had him turn back around to face me and added hydrogen peroxide to the cleaning regime.

"I need to call Burch," I said.

"To hell you do."

"Burch wasn't in that van; he's still alive."

Dillon grabbed my wrist. "I heard what he said to you, about the van of agents being dead. How would they even know about them?"

I blinked.

"They told you about the dead agents within a couple of minutes of spotting you. No way they found them *after* they spotted you. They knew about it all before they even walked in. You have a leak," he said.

"And Burch needs to know that."

I released the cloth. I gathered up all the gauze I'd gotten—squares of it, rolls of it. The antibacterial cream. I pulled the skin glue out of the box, pulled off the safety seal, and wiped Dillon's front wound again. "I don't even know if this'll do any good. This isn't meant for a bullet wound."

I frowned when I had to put the glue on his skin and press the openings together. Dillon tried to hide the pain, but I could see how badly it hurt him. And it didn't even work. Though the opening was small, once I let go of it, the hole opened up again.

"We do need to get you to a doctor. No matter how risky you think it is, your wound is more serious than you think."

I collected the gauze.

"Who knew you were going to be there tonight?"

I smothered some gauze in antibacterial cream. "Everyone involved in the operation."

"Such as?"

I pressed the dressing to the wound and put two pieces of tape on it.

"Me. Proctor. Shane. Burch. Burch's boss. The agents in the van, other agents who've been investigating the cartel's threat to move to the US."

"How much do you know about Burch?"

"I know tonight's going to end his career. He lost seven agents on one mission. There's no coming back from that." I pinched my eyes closed for a moment; I couldn't feel bad over someone's legacy when lives had been lost. "He was reluctant to let me work undercover tonight, but I pushed."

Shane was right: Burch had been too aggressive. Maybe even a bit overconfident after decades of experience, assuming he could thwart any complication.

"He never would have sent us in if he'd had any clue the cartel was going to be there." This one awful night would be the defining moment of his now-dead career.

Dillon hesitated as I bandaged the wound on his back the same as the front. "What about Shane?"

"What about him?"

"He knew about tonight."

*Glare* isn't a strong enough word for the look I shot at Dillon. "Don't even go there."

"I'm just asking if—"

"He's been my only friend for my entire life. He's my only real family, and he'd never, ever do anything to hurt me."

Dillon measured the resolve in my face. "What about Proctor?"

"He got killed."

"Obviously wasn't his plan. Any chance he was working for them?"

I didn't know. "There's another issue we found out about tonight..."

He waited.

"That fire was meant for you."

Dillon didn't reply.

"Why did they try to kill you?" I asked.

"Maybe they were getting ready for the cartel."

"But you hadn't done anything to piss them off? Break one of their rules?"

Dillon shook his head. "No."

"And if they did want to kill you, why'd they do something so unreliable? Why not do something simpler? Like shoot you?"

"No idea."

And when it failed, why didn't they try again?

"We need to find the mole," I agreed. "But we also need to figure out why they wanted you dead."

His troubled eyes looked to the ground, and he was silent for several seconds. When he spoke again, his voice was low. "I'm really sorry that you got tangled up in this," he said. "And it almost cost you your life."

I was in that elevator with him, but everything that came after had been my decision, not his. I was even more eager than Burch had been, more reckless in my determination to take down this organization.

"This is going to hurt," I said, pulling the roll of gauze to his arm. I wrapped it under his armpit, over the entrance wound, over the back, and wound it several more times.

"I need to call Shane."

"No. We need to keep our location off the books."

"We need money, gas, and clothes."

Dillon rubbed his jaw.

"I need your phone," I said. Mine was never part of my hooker outfit.

Dillon chewed the inside of his cheek.

"We can't escape the Baja Cartel all on our own. We need help."

A muscle in his jaw ticced. Breathing through his nose, he pulled the phone from his pocket and gripped it tightly. The muscle in his jaw ticced quicker as his hand slowly opened, and he dropped the phone into my open palm.

# 32

Dillon peered through the blinds as I called Shane and told him the bare minimum, calming his panic. The force had already heard of the murders and didn't know what had happened to me.

I was declared missing and endangered.

When I was done explaining enough to get him off the phone, I hung up.

"He's on his way," I said.

Dillon walked over to me and brushed the side of my cheek with the backs of his fingers. His lips turned down, and his eyebrows creased, his voice low. "If this doesn't end well," he started.

"Dillon—"

"I need you to know something." His baritone voice drifted across my skin like velvet and encased me in its warmth, his gentle touch against my cheek an ember, igniting everything in its path. "Before I met you, I had no purpose. I wanted to stay alive for my brother's sake, but fighting to exist and fighting to live are two very different things. I was trapped. Waiting for the hammer to finally come down—when I'd be killed. And the thing is, deep down? I really didn't care. Until you came along. You gave me a reason to live again, Fallon. You gave me something to fight for. After all those years of merely existing, you brought me back to life." He rubbed his thumb along my lip. "You saved me," he said. "And not just from burning up in that elevator. No matter what happens, I need you to hold on to that."

He was saying good-bye. Some part of him believed these were our final hours or minutes alive.

"I love you, Fallon," he said. "More than I imagined it was possible to love another person."

I wanted to eat those words. Feel them rush down my throat and live inside my body because his profession hit its mark, lighting the darkness that once shadowed my heart.

We'd almost died. Still might. But no matter what happened, Dillon had saved me; he chose me even though doing so might cost him his life.

Dillon made bad choices. I didn't agree with them, but I'd learned that he was also an admirable, devoted person. And at this moment, I consumed his love, and I let it envelop me and free my caged heart. We were two broken souls that had endured pain and uncertainty, and we saw each other's darkness as well as our light. The feelings we'd fought so hard against had become the cure our diseased hearts had ached for.

"I love you," I said. My eyes watered, and I took his hand and held it to my chest, willing him to feel my heartbeat, to feel how it thumped for him.

Dillon's brown eyes settled on mine.

"Why do you look so sad?" I asked.

He stroked my cheek, and I leaned into his touch.

"This isn't over," I insisted.

His bare chest rose and fell with each breath, and his lips parted as he stared at my mouth. He put his hand on the wall next to my head as if to steady himself, and his mouth was so close, I could feel the heat of his breath. I reached up on tiptoe, and when I grazed my lips against his, Dillon growled. And crushed his mouth to mine, unleashing all our worry, and fear, and pain. With death hanging over our heads, all the times we'd pushed each other away now seemed insignificant.

We kissed passionately, knowing we might never get to kiss again. We held each other for a long while after, knowing it might be the last time, and as I rested my cheek against his chest, a clarity crashed into my heart.

This whole time, I thought taking down narcotics organizations was the only thing that could make me whole. The only thing capable of filling my soul's painful crevices, left from the earthquake of my family's destruction. But no matter how many criminals I helped capture, it would never bring my family back. It would never unwrap the blanket of despair that draped me in pain when I was a little girl, crying in my empty bed, wishing my parents would love me again. I still wanted to help bring people to justice, but I didn't want to sabotage the rest of my life for it.

What I wanted was to feel *this.* This love extinguished the burns of my past and watered the hope for my future. It was the only thing with the power to heal my heart.

I loved Dillon. And despite everything he'd done, I trusted him with my life. I wasn't sure what our future would look like if we even made it out of here with our lives. He'd have to pay for his mistakes, but that wouldn't prevent me from loving him.

I looked up into his eyes, seeing a cloud of worry behind them.

Dillon traced my cheek. "I need you to promise me something."

"Anything."

He drew in a deep pull of oxygen, and the way he looked at me —with a profound, cutting sadness—sent a flood of unease over my skin.

"If something happens to me—"

"Dillon..."

"Promise me you won't go back to shutting yourself out from everyone," he said. "Even if something bad happens."

"Why would you say that?" I pulled back.

He offered a solemn look.

"If you're worried about your bullet wound—"

"I'm not."

"Then, what are you saying?"

Dillon's expression softened, and his voice was low as he grazed my jaw with his hand. "There's something I need to tell you," he started. He swallowed, and I could see his chest rise and fall quicker, his heartbeat clearly picking up in fear. "You're not going to like it, but you need to trust me."

A pounding on the door interrupted us.

# 33

The pounding came again. Louder this time. Angrier.

Dillon grabbed his gun, opened the blinds an inch, glanced out, and frowned.

"It's a guy in a hoodie," he whispered.

"It's probably Shane."

"He'd have had to drive like a bat outta hell to get here this fast."

"Well, I doubt the cartel would knock," I reasoned.

Dillon ran a hand through his hair and cringed. "You sure you can trust him?" he pressed.

I nodded, but Dillon didn't look convinced. In fact, he looked like he was questioning his sanity for letting Shane come.

If this guy was even Shane...

"This goes to shit"—Dillon grabbed the doorknob—"you take the gun. Kill whoever you have to, take the keys." He reached into his pocket, shoved them into my hand. "And you run like hell."

Someone pounded on the door again.

Dillon grabbed me around the waist and crushed his lips to

mine. Before he nudged me behind him, raised his weapon, unlocked the door...

And opened it.

Dillon didn't move, didn't speak. Didn't fire his weapon. I thought he might have a gun to his head, but he didn't lower his weapon, either.

Instead, he opened the door wider and allowed the guy to barge in with a black duffel bag.

"Shane!" I ran to him and wrapped my arms around his neck as Dillon shut and locked the door.

Shane only hugged me back with one arm; the other put the bag on the floor as he scowled at Dillon.

"Put the gun down," Shane demanded.

Dillon didn't move.

"He's not going to hurt you," I said.

"Gun. Down," Shane repeated.

I looked at Dillon, implored him to trust Shane. Grateful when he placed the gun on the nightstand.

"You'd better start telling me what the hell happened tonight because Burch has been calling me every fifteen minutes, demanding to know where you are. He's convinced that I know and that I'm lying to him, and up to an hour ago, I wasn't. So, start talking. Explain to me why I've been lying to my superior for *him*."

I explained everything I hadn't had time to do on the phone and how we needed help. But didn't know who we could trust. Who had tipped them off about the DEA working the party.

"Shit." Shane ran a hand through his hair and took a deep breath.

"Passed three dark SUVs in town," Shane said. "Every second you're here, the cartel gets closer. Probably setting up a grid right now if they haven't already. Get your stuff," Shane said. "We're leaving now. Hurry!"

I ran to the bathroom to get the medical supplies; Dillon's wound would need to be cleaned again in a few hours.

"I'm thinking we head north," I said as I tossed the stuff into the duffel Shane brought. "Once we're somewhere a little safer—"

"I'm taking you to the precinct," Shane announced.

"To hell with that!" Dillon said.

Shane ignored him. "I'm going to tell Burch what's going on. Get him to assign you protection while we figure this out."

I nodded. This made sense. I knew Dillon wouldn't like it, but—

"Screw that! It'll get her killed. We need to get her out of here."

"We need to call this in," Shane said to me. "You know that."

I considered it. "Maybe Dillon's right," I said. "Maybe we should lie low for a little while, do a little more digging before we involve authorities. If we call them right now, we might tip off the leak, and if we do that, we'd be giving the cartel a GPS on our heads."

"Fallon, listen to me," Shane said. "If Burch finds out you've been in bed with a Chicago captain?"

"I already told Burch about Dillon."

"That was before, when you broke it off."

"He wanted Dillon to be a CI."

Shane licked his teeth at that revelation. "But he didn't become one, did he?" He paused. "And now, seven men got killed, and the two of you went missing. When he finds out you've been with him the whole time, do you know what it's going to look like?"

He let a small silence pass.

"It's going to look like you were the leak. You got your agents killed."

"That's ridiculous."

"If you look at this from the bird's-eye, from someone who

doesn't know you, it's really not. You got in bed with a Chicago captain, and while seven federal agents were slaughtered, you somehow made it out, unscathed. Bird's-eye view: it looks like you were in on it."

"No one would—"

"Why would they *not* think that?" Shane pushed. "Put yourself in their shoes. Who looks more guilty than you?"

I shook my head and swallowed my shock.

"Think they're not going to look for someone to blame?" Shane pressed. "Someone to bring charges against? Could hold you accountable for the deaths of the men. Manslaughter charges. Maybe even murder."

I wanted to tell him he was crazy. But the scary thing was, he wasn't. Not in the least. Of course that was how it looked.

"You need to get in front of this, Fallon. Come clean now. Surrender yourself while they still view you as the victim, not the mastermind."

*Mastermind...*

"The longer you hide out, the guiltier you look," Shane warned.

"He's right," Dillon said.

I turned around.

"You need to go."

"What?"

Dillon scrubbed the back of his head. "Your odds are probably better, surrounded by federal custody, than running alone, especially if the cartel *and* the feds are hunting you down. And you can't let yourself become the scapegoat for what happened tonight."

That pain in Dillon's eyes returned—the pain that I'd noticed when he said he had something to tell me and that whatever it was, I wasn't going to like it.

"I need you to listen to me," Dillon whispered. "I need you to know I never betrayed you. I never worked you, Fallon. Fact is, I didn't even know you were in law enforcement when we first started dating, and when I found out..." He took a deep breath, looked incredibly depressed. "I'd never do anything to hurt you."

"I know that."

He offered a weak smile, his brows pushed together in pain.

"Fallon..." He closed his mouth, swallowed harshly. "I'm going to turn myself in."

It hurt. Thinking of the risk of him in prison, but I was relieved he'd chosen to do the right thing, taking responsibility for his crimes. And while I didn't know what that meant for our future—if we could even escape to have one—this was the only path that acceptably bridged the person he'd been to the person he'd become.

I nodded. "Burch's team will know what to do. You can go into wit pro."

"We can talk about that later," Shane interrupted, waving an impatient hand. "Fallon, we need to go."

"Wait," Dillon said, pulling me back. He gave me a sad smile, one that didn't reach his eyes, and his posture drooped.

"Fallon, I'm not turning myself in to the *cops*."

"I don't understand—" And then I saw it, the look in his eyes, and I pieced his intention together. That was what his earlier despair was about; he'd already made this decision, perhaps on the drive or when I was in the pharmacy or cleaning his wound. That was why he'd slipped and said *I* should get out instead of *us*.

"You can't." My eyes stung.

"I've thought of a million ways this could go down," Dillon said. "This is the only chance of keeping you safe."

"I see headlights." Shane peered through the blinds. "We need to go, Fallon."

I couldn't believe Dillon was even considering this. There was no way in hell I'd ever, ever let him do this.

"I'll let 'em chase me while you get away."

"They'll catch you!"

"But not you."

"There's no guarantee that sacrificing yourself will get me out of this! And they won't just kill you—you know that! They'll torture you!"

"Fallon!" Shane said.

"Stalling them is the best chance to keep you safe."

"While they torture you!"

"Fallon!"

"No!" I cried. I pressed myself into Dillon's chest, into the chest I'd fallen in love with. The complicated, twisted love that had no clear path forward, yet I couldn't breathe without it.

"It's going to be okay," Dillon lied.

I looked up into his now-tear-filled eyes. I couldn't let him die. Not like that.

"I can't lose another person I love," I said.

His whisper of a voice was full of sorrow. "I'm sorry I failed you."

I wiped a fallen tear from his cheek. "You didn't fail me."

But his lips trembled. "There's something I haven't told you yet."

Whatever it was, it was bad. I could see it plaguing his eyes, haunting him in a way that would keep a person up at night.

"What is it?"

"Fallon!" Shane insisted.

But it was too late.

Headlights swept through the blinds' cracks as tires screeched to a halt. A car door opened, slammed shut.

Dillon pushed me behind him as a fist pounded on the door.

"Open the damn door!"

# 34

Dillon grabbed the handgun and aimed its barrel at the hollow metal door that separated us from whoever was on the other side.

Which vibrated with each blow.

*Bam. Bam. Bam.*

"Open up!"

"Looks like it's just one guy." Shane squinted, struggling to see in the night. "But the SUV's dark."

So, who knew how many might be hiding inside of it? Or surrounding the place?

My throat ran dry.

*Bam. Bam. Bam.*

"Hernandez, open up!"

Confusion washed over Shane as he looked at me.

How did *he* know we were here?

"Hide in the bathroom," Shane hissed to Dillon.

"What?" Dillon said.

"Just do it!" Shane demanded.

Dillon looked at me and waited until I nodded my approval to follow Shane's order. He approached me quickly and afforded himself a second to silently proclaim what he didn't dare say out loud in front of Shane right now. By squeezing my hand three times.

*I. Love. You.*

Then, he placed the gun in my hand and vanished into the bathroom.

Shane took a deep breath, unlocked the door, and opened it.

Burch stood on the other side, alone. His eyes cut through the thick tension from Shane to me before he charged into the room. I'd never seen Burch this angry. His jaw set tight, his fists clenched. He barely resembled the methodically calm sergeant he'd always portrayed. Clearly a casualty of losing several men tonight.

Shane shut the door behind him.

"You said you didn't know where she was," Burch accused.

"I didn't until she called me," Shane said and then added, "How did you know we were here?"

Burch unleashed his anger onto me. "Why the hell didn't you call me? You know how many federal officers are looking for you?"

I set the weapon on the nightstand with a clunk.

"I can explain," I said.

"You'd better do it damn fast."

And so I did. I told him everything that happened at the party, how I escaped, and along with my suspicion—leaving out the part about Dillon helping me or being with me. I seriously needed Burch to calm down before offering that little bomb drop.

"You think we have a leak," Burch said when I was done.

"I don't know how else to explain it," I said.

Burch paced, hands on his hips, and as he did, Shane kept watch through a sliver in the blinds.

"Your car's runnin'," Shane said. "We need to turn it off; anyone driving past'll see the activity outside this room."

"Who do you think it is?" Burch asked me.

It had to be a hard consideration to hear because if there was a leak in play, his career wouldn't just end; it would end in disgrace. This would be scrutinized for years and would serve as a warning for investigations from this point forward.

What a horrible way to go down.

"I don't know," I said.

"Proctor?"

"Why would they have killed someone who was helping them?" I asked.

Burch rubbed his jaw. "Anyone else know about your theory?"

"Just Shane and..."

"And?"

I paused. "When I escaped tonight, I had help."

Burch tensed, looked at me like a parent who'd caught his daughter sneaking back into her window in the middle of the night. "From?"

Uneasiness thickened the air around me, and I worried that my boss might misunderstand the situation or look at me differently for accepting help from one of *them*. As pathetic as it might be, I savored his approval—approval that I'd worked so hard to earn. I didn't want to lose it.

But he deserved to hear the whole truth.

"From Dillon."

On cue, Dillon emerged from the bathroom.

Burch pulled the gun from its holster and took aim, provoking Dillon to put his palms up in surrender.

"It's okay," I said. "He helped me escape tonight."

But Burch didn't lower his weapon; if anything, he looked even more enraged.

"He helped you," Burch snapped. "As in the two of you working together?"

"I...no, not like that."

"Have you given him intel?"

"No!"

"How the hell can I trust that?"

"Because it's the truth! I'd never give up information that could jeopardize our case, let alone put people in danger!"

"Would you know if you did?"

"Yes!"

"Seven of my agents got killed tonight, and you think that's a coincidence?"

"I didn't give any info."

"How am I supposed to trust a word you say? You lied to me," he growled. "Said he refused to be our CI. Wouldn't work with us."

"He wouldn't."

"Bullshit! You've been with him the whole time! Feeding him information!"

"I haven't!"

"She hasn't—" Dillon started.

"Shut the fuck up!" Burch said, and then he told me, "Put your hands behind your back."

"What?" I asked.

Burch pointed the gun at me. At *me*. I hadn't just lost his favor; I'd become the enemy.

"Hands. Behind your back!" Burch repeated.

"Sergeant!" Shane started.

"Both of you." Burch motioned for Dillon and me.

"Sarge, Fallon hasn't—"

"Shut up, or I'll arrest you, too," Burch demanded of Shane.

"Then, arrest me," Shane said. "Because she hasn't done anything. I know how this looks, but she's dedicated her entire life to the war on drugs. She didn't flip, Sarge."

But Burch wasn't listening. A shield of anger wrapped around him, and as he stared at me, his right eye began to twitch. He'd lost everything tonight—his career, his reputation—and he looked like he was coming unglued.

Hopefully, at the station, I could prove my innocence. Hopefully, he'd have enough mercy to get Dillon and me some protection, so the cartel wouldn't get to us.

I nodded to Dillon, and then we both turned around and put our hands behind our backs.

As Burch clanked metal cuffs onto Dillon's left wrist, then his right, Dillon's chestnut eyes grabbed mine, emotion radiating with each beat of his heart. We had been through so much together, a war of our own, and I could see his anguish in the sagging of his shoulders and his fear in his widened eyes that, in the custody of someone so furious with us, we might not receive the level of protection required to keep us alive.

*I love you,* Dillon mouthed.

*I love you,* I mouthed back.

"Cuffs." Burch held his expectant hand out to Shane. Evidently, Burch had only come with one pair.

"I didn't bring 'em, Sarge. You don't need to arrest Fallon. Bring her to the station to ask more questions if you want, but—"

"I'm not asking for your damn opinion, Hernandez! You're in enough trouble for lying to me tonight!"

Was this how it was going to be? Burch would turn on anyone involved with tonight and try to throw us under the bus? I screwed up, no doubt. I wasn't ready for an undercover operation of this scale, and I was responsible for having convinced him I was. But Burch couldn't turn *all* of this onto other people and shoulder none of the responsibility himself.

"Sarge—" Shane tried.

Burch squeezed my wrists together and perp-walked me outside.

Dillon followed and kept his eyes on the lot and the main road.

Burch shoved me into the backseat of his SUV and slammed the door. It smelled like sweat in here, like he'd panicked the whole ride down.

How did Burch know we were here? Did Shane lie to me? Did he tell Burch?

"This is bullshit. I'm calling this in," Shane declared as he pulled his cell out.

"I wouldn't do that if I were you." Burch pointed the gun at Shane.

"What are you doin'?" Shane asked.

"Give me your weapon," he demanded of Shane.

"What?"

"Weapon!" Burch screamed.

Dillon glared at Burch.

I yanked the handle and rammed my shoulder into the door repeatedly, but it wouldn't open.

"Weapon!" Burch shouted.

I tried the other side. Same fail.

Shane and I exchanged a look through the window, one that silently communicated our fear. The cartel could come down this road any second, and anyone unarmed would be a sitting duck. As would Dillon, being cuffed. Shane's gaze hardened in disgust as he glowered at Sergeant Marcus Burch. It took several seconds before Shane reluctantly kicked his 0.40 caliber toward Burch, who picked it up and tucked it into his waistband.

We were all disarmed, but on the outside wall of the motel ten feet away was an emergency fire box with a fire extinguisher and an ax. Maybe I could blow the extinguisher in Burch's face or crack him over the head with it, giving us a chance to reclaim Shane's weapon. Get the gun from the motel's nightstand.

I'd have to get out of the SUV first, though.

Dillon took a furious step toward Burch.

"Get in," Burch ordered him.

With his hands behind his back, no shirt, Dillon moved toward the vehicle.

Shane took an aggressive step forward, his shoulders rounded in rage.

"Stay back!" Burch shouted, pointing the pistol at Shane's head.

The inside of the SUV was a sea of shadows with dashboard lights offering the only glow. The engine purred, waiting to move, to take me to my demise.

I tried the door again, but it was locked—child safety locks, I guess. The only way to open it would be from the front. I grabbed the front headrest and heaved myself over to the passenger seat, but before I could do anything else, the driver's door opened.

"Freeze!"

My former hero aimed the barrel of his semiautomatic at my head.

Burch eyeballed the guys, who were momentarily frozen.

I sprang into the driver's seat and threw the running car's gear into reverse. Burch dove inside and landed half on me as the SUV flew backward, its tires squealing along the asphalt. I squeezed the steering wheel, but Burch clenched his sweaty sausage fingers over mine, fighting for control as the vehicle jerked from side to side, careening toward the nearby field.

With the door still open, I elbowed Burch in the nose and kicked him with my free leg, but he hurled himself deeper inside the SUV and maintained his hold on both the weapon and steering wheel.

I tried to jerk the wheel to the right toward the building. If I could crash, maybe he'd fly out the door. But he wrenched the steering wheel back the other way, sending the vehicle into a fishtail toward the road.

Burch hit me in the head with the pistol so hard, it stunned me long enough for him to shove me into the passenger seat, stop, and clunk the gear into drive.

Forward this time.

I tugged the door handle, but it was also locked. I kicked the window.

"Stop."

The icy promise of death pressed against the back of my skull.

And as Burch closed the door, I glanced back at Dillon and Shane, who watched in horror as Burch sped down the country road.

# 35

"Open the glove box," Burch commanded.

As I turned to face forward, he kept his Glock 19 inches from my left temple.

The glove box opened with a click, and the interior yellow light illuminated stacks of papers and the car's owner's manual. On top of which sat a pair of plastic zip ties.

"Put them on. Now."

*I should go for the gun or grab the wheel and make us crash.*

But with death one squeeze away, my instincts cautioned me to wait to make my move. We were driving too fast with no seat belts, so I'd never survive the crash. And with the erratic look in Burch's eyes, I had no doubt he'd kill me.

Even if I had no idea why.

I wrapped the plastic restraint around my left wrist, then added my right. Which was tricky, threading the line through its end and pulling it closed with my teeth.

Burch grabbed the band and yanked it so tight, the ties cut into my skin.

I scowled at him—at the man who I'd once longed to impress.

"You're the leak," I said in disgust.

He said nothing, didn't even have the courtesy to look at me as we plunged ahead on the darkened road into whatever twisted fate awaited me.

"You led your men into an ambush. You sent them tonight, knowing the cartel knew we were coming. Knowing they'd kill us all."

"I didn't know they'd kill you; there was nothing I could do," Burch said.

"Bullshit. There was a lot you could do. They trusted you. Some had families. Kids that'll grow up without a parent."

"This isn't what I wanted, O'Connor."

"What did you want? Money? A cut of the take? What was the price tag for all those families you destroyed tonight?"

"This isn't about money," Burch said.

"Then, what?"

He swallowed. "They have my kids."

He made a left turn and got onto a four-lane road. In the middle of the night, the SUV's headlights pierced through the insidious darkness and lit a couple hundred feet in front of us. Only a few other vehicles sped along this road, and when they grew close in the oncoming lane, their headlights blazed so brightly, it hurt my eyes. No way anyone would see the gun Burch had aimed at me, diabolically hidden beneath the dash.

"Two men showed up at my house," Burch said. "Told me they had my kids." I recalled hearing Burch had two—both of which had graduated college recently. "They had pictures, proof they had them. If I alerted the FBI or anyone, my kids would be tortured and killed."

"What did they want?"

Burch gripped the wheel tighter as a bead of sweat trailed down his temple.

"They needed to know what we knew. What the chances were of being arrested on American soil. What evidence we had."

Right, in order to cross the border safely.

"So, you turned it all over to them," I said. "Including the undercover operation."

"If you have kids someday," Burch started but then caught himself, looking at me with a flash of pity. Realizing I'd never have kids because I wouldn't be alive much longer. "When you have kids, there's nothing you wouldn't do for them."

"So, you're trading me for them."

"When you got away, they offered an exchange." And then he added in a softer tone, "I'm sorry, Fallon."

I bit my lip. "How did you find me?"

He shifted. "Tracked Hernandez's phone."

Then, why didn't they just send someone to the motel to kill me? The thought made me shudder that Dillon and Shane could've gotten killed, too, but why have Burch bring me to them?

"Why didn't they just take a hit out on me?"

Burch sighed. "Can only assume they want to question you about your relationship with McPherson. Find out what he leaked and to who."

My stomach rolled with nausea. Of course that was what they wanted; they'd torture me for days, maybe longer, to figure out what I knew. Uncover any other threat they needed to mitigate to make their big move a success.

My mouth ran dry. "Did they know about us before tonight?" Before we'd been caught, escaping together? Because if they did, why didn't they kill Dillon before the party?

"I had to answer their questions, but I certainly wasn't going to volunteer information they didn't ask for. Protected as much intel as I could. Soon as I have my kids back, I'm going to work the case and personally make sure these animals are put away.

Besides," he said, glowering at me, "didn't realize you two were still together."

But now that Dillon helped me escape, they knew. So, what orders had been given for us?

"And Dillon?"

"If I found you two together, I was supposed to snag him, too." Burch looked nervous, clearly worried they might not let his kids go if he only showed up with me. But what choice did he have? When everything went to hell in the parking lot, he at least had me in the car. Returning to the motel to fight with Shane risked me getting away and Burch having nothing to bargain for his kids.

"How long have you been working with them?" I demanded.

He didn't answer.

"My dad's funeral? Were you working with them then?" When I invited Burch as a guest and thought he was honorable?

"No. Funeral was an intimidation tactic," Burch said. "To warn us they can get to any of us. And our families," he added.

Families. Usually present at a funeral, so yeah. That would have sent one hell of a message to everyone.

"How long have you been working with them?" I repeated.

Burch tightened his lips.

"Before we found Marks?"

He didn't look at me.

"And you didn't call off the undercover operation."

"Couldn't do that without tipping my hand."

"But they knew we were going to be there," I challenged.

"They had my kids."

"So, you just let us all walk into an ambush."

"The cartel is playing the long game, collecting people who'll feed them vital intel. If they killed agents tonight, it'd expose their plans, so no, I didn't think it was going to be a massacre."

But obviously, he'd been wrong in his assessment.

"You let your experience go to your head," I accused. All those missions he'd pulled off, with better stats than anyone in DEA history. "You knew it was dangerous, but with all the years under your belt, you thought you could still control this. Save your kids *and* salvage the case." Which wasn't just reckless; it was downright arrogant.

I blinked the stinging of immense disappointment in my eyes. After closing everyone out for years, over the last few weeks, I'd grown to trust two people—Dillon and Burch. And now, this man whose approval I'd savored, who I'd trusted with my life, was driving me to my certain death. His betrayal cut me deep.

Dillon would never betray me; he'd die to protect me.

I guess that was the gamble you took with opening yourself up to people. Some people would hurt you. But others would love you so much, it could make up for all those other hurts combined.

I burried my pain and focused on trying to convince Burch to let me go. "You hand me over," I said, "you really think they'll just let your kids walk?"

He tensed his jaw.

"Untie me, and we can come up with a plan. Maybe I can talk Shane and Dillon into—"

"No."

"You can give me a gun."

"I'm not risking my kids, O'Connor."

"Your kids are in danger, no matter what you do. We work together and maybe—"

"No!" Burch snapped. "I'm doing exactly what they say, period. I'm not deviating."

"You don't have Dillon."

"They can hunt him down themselves."

My throat ran dry. They *would* hunt him down. I had to think of a way to save him, save myself, and Burch was too emotional to listen to reason. Maybe I could get to his cell, call this in, like I should have done to begin with.

As we drove north in silence, Burch didn't take his eyes off the road in front of him. He didn't drive like a cop, looking at his surroundings—hell, the cartel could be following us for all I knew—but rather drove like a crazed father, desperate to get to his children.

I thought I could use that fevered focus to my advantage, but before I had the chance to make a move, he parked the car on a grassy field and led me down a slight hill to a dilapidated pier extending out into Lake Michigan.

The water, almost indiscernible from the dark horizon, was hauntingly calm, barely rocking the hundred-foot-long-foot boat tied to the pier's end. North of us, the city's lights glowed like a beacon of hope, and the moon's silver glow shimmered its reflection off the water, but right here, the shadows of hopelessness swallowed me whole as Burch led me to the armed men guarding the lone vessel.

One of the guys, who brandished spiderweb tattoos on his hands, patted Burch and me down and confiscated his guns before escorting us to the boat. Which had multiple levels to it, including one of those underground quarters.

I wasn't sure exactly where we were, but the area was abandoned, save for the psychopaths standing before us.

"The agent." Burch pushed me forward.

A three-hundred-pound man grabbed my elbow and looked at my face for confirmation.

Burch rubbed his ear. "What are you going to do with her?"

"Ain't no matter to you."

Burch looked at me with a silent apology before focusing on what he really cared about. "My kids," Burch insisted. "They said they'd be here."

"Did they?"

Burch tensed. "Bring them to me."

"Change of plans."

A gunshot blasted, and Burch's forehead split open, and his body collapsed to the wood.

I screamed in horror. When two men grabbed my arms and jerked me forward, I pulled and yanked so hard that I could feel my shoulder muscles tearing. But I was no match for their strength.

Once we reached the boat, one of them simply picked me up and threw me into a room on the lower level of the vessel.

Where I slammed onto the ground in a pool of sticky liquid.

Between two mutilated bodies of who I could only assume were Burch's grown children.

# 36

The bodies—one male, one female—were covered in cuts and bruises. But the most gruesome injuries—on their skin at least—were the inflamed welts that ripped their skin wide open in the shape of a *J*.

The smell was a putrid mix of sweat, blood, and burning flesh. Not decomp. They hadn't been dead long, though I bet they wished they had been.

A guy with two missing teeth pulled me up and shoved me into a wooden chair in the center of the room. A chair sitting on top of a fifteen-foot-wide plastic tarp. He zip-tied each ankle to a chair leg, slithered a zip tie through my currently tied wrists, strapped my right wrist to the right armrest, and cut the original zip tie loose with a knife. I took advantage of the freedom to punch him in his missing-toothed mouth, but he blocked it and shoved my left wrist against the other armrest so hard, I thought the bone cracked. He tied that one, too.

When he was done, he lumbered back up the steps and left me alone to take in my surroundings.

The room shouldn't be empty of furniture; clearly, it intended to hold a living room and maybe a dining room set in what I could only assume was a long-haul fishing vessel. But I guess they didn't need that, only this chair, what appeared to be a fire-burning stove in the corner—which crackled and offered the only light—and two hooks suspended from the ceiling's reinforced beams. One of the hooks splatted drops of blood onto the tarp below.

Footsteps thumped down the stairs.

I rocked the chair, hoping I could slip the tie off the leg, but there was no give with them.

Two men entered the room, but they didn't look at me. Instead, they dragged the bodies off to the side with less care than moving trash bags and jogged back up the steps.

*They wanted me to see that—the fate that awaits me.*

I rocked my chair to the side, getting a couple inches of air beneath the right leg, and I shoved my ankle down hard, trying to slip the zip tie off the peg, but suddenly, new steps descended the stairs. These clomps moved slowly, dragging out each step with measured intention. Whoever it was wore split-toned cowboy boots with a brown base and black top that rested on the calves of his black pants.

The man entered the room with the menacing confidence reserved for leaders, and as three other guys followed, I mentally compared the leader to all the faces of criminals I'd studied. I didn't remember anyone with a dark beard and mustache, bushy eyebrows. Plenty of guys were soft around the middle like this guy, though, like they hadn't seen the inside of a gym in a decade.

He fastened his unblinking gaze onto me.

"Fallon O'Connor." He rolled the sleeves of his blue button-down up to his elbows, seemingly unfazed by the blood splattered across his shirt.

His three henchmen took their stances—one on the wall to my left, near the fire, which popped orange embers from its engulfed logs; one to my right; and one behind me. So I couldn't see whatever horror he might inflict. A total intimidation tactic.

I clenched my jaw. These guys had me at their mercy, and there was nothing I could do about that at the moment. But I wasn't about to give them the satisfaction of showing my fear.

"Twenty-six years old. Police officer with the Chicago Police Department. Member of the DEA task force for less than two months. Career ambition: DEA field agent."

"Wow. You somehow managed to smuggle my task force application offline. Congratulations. If the whole satanic drug lord thing doesn't work out for you, you could become a PI."

He walked around me, pausing over my left shoulder as two more drops of blood from the hook splatted onto the plastic tarp.

The boat's engine rumbled to life, and I could feel the vessel pull away from the dock. Even if, by some miracle, someone figured out where I was, there'd be no way for them to help now.

"No criminal offenses on the books, not even a speeding ticket. Father and mother both deceased. Drug overdoses. Father recent."

"Your drugs kill a lot of people. Prey on the weak. But don't let that stop you," I said, looking up at him. "Money is far more important than having a soul."

"Roommate Shane Hernandez. Best friend since childhood."

I kept my face ambivalent. I wouldn't show him that it made me uncomfortable that he knew something as personal as how long we'd been friends.

"Recent boyfriend, Dillon McPherson." He made a tsking sound as he walked around my back and appeared over my right shoulder. "Federal agent and a drug captain. Not something a good DEA agent would do."

"Guess you kidnapped a dud, then. Sucks for you."

He moved to the front of me. "Shane Hernandez's father was killed in the line of duty, but his mother is still alive."

I scowled at his evil eyes.

"Cares a great deal for her. She lives in an apartment in Rockford these days, near his aunt. It'd be a shame if something happened to her, no?" He smirked. "Mr. McPherson has a mother, too. Must care a lot for her, seeing as how he bought her a house. Must care for his disabled brother, too. Paying for his place in the home."

"Are you ever going to get to your point or just continue with family trees? Because I have a cool family tree I could talk about, too. The Baja Cartel tree. You're Francisco Gutierrez," I realized now that he was close enough to see his ugly face with that scar on his cheekbone. Probably why he grew the beard—so he didn't show weakness. "Leader of the Baja Cartel and class-A asshole. Killed your own cousin to take ownership of the business *after* you bombed a rival cartel to take over their region."

"You've studied our organization," he said.

"Part of the job description." I looked away from him to his hired guns.

"Then, you know what we are capable of, Ms. O'Connor. And more importantly, what *I'm* capable of."

Yes, I was. Gutierrez murdered hundreds of people in the last few years alone, including innocent children—who he tended to blow up or poison. But the adults...he had fun with the adults. He had a reputation for getting off on the torture, not just using it as a tactic, but enjoying it.

"You took out four of my men tonight," Gutierrez chided.

"Let me kill three more, and we'll call it even." I nodded my chin toward the dudes around us. "These three'll do."

He chuckled and pointed at me with his finger. "I like you."

"Feeling's not mutual."

"I think you may change your mind when you hear my offer," he said, putting his hands into his pockets.

It was hard to not fixate on the blood on his shirt. What

exactly had been done to them to make the blood splatter like that?

"You leave here alive. You go back home, live out your life. In exchange for this, you simply provide us with"—he waved his hand—"a bit of information."

"You want me to tell you about the investigations."

"Knowledge is...valuable to any business owner, no?"

"No chance in hell."

He nodded and walked over to the fire-burning stove that didn't belong on a boat; its only purpose appeared to be heating up torture devices. "Thought you might say that. American law enforcement usually needs a little more...*motivation* to listen." He pulled a fire poker out of the flames. The black cast iron stick had a wooden handle that looked like a hot dog, and the bottom six inches of the iron was blazing red in the shape of a *J*.

Threat of branding me or not, I'd never help him. Why would he pick some new cop on a temporary DEA task force to help, anyway?

"Why me?" I asked.

"An agent who's in bed with the person she's supposed to arrest?" He cocked his head. "Is likely to be more...shall we say, willing to cooperate with us. Plus," he added, "you're new, so when you ask many questions for us, it won't raise suspicion."

"It doesn't work like that. I can't ask for details that aren't in my wheelhouse. They won't give me answers."

"You'll get answers," he warned.

"A higher-up would know more than I would."

"We tried that," he said, looking out toward the boat's entrance, where Burch's body had fallen. "Not as...complicit. Failed to disclose your relationship with McPherson. This information would have been quite useful to us."

Which they'd obviously learned about tonight. Yet...

"You tortured his kids for days." Not hours.

"Agreement was to keep them alive. Never said I wouldn't try to get information out of them," he said. "And now, *you'll* provide us with information."

I tightened my lips. "If you'd researched me better, you'd know I'd never work for you. I choose death, thanks." Which was obviously the price of declining his "offer."

"I haven't finished." He blew at the hot poker, watching the steam rise from its bright red tip.

"If you don't cooperate, I'm going to kill your boyfriend. *After* I torture him, of course. I'll start by sawing his legs off with a chainsaw," he declared. "Then, I'll do the same to his mother. His brother who lives in the Cold Springs Home. Poor bastard's mentally...what's the accepted terminology these days? Handicapped? So, when we torture him, he'll have no idea why. Imagine that'll make it scarier for him. Especially since I'll make him watch his mother go first."

An empty pit rolled in my stomach.

"Then, I'll move on to Hernandez. I'll really take my time with him—long line of cops in his family. Make sure he knows you had the option to prevent it."

He paused.

"Then, I'll slaughter his entire family."

He'd probably do that, no matter what I did. But the desire to protect those that you loved could be a dangerous force.

Gutierrez approached me and hovered the hot poker in front of my face. "Lot of death for a simple ask."

He pressed the poker onto my right forearm. The searing pain was so intense, it transcended me to another dimension, where only I and the pain existed. He held it there for what was actually five seconds but felt like an eternity before pulling it off.

Along with the skin it had touched.

The open wound still burned despite the absence of the poker.

"I'll make sure their deaths are...unpleasant," he warned.

I thrashed in my chair, but one of his men put a hand on my shoulder to keep me from tipping over. I turned my chin and tried to bite him but only succeeded in getting slapped.

My blood pumped rage through every cell of my body. If I didn't do what he said, I'd sentence everyone I loved to the most gruesome death imaginable. But I couldn't work with the cartel, either. Even if I could trust Gutierrez—which I never could after what he'd done to Burch—I couldn't help them destroy more lives and ruin this country.

"It's just a little information here and there," Gutierrez insisted. "That's it. You live. People you care about live, and their families live. You don't? We get the information, anyway—we'll convince someone else to cooperate. And everyone you love dies. Seems like a pretty simple choice, if you want my opinion."

# 37

A new man ambled down the stairs. As he entered the room, his impatient eyes assessed me. He was tall and tan with black hair that hadn't sprouted as many grays as someone his age should have, clearly unaffected by this violent line of work. There was something familiar about his face, something I couldn't place—not without getting a better look, at least.

"She gonna do it?" His deep voice possessed only a slight accent.

Gutierrez had spoken to the other men with superiority, but he spoke to this guy like an equal. "About to find out." He stared at me. "You gonna be smart?"

Evidently, my pause tested the new guy's patience because, after a breath, he walked back up the steps. "I'm going to finish setting up."

*Setting up what?*

Before I could speculate what he might be up to, a shorter guy set up something of his own. He wheeled in a metal cart out of the back room. Its wheels thumped along each plank of wood, rattling the instruments that blanketed its four-foot silver top—a

Craftsman twelve-inch hacksaw, Black & Decker cordless reciprocating saw, butane blowtorch, Oregon electric chainsaw, cattle prod, hammer, and pliers, among other things. Stained in blood, the tools hadn't even been cleaned yet from their last victims.

I swallowed.

Gutierrez glared at me. "What's your decision, Ms. O'Connor?"

It seemed like such an obvious choice. To never, ever help the cartel. But imagining Dillon and Shane and their families hanging from those hooks, suffering at the hands of those tools until death was a relief...holding the power to prevent it made the decision far less clear.

"And if I say yes, I can leave tonight?" And warn Dillon and Shane, give them a chance to get their loved ones to safety.

"Afraid you'll need to stick with us for a little while until we build up some trust."

"You said I could go home."

"I didn't say tonight. We extended confidence to your boss, and that didn't work out so well."

"I can't help you get answers if I'm held here. I need to go back to the precinct to ask questions."

"One thing at a time, Ms. O'Connor. That's a yes, I presume?"

I hesitated, looking up at the bloody hooks, wondering what exactly Dillon and Shane would endure—if not here, in another torture chamber of their making.

I shut my eyes and remembered everything that happened to my mom, my dad.

I had a choice—to either strengthen the cartel or not. And while they might be right—they might get what they needed, anyway, by kidnapping some other agent—I was not going to give it to them.

I could only hope that Dillon and Shane and their families would forgive me.

There was probably no chance I'd survive the night, but if, by some miracle, I did, maybe I could find out what Gutierrez had up his sleeve, so I could at least give that vital intelligence to the DEA.

"What kind of information would you be asking for?" I asked.

Gutierrez lowered the poker, unsurprised by the likely cooperation. I imagine that was why someone as powerful as him handled this; people probably rarely said no to him. And with so much on the line, he needed for this American operation to move smoothly.

"Whatever I ask, whenever I ask for it. After tonight, there'll be a lot of...shall we say, planning the US will do."

My stomach rolled because there was something far more ominous to his tone than the handful of deaths they had already caused this evening. "Why tonight?"

"Do we have a deal?"

"What do you mean, they'll be planning after tonight?" I pressed again.

"Let's just say, we're going to send one hell of a message to Chicago law enforcement. A little...how you say, warning to stop their war on drugs."

What could that mean? What was the guy upstairs setting up for? My mind raced. What could they pull off on a boat? Attacking other vessels—the Coast Guard perhaps? No. Too small. Crashing the boat into some landmark? Still, not enough carnage to send a message. And if the cartel wanted to send a message, it'd be big. The cartel would want to hit law enforcement where it hurt. Bomb a precinct or something, but we were on a boat, not a truck, so that wouldn't work unless...

*Oh my God.* Unless the target was close to the shore, capable of mass casualties.

Like Navy Pier, where hundreds of law enforcement agents—including the chief of police and the mayor—were attending that awards ceremony right now. The mayor, who'd publicly announced a fresh war on drugs.

"You're going to bomb Navy Pier."

A raised eyebrow.

That was what the guy was preparing upstairs—a bomb.

"You're insane."

This boat chugged closer to Navy Pier with each passing second. All those people would be killed, and it wouldn't just be law enforcement. One of the top tourist destinations in the city, Navy Pier attracted two million people from all over the world each year, and on a summer Saturday night like tonight? Thousands of pedestrians would be among the casualties, including children.

I couldn't let this happen.

I stared at Gutierrez and clenched my now-numb hands. "I won't help you," I declared.

His face darkened, and his lips moved into a pucker.

And then, in a move so quick his arm blurred, he raised his gun.

Pain exploded on the side of my head. I was sure I'd been shot. It was only after a few seconds that I realized I'd only been pistol-whipped.

As warmth dripped down the side of my head, he snapped his fingers to one of the guys, who rolled in a different table—a table hidden behind a door—ten feet away. On it was an HP Pavilion laptop.

Gutierrez vanished into a back room while the guy punched a bunch of keys, tilted the laptop's monitor this way and that until he was satisfied. When he walked away, I discovered what he'd done; he'd activated the laptop's camera. The video of me sitting in this chair stared back at me now. It had a white frame around it with an internet bar at the top.

When the cart rolled closer to my chair, it became clear to me what the plan was.

They were going to torture me.

And livestream it on the internet. Anyone watching the undoubtedly untraceable stream was about to get a front-row seat to the Baja Cartel's leader torturing a United States federal agent. What a horrific moment in American history this would be.

I needed to do something drastic and fast.

I hurled my body to the right and tipped the chair over, bashing my right shoulder into the ground when I landed.

The guy to my right laughed.

On my side, I arched my back and pushed my ankles down the wooden legs. It hurt like hell against the backs of my thighs, which dug into the seat's edge.

More laughter—the morons didn't catch on to what I was doing until my ankles slipped off the chair and freed themselves.

Internet-Setup Guy stopped laughing and marched toward me, but now, I had two free legs.

And I was going to use them.

I kicked him in the shin. Then the groin. And when he went down, holding his crotch, a second guy came at me with a knife.

He managed a swipe on my thigh, but I slammed the heel of my foot into his teeth and felt them break.

He grabbed his bloody mouth, screaming as Gutierrez walked back into the room. Now wearing a white shirt, primed for a bloody show.

Bloody Mouth lunged at me and cracked my temple with his fist as Gutierrez stood next to the instrument tray, debating what he'd use first.

He didn't even flinch when a second man had to join in my struggle, each pinning one of my legs down while the third guy cut my arms free.

I yanked, shoved, and thrashed but couldn't stop the three of them from binding my wrists together with new ties along with a chain.

They hung the chain from the hook and walked away, leaving me dangling directly in front of the camera.

Gutierrez picked his first instrument—a cattle prod.

And then he stood before the camera and pushed the button to start streaming.

"Good evening. My name is Francisco Gutierrez. Today, my colleagues and I were in the middle of a nonviolent business meeting when the DEA invaded and killed four of our men. Unprovoked."

As he lied, I swung my body and tried to kick him upside his vile, lying head.

But it didn't work.

Gutierrez turned around and shoved the cattle prod into my rib. A boiling heat sprinted through my body to my limbs, making my head jerk back. At first, all I could hear was the electric current ringing in my ears, but then screaming sounded in the distance—screaming that grew closer and closer.

It was mine.

Gutierrez looked pleased as he returned to his table, ranting more threats into the camera as he picked up a hammer and an ice pick.

A thump from upstairs made Gutierrez pause momentarily. The guy upstairs had to be almost done, setting up their massive bomb as the boat grew closer to Navy Pier.

I had to warn law enforcement. Maybe the DEA or some other American agency was watching right now. That was the whole point of his plan, was it not? To have them watching? Gutierrez was addressing them, threatening them, showing what would happen if they got in his way. I could use this livestream to warn the United States.

"The Baja Cartel is going to bomb Navy Pier tonight!" I screamed.

Gutierrez snapped his head back.

"They've moved to the United States!"

A hand smothered my mouth from behind. I bit it so hard, it jerked away.

"They killed Sergeant Burch and his kids! And—"

"Get a rag!" Gutierrez snarled.

"They're trying to infiltrate the DEA!"

"Turn that computer off!" Gutierrez snapped.

Another guy sprinted to the laptop and slammed it shut.

Gutierrez narrowed his evil eyes at me. Picked up the electric reciprocating saw and held it up to show off the sharp teeth of its blade.

"That was a foolish thing to do," he growled.

As I hung from the rafters of a boat out in the middle of the water, my executioner approached me.

# 38

Gutierrez turned the saw on. It buzzed to life with the earsplitting rumble of a lawn mower as its blade jerked back and forth so quickly that Gutierrez's hand vibrated. Tiny bits of what I could only assume were pieces of some poor victim's skin shot out from it, one pelting my cheek.

His three associates shifted into position—two on the wall to my left, one to my right, licking their lips as he prepared to cut me into pieces.

My heart pounded so hard in my chest, it felt like it might break through my rib cage as Gutierrez angled the saw toward my shoulder.

But suddenly, he jerked, and the saw crashed to the floor and stopped buzzing. Gutierrez thumped to the ground, groaning as he grabbed his bleeding shoulder.

The two henchmen on the left wall slumped to the ground with holes in their foreheads before I registered the sounds of gunshots as two silhouettes crouched in the stairway. Dripping wet.

It always amazed me what the police academy had taught us—that guns could fire, even when wet. Technically, they could even fire underwater, but I'd never been more grateful for that until now.

*How did they find me?*

As Gutierrez reached for his weapon, his only living bodyguard pointed his gun at my head.

And this time, when the gun fired, I heard the blast's *bam*.

I waited for the pain to come, but when the guy smacked to the floor, I realized someone else had fired faster.

Dillon. Still cuffed, but the chain connecting them had been broken, so he could move his wrists freely.

Shane approached Gutierrez and kicked his revolver out of reach.

Dillon closed the ten feet separating us in an impossibly fast second, his panicked eyes scanning my body. When he saw the burn on my arm, the cut on my thigh, his every muscle tensed into murderous rage.

Gritting his teeth, he shoved the gun into his waistband, wrapped his arms under my hips, and pushed me up until my wrists were free from the hook.

"I got you, Fallon," he said as he gently lowered me to my feet. Then, he cupped my face with both hands, searched my eyes, desperate for reassurance. "Are you okay?"

I nodded, provoking his shoulders to shrink in relief.

"How did you know I was here?" I asked.

But he was too preoccupied to answer; Dillon's eyes widened in rage-filled horror when he spotted the instruments they'd planned to torture me with.

"What did they do to you?" he growled, his voice primal and protective.

"I'm fine," I assured. "But we need to go."

It took Dillon a second to move. His jaw remained locked in

fury as he unraveled the chains around my hands and frowned at the zip ties.

"Fuck, these are tight," he said.

Shane checked the pulses of the cartel members and kicked their weapons out of the way for good measure.

"We need to hurry," I said. "There are other people upstairs somewhere, and they're heading to Navy Pier to bomb it."

Shane and Dillon exchanged a holy-shit look.

Dillon grabbed a knife off the table. "Hold still," he warned and then carefully cut my ties loose. He put his hand on my cheek and asked, "Can you walk?"

"Yeah, we need to hurry," I repeated, bolting toward the stairs, but it was too late.

The man from earlier, the apparent equal to Gutierrez, blocked our path as he descended the steps with two armed men.

One gun pointed at Shane.

One gun pointed at Dillon.

One at me.

# 39

Once he stepped closer, I finally got a good look at his face. Fourteen years of wrinkles had accumulated since our last photo of him, but I still recognized his eyes. He *had* been working with the cartel, and based on the way Gutierrez spoke to him earlier, he'd become a very high-ranking member of the Baja organization.

Rodrigo Ramirez.

And he stared right at Dillon, whose entire body tensed. I'd never seen Dillon quiver before, and I wondered if it was from anger, fear, or both.

Maybe it was from pain. Dillon was still shirtless, and the gauze I'd carefully wrapped around his wound sagged with water, and his wound lightly bled down his stomach.

Ramirez pointed his gun at my face. Dillon moved protectively in front of me, pointing his gun right back at Ramirez. Shane and the criminal to my left aimed their barrels at each other while the other guy with a bald square head aimed his Glock 19 at me.

Lots of guns. Lots of trigger-happy fingers one squeeze away from ending us along with any hope to stop the Navy Pier massacre.

"You look different," Ramirez said to Dillon.

*Different?*

Dillon's chest rose and fell three times. "I thought you were dead."

Ramirez's mouth twitched up on one side in arrogance. "What made you think that?"

"Not a word, not a dollar, no sign you were alive. Plus, your line of work. Plus, wishful thinking."

Ramirez's nostrils flared, and then he scanned me in a way he hadn't before.

"Your girlfriend's a cop," he accused.

Dillon took a step backward, closer to me.

Ramirez raised his eyebrows. "She know who I am?"

I could see Dillon's shoulders rising and falling faster as his breaths accelerated.

Ramirez smirked at me. "He didn't tell you?"

My stomach plunged.

Ramirez looked at his watch before regarding Dillon again. "You changed your last name," he said.

"You leave, and you think you deserve the honor of sharing a last name with me? Or Dex?"

*Holy crap.*

Ramirez straightened. "You can act as noble as you want, but you're just like me."

"I'm nothing like you."

"You sell drugs. Apple"—he pointed to Dillon, then himself—"tree."

"I sold drugs out of desperation to support Mom and Dex when you left like an asshole coward. You abandoned us. Let us think you were dead, but you've been there all along." Dillon looked between Gutierrez and Ramirez. "Moving up the ranks, evidently."

Gutierrez tried to get up, but Shane kicked him back down.

"Did you order the hit on me?" Dillon demanded of Ramirez.

"We might not be close, but you're still my son. They knew I'd never go along with it, so they tried to conceal it from me by going after you in public, but I wasn't stupid. Saw it for what it was. Dealt with the person who made that call."

*That* was why Dillon wasn't executed in the traditional way.

"Why was I a target?" Dillon demanded.

"They made your tattoo," he said.

I thought back to that first day in the task force when we'd seen the scorpion tattoo. The one Terrell had confirmed belonged to a captain. Terrell had been tortured for days before that fire; he must have confessed to leaking the tattoo detail during his torture session.

"Was only a matter of time before police picked you up."

"I wouldn't have talked," Dillon said in a low voice.

"They didn't want to take the chance. When the hit failed, *I* was the one that stepped in, so they didn't take a second shot at you! I kept you alive, and you jeopardize that chance on what? A girl? A fucking cop, no less? And not just any girl. You know where she lived when she was a kid?"

So, Gutierrez wasn't the only one with my file...

"Shut up," Dillon said.

"He didn't tell you who I am," Ramirez said to me.

No. But I'd caught up.

"You're his father."

"I used to live here," Ramirez said.

"Yeah, I got that by the whole deadbeat-father-walks-out-on-his-family thing."

Ramirez smirked at me. "All Chicago suburbs were part of my region at the time."

*His...region. As in drug region. Of course...*

Ramirez grinned as understanding sank my feet to the ground like anchors.

He was the boss when my parents became addicts, responsible for the drugs making their way into their hands.

"This isn't how I wanted you to find out," Dillon said in a tone only low enough for me to hear. "I was going to tell you."

"How long did you know?" I asked through burning eyes.

He hesitated, breathing only through his nose for several seconds, and with his gun still pointed at his father, his voice hardened. "Suspected it might be him when you told me where you lived. Didn't want to believe it could be...hoped the timing was off."

I thought back to that sickened expression on his face when we both confessed who we were. When he demanded I leave. I'd been so offended at the time, but looking back on it, Dillon must have wondered if his father could have been in charge of the drug region at that time, and that morning, I'd told him how they *pushed* the drugs out, giving freebies to keep them hooked. That was why Dillon looked so ashamed at that moment, carrying the burden of his father's vile choices.

"I wanted to tell you," Dillon said. "But I was hoping I was wrong. And by that point, I was more worried about your safety. That took priority over everything, and I was scared if I told you what I suspected, you wouldn't let me help you."

Ramirez interrupted our moment with a sneer. "Shame about your mom's death."

My mom was one of many to die because of people like him, and if I didn't do something, thousands more would die tonight.

# 40

I quickly assessed the situation in front of us. Ramirez stood with his pistol pointed toward Dillon; Gutierrez still lay on the ground, his breathing labored; a tall dude had his semi-automatic pointed at Shane; and the guy with the square head pointed his gun at me.

All while this floating bomb sped toward Navy Pier.

"You just confessed to dealing narcotics in mass quantities," I said, trying to throw his emotions off-balance. "A confession you made in front of federal agents."

Ramirez's face darkened.

"So, on top of being a piece of shit, not a smart one at that," I added.

His face morphed into full-on rage. "Step aside, son," he said in a tone that implied he wanted to be the one to end my life.

Shane tensed, which caused his rival to tighten his finger on the trigger.

Dillon backed up, covered my body with his. "If you're going to kill her, you're gonna have to kill me first."

An unacceptable outcome. After years of him not giving a crap about his son, I doubted Ramirez's hesitation had anything to do with how much he cared about Dillon. More about his ego. He stuck his neck out to save his son from a second hit, so killing him now wouldn't be a good look. It would undermine Ramirez's authority.

"Step aside!" Ramirez demanded.

Everyone tensed, their fingers tighter on the triggers.

The anticipation of the coming violence broke through the air like the humidity of an approaching thunderstorm, where the air thickened and ominous black clouds rolled through the sky with their threat of the forming tornado.

Dillon was a quick shot; there was a chance he could take out all three of them before this went to hell. But unlike before, when my death was temporarily delayed by an intended interrogation, these guns were one squeeze away from ending our lives.

Ramirez looked at his watch and frowned.

*Ticktock. Clearly, the bomb's live.*

"I'll give you one last chance," Ramirez spat in disgust. "You leave with me now, I'll make you a king in this organization."

Gutierrez groaned, coughed up blood.

"I don't want anything to do with your organization or any of this anymore. I'm out," Dillon declared. "And don't call me *son*."

Ramirez's gaze froze, but his humiliation morphed into vengeance with the widening of his eyes.

"You're just as pathetic as the day I left you." Ramirez's gruff voice was eerily calm.

We saw the intention in his eyes just before the gun fired. Thankfully, Dillon flinched, so the bullet missed center mass, but it still hit Dillon's arm and sent his gun flying several feet away.

The square-headed gangster realigned his shot to Dillon's back—Ramirez clearly wanted to be the one to kill me. I grabbed the hammer from the torture tray, lunged, and smashed it into the gangster's head. The crack of his skull sounded like a twig snapping, and his blood sprayed across my face. The hammer's head stayed lodged in his brain as the whites of his eyes grew larger before he crumpled to the ground.

Meanwhile, Shane tried to fire a shot at his assailant, but when his gun jammed, he tackled the guy to the ground, escaping a bullet himself while sending the other gun sliding. Shane kicked his attacker so hard, his body slammed into the stove. The guy screamed from the burn as it tipped over and ignited the wall.

Dillon shoulder-slammed his dad in his ribs, and the two of them thumped onto the floor as the flames grew.

In the chaos, Gutierrez—who had blood pooling in his lips and smearing across his teeth—managed to crawl and get a nearby Glock 19 that had been lying on the ground. I dove on top of his chest as he lined up the shot with Shane's head, and I grabbed the gun, twisting its aim away. I tried to yank it from his bloody hands, but somehow, his grip remained so tight, I couldn't get it away.

As we wrestled for control, Dillon's lips tightened with years of rage as he pummeled his father in the face with punch after punch. His dad lost the grip on the gun, which lay next to them, but he hit his son in the temple with a blow that stunned Dillon. And followed it with another.

Near the stove, Shane's battle escalated when his attacker jumped on top of Shane and began to strangle him. Shane tried evasive tactics and thrashed his arms up and out, but the man had a death grip on Shane's neck, causing Shane's face to turn purple.

I yanked two more times, got the gun from Gutierrez, and fired one shot. The guy on top of Shane froze for three seconds and then tipped over.

Shane coughed and rolled on the ground to reclaim his breaths.

The fire spread to a second wall. Any second, it would ignite the massive amount of dynamite on this boat, and I didn't know how close we were to the shore—to the thousands of innocent people.

With the flames crawling higher, Ramirez bucked Dillon off and began beating his own son.

I took aim and pulled the trigger.

Ramirez jerked and stilled long enough for Dillon to shove his father off him. Ramirez coughed up blood, a gunshot to his back rendering him a groaning pile of flesh.

"Come on!" I shouted. "We need to get out of here!"

Shane rose to his feet slowly, his nose and lips bloody and eye already beginning to swell.

I winced from the heat of the flames. It was so hot, I wondered if we were technically getting burned right now, and the smoke made it even harder to see and breathe.

I shuffled through the thick cloud toward the only escape—the stairwell ten feet away—and as I approached Dillon on the way, he stood up. Put his hands on his thighs, coughing so hard, I thought he might vomit.

That was when Ramirez made his move. He did it quickly, grabbing the gun and aiming it at my chest.

I pulled my arm up in a hopeless attempt to defend myself, but Dillon was faster.

He dove in front of me, blocking my body with his just as his father pulled the trigger.

Dillon collapsed with a hole in his chest.

"Dillon!" I screamed.

As flames engulfed the third wall, Ramirez's disgusting little lips turned up into a smug look of victory.

As I glared at the villain who'd supplied my mom with her fatal drugs, time seemed to stand still.

He raised his hand to line up another shot at me, but I pulled my trigger faster.

A look of shock spread across his face as a small hole opened above his right eyebrow, and his head thudded to the floor.

Flames engulfed the last wall and spread its heat to the ceiling.

I coughed and knelt by Dillon.

"Dillon!"

"We need to go," Shane said. "I don't know how long we have..."

*Before the bomb explodes.*

"Fallon," Dillon whispered. He was white, making a gurgling sound as he struggled to breathe. "Are you okay?"

"Hang on," I cried. "You're going to be just fine."

"Fallon!" Shane urged as the fire spread toward our only escape—the stairwell.

"Come on." I lifted Dillon's head. But he faded into unconsciousness and became dead weight.

"Help me!" I screamed at Shane.

He grabbed Dillon under his shoulders, and I grabbed his feet.

The fire was three feet from the stairwell now. It burned my skin, my face, my eyes as we lumbered Dillon's body up the stairs.

"Go faster!" I screamed.

I risked a glance at Gutierrez, who had tried to crawl to the stairwell but, choking and bleeding heavily, had collapsed onto the ground.

Fire spat embers onto my shoulder, but I wouldn't drop Dillon's legs. We had seconds, at best, to get off this damn boat before the whole thing went up.

"Arrggghhhh," Shane groaned with gritted teeth. A vein bulged in his forehead as he yanked Dillon's body over the last step and tossed him to the ground.

Dillon's eyes remained closed.

Shane looked over the edge of the boat.

"He's barely breathing!" I shrieked.

"There's an inflatable boat with a motor." The escape boat the cartel was going to take as their bomb sailed into Navy Pier. "Come on!"

I swallowed and grabbed Dillon's feet.

Shane and I could barely manage to put him on the metal banister, aiming the best we could.

"If he falls in the water..." I started. *He'll sink into the darkness.* "One of us needs to get in that boat first, catch him," I said.

Shane huffed an impatient breath; I didn't have the upper body strength to catch Dillon. Only he would.

I held Dillon's body, which was propped awkwardly on the banister, while Shane threw one leg over, then the other, and lowered himself like a pull-up before letting go. I heard a thump and the splash of a wave.

"Okay, drop him!" Shane said.

I looked down, pushed Dillon over, and watched him fall ten feet into Shane's waiting arms. It must have been too heavy, though, because it knocked Shane over, and Dillon landed on the bottom with a belly flop, rocking the lifeboat so hard, it almost tipped over.

But it worked. Both men were safely in the lifeboat.

I risked a glance around, horrified to see Navy Pier only a half-mile away. Within the blast radius, for sure.

And closing.

"You go!" I screamed. "I'll swim to you in a second!"

"What? Fallon!"

"Go!"

I ran to the front of the boat, found the steering wheel. The ship was on some sort of autopilot mode, heading right for Navy Pier.

"Fallon!" Shane shouted.

There was a control panel with the label CPT. A couple dials, one called rudder, one deadpan. Port and starboard side buttons that went from one to ten degrees, and in the center, a little green light beneath a switch that was flipped up to Heading Hold. That had to be the autopilot.

I flipped the switch to standby, and a little red light replaced the green. I could feel the rock of the boat as the autopilot's steering disengaged.

I pulled the steering wheel as far to the right as possible, so tightly, the boat almost tipped over, so I had to release it a bit.

"Fallon! What are you doing?"

The vessel turned out toward the open lake, and once it was pointed toward a safe angle—away from the shore—I flipped the switch back up to Heading Hold and ran to the banister.

Where Shane glared at me. I threw myself over the side and dropped into the boat.

Shane had already untied us from the main boat and started the motor, but he hadn't moved like I'd asked him to; only now, when I was safely inside, did he slam it into gear and speed away.

The buzzing engine increased in pitch as we picked up momentum.

To our left, Chicago's picturesque skyscrapers sparkled against the charcoal sky, branching in staggered heights toward the one-hundred-story John Hancock building with its white antenna-like towers glowing. The smell of musty grass grew faint as the warm summer air whipped past us, and to our right, the cartel boat headed toward the water's distant black horizon.

Shane kept the motor at full speed, so fast, the front end floated above the waterline, and one rogue wave could capsize us. We made it about ninety seconds before the immense blast rocked our boat and shuddered the water. I felt its vibrations all the way to my bones, felt its heat lick my back, and saw the ebony sky light up like a firework as engulfed pieces of the fishing vessel rained down in an array of flaming orange chunks.

One of which came right at us.

Shane jerked the steering so quickly, our boat almost rolled, and when a smaller piece shot toward us, he had to jerk the other way. The farther we got from the explosion, the smaller the balls of fire became until we finally made it far enough away, where we let the engine throttle.

I allowed myself a brief second to look back and see the fiery vessel's back end sticking out of the water as it went down. Balls of orange clouds glowed against the black water and sky so brightly, they stung my eyes, as if staring directly into the sun.

Navy Pier was still in one piece.

"Dillon!"

Shane helped me flip him over onto his back.

He wasn't moving.

His chest wasn't going up and down.

"I don't feel a pulse," Shane said.

# 41

I gnawed on my fingernail, tapping my foot on the linoleum floor.

"We got his heart started very quickly," I reasoned.

Shane said nothing.

"They had oxygen on him the whole time he was in the ambulance." An ambulance that was already on the shore, waiting for us, thanks to the Coast Guard, who had gotten to us within a couple minutes, drawn over by the explosion. "Those are all things working in his favor. Big things."

Shane rubbed my back.

"He's strong," I continued.

He looked dead, completely dead, his skin the color of my dad on that morgue table. And when I'd opened Dillon's eyelids, his eyes were a dull gray, lacking life. But his heart was technically still beating.

No, not technically. Why would I use that word? His heart was beating, period.

"Lots of people survive gunshot wounds to the chest," I continued. "Lots. Like every day."

I stood up and walked to the other end of the hospital waiting room. The space was neat and clean with its architecturally curved ceiling, pristine white walls, perfectly spaced windows, sand-colored carpet, and tidy rows of faux leather chairs. It was all designed to make it look like you were simply here for a medical appointment rather than awaiting the life-or-death news of someone you loved.

There were sixteen strangers in this waiting room, all looking at me. No, not looking. Gawking. I wore teal scrubs the nurse had given me, and I had a bandage on my arm with another hidden beneath the fabric on my thigh. Bandages, courtesy of a nurse that insisted to "at least" wrap the hideous, oozing burn and gash while I waited on news of Dillon. I'd cleaned the blood and dirt off my skin in the ladies' room with wet napkins, but I looked a mess. And I was clearly making the other people uncomfortable.

And Shane didn't look much better.

We'd been here for hours as they rushed Dillon up to surgery in hopes of repairing the damage caused by the bullet meant for me.

The bullet from his father's gun. His father, who'd put his son in the impossible position of supporting his family.

A few weeks ago, I thought I'd never feel an ounce of empathy for anyone who worked with narcotics. I'd judged them, just as I'd judged Dillon for his life choices. But I'd since learned that if I were in his shoes, I could've fallen prey to the slippery slope he did. Desperate to get his family out of the dangerously violent neighborhood—violence that threatened them every day and, on at least one occasion, resulted in the beating of his mentally impaired brother—he succumbed to the financial protection that dealing offered until he was in so deep, there was no way out.

"Fallon"—Shane put a hand on my shoulder—"why don't we go to the cafeteria? Get something to eat?"

"No."

"You look like you're going to faint."

"I'm not leaving until we hear from the doctor."

Dillon shouldn't have been there to get shot in the first place. While the cartel would've gone after him at some point, maybe the United States would have intervened before that could happen. Or maybe Dillon could've run after my death.

"How did you guys even find me?" I asked.

Shane rubbed his neck. "We followed Burch."

"I didn't see headlights."

"Didn't have 'em on."

"I didn't see a car."

"We were careful."

"Burch didn't even notice," I said. Or if he had, he didn't show it.

"Very careful. Watched Burch take you down that dock, to those...guards," Shane said. "When we saw them off Burch, took everything we had not to just go in, guns blazing, but we needed to be smart if we had any chance of getting you off that boat. Dillon and I scoped the place out, looking for a way in, but we had to keep our distance because of the guards. By the time they left the dock, the boat was already moving.

"Did the only thing we could—jumped in the water. Swam after it."

"Dillon had handcuffs on..."

"Used the motel's fire ax on the chain the second Burch left," he explained. "Grabbed the gun from the nightstand and my backup weapon from my trunk. The harder part was getting up onto the damn boat. Not the easiest thing to do. Felt like it took us forever, especially when we could hear you screaming."

And then they charged in, almost got killed themselves, especially when Ramirez showed up.

A doctor—female, short, arms like twigs, black hair in a ponytail—burst through the doors.

"Ms. O'Connor?" she called out.

I jumped up and half-jogged to her.

She took in my appearance but said nothing. "Are you family?"

"Girlfriend." I'd had police finally track down his mom, but she hadn't arrived yet. "And a police officer."

She nodded. "Dillon made it through surgery, but his heart stopped on three separate occasions. The bullet entered his left chest and caused a pneumothorax, which is a full lung collapse. The bullet also nicked his heart, causing a coronary lesion on his left atrium, and also damaged the aortic valve. His status is critical."

She let me process this, gave me a few seconds to try and remember how to breathe.

"We've done what we can, but the next few hours will be critical." She drew out her words slowly, in a quiet voice.

I didn't expect the pessimistic tone. The look on her face to be full of pity.

"What are his chances?" I asked.

"It's difficult to know how any one person's body will respond to trauma."

"But if you had to put a number on it?" Were his odds only, like, sixty percent? Fifty?

She looked from Shane to me before gently answering, "I'd estimate it at five percent."

The world swayed, and Shane was suddenly at my side, holding my upper arm to prevent me from falling over.

She had to be wrong. Dillon was strong, and if anyone could come out of this, he would. She was wrong. Doctors probably lowballed percentages to prepare you, just in case.

"Can we see him?" I asked.

There was that pitiful look again as she pursed her lips and nodded. "I'd advise you to call whoever you need to, so they can say good-bye."

*Good-bye?* I shook my head; there was no way Dillon could die.

Shane said, "I'll check on his mom's ETA."

I nodded.

"You can follow me," she said to me.

Some part of my brain told me that couldn't be good, that she was letting me see him. Visitors were usually confined to family only. Which probably meant she fully believed he wasn't going to make it.

With my head in a fog of dread, I walked with her through the doors, down a long hallway, around two turns, until I was in the intensive care unit.

The outside of the room was dark and intimidating, and the inside was stuffed with so much equipment, it felt like robots lived here, serving the one lone human in their center. The human with tubes coming out of every part of his body.

Dillon had a white tube down his throat, taped over his mouth, and a machine caused his chest to rise and fall with sounds of *shhh* and then *shaaaaaa* in perfect rhythm. Another tube extended out of his left rib cage. He had three IVs and other instruments strapped to his chest beneath his hospital gown. Every machine had colorful lines and numbers and sounds.

But only one phrase came to my mind: *life support.*

"Can he hear me?" I asked the doctor.

"I don't know," she said. "I'll leave you two alone."

Dillon looked so chilly, lying here with so much skin exposed. I pulled the hospital blanket up a few inches higher, making sure I didn't bump anything.

And then I sat next to his bed and reached for his hand.

His hand was cold, and my heart flashed to the other times I'd touched it. In the elevator fire, when he'd told me to save myself even though it meant leaving him behind to die. The first time he'd caressed my cheek, cupped my face before kissing me. The way he'd touched me when I professed my feelings to him, and after, when he touched my body. When he'd saved my life at that party and when he took me down from that hook. And now, this might be the last time I ever held it.

"I don't know if you can hear me," I started. "But I need to believe you can. Because I have some things to say to you."

I took a deep breath and leaned forward, so I could push my cheek against his hand.

"I once told you that the world would be a better place without you in it." My eyes stung, and my throat swelled. "That's not true. The world needs you, Dillon. I need you. Your heart is pure." I wiped a stray tear. "And I'm proud of you. For standing up to your father and having the courage to walk away from that organization."

I didn't want to believe he could die. But I couldn't ignore what the doctor said, either, and if, Heaven forbid, Dillon didn't make it, he couldn't pass away without knowing how much I loved him.

"Before I met you, I'd shut myself off from feeling things for people. I built my walls. Shut people out."

Dillon's heartbeat, beeping on the corner monitor, accelerated. His eyes remained closed, but a lone tear bubbled in the corner of his eye and dripped down his cheek.

I swiped it with my finger as my eyes blurred with tears.

"Maybe part of the reason I obsessed over my career was because it kept me preoccupied, so I didn't have to open myself up for relationships."

I paused. "I blocked everyone out until I met you. You made me feel alive again. And feel loved in a way I never had before. You were the rainbow after my storm, Dillon."

I swallowed the burning in my esophagus. "I don't know how this will all work..." His criminal offenses, my career. "But the only thing I do know is that I love you, and I can't live in this world without you, Dillon. I love you with every cell inside me. So, please, if you need a reason to live? Live for me. Fight for me."

Dillon didn't move. I don't know what I expected, but Dillon didn't open his eyes, his fingers didn't twitch in my hand, nor did he start crying. Maybe the tear I'd seen was nothing more than his body reacting to all the tubes and medication. Maybe he couldn't hear me at all.

Maybe it didn't matter how much his death would destroy his family and me.

A body could only sustain so much damage, and a heart could only take so much physical and emotional pain before it stopped beating.

I hung my head on his bedrail and sobbed.

And as I did, Dillon's hand tightened around mine. Three times.

*I. Love. You.*

# 42

Five days later, I paced in the halls of the hospital, where noises—sneakers squeaking against linoleum, the rumble of voices talking against the backdrop of monitors beeping—blended together like a now-familiar symphony, the smell of disinfectant growing weaker, the longer I'd been here.

Dillon's vitals had improved enough that the doctor decided to remove Dillon's breathing tube. It was going to take the medical team a few minutes, so I afforded my legs the stretch of walking all the way to the other end of the hospital, which was a treat. Aside from leaving for a shower a couple times and getting minor treatment for my burn and cut, I'd been by Dillon's side, sleeping and existing in the chair next to his bed. I'd even met his mom, who came every single day.

I rounded the bend to head back to the ICU room when something stopped me in my tracks. Well, not something...someone.

Jenna Christiansen.

It was impossible not to recognize her—sadly, the scars on her face were hard to miss. She probably thought that was why I was staring, but it wasn't at all.

It was admiration for the battle she'd fought. A battle that had made global news, the case Detective Fisher had worked. And while some people focused on the romantic aspect of her story—the sexy fighter willing to lay down his life to protect her—most focused on the dangerous side of it, referring to the unthinkable events preceding as a *Deadly Illusion.*

I couldn't believe I was in the same room with Jenna. Every news outlet had failed to get an interview with her. I'd actually met her briefly before, but when she was in the ICU in the aftermath of her tragedy, I didn't know all the details of what she'd endured. And now that I knew? I couldn't let this opportunity pass without telling her, from one woman to another, how proud she should be of what she'd overcome. She'd become a hero to women around the world.

And standing right next to her was another hero: Damian Stone, who kept his arm around her waist. They were in the maternity ward, with a smile that could only come from new parents.

As Jenna ambled down the hallway in a hospital gown, I approached her tentatively.

"Sorry," I said. "I didn't mean to stare. You might not remember, but we met in the hospital."

She must have been used to people approaching her by now because she didn't seem surprised; she simply offered a weak smile, while Damian watched Jenna's face, as if looking for any sign of distress.

"You're very brave," I said. "An inspiration to a lot of people. You saved a lot of lives."

Her eyes held mine for several seconds before she whispered, "Thank you," as if my proclamation chipped away at some of her pain.

She stood there for another moment before they walked to the end of the hall, where they turned out of sight.

I stared at the empty corner for a few moments and then headed back to Dillon's room, where two uniforms were posted outside his door for protection. The cartel was in mad chaos at the moment, but who knew if they might make a move?

Dillon's nurse emerged from the room. "You can see him now."

My pulse quickened as I jogged inside. The sight of him sitting up with a smile on his face was such a welcome relief. Dillon's facial stubble was a few days longer on account of him not shaving, and damn it if it didn't look sexy, complementing his tousled hair and chestnut eyes.

Dillon's voice was gruff, as if the tube rubbed his esophagus raw, but it only made him sound even sexier. "I'm cuffed to the bed." He tugged his right wrist that was handcuffed to the bedrail.

"You're kind of a wanted criminal at the moment."

I bent over and examined his gorgeous cheeks and jaw. The bruises on his face from his dad's blows looked less swollen today, his split lip closing up nicely.

Nice enough to finally give him a light, gentle kiss.

Lord, it felt good, like my center of gravity had returned.

I pulled my lips back, and Dillon tried to cup my cheek, but his wrist clanked to a stop. He frowned at the binding.

"You need to heal quickly," I demanded.

"Working on it."

I smiled and sat down in the chair. It'd be nice once he moved to a non-ICU room, where there'd be a window, where he could see the afternoon sun and the city landscape.

He stared at me, his eyes full of emotions so deep, they could dwell at the bottom of the ocean.

"I'm so sorry your dad's gone," I whispered.

"I'm glad you defended yourself, Fallon. Because I can't even comprehend a world where you don't exist in it. And now that I know everything, I'm glad he left. My mom and brother would've been in danger because the cartel uses family members. I'm just so sorry what he did to your family, Fallon."

I hated hearing the guilt in his voice. It was the same guilt that had laced his words when he insisted I *shouldn't* be with him the night I declared I was falling for him. He must have been battling his feelings for me, fearful of letting me get close to him, given his line of work. And when I met him in that basement after my dad's funeral, he'd said there was something he hadn't told me yet and that I'd never look at him the same. Looking back on it, he must have been trying to get the courage to tell me his suspicions about his father then and again after we escaped the cartel.

I took his hand and kissed it. I couldn't believe how much our tragic pasts were interconnected.

"I don't know how you can look at me and still love me, knowing that my dad is the one that destroyed your entire family."

"Because you're not your dad, and you're not responsible for his actions. I might not agree with some of the choices you made, but I understand why you made them."

I could see my words moving past his skin and the weight on his chest lift with the rise of his shoulders.

A slender nurse in blue scrubs came in and checked Dillon's IV. "Couple more days, Dillon," she said. "Then, you should be moved to a regular room."

When she left, Dillon stared at me in wonder.

"You saved me again." Dillon smiled.

"Shane helped."

"Don't let it go to your head," Shane said, walking in with the food we'd ordered. "I'd have preferred to let you explode. Considered letting your ass drown, too, but I'd have never heard the end of it."

Dillon's smile widened.

Shane set the bags down on the table and unpacked the burgers. The smell made my stomach growl.

"Damn, I missed real food," Dillon said.

"Heard you're going to live," Shane said.

"Sorry to disappoint you."

"Doc thought you were a goner."

To this, Dillon squeezed my hand. "You gave me something to fight for."

And he gave me something to fight for, too. My future would be bright, so long as we were both alive and safe.

Shane cleared his throat. He was probably uncomfortable with the emotional PDA because he changed the subject. "You guys hear of the string of burglaries in the city?"

"The criminals known as the Robin Hood Thieves?" I asked. "Yeah. Why?"

Shane shrugged. "Sounds like an interesting case."

I evaluated him. "You're thinking of leaving the task force?"

"Not right away," Shane said. "But I'm hoping to make detective soon. Those guys haven't hurt anyone yet, but they're escalating. Only a matter of time before someone gets killed."

I smiled, thrilled the passionate, crime-fighting Shane was back. "You'll make a good detective."

Shane's gaze fell to my fingers, laced with Dillon's.

"So, you two are really getting back together?" Shane asked, popping a French fry into his mouth.

I smiled at Dillon. "Yeah."

Shane popped another fry. "How's that going to work with you being in law enforcement and him being a"—Shane waved his hand in the air—"douchebag?"

I glowered at Shane, but he simply smirked and popped another fry into that big mouth of his.

# 43

"I love you so much." Dillon kissed my hand and my wedding ring that he'd slipped on a year ago at an intimate ceremony on Lake Michigan's beach.

"I love you."

"I'm so damn proud of you, Fallon."

I smiled and relished his lips against my temple.

"I'm going to deliver the good news," he said. "My mom and Shane have been here all night, waiting for an update."

Dillon smiled at me one more time, taking in the scene before him before walking out of the hospital room.

It was hard to believe how much we'd had to overcome to get here. So much had happened in the two years since the cartel's boat exploded.

As soon as the first and second-in-command died, a huge power struggle erupted in the Baja Cartel. All the leaders began killing each other in an attempt to gain control, but what they ended up doing was severely weakening their organization. The cartel members were too busy killing each other to pose a threat to my or Dillon's life, and soon, their organization was left in shreds.

Ripe for the picking when the United States stepped in.

With the cartel weakened, the United States formed a coalition and arrested dozens of cartel and Syndicates members.

The cartel and the Chicago Syndicates had been decimated. It would take decades for another group to take their place, if ever.

Dillon avoided jail time. He was a cooperating witness and received full immunity for it. He even became a consultant to the DEA. He was now on the other side of the fight, helping to stop people dying from drugs.

Still, while Dillon wasn't legally required to do so, he'd completed hundreds of hours of community service, wanting to atone for his mistakes. He'd also set up a community outreach program for families in financial distress, which provided opportunities for employment and prevention for teens who might otherwise get sucked into drug using or dealing. These programs had a significant impact on the Chicago communities.

As for me, I thought I was going to lose my job there for a while, especially when they put me on suspension, pending their investigation. But having a hand in saving the mayor, the chief of police, hundreds of officers, and thousands of pedestrians strengthened my standing with the DEA.

I officially joined a year and a half ago in an amazing role of analyzing cases behind the scenes. The responsibilities were so much more powerful than I imagined, connecting clues, solving mysteries, and investigating things that no one else had done yet. So far, two of my findings solved major cases in this country.

Meanwhile, Dillon and I settled into a beautiful home just outside the city, near his brother and mom, who we saw every Sunday for dinner. And now, we'd be adding another seat at the table.

I looked down, consumed with emotion.

A memory came flooding back.

*I'm two years old, and I'm in Mommy's arms, who's rocking me to sleep. I stare up into her blue eyes and touch my tiny fingers against her smiling cheek.*

*Daddy's face appears over her shoulder behind the rocking chair.*

*"Do you think she'll ever understand how much we love her?" Daddy asks.*

*Mommy shakes her head. "Not until she has one of her own."*

*Love*. A four-letter word, incapable of encapsulating the magnitude of what I felt right now. I never knew anything could be this powerful—more powerful than the strongest earthquake, more majestic than the rising sun. Instantly, my gravitational pull transformed, and the only thing anchoring me to this earth was her.

As I held my infant daughter in my arms, I couldn't explain how she had only come into this world an hour ago, yet it felt as if her beautiful soul had been tethered to mine for all of eternity.

There was nothing I wouldn't do for her.

From this day forward, my love for my child would be as constant as the stars in the sky and as unbreakable as the earth's core. And I knew, without question, that my love for her would even transcend time and space. That even death could not break this everlasting bond. Nothing could.

*You did love me, Mommy. Even when you couldn't show it.*

For the first time in a very long time, I could feel the gravity of how much my parents must've cherished me. I could feel their love wrap around me like a blanket on a winter night, and I now understood that it had been here all along. My eyes stung with the beauty of that realization, but also the sadness of it. To realize how suffocating their addiction had been, disrupting the current of affection between a parent and a child. My heart broke for them all over again, for what they'd lost.

"You know," I said to my newborn daughter, Kimberly, who

we'd named after my mom, "there are two extraordinary people who aren't here to meet you. But I know they'd give anything to hold you in their arms." A tear slid down my cheek. "And that they love you so very much. They're your guardian angels, looking down on you right now. And they always will."

I kissed her forehead and then whispered to my parents. "I'll tell her all about you both," I promised. "You'll never be forgotten."

I stroked my daughter's chubby cheek, overwhelmed with affection for her. "I'll love you forever," I vowed. "Even when I'm gone."

Dillon returned to the room, and the smile that reached his eyes was a brand-new one. The smile of seeing his wife holding his daughter. He sat next to me on the bed and opened his arms. Unlike the empty years when I'd pushed everyone away, I accepted his embrace and fell into him, letting his affection wrap around me.

"I love you," he said.

"I love you."

In each other, we found the light we'd always sought. Light we'd searched for in the wrong places, and now that we'd found it, we'd never let it go.

# EPILOGUE

## ZOEY

*She should be here any second.*

As I sat in the restaurant, I looked at the hanging television, and watched the top story on the midday news.

"The manhunt continues for the band of criminals terrorizing the community with a string of brazen armed robberies. Police say they struck again last night in the River North neighborhood, where the suspects broke into a condo, and made out with over fifteen thousand in valuables."

Fallon approached me. "Zoey," she said.

"Hi." I stood up and gave her a quick hug.

Fallon sat down opposite of me and glanced up at the television. "Can you believe these guys? My friend's working on the case. I hope they catch them before anyone gets hurt."

"Can I get you ladies something to drink?" a waiter asked.

We ordered beverages, and Fallon's eyes settled back on me.

"When I said we should do coffee, I didn't mean for it to take two years." Fallon smiled. "I'm sorry."

"Don't be. You've had a lot going on."

We'd had to reschedule several times. Fallon had been

swamped with work—with trial testimony, new cases—not to mention getting married and having a baby. Our coffee date kept getting bumped, but that didn't matter. We'd kept in touch via text and it was nice to see her now.

"Based on our texts, you do too," Fallon said. "Is your dad still staying with you?"

"I can't believe it's been months already; feels like he just got released from the hospital yesterday."

"It's admirable you taking him in like that. How's he doing?"

"His recovery's a lot slower than he'd like."

Than I'd like. What I wanted more than anything was for Dad to heal and regain his independence, and to find the bastard who'd hit him with his car, and then fled the scene.

I wanted Dad to get justice. And I would not stop until he got it.

But I had no idea that soon, the struggles that I'd faced over the past couple of years would pale in comparison to what I was about to go through—that three men would hold me hostage intending to kill me...

Nor could I have imagined the shocking truth of who had sent them...

* * *

THANK YOU FOR READING FATAL CURE! IF YOU LOVED IT, YOU'LL LOVE **LETHAL JUSTICE,** where Zoey gets her HEA and **Shane's story intertwines with a dangerous, forbidden romance between a captor and his hostage...**

**A CRIME LEADER HAS FALLEN FOR THE WRONG WOMAN. SHE'S HIS hostage in a heist, and if he leaves any witnesses, his**

**colleagues will kill them both.** ☆☆☆☆☆ *"Emotional... phenomenal!"*

**One-click LETHAL JUSTICE now!**

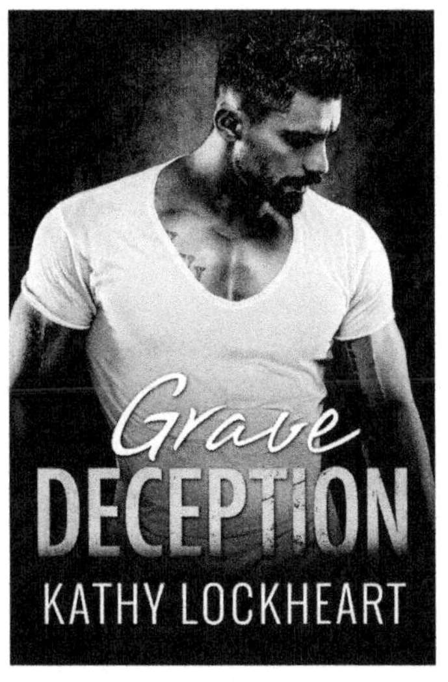


AND DON'T MISS GRAVE DECEPTION **where Shane gets his HEA.** My new neighbor is a scorching hot police detective—one I have a massive crush on, but I never wanted to get his attention like this: as the apparent victim of an attempted murder. ☆☆☆☆☆ *"An absolute must read!"*

**One-click GRAVE DECEPTION now!**

WHAT **JAW-DROPPING EVENT WAS ABOUT TO UNFOLD** WHEN FALLON showed up undercover at that party? And why did Dillon call his brother to say goodbye? Find out in this **exclusive FREE chapter from Dillon's POV** (KathyLockheart.com/DillonPOV). It will leave you speechless...

P.S. DON'T MISS **MY NEW DARK REVENGE ROMANCE, SECRET VENDETTA, which has dual POV and much more spice.**

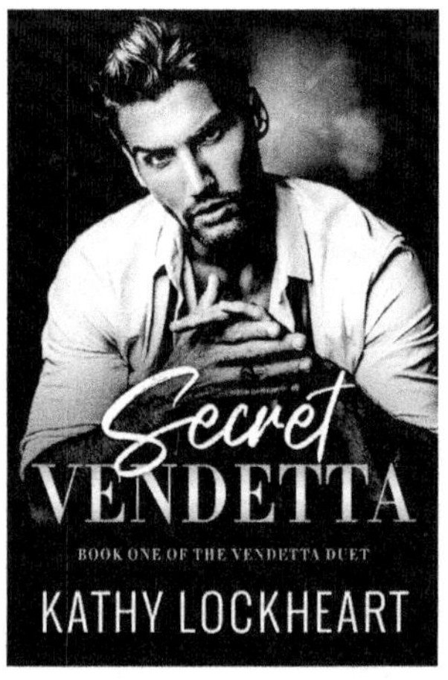


**LUNA**

Baptized in blood, I'm marked for death. Each time it comes, *he* appears. My masked protector. Saving me for reasons only known to him.

But the Vigilante is playing a deadly game. One I must stop before he claims another soul. My new love, Hunter, vows to keep me safe.

But will we survive the Vigilante's secret vendetta?

**VIGILANTE**

I'm the most dangerous man in the city. Hiding in the shadows, stalking my next victim. I watch them take their last breaths before bathing the city in their blood.

Now, I watch her. I end the lives of the men who come for her. But I fear my pervasive darkness...is about to make her its ultimate prey.

☆☆☆☆☆ "This book is beyond addictive!"

☆☆☆☆☆ "Sinfully Seductive & Suspenseful!"

☆☆☆☆☆ "...left me absolutely stunned and breathless."

**One-click SECRET VENDETTA now!**

# ACKNOWLEDGMENTS

First, **I'd like to thank you, the reader.** You have a ton of options when it comes to books. Your time is incredibly precious, and you gave *me* a chance. From the bottom of my heart, THANK YOU. **Readers mean the world to me**, and I'd love to connect with you! Please find my social media links at www.KathyLockheart.com.

Thank you to my husband for continuing to cheer me on, even when I wanted to give up. You've always believed in me more than I've believed in myself. Thank you to my children for inspiring me to go after my dream and for the endless happiness you've brought into my life. You are the sun in my solar system, warming my heart and soul.

To my family for loving and encouraging me. To my mother for your unending support, affection, and laughter. To my father, you've always been my hero, but witnessing how you treated people in your darkest hour made you rise to superhero status.

To my friends, Kristin and Sharon, for your never-ending support. You've always encouraged me to go after my passion, even when I was scared to do so. I can't tell you how much that means to me and how much I adore our time together. You guys keep me grounded when I start to spin.

To Katy for reading *Fatal Cure* long before anyone else and giving me honest feedback that motivated me to keep going. Readers like you inspire authors like me!

To my official beta readers and early ARC readers: Tracey (your email made my eyes sting!), Amy, Kristin, Amy, Sara, Kayla, and Ecaterina. Thank you for reading this long before it was ready to put into the dryer and for all your valuable insights that made *Fatal Cure* even better!

To my editors—Michelle Mead, The Novel Triage, Unforeseen Editing, and Judy's Proofreading—who made this story remarkably better than it was before! To my cover artist, Hang Le, for bringing such beauty to this novel!

To all the authors who came before me, your success paves the road for new writers to do what they love. Thank you.

~ *Kathy*

# INSPIRATION FOR THIS NOVEL

*This contains major spoilers. Please read AFTER the book.

The inspiration for this novel came from two separate elements: an emotional one and an entertaining one.

I'll start by explaining the emotional inspiration. Addiction is a disease as complicated as it is widespread. I think we all know someone who has suffered from addiction. I personally know someone who was dramatically affected even though they were not an addict themselves. As I thought about this person, I wondered about many things. I wondered what it would feel like to be a child of addicts and what effect it might have on your heart. I wondered what it would be like to be a parent struggling with addiction when you loved your child more than anything yet physically battled against a disease.

My desire to tell a story about addiction increased when I saw the opioid crisis sweeping our nation. I was haunted by stories of everyday people recovering from things like surgeries, only to find themselves physically addicted to the pills that were supposed to cure their pain. Most of these people never saw it coming, and yet, in some cases, their lives were destroyed. My heart broke for them, and I wanted to research this and tell a story about a character struggling with the aftermath of her parents' addiction. In particular, I wanted to take a character through a journey, from anger to compassion, when she unveils the truth of their suffering.

And as I thought about this character's journey, a love interest formed in my mind. This is where the entertaining part of the story comes in. Of all the people Fallon could have fallen for, this one presented the most tension and the most obstacles to their love—a person who made their living, selling the very drugs that destroyed her family. A forbidden romance seemingly doomed to fail.

I couldn't stop wondering how their love story would turn out. What would happen to a DEA agent who fell in love with the drug lord she was hunting? What would happen to her career? What would happen to their love story? Would it end in tragedy? I couldn't stop wondering about all of this, and I had to find out what would happen. Finally, I sat down to write it.

And thus, *Fatal Cure* was born. I hope you enjoyed it!

xoxo,

Kathy

Printed in Great Britain
by Amazon

43839986R00199